HIDDEN CONTEMPT

The Pull of a Specious Paradise

CELESTE SHIRECLIFFE

Entertainments
Press

Chapel Hill, NC

Published by Entertainments Press 2019
Chapel Hill, NC

First paperback edition May 2019

Edited by Lori Draft
Cover Art by Rachel Fuqua
Title Page Photo by Jeremy Bishop
Author Headshot by SAR Photo & Film

ISBN: 978-1-7335313-0-6 (eBook Edition)
ISBN: 978-1-7335313-1-3 (Paperback Edition)

[1. Romance—Fiction. 2. Suspense—Fiction.
3. Thriller—Fiction. 4. Political—Fiction.]
2019900524

Printed in the United States of America

Visit: www.celesteshirecliffe.com

To my husband, Dave.

I'll choose you forever.

✧ CONTENTS ✧

PREFACE

WHEN PEOPLE SPEAK of the future, they often envision a world they wouldn't recognize. They think they will be surrounded by inventions never thought of and ideas never tried. But as Chelsea Coremon's grandma had once told her, "The world is not so different as it once was. Our problems don't really change. At the end of the day, we all have to sit down and poop."

Although, if Chelsea's world were compared to the world her grandmother grew up in, things were indeed very different. It was, in fact, the future. Everyone owned self-driving cars—many even owned a personal flying pod to travel longer distances—and robots were a part of daily life. The breakthrough inventions that were only beginning to make an appearance during her grandmother's time were now common household items.

In many ways, life had more ease, but the world's most universal problems still existed. The added technology brought effortless results, and there seemed to be no end to the benefits of these creations. However, beneath the convenience, a world of complexity always accompanied them. And the facts still stood— humans still have their physical and emotional needs, and without a certain amount of resilience, even the most privileged could fall to the demands of the mind. Each person was fighting for a place in the world and a reason for living—same as always.

Chelsea Coremon was no different. For a long time, she wandered directionless, doing what any young girl would do. She survived high school, fell in love, got her heart broken, went to college, got her heart broken some more, decided on a master's program, and then hoped there would be a good job waiting for her when she graduated.

That was when all the robots came into the picture. She recalled watching an ad where a robot completed a variety of tasks with at least two times the speed and six times the accuracy of that of a human.

"Stop hoping Joe Shmoe will show up to work tomorrow. Get things done—and done right—100% of the time," the ad promised as it ended.

Chelsea contemplated the ad for a moment then shrugged her shoulders and went on studying for the exam she had that day.

But she never would've guessed just how much that ad would affect her life in the years to come. Because when her time came to toss her cap into the air, there were no longer any jobs for her to fill. Robots now completed most of the jobs she would have qualified for, and after months of searching for steady work, she finally had to give up when the first payment on her student loans came due.

She cringed as she called her mother to admit that she needed to move back home—indefinitely.

"I'm sometimes able to get work," she told her mother, "but all the old-timers hold the permanent positions, and I have to spend all my time applying to every temp job possible just to get *any* work."

"Okay," her mother agreed. "I'm sure something more permanent will come up eventually, and living at home will make it so you can afford a house once you do find a job," her mother

❖2❖

assured her.

But in the four years Chelsea spent at home, she never did find a full-time job. Instead, she found The Societies.

❖3❖

1. THE SOCIETIES

I T TOOK SOME PERSUADING—a few well-placed ads, some moving speeches accompanied by applause, and chanting crowds calling for a solution to their problems—but with time, the government had everyone excited and convinced. All they had to do was come.

So Chelsea Coremon prepared her application to live in one of the facilities the government was calling *The Societies.* Her excitement was piqued. She knew her struggles were almost over, and the new life she would have was the life of the future—a life of sustainability and ease. Four weeks after submitting her application, an uncontrollable squeal of anticipation escaped Chelsea's lips as she read the announcement of her new citizenship in the *Hawaii Society.*

"I got in! I'm going to Hawaii!" Chelsea yelled down to her mother and younger brother from the banister of their small three-bedroom home.

She ran down the stairs, jumping down the last few and landing with a thud before whirling around in the direction of the kitchen.

"You did?" her brother Glenn asked in surprise through a mouthful of breakfast casserole.

"I just got the invitation in my email," she explained. "Quick, check yours."

"Your top pick! That's great, Chelsea," her mother said with a smile. "When do you leave?"

"Less than three weeks!"

"Well, that's soon," her mother said and her smile turned to a look of contemplation. She began thinking of a list of all the logistics that needed to happen before Chelsea had to leave—forever leaving behind the life she knew on the outskirts of Las Vegas.

"Mine hasn't come yet," Glenn said as his shoulders slumped down.

"It hasn't?" Chelsea asked in disbelief.

"I'm sure you'll get yours soon," their mother assured him.

"Yeah—maybe mine just processed faster than yours. I'm sure you still have a chance of getting into Hawaii too," Chelsea said, hoping that was actually true.

"That's possible, I guess," he said, trying to remain optimistic. "But, hey, at least we know *you* got in. You get to live in Hawaii like you always wanted! I'm happy for you, Sis."

"Thanks, Glenn," she said as she squeezed him tight.

"Well, Chelsea, you had better pack up anything you want to put into storage."

"They said I'm only allowed one small bag. I won't be able to bring much with me," Chelsea told her mother as she dished herself up a serving of their family's traditional New Year's Day breakfast.

"Well, if it can't fit in your closet, then get rid of it," her mother said. "And please don't get rid of any of the items you know I'm sentimental about. I'll need something to look back on to remember my little girl when I miss you."

Aw, she will miss me, Chelsea thought with a little smile. Usually, her mother didn't express much affection—she was all business. Chelsea supposed that was the accountant in her. Although ever since her father walked out, her mother was more calloused to emotion in general.

"And when is the two hundred thousand deposit due?"

"End of next week or I lose my spot," Chelsea answered her mother.

"Well I'm glad you had enough saved up for the entire deposit," her mother said with a small sigh. "I'm sure we'll have to start making payments as soon as Glenn's invitation comes."

"Sorry, Mom."

"Oh, don't be sorry, Glenn," she replied. "Chelsea had more time to save than you, and your dad said he would help with the payments. I'm glad you'll be with people your own age, and at least we won't have to pay either of your student loans anymore. I really hope you'll both be happier at the Societies while we figure out how to live in this new world of robots." She rubbed her forehead and pushed her hair up out of her face as she wondered what life would be like without her two youngest living with her. "It will be an interesting year here without you guys."

"We'll miss you, Mom."

"Yeah," Chelsea agreed.

"Thanks." She smiled. "I'll miss you guys too." She poured each of them a cup of orange juice before picking up her own glass. "Well, Happy New Year. You both have a very exciting year ahead of you," she said, and then raised her glass in the air while tilting it toward them.

Beginning the next day, thousands of others in Chelsea and Glenn's age group were headed for a new life in one of the twenty newly established Societies located throughout the United States. Everyone was hopeful that these Societies would provide some relief for the nation's young adults—who were barely limping along, but with valid reasons.

Starting a life outside of The Societies was tough. The first of a long list of well-known adversities was that it was nearly impossible to find good housing. Rental prices rose daily, and very few could afford to buy a house or land. Even the most basic one-bedroom condo ran for a million dollars or more. Chelsea's mother often vented her frustrations when paying the mortgage for their two million dollar home on her one salary after Chelsea's father left her. "It's ridiculous our little house was two million dollars when my parents were able to get a nice home for three hundred and fifty thousand," she would complain.

At which point her brother would often attempt to invite perspective by saying something like, "Didn't Great Grandma say they only paid sixty-five thousand for their five-bedroom home? Housing has constantly been on the rise."

But his logic offered little consolation when she felt so financially burdened. Chelsea hoped that with Glenn and her taken care of at The Societies her mother would be able to relax a little— maybe even have time to meet someone and find love again.

Of those who could afford to buy a home, aggressive bidding wars and lavish blind offers were waiting for every house that hit the market. Within an hour of posting, any somewhat affordable option was usually locked into a contract. Homes that were too expensive for the market defaulted to the government. These houses were then converted into hostel-type residences that were subsidized so people could afford rent—allowing the government to provide some relief to a small number of those affected by what would later be known as the Housing Crisis of 2065. Most, however, avoided the hostels, as they were usually poorly maintained and overrun with crime. Everyone knew they were a Band-Aid fix to the gaping wound that was the United States' housing market.

The older, more established generation did not feel the hurt like the younger generation—they usually had homes at least. And though life was not easy for the majority of US residents, the unestablished suffered from an acute sense of paralysis.

High rent bills made it difficult for most young adults to meet their financial goals, but even those living with relatives struggled to save enough money to afford a house because of the large student loans most had accrued through many years of advanced schooling. Unfortunately, all the hours of coursework and the diplomas did not change the lack of jobs though. Over half the jobs that once existed were now completed by the predominantly superior abilities of artificial intelligence. Given this fact, most companies had no need to hire anyone inexperienced. Robots completed the tasks that had once allowed youngsters to gain experience in the workforce, and even the more advanced positions that Chelsea's generation had been preparing for were now performed by robots.

To make matters worse, very few people were retiring. Unprecedented inflation rates and the end of social security funds meant most could not afford to retire as planned. Continuous advancements in remarkable medical technology also made it where the elderly were living longer and maintaining high levels of functionality their entire lives, which allowed them to maintain employment even in their old age. Job openings were simply not available as quickly as the workforce was growing.

Government officials assured the public that the employment problem would eventually subside with the onset of slow population growth over the previous ten years. In the meantime, however, the young adult population found itself with nowhere to live and no means of providing for themselves. Steadily, more and more people were realizing something had to be done to help, but no one seemed to know exactly what until Senator Liam Travis seized the opportunity to become the icon of hope.

He was rating low in the polls, and with another election approaching, he decided *he* would be the one to provide the answer to this hopeless scenario in order to persuade young adults to vote in his favor. For months, he and his brain trust mulled over various strategies that would make young voters like him enough to guarantee his victory. Eventually, they developed a plan based on a vision of ease-of-life that would resonate with the ideals of downtrodden youngsters hoping to catch a break from their disheartening reality. On Tuesday, January 5, 2066, he presented his idea—the original plan for *The Nationwide Society Program*—to Congress.

Naturally, there was pushback, but the numbers were there to show that if the government invested in these self-sustaining facilities to provide for the needs of their disgruntled youth, then they would save taxpayers billions of dollars of government aid in the long run. In the end, the plan was approved, and anyone within the age range of twenty-five to thirty-five, without a home and without adequate income, could apply to any of the twenty Societies that would be built across the United States. Of those who applied, one hundred thousand people per Society would be randomly selected to become citizens, and if the program found success, then plans for more Societies would soon begin.

Applicants' top preferences were factored into the random drawing as much as possible. If the invitation to live within one of The Societies was accepted, new residents could move into their living quarters in four weeks or less. There was no variance in accommodations, no premium package—every resident's room was exactly the same. Outside of that small, private living space, the rest of the grounds and infrastructure were considered public to all who lived within The Society.

Any government-supported loans were forgiven upon accepting residency, and aside from the deposit of two hundred thousand dollars per person, everything was free. Two hundred thousand was a sizable amount for this struggling population to pay but was comparable to the down payment required to purchase a house, and nothing compared to the normal costs accrued throughout the course of a lifetime. Sponsors, usually desperate parents hoping for a better future for their child, often provided the financial backing for applicants who were not able to foot the bill themselves. Interest-free payment plans were available for those parents who couldn't afford the initial cost.

Additionally, residents had to agree to complete a minimum of two hours of work each day in order to eat and live in The Societies. The grounds were designed to be virtually self-sustaining, but these two hours provided upkeep of the facilities and opportunities for learning to the residents. And though Chelsea had not read through the *entire* 346-page contract, she did study the list of requirements and rules to live in The Societies and felt she could live within the mandated expectations. She scanned her thumbprint to agree to the contract, and her acceptance was finalized.

Unfortunately, when her brother Glenn's invitation came a week after hers, it wasn't to the Hawaii Society as they had hoped. He was assigned to his third choice, The Houston Society. He had decided to apply separately in order to increase Chelsea's odds of getting into Hawaii. However, they had unrealistically hoped that by fate they would still end up together, but it was not to be. In fact, Chelsea came to find that none of her friends or family had been placed in the Hawaii Society with her—despite the fact most of them had applied for it.

In some ways it seemed fitting she would be placed on her own. She had always felt like a loner, even among her circle of friends. This opportunity merely provided the means for her to graciously break away from her childhood ties. She was only sorry to say goodbye to Glenn, whom she had grown very close to over the last three years of living with their mother following college as they both tried to find steady work.

"I really hope you like it in Houston," Chelsea said sincerely on the day of her departure as she gave Glenn one final hug before boarding the transporter pod to the Hawaii Society.

"Just don't forget to call me sometimes," he reminded her. "I know you suck at phone calls, but that doesn't mean you get to forget about me while you're living it up in Hawaii."

"I couldn't forget about my little brother," she said as she pulled back and gave him a smile.

"Younger brother," he corrected.

"You're only twenty-five, Glenn. I've got a full three years on ya. I'm afraid you're my *little* brother *forever*."

"Yeah, but I'm a whole head taller than you, sis. Younger brother is more accurate."

"Oh, shut up," she said teasingly. Then she became more solemn as she realized this could be the last time she would see her brother in person for a very long time. Traveling from The Societies to visit family was extremely expensive, and she knew it would probably be years before her parents would be able to save up the money. "I'm going to miss you."

Glenn hugged her tight. "I'm going to miss you too." As they embraced, his shoulders began to quiver, and he sobbed at what felt like the loss of his best friend.

Listening to his quiet sobs made Chelsea regret not applying together in a group application. Realizing the extent of his sorrow, she allowed her own tears to fall—even though she hated to cry.

"No need to cry now, Chelsea," her father said as he walked up behind Glenn. "You're getting outta here and going on an adventure!"

"Dad—you came?"

"Of course I did," he said as if his coming had never been in question. Chelsea's mother looked away just in time to avoid eye contact with him when he glanced over. "Plus, your mother called and told me you wouldn't be able to come back for a long time, so I figured I'd better come to say goodbye. Now—get over here and give your dad a hug before you go off and leave us all here to fend for ourselves."

Chelsea quickly wiped away her tears and her father squeezed her firmly in his arms.

"Final boarding call. All new residents of the Hawaii Society please board the transporter pod," an announcement called from the brand-new, high-speed, hydro-propelled pod that commuted across the breadth of the Pacific Ocean to the Hawaii Society each day.

"Hurry now, Chelsea," her mother called, "I haven't even had a chance to hug you."

"I need to get back to work anyway," her dad said as he let go. "Go have some fun! We all know we won't have any here. Goodbye, little thing," he said, taking one last look into Chelsea's chocolate brown eyes. He turned to Glenn, who was working to hold back any more tears. "I'll be there in a week when you leave for Houston," he said before running back to his self-driving RV. Chelsea could hear him answering a sales call as he left.

"Quickly, Chelsea," her mother said after her father disappeared. They hugged briefly and her mother gave her a short kiss on the cheek before stepping aside for her to join the others who had already boarded the transporter pod. Chelsea ran on board and turned around just in time to wave to Glenn and her mother before the doors shut behind her.

The pod soon lifted into the sky and used battery power to fly over dry land until it reached the ocean water where it submerged its front lip to provide a source of energy and propulsion for its microcombustion hydrogen jets. As Chelsea walked around in the pod, perusing the crowd, she did not feel particularly drawn to anyone, so she found an open seat and quietly took in the scenery for a long while.

"Mind if I sit down?" a tall, slender man in his late twenties asked Chelsea as he gestured to the seats beside her.

"No. Go right ahead," she said.

"Thanks," he replied while carefully taking a seat. "You excited to get to The Society? I hear it's going to be amazing. From the pictures, I can't think of a more beautiful place to live." They sat looking out of the huge window of the pod over the vast Pacific Ocean.

Dreamily envisioning Hawaii as she spoke, Chelsea replied, "I'm so excited. I've always wanted to live in Hawaii. But who wouldn't want to live in paradise, right? We're just lucky we were chosen."

"That's true," he agreed. "Thank goodness the government stepped in to make something good happen—finally put our tax dollars to good use. Or other people's tax dollars, I should say," the man chuckled. "I never made much, even as a graphic designer. It's a very competitive job market," he explained. He then extended his hand to Chelsea. "Name's Hammond."

"Chelsea," she said as she shook his hand and their eyes met. His mocha skin was warm to the touch and his grip was gentle but firm. She found his face quite handsome and wondered if he was available.

Not knowing a graceful way to ask, a painful moment of silence ensued as Chelsea awkwardly turned away to look out the window while trying to think of a new avenue of conversation to pursue without blurting out her relationship status. As the two of them watched the ocean rapidly pass as they rushed by, they unexpectedly witnessed a whale breach the water and land hard with a big splash. Hammond and Chelsea looked at each other and smiled with delight, acknowledging the fortuitous sighting while traveling over four hundred miles an hour.

❖14❖

Just then, a woman abruptly plopped herself between them. "How's it going, darling?" she asked while cozying into Hammond's chest. "Sorry I took so long. I decided to change my up-do to some braids so I could have wavy curls when we arrive on the beach," the woman explained gleefully, her shoulders bouncing up and down in a playful manner.

"The most beautiful girl, with wavy hair, on a pristine beach— sounds like a vision," Hammond commented, completely lovestruck, as he ran his hand down one of the woman's braids. "You don't need to worry your pretty little self about me though. I wasn't bored. I was just talking with this nice woman here. Chelsea, this is Sara."

"Nice to meet you, Sara." Chelsea nodded in acknowledgment, and then quickly tried to think of a way to continue the conversation. "So, what did you do back in the states? Hammond was just saying he was a graphic designer."

"Sara's the best video editor out there," Hammond jumped in while smiling brightly at Sara. "Most creative mind you'll ever meet."

"Bit too creative according to my *many* past employers," Sara added while laughing. "And you? What did you do for work, Chelsea?"

"I was a video engineer back in Vegas," she explained. "Although I can tell you I'm happy to be done with that for a while. I've been completely burnt out from working awful hours at events or not being able to find steady work."

"Mmm-hm. We know how that goes," Sara responded. "We've both worked live events before, and they can be brutal hours."

Hammond got a pensive look on his face. "It's interesting. Everyone we've met today either worked in live events or has some kind of creative background."

"Hm. That is interesting. It's not often I meet a lot of people who work events that I've never met before. Although in Vegas, there are a lot of us, so I suppose I couldn't know everyone."

Chelsea watched Hammond begin nuzzling into the side of Sara's face and felt awkward that she had hoped he would find her attractive when he was so obviously into Sara, who was the exact opposite of Chelsea—Sara was tall, blonde, and skinny as a stick. However, part of her was grateful that Hammond was unavailable—it relieved her of any pressure to impress. He was automatically in the friend zone, and she desperately needed some friends. "So, how long have you two known each other?"

"How long has it been, love?" Hammond asked Sara with a smile.

"Well, I suppose that depends on what you mean by 'being together,'" she said teasingly. "I first met Hammond in a dessert shop when we were about ten. He was buying grape flavored mochi balls, same as me, and I knew we were destined to be together. But we weren't romantically together until about thirteen."

"I don't think I've left her side ever since," Hammond said, sheepishly happy. "We eloped as soon as we could and have been together ever since." Seeing the shock on Chelsea's face, Hammond responded quickly with the usual blurb he told people about their surprising love story. "I know we're kind of an odd case these days. We just found exactly what we were looking for very early on, and after they ended marriage, we just decided to keep going as if nothing had changed."

About twelve years prior, the government had dissolved the institution of marriage. They had deemed it unnecessary and decided it overcomplicated the system. Not many young people were choosing to get married anyway, so it changed very little for the unwed. But for the older generations, not having marriage as an integral part of society was a hard adjustment, especially for those couples that had been married for many years. They resented the government's sudden legal indifference to their union. And though Hammond and Sara had only been married for one short but blissful year, at the time of the nullification, they couldn't help but feel robbed of something truly special. But due to the debate on the definition of marriage growing more complex and heated throughout the years, the Supreme Court felt its best solution was to rule it a nonissue and nullify marriage altogether.

Personally, Chelsea liked the idea of marriage—though if she would admit it, her opinion was mainly due to the fact that marriage was the factor that had kept her father around when she was younger. She still remembered a time when her mother was joyful and her father at least *tried* to be a good husband. And as an adult who knew what it was like to have a father around when she was a child as compared to Chelsea's life now where she felt her father couldn't care less, she resented the ruling that gave him his out. She often replayed in her mind the words her father spoke as he left during her senior year of high school. "I don't have to put up with this anymore. You're not my wife. You want me to help out more? I'll help myself out the door." Seeing how hard it was on Glenn to be passed back and forth between the stable life he knew at home with their mother and the unpredictable life on the road with their father, she felt marriage at least made things less complicated logistically when it came to children.

However, most people weren't choosing to have children either. This was due to the release of a new drug fourteen years prior that was invented by Timothy Scott. He was a college dropout who had rediscovered a primitive one-time oral contraceptive and developed an antidote to its effects. The drug was made from the root of a plant found in Brazil. It made women completely infertile until they took the antidote. The root had been used anciently for the same purpose, but the formula for the antidote had been lost for hundreds of years, and since few women wanted to be permanently infertile, the root was forgotten. That is, until young Timothy Scott, studying biology, read about it in a doctoral dissertation about tribal communities in the library of his university. He packed his bags the following day and left on the next available flight to Brazil, determined to find the antidote and become rich. It took him ten long years to track down the correct ancient medical text found in a remote tribe before he uncovered the formula for the antidote and another three years of research to get the drugs approved for public release. But in time, he became a success and eventually gained his fortune.

Shortly after the drug became popular, a mandate was passed requiring that all female residents of the US take the contraceptive within a month of puberty to avoid unwanted pregnancies. This approach to birth control was highly praised throughout the country. Abortions fell to almost zero, and seventy-four percent fewer children were placed in orphanages each year. In the short run, it was an obvious success—a win for humanity, and a win for children. But many women never felt completely prepared to step into parenthood until after the effects of the root became permanent. There were twenty to thirty years before the results became irreversible, and since everyone begins puberty at a different age, some had more time and some less before it was too late. Most of Chelsea's generation never even considered parenthood as an option—as they could rarely take care of themselves. Either way, the population growth was declining, and fast.

"On the contrary," Chelsea replied upon hearing about Hammond and Sara's early and long-lasting relationship, "it's refreshing to see some consistency nowadays. It seems like everything changes every day—including all my friends' lovers. It's nice to see some of my friends who just genuinely enjoy each other."

Most people their age spent their time with many different partners simultaneously, either trying to determine which was the most compatible with them or simply indulging in their own physical pleasures with as many people as possible.

Chelsea's grandmother once told her the dating scene reminded her of a show they used to watch when she was young—a reality TV show where one person was openly dating multiple people, trying to determine which one of the group they truly wanted to be with. They all knew the contestant was dating the other candidates, and one by one, they would be narrowed down. But her grandmother said the final couple rarely stayed together very long after the show ended. Because of that, Chelsea decided it was a flawed method and chose to date one man at a time. Although finding someone who was interested in more than a one-night stand seemed impossible. She envied Sara.

"So I guess that means you consider us friends?" Sara eagerly asked Chelsea.

"I mean, if you want to be," Chelsea replied, realizing she had insinuated they would continue their brief association beyond the pod.

"Of course! We were hoping to make some friends sooner than later," Hammond said with a friendly smile.

Sara's supportive nod was quickly disrupted as her focus changed to the panorama behind Chelsea. Her eyes widened in awe, and she pointed excitedly. "There it is! We're here!" she exclaimed as the Hawaii Society appeared in the window of the pod.

2. UNDER THE PEACH TREE

∞

THE INITIAL SIGHT of the Hawaii Society building was a vivid tropical splendor. A luscious mountain with a waterfall running down it encircled the backside of The Society's mammoth buildings. To the left of the mountain, a pristine beach was visible with a row of palm trees and an endless view of the open ocean. To the right of the mountain was a vast tropical forest. A large garden and an orchard, with row upon row of fruit trees, were planted at the edge of the forest in close proximity to The Society grounds.

White buildings in the shape of oval cylinders were packed next to each other and reaching up to the sky to almost match the height of the large mountain behind them. They were lined with rows of windows from top to bottom and roofed with solar panels to absorb the sun and produce their own electricity. Between each building, the grounds were engulfed in a myriad of trees and plant life with walkways running through them for easy passage. In the center of these buildings, four ginormous square frustum-shaped towers supported the base of a stadium-like building. The towers resembled the legs of a table with the stadium-like building acting as the tabletop. The huge oval building on top had a dome-shaped, glass roof that was reinforced with clear solar panels that added strength to the dome's design and supplied a large amount of electricity to The Society. It was modeled after a football stadium in order to accommodate the entire population of The Society at once. Nestled under the dome and between the four towers, more cylindrical oval structures stood hidden beneath the protection of the domed building overhead.

Unbeknownst to Chelsea, this stadium-like building was the reason she had been clandestinely selected from the millions of other candidates to live in this tropical paradise. Even though the selection process was supposed to be completely random and fair, Hawaii was a special case in which the government saw fit to give preferential access to those with skills in events and showmanship. The Hawaii Society had been specially chosen to represent the quintessence of Society living. This dome-shaped building would be the arena that would broadcast to the nation the success of The Society program—reassuring taxpayers and concerned parents that their money was well spent and their young people taken care of.

Once the transporter pod came to a stop in front of The Society, everyone rushed for the opening doors. No one had luggage to grab since everyone was allowed only one bag of minimal personal belongings and the clothes on their back. In Chelsea's bag was packed a neatly folded, cloth-like LED screen to display pictures of her family and friends on her wall, some lip gloss, her favorite perfume, and her PED.

Everyone owned a PED to replace the laptops, computers, cell phones, cameras, projectors, and other electronic devices that had become essentials in the early twenty-first century. PED stood for Personal Electronic Device. It was about the size of a woman's pocketbook but could expand to the size of a small tabletop if needed. Made out of collapsible, self-healing, durable glass, it could run an indefinite number of programs, applications, and controls and was built to last a lifetime. Most often, the PED itself was left at home in a secure location. It did the complex computations while wearable devices served as the everyday, on-the-go devices that synced with the PED. A wristband and an earpiece were the most commonly used portable options.

When activated, wristbands projected a laser image, sensitive to touch, onto one's forearm or palm for a more limited but portable use of the PED's technology. Wristbands were also everyone's means of identification and money. There was no longer any tangible form of currency. All transactions were electronic, and money was spent with a tap of the wrist. They also served as a way to track health so that hospitals could be alerted immediately if any signs were detected that the wearer needed medical assistance. By age two, most children had their first wristband. It was used to help guardians locate and communicate with them. Between ages ten to sixteen, they usually received their first PED and an earpiece to couple with the wristband.

The earpiece sat snug in the ear and was invisible to the naked eye. It was tiny and custom fit to the inner ear, making it barely noticeable to the wearer. Special technology was created that allowed it to grip the inner ear, ensuring it stayed in place, and if a fingertip were placed on the opposite end of the device, its grip would transfer to the fingertip for safe removal. It served as the audible communication with the PED system. Its ability to decipher exactly what the wearer was saying while tuning out all outside noise was perfectly accurate, and only the wearer could hear sound from the earpiece.

These devices were shockproof and waterproof. All electronics could be charged wirelessly via the wireless charging hubs found in every room of any modern building. This made it so Personal Electronic Devices, wristbands, and earpieces had an almost constant supply of power, and even if there was no nearby charging hub, the batteries could last for several days.

The majority of employers and private entities often required people to wear their wristbands and earpieces so that video recordings could be taken in case of an incident. By referencing footage from multiple PED devices, ninety-five percent of incidents could be confirmed and handled with complete accuracy in the court systems. Wristbands and earpieces were usually only removed for moments of privacy or to sleep, but the majority just turned them to privacy mode and left them on for convenience. However, among Society citizens, wristbands were required to be recording and within eyesight at all times—though people would only be held accountable for not wearing their wristbands and earpieces in a case where they were prosecuting another person for something they did without the PED footage to prove what had happened.

Most wristbands were a thin black wire that was barely noticeable. This made it comfortable to wear on the wrist both day and night. Those with money had multiple wristbands of varying styles to match different outfits or provide them with an assortment of styles to choose from. Chelsea's parents could afford only a basic black wristband for her in her adolescence, but since she had a particular liking for bracelets, she decided in her adulthood to construct her own by weaving strands of copper into a wide woven band. Months of collecting copper from old cables that were no longer used at her previous temp jobs eventually accumulated into enough metal to construct her design. She herself embedded into the copper weaves both the PED-linked microchip and the microscopic laser projector to project onto her wrist. It took her four years to complete, but she was quite pleased with the end result. Her mother felt it was far too bulky and showy for a PED wristband, but Chelsea wore it proudly just the same.

Once everyone had exited the pod, a robot about four feet tall stood blocking the crowd with a projected barrier that read, "Do not cross—your tour of the Hawaii Society will begin soon." The head, arms, and chest cavity of the tour bot were perfectly formed and rounded to mimic the body of a human, but instead of two legs, it had track tires to move around. As the last of the passengers stepped in front of the robot, it publicized, "Welcome, newcomers. All one hundred and thirty-six passengers of phase thirty-one of the resettlement have been accounted for. Initiation of the welcome message will commence."

Great, Chelsea thought sarcastically. *More robots. Just what we need. They're the reason we're all out of a job in the first place.* But despite her feelings toward robots, she knew they weren't going anywhere. No company could deny the efficiency of a bot over paid workers, and as she looked over the grounds and saw a variety of bots, Chelsea realized that fact must hold true at The Societies as well.

A hologram of the Vice President of the United States, who had helped endorse The Societies Program, projected from out of the robot's aluminum chest plate and played a prerecorded greeting. "Welcome, new residents of The Societies! We hope you find your new home comfortable and pleasant. In The Societies, you will find a peaceful and prosperous community where all are equal, and the necessities of life are provided. Shelter, food, clothing, recreation, and healthcare are all readily available to everyone. Things found within your Society belong equally to every resident. Discrimination and privilege do not exist within its walls. You have been chosen at random from millions of hopeful residents to test and enjoy this Society—to live life as it should be. Relish in what lies before you. Your resident information bot will now lead you on a tour of the facilities."

At the close of the message, the hologram disappeared, and the information bot's digitalized and rudimentary face reappeared. Robotics engineers found robots with overly humanized features made people feel uneasy, so they purposefully made robots with computerized facial features that showed no negative emotion.

The electronically formed face smiled at the crowd of newcomers. "As Madame Vice President stated, I will be giving a tour of The Society during which we will discuss Society living. Let us begin. Follow me closely, please."

Sara quickly unraveled the tight braids she had made in her hair while in the bathroom of the pod to showcase her dirty blonde hair that now had a slight wave to it. She grabbed a bright-colored hairpiece from her large handbag to pull back the hair draped over her left temple. She then cozied into Hammond's side, squeezing his arm as they walked. Her long, slender legs easily kept up with Hammond's. "We're actually here, baby. It's happening!" she said as she jumped up and down ever so slightly. He put his arm around her and happily nodded at her enthusiasm.

Chelsea saw Sara as a little girl bursting out of a grown woman's body. She displayed endless amounts of energy and was enthusiastic about the most bizarre things—her hairdos for one. Chelsea would soon come to find that Sara often had as many as four hairdos within a day, each one uniquely different from the next. Judging from Sara's neon yellow top and flashy legging, it was obvious she also seemed to prefer brightly colored clothing, along with hair trinkets to match. Her light skin was slightly tanned, and freckles dotted her face and arms.

Hammond, on the other hand, was far more subdued. His attire was most comparable to that of a golfer. He preferred collared shirts with little color and a neutral pant. He had a composed demeanor that made others feel safe and calm. His brilliant smile appeared most often around Sara, and his laugh was timid.

They were a bit of an odd couple, Sara and Hammond, but Chelsea considered herself lucky to have met them so soon and hoped they would remain friends. Considering herself a bit offbeat as well, Chelsea liked their distinctiveness.

"When the United States government originally bought this island, it was in hopes of preserving the nature of one of Hawaii's most richly blessed small sister islands. But with the development of scare real estate prospects, it has now been repurposed as a way to enhance the lives of America's young people through these trying times, while still preserving the majority of the landscape of Hawaii's natural beauty. We thank you for being a part of this catalyst program and ask that you show great respect in your care of both the nature and the newly built, high-tech facilities found on this island," the bot shared before beginning the walk-through. Extending its robotic limb to the south, it continued. "If you would direct your attention to the right, you will see The Society's blossoming orchards and garden. The outside garden grows a variety of fruits and vegetables that require two feet or more of vertical growth. Smaller, less expansive plants are grown inside Tower Two, which you will see later in the tour. Small robots patrol the gardens to rid the soil of small weeds and insects and to plant seeds as needed to ensure constant growth. An intricate compost watering system is in place to ensure each plant is watered the optimal amount—taking into account any rainfall. Additionally, each tree and plant has been genetically modified to possess the accelerated growth rate of a weed. Each resident is allowed to pick two items directly from the gardens each day if you wish for a snack in addition to the three provided meals. Please take the next five minutes to sample any fruits or vegetables found within the gardens. Use your wristbands to check the ripeness of each sample to ensure a ripe pick."

Following a long row of orange trees, Chelsea started down a path in hopes that she would locate a peach tree where she could sink her teeth into a fuzzy, ripe sample of her favorite fruit.

"Mmmm, these pears are amazing! Do you want to try one, Chelsea?" Sara called out from a nearby pear tree. Hammond, his mouth full of pear, was nodding beside her.

"Oh, no thanks. I really want to try a peach," she called back to them. Though she didn't mind the taste of pears, Chelsea couldn't help but have a certain disdain toward the fruit after someone in high school told her that her body resembled a pear—she could tell it wasn't meant to be a compliment. Every time she looked at her reflection from that moment on, she envisioned a pear outlining her body.

Just past a row of very copious apple trees, she spotted the peach trees she was hoping for, which were healthy and plentiful. But as she examined them, she noticed all the peaches on the lower branches had already been picked. The only remaining peaches hung on the taller branches that were just out of her reach. So, as short girls do, she got creative. She walked up to the nearest tree, reached for a branch near the trunk and pulled herself up to the closest peach in sight.

"Examine peach ripeness," she said as she placed her copper bracelet against the skin of a ripe-looking peach.

"Tropic Sweet Peach. Ready for picking," her wristband indicated to her through her earpiece.

She pulled the soft peach from its branch and jumped down, careful to avoid the patrolling garden robot below, and took a large bite. The juice ran down her forearm, and she savored the sweet, succulent flavor she had been hoping for.

"You know, there's a better way to do that," a voice interlaced with a light chuckle said to her from behind.

Chelsea whirled around, startled to know that someone had been watching her. A striking man, who had obviously just returned from the beach, was walking toward her. He was holding a step stool in his hand and smiling. His dirty blond hair was damp and chaotic from having been briefly dried with the shirt that he was holding in his other hand. He wore his unkempt look well and had a face that could dazzle any woman. His sharp jaw and brilliant eyes only briefly distracted Chelsea from his perfect smile. Sand still clung to his muscular back from an afternoon of sunbathing.

Chelsea had had her share of run-ins with this kind of man—the type who exuded a sense of irresistibility. She promised herself that she would not so easily fall prey to his charm like she had with other men in the past—though she found her heart pounding the closer he got to her.

She simply responded, "Well, I got my peach. So my way worked just fine. Thank you." She walked past him toward the group, taking a large bite of the peach to avoid having to talk to him further.

She looked back briefly to see him being approached by another woman. The lanky brunette in a damp bathing suit walked up beside him and handed him an apple. Chelsea rolled her eyes. *He has the nerve to tell me how to do something when he clearly doesn't do anything for himself,* she thought in disgust.

The man stood frozen—slightly perplexed by Chelsea's response to his suggestion. He hardly noticed the apple placed in his hand or the usual slew of questions Lola began asking him. He just watched Chelsea's beautiful hair blow gently in the wind. Its color matched her copper bracelet, and it was cut in a unique undercut bob that showcased a small infinity symbol that was shaved into the hair on the nape of her neck. Distracted by the gentle sway of her hips, he also noticed her peculiar walk, which he could only describe as a sort of strut. When he came to his senses, he couldn't help but smirk at the feisty woman who had climbed the peach tree. Utilizing Chelsea's trick, he too took a large bite of his apple to avoid having to answer his newest agent's constant flow of inquiries.

3. HAWAII SOCIETY TOUR

CHELSEA WAS QUITE pleased with her peach. Knowing that peaches were not a fruit native to the region, she was impressed by its robust flavor. She wasn't too surprised though. One rarely encountered less than exceptional produce options because of the plethora of new discoveries from agriculturalists that had propelled the horticulture industry forward significantly in the last twenty years.

In Chelsea's eyes, there were few better things than biting into a perfectly ripened piece of fruit. It was pure, untainted sweet, straight from nature. Her rather spiteful encounter with the man under the peach tree only slightly dampened the delicious moment. She was rather pleased with herself for telling him her mind. It was a trait of hers she knew she should probably rein in a bit but, in view of her past failed attempts, had ultimately decided to embrace instead.

"I hope everyone enjoyed a taste of our endless selection of succulent fruit and vegetables. We will now continue our tour of The Society," the tour bot said. "Directly in front of you, you will see the front rightmost column of The Society building where we will visit the welcome desk and reception area. We refer to it as Tower One."

As the group entered the first of the four towering columns, Chelsea caught a glimpse of the bridge that led to the other side of the river where the foot of the waterfall was showering mist around the base of the mountain. She wanted to dart away and stand under the rushing water and feel its gentle mist moisten her skin. It was the perfect day to do so, with the hot sun bearing down. But with the information bot tracking everyone's wristbands, she knew it would not be allowed. She had to follow instructions and finish the tour. The Society Agreement she had signed made it very clear that all residents were to follow "Society Rules and Instructions" or be removed.

Inside of Tower One was a large, open area with some sizable pools and hot tubs situated at the far end. The towers were made of thick glass panes to allow residents to look out over the mountain and adjacent forest. There was a welcome desk close to the entrance where a variety of snacks and drinks were laid out. An LED wall was located behind the desk, and a large interactive interface with a map of the facilities stood vertically to its right. As the group approached, a beautiful Hawaiian woman dressed in a traditional Hawaiian grass skirt and a colorful headdress filled the LED wall.

"Aloha, Hawaii Society Residents! We welcome you to the Hawaii Society. I am Kona—your facility's local citizen. I too was randomly selected to live among you on this beautiful island, not far from the beloved islands of Hawaii. I grew up in Maui and love the great state of Hawaii and all its beautiful features. I was chosen to act as an advocate and leader for our community when I became a citizen here. Our Society is a new hope for the world—to demonstrate how to live in a place of harmony where *all* needs are met for *every* resident. If you would like to view the map of the facility or ask a question, please approach the interface pad so it can answer any questions you may have."

A young man with dark spiked hair stepped forward and called out, "Where can you find a bathroom in this place?"

"The community restroom can be found five hundred meters behind the welcome kiosk and to the right. Please be aware that we do not have gender-specific bathrooms at our facilities. Feel free to use any restroom on the premises," the Hawaiian beauty on the screen replied without hesitation.

"O-okay," the man said and walked past the monitor.

"After relieving yourself, you will return and finish the tour with the rest of the group, sir. That is an official instruction. Do you comply?" the bot asked in a singsong voice.

As the tour bot asked, the man froze in his steps. His fists clenched, and he turned around to face the bot before replying.

"Yes," he said. Chelsea noticed a slight grimace cross his face as if he hated himself for agreeing to comply, and then he turned back around to walk toward the restroom.

"While Mr. Wong relieves himself, those willing to comply with those same instructions may also join him. We will resume our tour in five minutes. Anyone remaining may study the facilities map found on the screen."

The map showed the four large towers with each having three levels. The oval cylinder structures were labeled as living quarters. The circular dome building had an inner and outer circle in its interior. The inner circle housed an auditorium with a large stage and seating for the residents to attend events. The outer circle, within the dome, consisted of a number of rooms to assist in pre- and post-production for filming videos and producing live events. As a video engineer by trade, Chelsea was particularly anxious to make her way up to the dome and see what kind of technology it housed.

After people returned from the restroom, the tour bot went immediately into the next part of the tour. "The rest of this level consists of an open social area with plenty of seating and tables for those who would like to mingle at any time of the day. The pool facilities are located just past the social area as well as outside the back doors. We will visit the pools later in the tour," the bot explained. "In the center of the room, you will see a large pillar with a ramp leading up to the elevator that can take us to the second and third floor. You will also find the Society Rules displayed for all to see. You should have already read the rules when you signed the Society Agreement, but I would ask that everyone take a minute to reread them to refresh your memories of the statutes you will need to live by as long as you remain. Thank you for complying. Once read, please make your way to the elevator just up the ramp." The tour bot headed to the entrance of the elevator to wait while the group circled around the large silver plaque that hung on the wall.

❖Society Rules❖

❖Every resident must comply with official instruction.

❖Every resident must contribute at least two hours of work and/or training daily. If physically unable, a suitable substitute must complete those hours.

❖All public facilities, equipment, and resources belong equally to everyone on a first come first serve basis. Private living quarters and belongings should be labeled as such.

❖No prejudice, hate, or discrimination will be tolerated.

❖Wristbands and earpieces should be actively recording video footage and be worn or within eyesight at all times.

❖Follow any safety instructions found throughout the facilities.

❖Residents are not allowed to request additional accommodations or special treatment beyond the basic needs already provided for, which include health, food, water, clothing, recreational activity, learning, and respect.

Any resident who does not comply will be relocated immediately. Any suspected violations of rules will be submitted to the government offices to verify through video footage.

While making their way to the elevator, the group broke out in whispers, discussing The Society's rules. One man was particularly amazed that they were only required to do two hours of work a day. Chelsea was also excited about that fact. She couldn't make out what exactly Tray Wong had to say as he muttered under his breath, but as the elevator doors opened to the second floor, their conversations quickly ended when they smelled the aroma from the kitchen.

The elevator chimed, and a recording said, "Second Floor. Kitchen, cafeteria, and dining area." Everyone quickly unloaded from the elevator, excited to taste the food that was producing such a wave of delicious smells. "This entire level is dedicated to providing healthy and well-balanced meals to the residents of the Hawaii Society. Please follow the lit indicators on the floor and treat yourselves to one of our kitchen's wonderful meals. Feel free to sit at any available table. We will convene in one hour." After finishing the brief announcement, the tour bot situated itself at the side of the elevator to wait for the residents to eat.

As they stood in line, they could see a robotic chef in a massive kitchen behind a glass panel, busily working to prepare and cook the food that was currently being plated for residents to consume. The robotic chef looked like a metal octopus hanging from the ceiling, but it had ten limbs instead of eight. Three of the arms worked together to prep the food, while three more cooked it. Two of its metallic hands meticulously plated each meal, and the other two whirled around doing whatever cleaning or stirring or pouring needed to be done.

Chelsea watched in wonderment as the robotic hands blazed around the kitchen at an alarming rate with perfect coordination. She had seen robotic chefs many times before, but most only had two limbs. The added coordination for the ten limbs to dance around each other with ease was very impressive.

"Now that's a robotic chef worth posting about," someone commented while sharing a live video of it on his social media account via his wristband.

A conveyor belt with plated meals on it rotated slowly beside the line of people, allowing everyone to grab a plate of his or her own. A small slice of roast, fresh pineapple, a garden salad, and a helping of sweet potato casserole were accompanied by guava juice for that day's lunch. As Chelsea picked up her plate, the fragrant steam coming from her platter made her mouth water. It was the perfect hybrid of a home-cooked meal and the kind of fine dining found at a five-star restaurant. Everything tasted amazing and was cooked to perfection. The meat easily fell apart with just a fork, and the seasoning that accompanied it was the perfect pairing for the mild flavor of a pork roast. It was near impossible to catch all the sweet juice that ran from the sides of the pineapple as people took their first bites. The freshest and crispest lettuce and vegetables were in every salad, and the sweet potato casserole was a rare combination of flavors that Chelsea had never tasted before. The usual brown sugar and nut combination she was used to at home was replaced with an earthy seasoning and what she could only guess to be bacon. And to wash it down, the guava juice was a creamy nectar from the ripest of guavas.

Besides having an abundance of outstanding fruits and vegetables from the Society's gardens on hand, the robot chef's exquisite meals were also the results of its ability to scour the internet for the best recipes with the highest ratings. After cross-referencing the available ingredients, menus were selected to accommodate the majority of people's food preferences and use the ingredients at The Society's disposal in the most effective way possible. Having a robot chef was an ideal combination of efficiency (where it wasted no food) and quality (where every dish was a top-rated culinary masterpiece).

When everyone had finished their meal, they placed their plates and cups on a conveyor belt with cutouts that gripped the dishes securely and sent them to the dishwasher to be power-washed with steaming hot water on each side. After all the dishes were scanned and confirmed clean, they were placed neatly back on the conveyor belt to be used again during the next meal.

"I trust everyone enjoyed their meal. We will now go to the third and final level of Tower One to view the hospital facilities."

The group did not see much of the hospital. Everyone stood in the lobby as the tour robot pointed out the check-in desk and the pharmacy and gave a short spiel on the excellent care everyone would receive if they ever had need of it. Body scanners were available to scan people for any injury, sickness, or disease known to man. Medical bots performed any known, nonexperimental procedures. Those with more complex or unknown issues would have to be sent back to the mainland to visit a specialist.

As the group left Tower One to proceed to Tower Two, they walked past the open-air pools that were directly outside of the social area and the indoor pools on level one. The outside pools were various sizes of circles that were spread out over a large area. The circles were connected with strips of pool—a design that resembled the structure of molecules. This allowed for more intimate groups to enjoy the pool in the smaller circles while larger groups could swim in the bigger sections. Only twelve people soaked in its clear waters as they passed. Since only a few thousand people had been brought to the island at this point of the resettlement, The Society grounds still felt very empty compared to what it would be when all one hundred thousand people were living there. As she impatiently followed behind the tour bot, Chelsea hoped she would soon be enjoying the pool water too.

Tower Two's first level was a cluster of gym equipment and other "self-help" services. Chelsea counted ten people using the gym equipment, most of whom decided to take a water break shortly after seeing the tour group enter. The gym equipment was designed to convert the energy produced from residents' exercises into electricity to add to the power produced from the solar panels on the roofs of the buildings. The other self-help stations included a hair cutting station, a nail salon, a massage station, and a tattoo station. Each service was completed by a special machine or robot. Makeup tattooing was a very popular practice to save on the time and hassle of daily application. It was common to contour the face with extensive tattoo artistry in order to appear more chiseled, as well as having colorful eyeshadow or extravagant eyeliner designs to stand out as unique. Chelsea had had a modest, natural look tattooed years ago and didn't have any plans to add to it.

The second level of Tower Two was also a kitchen and cafeteria. Given that it was an exact replica of Tower One's kitchen and cafeteria, the tour bot said they would be skipping that floor, but all were welcome to visit it during another meal break. Eventually, everyone would be given suggested time slots and towers to visit for meals via their wristband to keep from overcrowding the cafeterias. But since people were arriving in phases, it was known that those suggestions would not be given until the majority of the residents had arrived.

The third and final floor of Tower Two was a vast indoor garden. It was barely recognizable as an indoor facility because the majority of it was covered in green plants. Levels of shelving large enough to walk on were stacked atop each other and housed the plants in large trays of water. Using hydroponics and pink UV lights, a variety of fruits, vegetables, and herbs were grown that stocked The Society with any produce not being grown outside and small enough to contain within a two-foot perimeter. Everyone was invited to walk the aisles of the ginormous indoor garden facilities and try a sample of something.

"If there is no dirt, how do the plants get their nutrients?" Chelsea asked the information bot as she walked down one of the aisles.

"On the far end of the indoor gardens, there is a large tank full of fish that supplies the kitchen with fish for your meals as well as providing nutrients from their waste to the plants."

"That's kind of gross," Sara whispered to Chelsea. "Our food is basically grown from fish poop."

Chelsea chuckled, and despite her very full stomach from the feast served at lunch, she looked over the selection of bright fruits. They all looked so succulent, she couldn't resist. She tried a strawberry and was not disappointed. It was the sweetest strawberry she could ever recall tasting.

The first floor of Tower Three was an entire level full of classrooms where residents could go to learn more advanced training for some of the jobs that had to be done around The Society. There were classes to learn advanced networking, robotics, video editing, audiovisual engineering, mechanics, computer science, hydroponics, agriculture, and livestock, plus a number of miscellaneous classes to build off those skills.

Chelsea had interest in some of the subjects but felt little urge to sign up for any the next day when she was so looking forward to spending her days lying on the white sand—not having to study or stress about getting work.

"You going to sign up for a class?" Hammond asked as he looked over the list of available options for the following day.

"Maybe I'll look into classes later, but for now, I'm just going to relax and do something easy," Chelsea answered.

"This next level is where you will find the childcare and grade school facilities for those members of The Society with children," the robot said as they entered the second level of Tower Three. An audible groan could be heard from a few people in the group. Two people who had been trying to corral their children during the entire tour immediately perked up and stepped forward with their young children.

Very few families, groups, or partners would be found within the popular picks of the Societies once all the residents moved into their assigned locations. Since only one application could be turned in for people wishing to apply as a group, applying together meant lower odds of getting paired with an individual's top preference.

Had Chelsea applied with her brother, she knew how unlikely it would've been that she would still be placed in Hawaii. She felt bad knowing she had abandoned Glenn for the sake of her own selfish desires. The fact that Hammond and Sara got in together made her feel that much worse. *Maybe we would've had a shot after all,* she thought. Chelsea wanted to blame the system for not allowing families to stick together, but she knew it was the price that had to be paid in the name of fairness—a price she shamefully admitted she hadn't wanted to pay, for fear of losing out on Hawaii.

The two people with children eagerly walked off the elevator onto the second floor. "What are the hours for the childcare center?" one asked.

"A robotic caregiver will be available at all hours of the day and night. Society members will be able to sign up for caregiver task hours from 8 a.m. to 5 p.m.," the tour bot answered. The rest of the group lagged behind the two eager parents. Most everyone began checking their PED notifications using their wristbands.

"As you can see, the daycare center is equipped with toys, books, movies, games, and play structures for all ages. From one month to fifteen years of age, children will be provided with guided supervision and education 24/7—apart from mealtimes. Because this floor is not equipped with a chef and cafeteria area, we do require that parents take children to each mealtime. Depending upon the age of your child, more or less time during the day is mandated to ensure learning and proper mental development. And unlike the adults, children's sleeping quarters can be found right on this floor to ensure proper naps during the day and age-appropriate bedtimes. We will pass the sleeping pods for the children on our left as we continue walking toward the education centers ahead. I invite you to take a quick look at the various accommodations as we walk," the tour robot said.

One of the parents appeared displeased upon hearing the schedule for the children and seeing the separate sleeping pods. She looked with a questioning expression at the wall of small coves for the children to use for beds that were stacked atop each other, making the wall look like a piece of oversized honeycomb. Small doors were affixed to the front of the pods to keep the younger children from falling out.

The education centers for the children consisted of multiple rooms with row upon row of tabletops with a screen at each individual station. The tour robot went on, "These interactive monitors are where each student sits to complete the necessary hours required for each grade level. Academic activity is catered directly to their performance needs. The level of customization for each student has proven very effective in teaching students to build on their strengths and overcome their weaknesses in all educational subjects."

After realizing all the educational rooms were identical, the crowd steadily turned and headed back to the elevator. The floor had been so irrelevant to most that the tail end of the group was still lingering near the entrance of the elevator as the rest of the group made their way back from seeing the educational stations.

As the elevator rose, Chelsea overheard one man saying, "I don't even know why they let people with kids in The Societies in the first place." She hoped that the kids on the elevator didn't hear his rude comment. She wanted to reprimand him, but as she thought of her rebuttal, the elevator opened on the third floor to a smiling figure ready to greet the anticipated visitors.

"Thank you so much for coming to the Hawaii Society. I am Sandra Waverly, your government official tasked with running this Society. Our goals are to maintain a self-sustaining system and contentment among our residents. Behind me, you will see the government offices that assist in running The Society and corresponding with Washington. If you ever have any concerns or legal issues, please visit this floor and enter your name and issue into the touchscreen to my left. Whoever can best assist you will be with you shortly. Does anyone have any questions?" She waited briefly, and then her crimson lips perked up into a tense smile. "Excellent. Make yourselves at home and enjoy the rest of your guided tour of our beautiful facilities." After her speech, she promptly turned to walk down the hall back to her office.

No one had the chance to exit the elevator while she gave her speech, so the doors closed without anyone making a move. A baby's fussing broke the silence that formed while everyone worked to mentally process their first encounter with their Society's government official. Nothing was particularly bizarre about it—it just lacked sincerity. It felt too rehearsed.

Instead of returning to the ground level to explore the next tower, Chelsea was thrilled to see the elevator rise to the fourth floor where they would explore the stadium-like building with the glass-topped dome. The elevator doors opened to a large hallway that curved with the oval shape of the building. Past the hallway, they entered a tunnel where Chelsea could see a portion of a brightly lit stage and a small section of stadium seating in the distance. As they walked through the tunnel into the gigantic arena, they moved toward a curved fifty-foot LED screen that spanned the wall above the stage and was alight with the message *Welcome to the Hawaii Society*. The stage protruded twenty feet from under the screen. The arena seating circled the entire room and removable chairs were lined directly in front of the stage on the ground floor. In a moment's notice, these chairs could be flipped underground to provide an open floor for a variety of activities, ranging from sporting events to dances.

"The dome, as we call it, is a building unique to the Hawaii Society. No other Society has an arena on its grounds. This arena was specifically made to broadcast to the world the successes of The Societies Program. The stage you see before you is the backdrop where the majority of broadcasts will be filmed. You will also have the occasional chance to view live entertainment, attend events hosted by movie star Davin Chapman, get updates and news from our Society leaders, and possibly perform in talent shows to showcase your own artistic abilities. When it is not in use, the stage and floor seating can be removed remotely. As a whole, the arena is large enough to seat all one hundred thousand members of The Society at once. Events will begin here in six months' time after more members arrive." Everyone stood still for a few minutes, in awe of the colossal arena.

"We will now make our way to the outer rim of the dome. We will do a quick walk-through of the media rooms where the behind-the-scenes of the arena takes place."

This was the part of the tour Chelsea was most excited for. They saw edit bays, green rooms, recording studios, networking rooms, and the backstage area. All had the latest and greatest technology available to the market. This was the kind of stuff that got Chelsea's blood pumping. She was anxious to get her hands on it—after she had her fill of soaking up some Hawaiian sunshine, of course.

Tower Four was soon dubbed The House of Fun. Level one was a huge storehouse that contained water equipment and recreational vehicles. Boats, surfboards, quad skis, paddleboards, and every other piece of beach equipment that could be imagined were at their disposal. Chelsea was particularly intrigued by the flyboards. She had participated in a one-hour flyboard lesson on a family vacation when she was seventeen and had been itching to get on one again ever since.

At the far side of the equipment room was a large rolling door that opened to the waterway, which provided easy access for equipment and vehicles to be launched into the river that ran directly into the ocean. A large cutout in the floor was full of water and had lots of docking stations with a long line of speedboats. In the far left corner, there were also showering stations where people could clean off equipment and wash the sand from the beach off of their bodies.

Level two was dedicated to entertainment. The majority of the floor housed large empty rooms where groups or individuals could play out virtual reality games. From bowling to laser tag to all-out combat games, there was a virtual reality for almost any game ever invented.

Hammond told Chelsea all about the time he played his buddy in a virtual reality game of wizard's chess. He said it easily rivaled the match played in *Harry Potter and the Sorcerer's Stone*. Chelsea had never read the Harry Potter series but knew it was considered a classic. She felt embarrassed not knowing what Hammond was talking about, but between looking for work, competitive schooling conditions, and long workdays at her temp jobs, she had had very little extra time for leisure reading—although now there would be plenty of time to enjoy pop culture and literature with her workload requirement down to two hours a day.

The rest of floor two had movie theaters and a large club. Most everyone was excited about the club, but Chelsea hoped to visit the theaters. She loved movies—sitting in a dark auditorium, relearning life lessons, and experiencing a thrilling adventure. It was among her favorite guilty pleasures.

Level three had a long row of shopping kiosks, multiple PED repair stations, and general supplies dispensers. "Everyone will now enter a shopping kiosk and select a nightwear option for tonight and one outfit for tomorrow. In the coming days and months, you are welcome to visit the shopping kiosks at any time to select your remaining outfits until each person has the allotted wardrobe. Each outfit is branded with the Hawaii Society logo. The clothes you came in can be disposed of in the morning. The first group will now enter the shopping kiosk and select their outfits," the tour robot instructed.

Everyone quickly formed lines to enter the shopping kiosks, and the first group entered. Chelsea got in line on the far side of the row of kiosks. The man in line before Chelsea exited just as a pair of spandex shorts, a sleeveless shirt, some briefs, and a pair of sandals dispensed out from a tray on the side of the kiosk. Each item had a small tag attached with the logo as described. The man paid no notice to Chelsea as he took his things and moved out of her way so she could enter.

As she walked into the private kiosk, blue lights lit the sides of the cubicle and a screen displayed a message telling her to scan her wristband. She placed her bracelet against the screen. Just as she did, her description popped up on the screen.

```
Name: Chelsea June Coremon
         Age: 28
       Height: 5'3"
    Weight: 125 pounds
        Hair: Red
    Eyes: Dark Brown
```

The system began a 360-degree scan of her body, and a digital 3D outline of her body with exact measurements appeared next to her description. *A pear,* Chelsea thought with a sigh as she looked at her 3D outline.

For her outfit, she selected a simple tan T-shirt with a modest V-neck and some jean Bermuda shorts, accompanied by a pair of flip-flops. Her nightwear was light and simple. The selection in the kiosk was fairly minimal, but Chelsea didn't have an overly exuberant sense of style. She was sure that in the next kiosk over Sara was having a small meltdown with the lack of selection. After finalizing her outfit, the machine immediately went to work crafting Chelsea's custom-tailored apparel. Within a few minutes, her clothes, perfectly made and pressed-to-wear, came down the dispenser.

Chelsea was surprised to discover that Sara had somehow found a rather unique lime green skirt pattern, which she paired with a bright pink crop top. She wouldn't have picked that outfit for herself, but she imagined anything would look good on Sara.

Once everyone had their clothing for the next day, they were instructed to pick up their general supplies at one of the dispenser stations and then visit one of the PED stations to ensure their PEDs were working properly and correctly linked to the network. Once connected, they would be able to receive notifications and sign up for their daily two-hour task.

At the supplies dispensers, all necessary hygiene products were available to choose from. There was lotion, shampoo, face cream, hairspray, deodorant, a mouthpiece that scrubbed teeth as it dispensed a substance to prevent cavities and activated the stem cells for tooth structure regrowth, a hairbrush that tripled as a blow-dryer and straightener, and miracle mousse that could give the perfect wave to the most stubborn hair. Women were given a menstrual cup, and anyone was welcome to take an electric razor if needed. Only a few men took the razor though since most women and some men had any unwanted hair follicles removed at puberty. Makeup was not available, because everyone's makeup was tattooed on. Any additional makeup would have to be specially ordered at a premium price from the mainland.

At the PED station, Chelsea had to give multiple permissions to the Hawaii Society system that she previously had turned off. Permissions such as video recordings in all public and private locations, automatic money withdrawals, and automatic updates to her contract with The Society had her worried. She was reluctant to say yes. But as she contemplated the possible repercussions of selecting no, a pop-up notification appeared that informed her that she would be removed from The Society if she did not agree to comply. Not wanting to cause a scene or be forced to leave, she checked *yes* and continued without further thought. Mr. Wong, however, did whisper a few choice words before giving his permission.

"I will now show you to your individual living quarters. I hope you have enjoyed your initial tour of the Hawaii Society." The robot took everyone down to the main level of Tower Four and out onto the winding sidewalks that weaved between all the buildings. Beautiful plants and trees accompanied by large patches of green grass decorated the areas between the pathways. Chelsea looked up at the cylinder buildings nestled between the four towers and under the dome. The sun glistened off the pristine white sides of the building where her group had been assigned rooms. One by one, they were guided to their personal living quarters.

Society coordinators were supposed to be careful to try and place groups and partners in rooms that were next to each other, since there were no rooms to accommodate multiple people. Each person got one private room, whether they wanted to share or not. Rooms could be connected by unlocking the adjoining wall's door, if desired, but no accommodations were made for groups or partners beyond that. Hammond and Sara were among the first to receive their room assignments. "We'll see you around," Hammond said to Chelsea as he walked alongside Sara into her living quarters, ignoring the room he had been assigned to.

Chelsea was one of the last assigned a room. Her name was displayed brightly on a small LED to the right of the door. As her bracelet came near the door handle, the deadbolt unlocked automatically. She said goodbye to those who were left in the group and walked into her new room for the first time. It was a very small room. To her immediate right was a tiny bathroom with a toilet, a sink, and a shower. Just past the bathroom door was a narrow closet with three drawers, two shelves and a hanging rod that could only accommodate a small number of outfits. Chelsea placed the clothes and hygiene supplies that she had been holding into one of the drawers of her closet. On her left, across from the closet, was a full-length mirror. Near the end of the room, there was a simple desk with shelves above it, and a full-size bed near the window.

Chelsea placed her handbag on the desk, got out her small LED screen, and unfolded it to its full length. She pressed the adhesive edges against the wall across from her desk. Then pictures of her family and friends suddenly appeared on its display. She stared at it for a moment and then looked out the window to the beautiful vista outside. She shut the blind.

She wasn't sure why, but despite being exactly where she wanted to be and happy to be free of the grueling obligations of her past life, she could not bring herself to smile. She simply lay on the bed and stared up at her reflection with what light was coming from the LED screen—her hair fanned out around her head, her subtle makeup was barely noticeable on her face, and her disenchanting lips pursed at the thought that she would have to look up at herself each night as she fell asleep. *Of course they would put a mirror on the ceiling,* she thought. It seemed to serve only as a cruel, visual reminder of her lonely existence as pictures of her distant family and the outside world flashed on the wall.

With that thought, she closed her eyes to go to sleep. Despite the dinner alert her bracelet gave her or the hundreds of activities she had waiting for her to try, she had no trouble sleeping away the evening and then on through the night. Her last view of herself, so undeniably empty, left her tired. *Besides,* she thought, *I have the rest of my life to explore this island.*

4. LAZY DAYS ON THE BEACH

THE NEXT MORNING Chelsea woke up feeling better about life. Her melancholy attitude melted away in her sleep as she dreamed of surfing the turquoise waters of Hawaii. She woke up before dawn to catch the sunrise on the sandy beaches. People must have stayed out late partying the night before. Cleaning bots were still scouring the shore, picking up cups and dumping them into the ocean. Each cup was made out of a plant-based substance that provided a food source for fish and could completely decompose in thirty minutes in salt water, so it was most effective to put the cups directly into the ocean.

Chelsea sat down on a part of the beach that had already been cleaned. She took off her shoes and let her toes run through the powdered sugar-like sand and stared out over the ocean as a heart-stopping sunrise rose above the water. It was her first sunrise in Hawaii. She spun around for a quick photo in front of the mesmerizing pink and orange swirls that the sun was slowly engulfing. She didn't want to forget this moment. Holding out her bracelet, she called out, "Cheeeese," and it captured a photo. The picture appeared on her arm to preview. It captured the sunrise perfectly. She smiled. Her first full day on her Hawaiian island had a perfect start.

The next thing on her list to do was go back up to the shopping kiosks and get a swimsuit before the lines formed. Thankfully, it was still too early for most people to be out of bed. She quickly popped into the nearest kiosk and scanned her bracelet. She selected a swimsuit, rash guard, board shorts, and water shoes. She wanted to make sure she had the proper attire for all the water activities. She was quite pleased with the end product as her order came down the shoot. Her bathing suit top had a high neck and was made out of a slightly see-through, woven material in a pleasant deep blue color and had a piece of cloth that wrapped around her abdomen. Its beautiful and unique design was of little consequence, though, as Chelsea planned to spend most of her days in her black and white rash guard and board shorts doing every possible water activity imaginable.

She immediately changed into her rash guard and board shorts and rushed down to the Outdoor Recreation Supply Room, where she picked out a surfboard. She sat for ten torturous minutes to view the instruction and safety precaution video. After watching it, she stopped by the shark repellent bracelet station and grabbed four—one for each limb. A tiger shark paying her a visit was the last thing she needed to mar her first time in Hawaiian waters.

As long as she was able to catch a wave, she discovered she was not half bad at surfing. However, after a few unexpected mouthfuls of seawater from a wave catching her off guard, she decided it was time to move on to the next activity. She returned her surfboard just as the first few residents were making their way to the Outdoor Recreation Supply Room.

"Good morning," she cheerfully greeted them. Once they were out of view, she broke out into a full sprint. She ran straight for the waterfall. Her fingers tingling with anticipation, she could hardly contain her excitement. She weaved through the walkways of The

Society grounds and over the bridge to the majestic waterfall's powerful flow that crashed into the calmest portion of the river. As she stepped into the pool of water by the waterfall, the mist swirled around her—just as she had envisioned when she first spotted the waterfall during the tour. A small rainbow could be seen in the mist, and the mist produced a sort of haze that made it feel as though she were in a dream. She looked up, admiring the accumulation of vegetation and vibrant flowers surrounding the waterfall and the adjacent mountain ridge.

She stretched out her hand to feel the water crash on her skin, and just as she did, *beep beep beep beep*. She jumped, startled from the unexpected noise sounding in her ear. Her bracelet lit up on her wrist with a list of available tasks. "It is eight o'clock and you have yet to select your daily task or training. Please view the available tasks and trainings and select from those available." She had almost forgotten that she still had a responsibility to fulfill. Hoping to have a relaxing and carefree first full day, she selected an easy, mundane task. She would wipe down tables at the end of dinner in Tower Two.

Until then, she wondered what she should do to fill her time. But when she turned and looked behind her at the beautiful river running through the thick forest grounds and alongside The Society building, she wondered no longer. She felt the river beckoning her to explore its rippling water.

After making a quick stop in the cafeteria to eat breakfast, she went to the Outdoor Recreation Supply Room. Looking over the wide variety of water equipment, she debated which craft to choose to make her journey down the river. The kayaks and canoes tempted her. A relaxing venture down the river on an air tube sounded quite tranquil as well, but when she spotted the long white paddleboards, she quickly made her decision. She scanned her wristband across the checkout station and selected a paddleboard and waited for it to drop down to her from the storage compartment it was displayed in above her on the wall. Large chains running vertically up the walls rotated horizontal shelves that held some of the water equipment. When the paddleboard dropped down in front of her, the lock that kept the board in place unlatched. "Proceed to The Society bus if you'd like to begin paddleboarding farther up the river. Otherwise, proceed to the docks and place your paddleboard in the loading and unloading station just left of the speedboats. Enjoy your day," a prerecorded sound bite instructed her via her earpiece.

Chelsea quickly ran to catch the self-driving bus before it made its journey through the forest to a spot farther up the river as it was programmed to do every half hour. After loading her paddleboard on the bus, she walked on board and sat down near a group of people.

"Why do you guys want to go paddleboarding again? I prefer a sport with a motor behind it. Something a bit more exhilarating," one of them said.

"We can always quad ski again later," another man said.

"But this time, I'm getting my own. No way I'm letting you throw me again," another one said while rubbing his head.

"I'm still mad that you told Mom about that."

As they continued to talk, Chelsea realized the group she sat next to were siblings—three triplet brothers and their younger sister. Hearing them bicker and chat made her think of Glenn, and she found herself wishing he were there with her. She needed to remember to call him, so she added a reminder to her calendar to call him in two weeks when she could ask him if he was enjoying the Houston Society.

When the bus stopped, she waited for everyone to unload and then she walked off and grabbed her paddleboard. Hiking down the paved path to the river, she saw pastures of livestock in the distance. From her perspective, she could only see the cows, chickens, and pigs. Around the cows were fences and posts that would reposition at a specific time to move the cows into position to be milked. Chickens had special nests to lay in that would gently suck the eggs in the nest down a pipe to be packaged for delivery to the kitchen. Leftover food and scraps from the kitchen were transported to the pigs using an underground system that linked directly to the cafeterias.

Only a small portion of the animals was raised for slaughtering to preserve livestock numbers, which meant small helpings of meat at The Societies. Most didn't mind though as people had generally cut down their meat consumption in the past twenty years to lower the environmental impact of agriculture and after it was discovered that lab-grown meat, which was meant to be the meat of the future, caused many to eventually develop large tumors in their muscle tissue. Slaughtering was automated to avoid the unpleasantries that accompanied the task, but supervision and upkeep were required to ensure the animals received the proper care and the facilities functioned properly, as was the case with all aspects of the facilities at The Society.

Chelsea placed her paddleboard in the river and felt the gentle tug of the current around her legs and on the board. Before the board could float away from her, she quickly jumped on and positioned her paddle across her lap. The river pulled her downstream easily without the need to paddle, so she lay down on her back and looked up at the trees and foliage around her. The whole island was blanketed in green. When there wasn't sand underfoot, the earth was covered with dark brown soil, and large rocks were scattered throughout. Being a fairly small island, the river was not wide. It barely accommodated Chelsea's large paddleboard at parts. Soft ferns brushed up against Chelsea's arms as she floated down the narrowest parts of the river. The vegetation that covered the grounds was more beautiful than any of the manmade botanical gardens she had visited in the casinos of Las Vegas. Small vines wandered up the trunks of trees, and large-leafed plants spurted out from among smaller plants that were sometimes sprinkled with colorful flowers. The unkempt beauty that graced the island's grounds was unmatched.

The journey down the river was not long, and soon Chelsea emerged from the forest on her paddleboard to see the view of The Society buildings and the river opening up to the sea. Coconut trees dangled their fruit overhead, and the river widened and became slightly deeper the closer she came to the ocean. The current slowed and allowed her a moment to pause and take in the beautiful scene before her—the river winding down to the blue ocean that stretched out across the skyline, the majesty of the huge Society buildings towering over her on her left and the picturesque waterfall running down the breathtaking mountain on her right.

After taking a moment, she stood on the board to paddle the rest of the way to the ocean. When she propelled herself forward with her paddle, she rocked back and forth a few times, trying to keep her balance. A pair of lovers stood on the bridge, taking in the scene and stealing kisses as she paddled underneath them. *That's romantic*, she thought. Then she thought of how few couples shared in anything more than superficial romance, and she rolled her eyes to herself. *Well, a girl can dream.*

Passing the waterfall and the bridge, Chelsea steered herself along the far edge of the river, away from the docks of the equipment room in Tower Four to avoid any outbound traffic. The current picked up, and it pushed her out into the ocean. She quickly paddled and somehow managed to stay on top of the board to make her way out and away from the crowds. When she was far enough out, she bobbed on the gentle waves and let her arm dangle off the edge of the paddleboard in the water. She soaked in the warm sun and drizzled water over her stomach to cool down when she needed to until an alarm went off in her ear to tell her it was time to go in for lunch. She reluctantly picked up her paddle and began paddling toward the waves to ride them into shore. As she did, a large turtle popped up out of the waves and greeted her with its leathery grin before floating back down under the turquoise water. She smiled at the visit from her aquatic friend—it was the climactic note to her all-too-perfect first morning in paradise.

At lunch, Chelsea munched happily on her fruit salad and zucchini boat pizza before completing some of the errands she had to do that day, which included getting another outfit for the next day and writing her parents an email to let them know she had made it safely and was enjoying her time at The Society thus far. Then after dinner, she spent her two hours of task work wiping down tables in the dining area and listening to a playlist that left her feeling light and happy. The two hours went by relatively quickly as she focused on the words of the music quietly playing in her ear—though it took everything in her not to sing aloud.

That night before bed, Chelsea went to soak in the pool. Hoping to make some new friends, she found a friendly-looking group and waded in toward them.

"You one of the newbies?" a man asked.

"Yeah. I just got in yesterday," she answered.

"Well, come join us, girl," he said as he spread his arms out wide and smiled. He had dark hair that he pushed back behind his ears. It was wet from the pool and his arms were covered in a tiger print. "How was your first day?"

"Great," she said. "Saw a sea turtle while I was out paddleboarding, caught a few waves surfing, and got to see more of the island. It was perfect."

"Wow. You did a lot for your first day," he said. "You might want to slow down so you don't wear things out too fast."

She doubted she could ever tire of the island. "I did save flyboarding for later. I'm really excited for that."

"That's cool. My name is Drake Pomley by the way. What's yours?"

"Chelsea. Chelsea Coremon."

"Cool. This is Truman and Daphne and Rad." His small group of friends turned and waved to her and then returned to their conversation. "Want a turn?" he asked her, pulling a floating lounge pad into the pool.

"Um . . . sure," she said, not wanting to ruin her chances of making a friend.

He pulled the float toward her and as she went to jump on, he grabbed her waist and hoisted her on. "I got you," he said, smiling.

Chelsea almost smacked him when he grabbed her unexpectedly, but she managed to stay cool and returned his smile with an awkward, "Thanks." She lay down, and he brought his elbows up on the mat to talk with her more intimately.

"So did you come with a group or are you alone?"

"I came alone. What about you?"

"Same."

"How long have you been here?"

"About two weeks. Thankfully, I'm starting to make some friends here and there, and I'm getting used to how things operate at The Society, but honestly, it can get a little lonely sometimes."

"Well, if it's only been two weeks, I'm sure you'll only make more friends with time, and then it won't be so lonely," she said, trying to comfort him.

"Well, I can already say it's starting to feel less lonely with you around," he said with a wink. Chelsea silently rolled her eyes. "So . . . what are you into, Chelsea? Any particular games you like? We could go up to my room and play around. I have a few in mind I'd like trying on you."

Chelsea immediately knew the kind of games he was referring to as he stroked her hip with his fingertip, and since she had absolutely no interest in him romantically, she knew it was time to end the conversation. "Not really," she said as she rolled off the mat and into the water. "What about you guys? You like board games?" she asked Drake's group of friends. "You guys want to meet up to play some board games on my PED sometime?"

"Sure," the man Drake introduced as Truman said. "We like board games."

"Great. Let's do that sometime then," she said as she pulled herself out of the pool.

"You leaving already?" Drake asked.

"Yeah. Like you said, I think I did too much today. I'm tired. You have a good night," Chelsea said as she excused herself.

"What about you, Daphne? You want to go play some games with me in my room?" Drake asked the other girl.

"Sure," she said before jumping up on his back and giggling with excitement.

IN THE FOLLOWING DAYS and weeks, she rediscovered how much she loved flyboarding. She spent most of her days working to master it and the rest of her time lying lazily on the beach or immersed in the pool. After years of looking for work or working tirelessly with little pay and no glimpse of reprieve in sight, she felt so relieved to spend her days relaxing and doing what she wanted without the concern of money in the back of her mind.

She often met Hammond and Sara for meals or for some activity out on the water. However, being with them often left her feeling very lonely as they cuddled with each another and smiled gleefully repeatedly. She really did enjoy their company and appreciated their friendship, but she kept her time with them limited—mostly for her own sanity, though she assumed they preferred it that way as well.

About two months after Chelsea arrived, she met and became friends with Finley. She was a lighting guru who spent most of her time doing the lighting for many of the promotional videos for The Society, and eventually, she also worked the live events on the big stage that started to occur soon after her arrival. Chelsea and Finley seemed to understand each other, given their similar career backgrounds.

Whenever Finley had the chance, they would meet up to go paddleboarding. During these excursions, the majority of their time was spent drifting atop the water talking about Finley's work or the various boys she was involved with. Her work stories were often repetitive. And since Chelsea had worked in her same industry for years, she had heard or seen most every scenario or complaint there was to be had from a lighting engineer—"so-and-so obviously doesn't understand how electricity works" or "I'm going to go crazy if I hear another person complain that the lights are too bright for them to see the audience"—the usual stuff.

Finley's dating stories were always intriguing though. She was only slightly interested in two of the men she was seeing. The others were merely fun, wild, and interchangeable. Like a drama-filled reality TV show, Chelsea found Finley's relationship stories entertaining enough. But she mostly listened to them because she knew it helped Finley sort through the mess of feelings it left her with. Finley didn't consciously realize it herself, but Chelsea observed that the more men her friend became involved with, the more irritable and snarky she became. Talking through it with Chelsea usually helped Finley refocus her energies on the men she honestly cared about.

For Chelsea, there was only one man she had met at The Society that she had contemplated getting serious with. His name was Zag. He was the stereotypical dark and handsome, and he maintained a toned physique to catch the ladies' attention on the beachfront. His ability to captivate a woman brought him great satisfaction.

For a few months, Zag had occasionally come running to Chelsea's side, saying, "So what are we doing today, sugar?"

"Well, *I* am going to go kayaking," she would always say— or whatever other activity she had planned for her day.

To which he would reply something to the effect of, "Great! Let's go."

But the morning after one of their fun-filled days together, Chelsea observed as he ran up to another girl and said to her, "Shall we spend the day together? You're the only girl on this island I want to be with."

She already knew it deep down, but she had to remind her heart that their relationship was nothing more than playful banter and flirting. And after how angry he became with her when she refused to finish one of their days of dalliance wrapped in his arms, she became convinced he only returned afterward because he was determined to break her—like a rancher trying to break a young mare into submission. So the next time he asked, she bluntly told him she wouldn't be sleeping with him—ever—and he never approached her again. She knew it was probably for the best, but she secretly missed his attention.

"Can't say I blame him," Finley commented after Chelsea finished telling her about Zag. "You don't seem to put out very often—though I'm sure you have your reasons—but most people just don't appreciate that. I mean, it's not like it would hurt to test the waters and see what Zag has going for himself, if you know what I mean," she said with a wink.

"I just can't bring myself to do that. I want to know he loves me, and I want to be in love with him if I'm going to sleep with him," Chelsea retorted, having thought about the topic a lot after being too hasty in past relationships. "Zag is just a flirt. He makes you feel like a trillion bucks when you're with him, but he doesn't mean anything he says. I'm fairly certain his main goal is to sleep with every girl on this island."

"You may be right—but what does it really matter? What exactly is *love* anyway? If you ask me, it's just the sexual passion you feel toward someone twisted in your mind to be something more. A primitive mindset to get men to stay with girls once they get them pregnant, and they need help surviving birth and raising a child. That's a problem of the past, girl," Finley said, looking over at Chelsea mockingly. "So you don't have to be such a stiff about it, Chelsea—live a little. Have some fun. If not with Zag, with someone." Finley rolled over in the sand and took a long swig from her cup before throwing it to the ground. "Speaking of which, I'm going to go meet up with Terrance. I'll see ya in the hereafter," Finley said while standing up to leave. "And in the meantime, forget Zag. There are other guys you can fall for who might be interested in something more than a one-nighter. Or you could just loosen up and get your feet wet. Like literally, you may want to get your feet wet. There were so many cool fish out there today. Plus, it will remind you there are plenty of fish in the sea." Finley grinned goofily and nudged Chelsea with her elbow. "Get it? See what I did there?"

Rolling her eyes and cutting Finley off before she could continue, Chelsea teased, "Go—go see your lover boy. Get out of here! Don't make me suffer through any more of your awful puns."

Chelsea did end up taking Finley's advice—she swam around the reef. The vivid colors of the fish were hypnotic as they drifted in the cool waters around her.

She found it odd that the schools of fish stuck with their own kind and rarely mingled, yet together the many species formed an interdependent ecosystem—each had their role, and each did their part. She found it beautiful that within nature, everything worked together, and each part was able to integrate into the system without much intervention.

That thought somehow spiraled into her wondering how her generation was somehow unable to integrate into normal society—each generation before them had. But without the death of one generation, a new one couldn't seem to thrive. It appeared that human intervention had actually disrupted the natural flow of life, and because of it, her generation was forced into a sort of isolation instead of assimilating. They were sent to live their lives in a separated space and in a completely different manner. *It was voluntary though,* she thought. *And isn't it a luxurious and wonderful life to live?*

She turned on her back to float and took off her mask as she pondered that thought. She knew very well her life at The Society was luxurious. It was comparable, if not better, to her family's most extravagant vacations. And yet, each day seemed a little harder to wake up in the morning. *Am I just unexplainably ungrateful for this beautiful life that has been handed to me?* That thought lingered with no answer until a rush of water rolled over her body from a speedboat that someone had steered too close to the reef.

"Get away from the reef! You're going to kill somebody!" someone nearby cried out.

IN THE NEXT FEW weeks, Chelsea read a lot of the books that she had been hoping to read for years, including the Harry Potter series. She also spent more time at the gym than normal. She found it soothed her troubled mind more than the calm of the sea. Or maybe she was just distracted by the pain. Her muscle tone improved steadily, and her time at the gym became the best part of her day.

One morning, after lifting weights and spending some time on the sandy shore reading the last book on her list of must-reads, she went to complete her two hours of task work. That day she had signed up to watch children at the childcare center. There were now twenty newborn-to-toddler-aged children at The Society. She would be helping the childcare bot watch them for the afternoon. She couldn't wait to see what hilarious things the toddlers would have to say.

But after two hours of chasing a three-year-old, a six-month-old wanting to be constantly held, and a two-year-old wanting to be her playmate, she decided childcare was more difficult than she had realized. For the first time since she arrived at The Society, she felt completely drained. She wondered if she would ever be cut out to be a mother—though she supposed if she ever did become a parent, the childcare bots would do most of the work at The Societies anyway.

At the end of her time, one of the two-year-olds' mothers came running in, and she hugged her daughter tight. "I missed you so bad, sweetie. Have you been enjoying yourself today? Are you ready for lunch?"

"Yes, Mama, but no leave more," the two-year-old struggled to say.

"I wish I didn't have to leave you here all day. I'm going to talk to The Society leaders about taking you with me more. I miss you too bad."

"I don't know why there's a minimum for childcare," Chelsea interjected into their conversation. "Sorry to interrupt. I'm just surprised they have a minimum."

"Oh yes, and six hours is just the minimum until they're three. After three, they have to be at the childcare center for at least eight hours," the mother explained. "They say they have to take the necessary time to educate them for when they can leave The Society after they're grown, and there are more jobs available. Plus, most of the activities here aren't exactly kid-friendly, if you know what I mean, and everyone looks down on anyone who brings a kid along anyway. Most parents are quite happy to leave them and enjoy the activities on the island kid-free. I just miss my little Tassy so much. I would love to spend all day with her if I could," the mother said, giving Tassy a short squeeze. "I take a shift every day so that we don't have to stay away too long, but hey, it beats living place to place like we were doing."

Huh. Chelsea found it odd that they would require that much time for the children to be away from their parents. *Though they do need to get an education, and the parents may not be equipped to do that*, she thought. Despite her justification, she still left feeling heartbroken for the mother and her child. *At least they're better off,* she reminded herself.

That afternoon she watched one of the last movies filmed in Hollywood before the earthquake happened. She had seen it once before, but it had been over a year, so she was excited to see it again. It was an action-adventure film set in the center of a faraway planet. She enjoyed the temporary escape from the gravity of her own planet, and when the two siblings in the movie embraced at the end of the film, it reminded her she should call Glenn again and see how he was doing.

It's still early enough to call him, she thought, looking at the time and calculating the time in Houston.

"Hi, Chelsea," Glenn answered.

"Hey Glenn, how's it going?"

"Great! You actually remembered to call again. I'm impressed."

"Yeah, yeah," she groaned. "I told you I wouldn't forget about you."

"Yeah, but this makes twice in one month. That's a record for you. You doin' alright?"

"Yes, I'm fine," she said. "Have you ever considered that maybe I'm just not as bad at this long-distance thing as you thought I would be?"

"Chelsea, I've talked to Mom *and* Dad. One email is hardly what they would consider keeping in touch."

She knew he was right, but she still defended herself. "Well, Dad still hasn't even answered my *one* email. I'm not about to feel bad that I haven't contacted him *again*."

"You know how he is. He's just busy with work and gets caught up in things. I'm sure he means to respond, and you should at least answer Mom." Chelsea was beginning to regret calling Glenn. She wasn't expecting to get a lecture.

"Fine. I'll email her back tonight. Can we drop it now? I didn't call to talk about Mom and Dad. Tell me how Houston's been. You hardly gave me any information last time I called."

"Sorry," he said. "Things have been good here. I've met a ton of new friends, and life is just *so* stress-free. It's really nice. Though it's a little hard for me to have to stay on the grounds. I'm not used to being stuck in one place all the time, but I have everything I need here, so I guess I can't complain. Oh, okay. Be there in a minute," Glenn suddenly called to someone in the background. "Hey, I got to go. I'm doing really great though. We're all going virtual bowling tonight, so I need to head out. You'll have to call me or email me something more about Hawaii and all the fun stuff you've been up to."

"Alright." Chelsea sighed. *Sounds like he's doing just fine without me.* "Have fun."

After dinner, Chelsea sat down at her desk and wrote her mom and Glenn a long email all about Hawaii. *That will keep them happy for a while,* she thought. She really did hate long-distance communication. Then she turned in early so she would be rested for a full day of flyboarding the next day. She planned to go out early in the morning to get a flyboard before anyone else. The Society was also holding a mandatory event the next evening to talk about a party they were planning to host when all the transports were complete. That alone made for a more eventful day compared to the rest of her days, so she closed the blind and turned out the lights to get some shuteye.

5. THE MAN IN THE PINEAPPLE SHORTS

CHELSEA WOKE BEFORE dawn and went to the beach to experience another breathtaking sunrise. She had not done so for a few weeks and enjoyed those rare times where the beach was mostly empty and quiet. As she strolled down the path to the banks of the shore, she spotted a man sitting alone, looking out over the ocean. Something seemed odd about him, but she couldn't quite place what it was that struck her as so unusual—he just looked out of place somehow.

As she got closer, she noticed his shorts were made of a vibrant pineapple-themed print that she hadn't seen before. *Maybe it was an option in men's clothing that few men cared for?*

That didn't seem likely, though, since she knew Rad and a number of other colorful characters living at The Society would be delighted with the print. She also couldn't find the Society's clothing tag that was supposed to be on all the residents' attire. *Maybe he cut it off?* she wondered. After studying his face, she was sure she had not met him before—so she went to introduce herself.

"Mind if I join you?" she asked as she sat down. The man almost fell over, not knowing there was anyone around while he had closed his eyes and was enjoying the sound of the ocean waves.

She looked down at his hand as he caught himself to see worn, wrinkled fingers. His peaceful smile left, and a concerned frown replaced it.

"Suppose not, seeing you already sat down," the man grumbled and then continued his meditation.

"Oh, I didn't mean to bother you. I just didn't recognize you and thought I'd come introduce myself. My name is Chelsea—but I can tell this may not be a welcome visit, so I'll find another spot so you can watch the sunrise in peace, Mr. . . . ?" Chelsea stuck out her hand to make for a friendly parting.

"How about we skip the name, and you're welcome to stay— *if* you don't ask any questions," the man offered. "It would be nice to talk with someone for a change."

"Why haven't you spoken with anyone?" The man turned to stare at Chelsea with a displeased expression. "Right. That's a question."

"Suppose you've been to grade school then, huh?" the man said sarcastically. "Say, how about you tell me about Hawaii and any of the sights you've seen. That sounds like a conversation I wouldn't mind having during my first Hawaiian sunrise," the man suggested.

He spoke as if he had never been on The Society's beach. *He must have been shut up in his room or some such thing if he has been at The Society but hasn't had the chance to explore it.* Numerous inquiries buzzed in Chelsea's mind like annoying honeybees, but remembering that he had said no questions, she reminded herself that she wouldn't be getting any answers. To distract herself from the buzz, she decided she had better tell him about Hawaii as he had requested.

"Sure. Where to begin?" She silenced the questions in her mind and reflected on her past eight months in Hawaii, trying to focus on only the most positive aspects. "Every Hawaii daydream I could have imagined before coming here has come to life on this island. I've surfed turquoise waves while dragging my fingers through the cool waters at my side. In this ocean, dolphins swim with you while vibrant fish and wildlife drift around your head. I've soared over the waves on a flyboard with nothing to constrain me or hold me back. It's like experiencing a total sense of freedom and power while still struggling to catch your breath from the staggering vista before you. I've climbed to the top of that monumental mountain and looked out over a never-ending ocean that seems to say, 'There is no end to the beauty of this place.' *Kala*—in Hawaiian Huna tradition, it means 'there are no limits.' That's how I would describe this place. It feels like everything good can be found here if you are open to it."

As she finished, the sun crested over the water to unveil a vibrant orange that gave light to the blue sky above. When she looked over at the man, he had a smile stretched across his wrinkled face, and he closed his eyes to breathe in one more breath of fresh ocean air. "A nice finish. Thank you," he said. "Though you were wrong about one thing," he continued as he stood. "At these Societies, you can only go so far. Well, I have to go, Chelsea. It was nice meeting you, but it's time I got back to my family."

The man left the beach to enter the towers just as the first few people were making their way to the sand. *What an odd encounter,* Chelsea thought. She set off to the Outdoor Recreation Supply Room to get her flyboard. Thankfully, there was still plenty left, and she grabbed her usual four shark repellent bracelets.

She took her supplies to the docks and strapped the boots of the flyboard onto her feet and then pulled on her life vest. She then grabbed the intake tube that would suck up the water and shoot it out from under the board using an invention called oxidane microblasters. She lowered it into the river to give the flyboard the water supply necessary for it to thrust her into the air. After switching the microcombustion engine on, she took the control switch that was attached to the board by a cord and pressed the button a quarter of the way down. She shot up two feet above the water and leaned her weight forward to edge herself out. Once through the dock's open doors, she skillfully jetted out down the river toward the open ocean. For the next hour, she flew over the water, occasionally diving in headfirst and emerging some feet away. It had taken her a few weeks to master that trick, but she was finally feeling confident with the move. Her next step was to master a backflip. She reasoned it would take her much longer to master that maneuver.

As Chelsea finished her last bit of flyboarding, she spotted the transporter pod zooming across the horizon toward The Society to make its first delivery of new residents for the day. After returning to the Outdoor Recreation Supply Room and placing her things back at their appropriate stations, she headed in the direction of her living quarters. She needed a shower before she got breakfast. Then later, she would have to complete her task sometime before dinner so she could attend the mandatory Society-wide event. She came to the main walkway just as the new residents were entering Tower One to begin their tour of the grounds.

In the distance, she saw a man with vibrant shorts walk into the transporter pod just before the doors shut, and it took off for its return voyage to the mainland. She stood in disbelief as she realized the man who entered the pod was the same man she sat with on the beach that morning. *Why would he be leaving?*

Though it was obvious he couldn't possibly be within the twenty-five to thirty-five age restrictions, she had not considered he might be visiting from the states. She thought he might be a worker in the government offices or some other explanation that would justify his presence. The Societies were not supposed to have visitors from the mainland. Apart from special events, only residents were supposed to be aboard the transporter pod.

Maybe he snuck on for a free visit to Hawaii? she thought, despite the unlikelihood.

6. BACK TO GIG LIFE

THAT NIGHT, Chelsea went to the mandatory event held in the dome arena—but she didn't pay attention to a word of it. She was distracted by how bad the video engineering was the entire time. One of the panels on the LED wall had gone out, leaving a hole in the host's chest for the majority of the show. A camera was not properly set up to follow one of the hosts, so whenever Davin Chapman spoke, the camera focused on an empty part of the stage. From her vantage point, he looked like a small figurine. And lastly, the screen had a full four feet of blank black space on stage left.

During the whole event, Chelsea sat whispering her disapproval to Finley, who had decided not to do the lighting that evening.

"Yeah, this is awful," Finley agreed with a grin. "You know, they've been hoping an experienced video engineer would take over, especially before the Grand Welcoming event. You ought to come in tomorrow and fix things. You could show people how a show should really look. I've heard you're pretty good."

"Maybe you're right." Chelsea paused to think. "I am getting kind of sick of doing the mundane tasks on the island, and it would give me something more challenging to think about." Chelsea took one last painful look at the screen before making up her mind. "I don't think I can take another event like this anyway. Maybe it is time I get back into it." Chelsea pulled up her task schedule and signed up for a video engineer shift in the dome for the next day.

❖

HER TASK WASN'T UNTIL eleven the next morning, but it was a little easier to wake up that day—almost like the thought of returning to her work gave a small boost to her step. Eight months prior, she had been so unhappy as a video engineer that she had feared she would never be willing to start again, but now she found she was eager.

At thirty minutes to eleven, she began rushing to the dome to begin. She walked backstage just as a squirrelly man named Roland was finishing his shift. Chelsea had heard about him before from Finley but had yet to meet him. He had dubbed himself an overseer of the dome's live events, and Finley despised him.

"Hi. I'm Roland Sims," he said, extending a hand to Chelsea.

"Hi."

"You headed backstage for a shift?" he inquired.

"Yes. I'm Chelsea Coremon. I'll be signing up for video technician tasks to help with your video engineering."

"Are you that girl Finley was telling me about? You used to work as a video engineer in Vegas, right? She told me a few weeks ago you'd be helping today. Good thing—no one volunteering for video tasks knows what they're doing. It's been a disaster."

"I'll get things in order," she said, slightly amused that Finley had predicted she would come. *She must have guessed I would want to fix things after seeing the disaster of a show that happened last night.* "When's the next event?" Chelsea asked, trying to get an idea of how much time she had to fix things.

"It's in two weeks. They're putting on an hour karaoke show for an entertainment night. Davin will be the host. He usually

❖70❖

comes by a day or two before to go over his lines, but its policy to not have any formal tech rehearsals," Roland said. "Make sure you sign up for the show ASAP so we don't end up with some random person wanting to 'try out a new task,'" he said, making air quotes with his hands and rolling his eyes as he walked away.

Chelsea chuckled under her breath a little. She saw what Finley meant when she said Roland considered the dome as his territory—even though he spent most of his task time messing up her settings on the lighting board according to Finley.

The Societies didn't have the resources to check if tasks were completed correctly, and many tasks were done with little qualification or only half-heartedly. That was Chelsea's biggest frustration about the tasks. People took no ownership of what they did. The tasks were too often neglected or, even more problematic, improperly done.

In the dome, that didn't usually mean anything too catastrophic—a show would go poorly or a fuse would pop. But around The Society, it sometimes created trouble. Chelsea thought back to a few months prior when the robotic chef in Tower Two was getting the salt and pepper confused in some recipes. What should have been a simple fix of correcting the computer programming for the ingredients turned into no meals produced in Tower Two. Someone signed up to fix it and decided it was an opportunity to take the robot apart and explore its inner workings. When he was unable to put it back together, it meant a whole week of sitting in a horrendous line for food in Tower One, which was the only tower producing meals because of it. On the eighth day, everyone woke up expecting more long lines and angry people, only to find that the robotic chef in Tower Two had been repaired—seemingly overnight. No one knew who had fixed it, but everyone was so happy to have two functioning cafeterias that no one really cared who did it or why the person didn't take the credit. Then, a few days ago, someone who was supposed to be servicing the internet connection ruined all the settings so that no one was able to get connection. People were irate at first, but when connection somehow returned two days later, everyone settled back into their routines. Chelsea was just glad there wasn't too much chaos because of it like the incident with the robotic chef.

Although she had been meaning to come and see the video equipment in action for some time, aside from the mandatory meeting the previous night, Chelsea hadn't attended any of the events held in the dome. She enjoyed her water activities far too much to be cooped up inside. But now, she felt bad everyone had been living with such subpar video standards for eight months when she could have easily fixed things.

She was very pleased to see the video engineering station backstage was equipped with a top-of-the-line video switcher and HD hover cameras. There was a recording system and a small but highly sophisticated broadcast system that could broadcast to any news channels on the mainland with a click of a button to allow people outside of the Societies to view their shows and advertisements.

However, Chelsea was less pleased to discover the inner programming of each of these pieces of equipment was in complete shambles. Most of the signals were routed incorrectly, and it was obvious that the previous operator had messed with the settings to create the strip of blank screen that Chelsea had observed the night before. Over the next two weeks, she spent her two hours of work a day troubleshooting the issues. And along the way, she found numerous additional items that needed some fine-tuning as well.

Roland often showed up during Chelsea's tasks to "supervise" as he called it. She found it very irritating and often tried to get him to leave. Unfortunately for her, he felt it was his duty to make sure she knew what she was doing. He would usually come up behind her and ask what she was working on. She couldn't tell if he just didn't know anything about video and was masking his curiosity behind a "supervisor" role or if he was just checking to see if she had something that sounded logical to respond with. Either way, she often responded with little patience for his scrutiny, and one time they even got in a small argument about the correct color balance on the cameras. Roland was quickly becoming her least favorite person at The Society.

The day before the karaoke night, she had one last thing to do before completing her list of things that needed repair in the dome. She had been waiting on a new panel for the video screen to arrive that would replace the one that been damaged on the LED wall. From the looks of it, someone had crashed into the panel with the hover lift and chosen not to report it. She would have to use the lift to get the old one out and replace it with the new one, but she felt confident she could do it in her two-hour allotment.

She found the lift hiding behind a curtain backstage and maneuvered it to the LED wall. Then she raised it up to float in midair beside the screen. She began detaching the broken panel just as Davin Chapman, Roland, and a posse of women trailing behind them whispering about Davin walked onto the stage.

Chelsea huffed and tried unsuccessfully to concentrate her thoughts on her work. *How can people be so obsessed with movie stars without knowing anything about who they really are?* Davin looked like a typical player to her, and most performers were so obsessed with themselves it was nauseating. Still, she found herself glancing down at him one more time. *He is handsome— I'll give him that.*

Just as Chelsea looked away, Davin looked up to see her in the lift for the first time. He looked again. He recognized her. *It's the girl from under the peach tree!* He hadn't seen her since that first day she arrived at The Society. He had been hoping to bump into her again, but somehow, he never had. Or if he had, he hadn't recognized her.

"Who is that?" he asked Roland as they walked past.

"Who? Chelsea? She's the video engineer who started working in the arena this month," he explained. "I think she knows what she's doin', but don't expect any favors from her. She's a stubborn lil' spitfire. I had it out with her the other day 'cuz I told her the cameras looked too blue, but she went on about the proper coloring for such and such a lighting . . . "

Roland kept talking, but Davin had stopped listening. He just chuckled to himself as he recalled his first encounter with the "stubborn lil' spitfire" at the orchard. He wasn't surprised she'd told Roland off. *Knowing Roland, he probably deserved it too*, he thought to himself.

Considering Chelsea was fifteen feet up in the air and he had lines to rehearse, Davin tried to collect his thoughts and concentrate on the run-through. He would find another time to talk to her now that he knew she would be working in the dome.

As he rehearsed his lines, he explained what would be happening on stage to the girls who had shown up for the run-through. Even though formal rehearsals were not protocol, Davin tried to do a short, informal rehearsal off the clock to make sure everyone on stage knew what they were supposed to do. Most people, especially women, were happy to oblige.

After the rehearsal, Davin went to look for Chelsea, but she had already left. He decided he would try again after the karaoke night so his pre-performance nerves would not get in the way of speaking with her. Being on stage and in front of a live audience was still very nerve-racking for him—despite his seemingly natural ability for it. He preferred film acting where he knew he could do another take if something went wrong.

AFTER THE KARAOKE EVENT ended the next day, Davin went straight to the video workstation to introduce himself to Chelsea. He had been anxious all night for the show to end so he could officially introduce himself. But when he got there, she was already walking away with the lighting designer. He went to chase after them when a phone call suddenly popped up on his wristband. He answered it.

"Davin Chapman?"

"Yes?"

"It's Dr. Hansen. I'm sorry to say I have some bad news . . . "

Davin froze, and his heart sank. He knew Dr. Hansen wouldn't call unless it was serious. As he turned to run to his room and pack, he heard Finley say something about Roland.

"Ugh, Roland is such a jerk!" Finley had said as she and Chelsea exited the stage.

"What did he say this time?" Chelsea asked.

"He sat behind me the whole show telling me how useless my job is. How no one even notices if I miss a cue unless I turn the lights off completely. I missed one cue! One blasted cue—and now I'm useless! The worst part about it is, I only missed the cue because *he* threw me off when he suddenly sat next to me, all creepy like, right as my cue was coming up! Ugh, he drives me nuts sometimes."

"He just does that crap to get a rise out of people. Don't let him get to you," Chelsea told her.

"I just hate being called useless. I have so little creative control over what I can do with the dome's minimal moving lights anyway!" She took a deep breath and tried to calm herself. "I know I shouldn't let it get to me, but I already feel useless the rest of my day. I at least want to feel useful when I'm doing something I went to school for," Finley said.

Chelsea knew exactly the feeling Finley was talking about—feeling useless most of the day. The feeling was surprisingly overwhelming at times.

"Listen," Chelsea said as she stopped and looked Finley in the eyes. "You're good at what you do, no matter what Roland says.

I've worked with other lighting engineers who aren't half as good as you are. And the way I see it, you have to remember that events are like a cake. Audio is the cake itself—without it, you don't really have a show, because the audience couldn't hear what's going on. Video is the frosting—it's a must-have combination with the cake to engage the audience. But lighting . . . Lighting is the sprinkles and the decorations on top of the cake. It's what makes the cake impressive! Without the sprinkles and the decorations, it's just another cake. People don't always recognize what the lighting adds to events, but it's true. And it all comes together to make an extraordinary combo. So who cares what Roland has to say? We made people scream and jump up out of their chairs and have an awesome time tonight! There are very few jobs out there that command a crowd like that. The show was awesome—and it was in large part because of you," Chelsea finished with a reassuring smile.

"Yeah, you're right—thanks." Finley looked up and smiled. "Screw Roland!" she yelled into the sky and let out a big sigh as she put her arm around Chelsea's neck. "Let's go do something fun."

FOR THE NEXT SIXTEEN months, Chelsea did the majority of the video engineering tasks. She fell back into the routine of working events, though at The Society it required far fewer hours. Instead of clients that required twelve- to sixteen-hour days, she only had her two-hour tasks to fulfill each day.

But during that time, she never saw Davin again.

He had returned home to Oklahoma where his mother had fallen deathly ill. The sickness had come on suddenly. It had progressed so fast that Dr. Hansen had been fearful Davin would not make it in time to see her. She had encountered a bacterium—a powerful superbug that had developed quickly.

With less sickness and more medical advances in the world, the trade-off manifested with more and more superbugs beginning to materialize. Thankfully, doctors were able to kill them off within a few months of surfacing. It was truly astonishing how quickly the advances in medicine allowed doctors to find a cure to these horrendous sicknesses and stop their spread. But with the evolution of superbugs, sometimes they still weren't able to save everyone. The unlucky few who caught the first wave of the superbug were sometimes lost.

Fortunately, Davin was able to make it in time to see his mother. And with him by her side, she had experienced a miraculous recovery. She was so glad to have her sweet son by her side and was certain that was why she was able to heal. She missed him and his handsome face that reminded her so much of his father. However, the severity of the bug had left her partially crippled with symptoms similar to that of a stroke.

Davin had wanted to stay until his mother could walk normally again—hoping that regaining her mobility would lift her spirits before they had to say their goodbyes once more. He had to plead with The Society leaders to negotiate a new contract that would allow him to stay so he could be with his mother during her recovery. They almost refused him and opted to get someone else to work for them, but Kona and Davin were getting wonderful reviews from everyone on the mainland. People specifically raved about the two pairing well together. Not wanting to lose any support from the general public, they agreed to Davin's terms. He had to return to The Society every few months to shoot a new promotional video, but besides those few visits, he was allowed to stay with his mother either until she had made a full recovery or until it was time to return to The Society for the Grand Welcome Celebration.

7. THE GRAND WELCOME CELEBRATION

AFTER TWO YEARS of commuting people across the sea, the round white transporter pod had made its last voyage across the Pacific. All one hundred thousand residents of the Hawaii Society who had been chosen to live out their days on the beautiful island had arrived. The current residents were asked to meet the newcomers at the unloading station to welcome the last of the arriving Society members.

With cheers and celebratory music, the residents walked off the pod in awe of their new reality. The usual guided tour from the resident information bot for the last arrivals was postponed until the next day so that a special welcome party could commence to celebrate the transport completion. Camera drones from the press arrived for the day to showcase The Society and allow news reporters to make comments on the Grand Welcome Celebration. The head government official, Miss Sandra Waverly, who was in charge of running the Hawaii Society, wanted to communicate that with all of its members present, The Society was now finally whole.

All members were to live and operate together in a self-sustaining and harmonious paradise.

The last ones to step off the spacious transporter pod was Senator Liam Travis, the mastermind behind The Societies, and Madam Vice President herself. The cameras pointing in every direction quickly refocused on the articulate, high-energy woman with bright red lipstick and a red Hawaiian hibiscus delicately placed in her long dark hair. Senator Travis stood at her side, smiling and waving when cameras focused on him. He had an average build, standing at 5'11", and jet-black hair that was perfectly parted and combed. The senator had recruited the vice president to back The Societies because of her likable personality—something he was not so fortunate to possess. The whole country was in love with her energy and grace. She raised her hands to the sky with an exuberant "Aloha!" The crowd erupted into a cheer and the elaborate celebration began.

The Grand Welcome Party was an event unlike anything The Society had seen before. Dancing, games, and water activities filled The Society's sandy shores in the daylight hours. A roasted pig and tropical drinks were passed out in full luau fashion. The vice president was broadcast driving a quad ski over the sand and into the clear, cool water. Robotic dolphins that could have been easily mistaken for real ones from afar put on a mesmerizing show for the onlookers on shore. As the deep blue night sky melted over the orange sunset, everyone made their way to the large dome that sat atop The Society towers for a night of entertainment. The event was to be hosted by the usual island beauty, Kona, who had been hosting the shows solo for the last sixteen months, and Davin Chapman, The Society's resident star, recently returned from his stay on the mainland.

Chelsea knew how important the event was to The Society officials and looked forward to working a larger, more challenging show. She made sure to sign up to work the event as the video engineer and came in the day before to ensure all the equipment and settings were properly set. She came dressed in her all-black clothing, as is custom for technicians to do in order to blend into the dark backstage environment. However, when she got to her workstation, she found someone had changed all her settings!

A moment of sheer panic overcame Chelsea before she was able to take a deep breath and go to work to reprogram the switcher before the show would begin. *Why did I not backup my programming?* she thought as she cursed herself. Knowing she would be hard-pressed to finish in time, she tried to make a list in her mind of all the necessary steps she would have to take to get the other equipment ready as well.

When she finished reprogramming the video switcher and turned on the broadcast signal, the next item on her list was the cameras. She opened a drawer of tiny HD hover cameras and counted out ten. At that point, there were fifteen minutes until the show would begin—just enough time to configure the camera trackers to sync with the talent and turn on the backstage monitors before the show would begin.

Hover cameras were tiny high-definition cameras that floated in midair in front of the stage and followed a designated individual. This equipment made it unnecessary to have human camera operators. The tracking mechanism in each hover camera could be programmed to track PED wristbands so the camera would follow whomever it was assigned to monitor. There was one camera designated to each talent on stage and one camera for a wide shot of the whole stage. When a performer walked offstage the cameras defaulted to different parts of the stage to provide a variety of angles to cut to. Chelsea entered each individual's PED IP address and waited for the cameras to sync to their designated performer.

Davin and Kona's wristbands synced up immediately. The luau dancers' did soon after, but the special act's wristband was not syncing. Chelsea's heart sank as she realized the show was about to begin and she needed to locate the special act to troubleshoot the problem. Thankfully, she knew the special act was a dance that would be performed at the end of the show, which would hopefully allow her enough time to locate the performer mid-show and resolve the problem. She would have to leave the switcher on autopilot and count on it to switch between cameras to whoever was speaking at the time—a risky move considering the system could easily get confused if more than one person spoke at once.

With what little time she had left before the show began, Chelsea jumped up to turn on the backstage monitors. Normally, she could do this remotely, but since the switcher's settings had been erased, she would need to re-network the monitors later when she had more time.

Davin and Kona were already waiting to enter stage left by the unlit backstage monitor. "Excuse me, I need to turn on this monitor," Chelsea said as she weaved between Davin and Kona.

Recognizing Chelsea, Davin quickly stepped to the side and gave a pleasant smile as he motioned to the monitor. "It's all yours."

He watched as she bent under the television screen to find the small button on the back to turn it on. Inadvertently, he found his eyes trailing down her back, down to her waist and farther. Then he felt a peculiar urge to step toward her and touch her—like some unknown force wanted him to be as near to her as possible.

"Goodness, Davin, you could at least *pretend* like you have your mind on the show," Kona said, trying to cover her resentment with a polite snicker. Davin had never shown her any interest—a fact she resented, considering most men fawned over her.

Chelsea spun around, having finished what she needed to do, and realizing the situation, she gave Davin a disapproving smirk.

"I'm sorry—I'm usually more of a gentleman," he said, hoping he hadn't ruined his chances when he was so hoping to make a good impression on her. "I could've turned that on for you if you needed."

A small laugh escaped Chelsea's lips at the thought of a gentleman, since she was fairly certain "gentlemen" no longer existed. "Right . . . Well, you're all set now. Excuse me, I have to hurry."

Davin groaned inside as she walked away, in part because of his disappointment at his distasteful encounter with Chelsea, but also because he still had an irresistible longing to touch her. *Get a hold of yourself, man. What is it about this woman?*

"Showtime, Davin," Kona said as their wristbands lit up, cuing them to enter the stage. Their microphones automatically went live when they passed the backstage curtain. "ALO-O-HA Hawaii Society! Welcome to tonight's Grand Welcome Performance! Weren't today's celebrations amazing?" Cheers ensued from the crowd. "I'm Kona Palakiko, your MC tonight, along with the yummy Davin Chapman. Let's give him a big round of applause to welcome him back to the Hawaii Society! We have certainly missed him," she said over thunderous applause.

As Davin spoke, Chelsea rushed over to stage right to find the special act, Lacie Sharp. She was in a corner doing some last minute rehearsals.

As Chelsea ran across backstage, she passed the producer who was directing cues for the show on his fully extended PED. He was a large, gruff man, with long brown hair pulled back in a low ponytail. His name was Ben Sharp, but most referred to him as Big Ben. He had been specially flown in from the mainland to direct the Grand Welcome because he was known to pull off any show handed to him. He was stern and prided himself on his intimidation tactics. He sent out a message the day he arrived with all the details for the show so everyone knew what he expected for the workers on his show. In that email, he laid out the details of the show and specifically emphasized the importance of the special act going well. It was to be performed by his daughter, and it was her first show to a national audience. He expected perfection to ensure his daughter's success and, of course, the overall success of the show. Ben was especially miffed that no time had been allotted for formal rehearsals in The Society but, unable to pass up the opportunity to allow his daughter to perform in a nationwide performance, he agreed to the terms.

"Aren't you the video engineer? What are you doing away from your station?" he yelled as softly as his anger would permit him without the front row of the audience hearing him from backstage.

Not immediately answering, Chelsea quickly turned on the stage right backstage monitor. Then she turned to Big Ben. "Lacie's camera isn't syncing to her wristband. I need to find out why. I'll figure it out and be back to my station shortly."

Looking at Lacie's wrists as she whirled them above her head during her solo rehearsal, Chelsea saw no sign of her wristband.

"Where's your wristband?" Chelsea asked Lacie as she approached her.

"I took it off. It doesn't go with my outfit, and I didn't want it distracting from my performance."

In disbelief of how unaware Lacie was of the technical needs of the show, Chelsea insisted, "Lacie, you'll need your wristband for the camera to get a good shot of you. Please put it back on."

"I left it in my dressing room," she replied whimsically as she continued to rehearse.

Ben could barely contain his anger. His face turned red, and he struggled to remain seated as he directed the show. "Get your crap together, video lady! Your switcher's autopilot is about as competent as you are!"

Furious that Ben could be blaming *her*, she barked at Lacie, "Hurry and get your wristband from your room. Then come see me, and I'll sync your wristband before you go on stage."

"But I need to rehearse!" Lacie called out as Chelsea ran back to her station.

Chelsea reached her station just as Davin was introducing the luau dancers to the stage. She took command of the switcher and made sure to get the best shots on screen to hopefully appease Ben's temper before the end of the show.

The dancers were finishing their number, and Davin and Kona entered the stage again to perform their short duet before introducing Lacie—but Lacie *still* had not come to see Chelsea to sync her wristband. Chelsea connected a communication line to Big Ben's earpiece. "Ben, I haven't seen Lacie. Where is she?"

"She has been rehearsing like she told you she would. Have you got her wristband sorted out yet?" he spat back at her, impatient with her for bringing up the same problem again.

Frustrated that Lacie had ignored her instructions, Chelsea replied with a short, "I will."

She sprang to action, running to Lacie's dressing room. Luckily, she spotted the wristband quickly and ran across backstage to deliver it just as Kona was introducing Lacie as the final performance before the vice president would address the crowd and close the Grand Welcome.

"Hurry up! I'm going to miss my cue!" Lacie screeched. Chelsea turned on the syncing capability for Lacie's wristband and slipped it on shortly after the music began. Discombobulated from missing her start, Lacie stumbled on stage and struggled to find her place in the dance.

Chelsea ran to her station to try and sync Lacie's wristband to the camera in record time so she could get some good shots of the beginning of the routine. Thankfully, it synced without a problem, and Chelsea began cutting between the best shots. Lacie eventually found her place in the routine. Then in the last few seconds, Lacie suddenly raised her hands to the sky, and her wristband went flying off her wrist and landed at her feet. Chelsea watched in dread as the wristband flew off, the camera following it in midair, to end her performance with a close-up shot of her feet on a fifty-foot wide video wall.

Lacie left the stage fighting tears, and some chuckles were heard throughout the crowd. The vice president walked on as Lacie left, and the room silenced for an inspiring and epic monologue about the bright future for America's Societies residents.

But Chelsea did not hear her stirring speech. She sat at her station mindlessly switching between cameras as she prepared herself emotionally for the scene that was about to ensue. She could see Big Ben fuming as he cradled his crying daughter in his large arms. *How could I have been so stupid to leave Lacie to get the wristband? I should have at least quickly tightened it before she walked on stage. If they only knew how much I had to fix before the performance began, they would understand!* So many pointless regrets flew through Chelsea's mind as the night came to a close and the crowd applauded the vice president's speech and music thumped through the speakers as people exited.

Davin was happy the show was done. It was the largest and most critical performance The Society had planned for him to do. He felt quite pleased with how well it went and thought he had performed his best. Now if he could make a quick break from Kona and avoid his agent, Lola, maybe he would get a chance to sit down and properly speak with Chelsea. He looked over just as Big Ben was closing in on Chelsea at her station.

"You threw my daughter's performance under the bus! Jeopardized the show on multiple accounts and made us look like complete fools! You'll be lucky if The Societies get any more funding with such a sorry excuse of a performance as the whole world watched *you* fail! And to think you're a trained video engineer—you are a sorry excuse for a professional. No wonder you couldn't cut it in the real world."

"You completely ruined my performance!" Lacie piped in.

"Let's go, Lacie. The pod leaves soon, and Madam Vice President will want a word, I'm sure," Big Ben said, and he and Lacie stormed off.

Chelsea couldn't reconcile her feelings of complete injustice and utter failure. She sank in her chair as they walked off without hearing any of her side of the story. Knowing she would have to deal with these unresolved feelings for the next week or more, she suddenly felt very tired.

After watching the whole scene play out, Davin ran over to try and console Chelsea and figure out what could have possibly elicited such a response. He hadn't noticed anything go terribly wrong besides, possibly, the rather humorous flying wristband. He couldn't help but chuckle as he thought of Lacie's face when she realized she had just sent her wristband flying into the air.

"Wow! What was that about, right? Can you say blowing things out of proportion much?" Davin said, walking up to her and trying to lighten the moment.

Chelsea looked up at him with what he could only interpret as irritation. She managed to get out a small "Yeah" as she spun her chair slightly away from him.

Wondering if she maybe needed a more empathetic approach, he knelt down next to her and put his hand on her chair. "Hey, don't let them get you down. I've worked with them before, and all they care about is *them* looking good. No one even realized Lacie messed up her stupid dance, and it's not your fault about the silly wristband thing." He gave her a half-smile and waited for some response. He half expected her to lean in for a hug, or maybe he was just hoping she wanted to be as close to him as he did to her.

To his dismay, she leaned forward, not for a hug, but to stand up and walk away. "Thanks, but I don't want to talk about it. I'm going to bed. Have a good night, Davin."

8. WITHOUT CONSENT

AFTER THE GRAND Welcome program was over that night, everyone was exhilarated from all the fun and the thought of living out their lives in the beautiful paradise that was the Hawaii Society.

All but four residents:

Chelsea—who went immediately to her room and spent the rest of the night trying to process the evening's events—from Ben's harsh and unfair rebuke to Lacie's maddening disregard for the technical needs of the show to Davin Chapman being so unexpectedly concerned for her. Her emotions felt dismantled.

Davin—who felt both annoyed at Chelsea's lack of warmth at his best efforts to console her, as well as feeling a disheartening worry that she may *never* warm up to him. He attended the after party at the club, but he was only present physically. As the music blared and the lights flashed around him, he remained emotionally unconscious to his surroundings.

Hammond—who had enjoyed the long day of celebration but ended the Grand Welcome Performance sitting alone, wondering where Sara was. She left to use the restroom near the beginning of the luau performance and never returned. She had declined all of his calls, and he had searched every bathroom but could not find his Sara.

And Sara—who had retreated to one of the small video editing bays on the outer circle of the dome to cry. She cried harder than she ever had that evening. Her eyes were long since swollen from her tears of dismay and feelings of shame as Hammond searched for her in the empty bathrooms nearby. She wanted to somehow be strong but felt completely broken inside at the same time. Her normally done-up hair was ratted and unkempt. It somehow felt like she had ruined her sweet and genuine love for Hammond. It had been crushed, tainted, and she could not find the words or the courage to leave that room to tell him.

As the last of her tears hit her wet skirt, she looked up at the dark edit bay computer screen to see her disheveled reflection. It was not her reflection anymore. It looked unfamiliar. It angered her, and she felt a rage inside that she had never experienced before. She took her hair out of the marred braid she had made for the night's festivities and twisted it in a tight bun on the top of her head. She dried her eyes and straightened her clothes. She would not be defined by that night. She would tell Hammond, and he would understand.

She found him on his way back to their living quarters, still searching for her as he had been for the last half hour.

"Hammond," she barely managed to get out.

"Sara! For goodness sake, where have you been? I've been looking everywhere for you, and you kept declining my calls. You missed seeing the video you edited," he said as he reached out to hold her. Then he took note of her swollen eyes and flushed skin, and he saw past her masked smile. Something was wrong. Her usual bubbly self seemed rattled and withdrawn. "What's the matter, love? Is everything all right?"

She felt awful for how long she had been ignoring his phone calls when it was so apparent he had been worrying about her, but she also felt a strange resistance to his touch that she had never experienced before. For the first time, his touch did not give her feelings of comfort and safety like it always had in the past. "I'm sorry. I went to the edit bay. I need to go to my room. I really just want to sleep," Sara said.

"Okay," he said, brushing his hands across her cheeks and feeling them warm from tears. "You sure you don't want to talk?"

"Hammond, please. Can we go?" She looked angry.

They went to Sara's room without saying another word. This was so unlike her that he was completely unsure what to do. He felt stiff and uncomfortable. *Why is Sara acting like this? What happened? And why won't she tell me?* he wondered in agony.

As soon as they reached her room, Sara ran for the bathroom and closed the door. Hammond stood at the empty door with wide eyes as he tried to reason the cause for Sara's behavior. He wasn't sure what to think, but he knew that whatever it was, he had good reason to be concerned.

In the bathroom, Sara took her hair down from the tight bun she had put it in. She quickly got into the shower as fast as her body could move through the stiffness. She used all the soap she could manage to gather in her palm without it spilling over, and she feverishly scrubbed her entire body.

After her shower, she felt a small amount of relief—like somehow the night could have been washed down the drain. She used the insta-dry shower feature to dry off her body, which eliminated the need for towels at The Society. Normally she enjoyed the feature, but after using it this time, she realized she had forgotten to grab her nightwear before entering the bathroom. Though she knew how irrational it was, a small amount of panic rushed over her. She opened the door to the bathroom—hoping she could somehow retrieve her nightwear without notice.

But to her shame, Hammond stood in the doorway, waiting for her to exit so he could get ready for bed. She froze. Unshaken by her familiar body, he went to retrieve his mouthpiece, and almost by muscle memory, he lightly kissed her familiar lips as he passed. Her body went stiff again, and she pushed her hand against him while cowering against the wall. He pulled back, and she quickly ran for her closet to retrieve her clothes.

"I'm sorry," Hammond stammered, feeling a rush of concern and a small sense of betrayal from Sara's reaction to his innocent kiss.

"No, no," Sara tried to assure him as she got dressed. "Just wanted to get my clothes on before I get cold is all," she said, trying to make Hammond feel better about her unwarranted response with a feeble lie.

Sensing her lie and feeling hurt that she felt she needed to, Hammond hung his head low and eased his way into the bathroom to get ready for bed in order to give Sara the space she clearly desired. Sara lay on the bed, hoping when Hammond cuddled up next to her, as he did every night, she would feel right again about being wrapped up in his arms. And that while being held tight, the whole story would come spilling out.

But when Hammond's arms wrapped around her as he crawled into bed, she went rigid again. And to her dismay, she found it still felt wrong and uncomfortable to be so near to him. She pulled away. "Sorry. I think I'm too hot to cuddle tonight," she said as she scooted away from him. She gave him a forced smile before she whispered, "Goodnight," and then she turned away and clung to the edge of the bed.

Hammond stared down at her in bewilderment. Sadness overcame him as he lay back on the far side of the bed. Sara had never been so cold to him. Everything he did that evening seemed to upset her. He stayed up for hours trying to think of what he could say when morning came to help her open up to him. He wanted to choose his words carefully, but every phrase and every thought that came to mind left him feeling unsure it wouldn't just upset her further. Without his consent, sleep eventually overtook him as he lay thinking.

THE MORNING SUN EASILY awoke him the following morning, and he lay motionless, waiting for Sara to wake so he could talk with her. He still wasn't exactly sure what to say, but he knew he had to try something.

Sara lay asleep next to him—peaceful and still. Without the rigid body language from the night before, she looked to be her usual sleeping self. However, he did notice her eyebrows furrowed occasionally, which was unusual compared to the many other times he'd gazed on her sleeping face. He wondered if he could touch her. Knowing how opposed she had been to touch the night before, he was hesitant, but he so badly wanted to touch her and feel near to her again. He reached out and lightly stroked his finger across her arm. Her eyebrows furrowed again just as his skin touched hers. His heart sank, and he lifted his fingers and let her be.

After a few minutes, she began to wake. "Good morning, beautiful. How are you doing?" Hammond said as he saw Sara's eyes open.

She curled up into a tight ball as the flood of memories from the night before came rushing in on her. But just as she did, she remembered the promise she made to herself. She would be strong, and she would tell him. But as she stared at his worried eyes, gearing up to tell him, her determination faltered as she began to quiver inside—reliving the moment in her mind's eye. She blocked out the memory as quickly as it came. Somehow, she still wasn't able to tell him what had happened. *I will*, she thought. *I just can't right now.*

"I'm sorry about last night, Hammond. Really." She popped out of bed and ran for the bathroom. She put in her mouthpiece to brush her teeth. When she finished, she popped her head out of the bathroom door. "We should go out and do something. I could really use a good pick-me-up. We haven't been windsurfing in a while. We should go windsurfing, Hammond! That sounds so fun!"

He wanted to stop her, hold her down, and insist she tell him what had happened. She was hiding something, and he knew it. But he also saw the hope in her eyes—the hope that he would say yes and let her avoid the conversation just a little longer.

"Sure, love. We can go windsurfing."

FOR THE NEXT DAY and a half, Sara filled every hour with activities. Hammond began to notice the activities chosen were ones where little conversation could be had. Sara also spent extra hours sleeping in, and she never stopped for a breath as she crammed food in at mealtimes to avoid having to talk. Hammond soon realized he needed to step in if he wanted to know the truth.

"Sara, I was wondering if we could hike to the top of the mountain tonight before the sun goes down. I'd really like to go. Will you please join me?"

Sara was caught off guard. Hammond rarely made requests. She usually had the demands, and she made the plans. But she'd always told herself that whenever he did ask for something, she would be sure to make it happen. "Okay," she reluctantly agreed.

On the mountain, they hiked in silence and moved at a brisk pace. Hammond stayed a few steps behind Sara. He remained conscious of her footing and reached out to support her whenever he was concerned about her falling. Even though he normally considered her a very strong woman, he couldn't help but feel like she was suddenly fragile, at least emotionally, and it translated to how he treated her physically.

The distance Hammond felt between them was heart-wrenching. Her familiar voice and touch were missing—something that had been a constant since the day she first approached him in the dessert shop. She was never short for words. She was always running up to him and tugging on his arm, dragging him to do some activity she'd thought of. He never minded, though. Anything with her was enjoyable, and he loved that he never tired of her. He couldn't help but smile at every thought and idea she shared with him. She was the light in every room, but that part of her had been locked away.

When they reached the top, Hammond found a rock big enough for the two of them to sit on, and he motioned for her to sit. No one else was on the mountain that evening, which Hammond was grateful for. He knew she would need the privacy if she were going to open up to him.

She sat next to him with hesitation but without protest. He grabbed her arm gently and removed her wristband, and then her earpiece, and then his own. He placed them in his pocket. He hoped this would create a sense of privacy that they had not experienced since before coming to The Society. He knew this was not technically allowed, but he also knew they would not be accountable unless something happened that they would need the video evidence for.

"Now it's just you and me, Sara." He turned to straddle the rock and face her directly. "You know I love you more than anything in the world. I always have. That will never change, no matter what. I've been with you long enough to know you're hurting. I don't know why, but I can't help but feel like you need to let this go. Whatever it is, it's crushing you." Sara felt warm tears trickle down her face, and she tasted their salty flavor as they reach her open lips. "I *need* my smiling, bouncing Sara back. I want you to tell me everything you're thinking again—every obscure and intricate little thought. I can't take the silence. So please, I won't talk the rest of the night if you don't want me to. I'm here just to listen." He sat holding her hands gently in his and waited patiently for her response.

Sara took a slow breath in. She knew she had to tell him, though she knew a day and a half ago was when he deserved to hear it.

"The other night during the show, the society coordinator guy came onto me. I told him no, and I tried to get him off, but . . . I couldn't." As she spoke, the words began to fall out of her mouth faster and faster. "I'm sorry. I ruined it for us. I just wasn't strong enough. I've never been pressured like that before—"

"Whoa, whoa, Sara, what happened? The society coordinator? Like Branch Willix—society coordinator?" She nodded in affirmation as tears began to well in her eyes. Hammond's face turned hot with fury. "What do you mean, he 'came on' to you? Did he rape you?" Sara went quiet and hung her head low.

Cases of rape were much more rare after the *Sexual Harassment Cases of 2020*. They were a series of cases against prominent men of the time and ultimately resulted in very strict sexual harassment laws. Society went through a long phase of saddling men with the ails of civilization after very harsh rulings were made. Men were often hastily condemned and prosecuted in *any* sexual disputes, with very few exceptions.

However, because of permanent birth control, women became more open to sexual promiscuity. And seeing that men were often unjustly persecuted, more women began to speak out against this practice. The perceived gap between men and women's sexual drives grew smaller. A mutual arrangement between the genders emerged to counter any confusion of consent. It became a cultural norm to verbally ask one's partner, "*Is this mutual?*" before making *any* sexual advances. If the answer was not an explicit *"yes,"* then whoever advanced without consent was held responsible with little leniency in a court of law. This was made more viable with the adoption of the PED wristband and the ability to enable its continuous recording system. Video footage could be referenced and compared to confirm incidences. Even within a committed relationship, partners usually continued to ask before moments of intimacy.

Hammond reached for Sara and pulled her to his chest. He felt her tears dampen his shirt as he held her, and he tried not to let his anger cause him to squeeze too tightly.

"I'm sorry," she sobbed. "I was just coming out of the bathroom stall, and he caught me off guard."

"Sara, you don't need to say sorry. Why do you think you need to say sorry to me? Rape isn't your fault."

He pushed her away and looked into her eyes as she answered. "You were supposed to be the only guy I was ever with," she explained.

He smiled his kind, soft smile and kissed her forehead as he pulled her again into the safety of his arms. "I'm glad that's what you want, but it doesn't make our relationship any less because of what *he* did to you."

As he said those words, the anger curdled inside him once again, and despite his desire to hold her longer, he let go and stood. "It's time to go. Come. I need to get you back to your room." Hammond took their wristbands and earpieces from his pocket and repositioned them back where they belonged. Then he took Sara's hand and began leading her down the mountain. He thought hard as they hiked down the mountainside about how he wanted to handle the situation and make Branch suffer the consequences that awaited him.

"It's been a long day. I think you should lie down and get some rest," Hammond suggested as they walked.

"What are *you* going to do? Will you be coming to bed with me?" she asked with concern in her eyes.

"Don't worry about me," he said, though he could tell from her facial expression that answer would not suffice. "Of course, I'll lay down with you if that's what you want. I just think you need to rest and have some time to let this sink in now that I know what happened. It's too late to visit the government offices now. In the morning, we'll head to the security department, and I'll have him prosecuted. He'll pay for what he did to you. I'll make sure of it," Hammond said crossly.

"No!" Sara said, stopping abruptly on the trail and ripping her hand from his. "If anyone is going to get him prosecuted, it needs to be me. I need to do it—alone. I *need* this," she said sternly, successfully holding back the tears that threatened to form. "I want to feel strong again."

Hammond's heart hurt for her, and he realized how helpless this experience had made her feel. He tried to suppress his anger and hold back the urge he felt to run in and save her. He could see in her eyes that she wanted to save herself. He took a few deep breaths to settle his fury. "Okay."

THEY WENT TO BED together, and for the first time in days, Sara allowed Hammond to cuddle in close to her. Feeling her near to him again was an immense relief to the tension that had built up between them. Hammond was grateful to feel the walls she had built crumble after they spoke, and Sara was appreciative that Hammond had taken the initiative to help her open up. She went to sleep, hopeful that she would experience restful sleep again without images of the society coordinator haunting her dreams.

Feeling especially protective, Hammond purposefully positioned himself between Sara and the door. He tried to sleep, but once Sara was peacefully slumbering, Hammond couldn't stop his anger from festering inside him. As the minutes passed, he couldn't stay in bed any longer. He had to find Branch and let him know he was *never* to lay a hand on Sara again. He sneaked out from between the sheets, careful not to wake Sara, and left to find Branch.

"Locate Branch Willix," he whispered, and his PED responded in his ear, "Branch Willix is currently in the self-help room of Tower Two level one." It was early enough that he knew there would still be people out of bed—he would have to be somewhat discreet about the encounter if he didn't want word to get back to Sara before she prosecuted him in the morning.

"HOW DARE YOU TOUCH Sara against her will!" Hammond said as he neared Branch, loud enough that only Branch would be able to hear.

Branch looked up from his exercise equipment, slightly perplexed. "Are you talking to me? I don't even know what Sara you're talking about."

"Sara! *My* Sara! The beautiful blonde with long legs and golden hair. The girl you raped the other night at the—"

"Whoa, whoa, those are some serious accusations, buddy. You talking about the girl from the night of the Grand Welcome Celebration?" he inquired, standing to match Hammond's stance.

Hammond was caught off guard by Branch's confident approach. A very non-confrontational man himself, Hammond struggled to keep his composure as Branch challenged him.

"Not sure who you are or what she told you, but that girl wanted it. I asked and everything. What can I say, not many girls say no to this," he said haughtily as he gestured to his physique.

Angered by his arrogance, Hammond regained his courage and moved in close to Branch's face. "You are such an arrogant liar. She told me everything. And in the morning, we're going to the justice department, and she is going to turn you in. You may be the society coordinator, but you are not above Society rules! Government official or not, it's over. In the meantime, you keep your hands off my wife."

Branch let out a slight chuckle, despite Hammond's threats. "Hate to break it to you, but she's not your wife. You don't own her body like you think you do. We did away with that kind of thinking for a reason, and apparently, you aren't doing her right, because she didn't even hesitate." It took every ounce of self-control for Hammond not to punch him. "You don't believe me? I'll prove it to you *right now*—perks of a government official. Why wait until morning? I'd like to clear my name now," Branch said, motioning for Hammond to follow. "But I'm warning you right now, you won't enjoy what you're about to see nearly as much as I will," he said with a conniving smile.

They headed for the government offices. Hammond was furious and concerned at the same time. Anger still consumed him, but Branch's overarching confidence left him worried—maybe he didn't have the whole story? *Would Sara lie to me to cover up a lack of fulfillment in our relationship? Is that why she insisted she should prosecute him alone?*

Ding. The elevator chimed as they reached the third floor that housed the government offices. Everyone had left for the day. It was empty and dark. When Branch walked in, the lights popped on. "Come on," he said. "Let's go to the security room. We'll watch a little porno together," he said with a wink. Hammond's fists clenched.

In the security room, Branch sat down at a desk that faced a wall with a mammoth monitor on it. He pulled his PED from his pocket and expanded it to its full size before connecting it to the security system using his government clearance. As he did, the monitor in front of him lit up to show hundreds of cameras' footage in real time. Branch pulled up a search bar and searched three things—Branch Willix, Sara, and west bathroom dome cam.

He scrolled through the recorded footage of the last two days until he reached the night of the Grand Welcome Celebration.

Branch and Hammond watched together as he saw Sara from her wristband camera getting up to leave and use the restroom the night of the show. "Is this your girl?" Branch asked. Hammond did not answer. He stared intently at the screen, wishing he didn't have to see what he feared he was about to witness—but he had to know.

He observed as Sara walked to the nearest restroom in the west side of the dome and entered from the right entrance. Branch could be seen from the bathroom's wide-angle security camera looking at himself in the mirror as she walked in. She looked at him and gave a slight smile and walked into a stall. Branch slowly made his way to the entrance of her stall, and as she exited, he grabbed her around the waist. He could be heard asking, "Is this mutual?" Then he shut the stall door behind him as Hammond heard Sara's voice saying "yes" over and over. The wristband cameras didn't show much, but enough that Hammond had to look away in pure agony from the sight. Branch looked at Hammond and smiled as he turned back to the monitor to exit out of the security footage.

"Oh, don't take it too hard, man. I'm sure she still loves you—no harm, no foul. She probably was just up for a little extra fun that night. You just go show her a good time tonight, and I'm sure she won't come looking for more."

Hammond slumped in his chair, brokenhearted, unable to think or move. Branch wasn't sure what to do to get him to leave, so he tried to console him with his logic. "It's really normal for people to want to explore their sexuality and try out new partners. I mean, you can't expect to have Sara all to yourself all the time, right?" Branch said, smiling and patting Hammond on the shoulder.

That comment cut deep for Hammond. He *did* expect to have *all* of her forever—that was what Sara promised him in her wedding vows years ago. *Maybe our vows don't mean anything to her anymore after our marriage was ended?* Hammond thought.

Seeing that Hammond was still stuck to the chair, Branch decided to go with a more direct approach to get him to leave. "Well, we saw what we came here for. I'm afraid it's time to clear out. I'm not technically supposed to bring people in here, but I figured you had a right to know the truth. I'm sorry to be the one to break it to you, man."

It's too bad it had to be his girl that I ran into that night, Branch thought to himself as he walked with Hammond back down the hall to the elevator. *Most men aren't so possessive of their girls.*

When they reached the elevator, Hammond walked on—still distraught. Branch stayed behind. "I have to go back to get my PED, but I tell you what, I can see you're real beat up about this. So, if you ever need anything, you let me know, and if she ever comes around again, I'll tell her no thanks—out of respect for you. You have a good night, man." The doors to the elevator shut, and Hammond rode down.

Hammond found a bench on The Society grounds and sat on it, unable to think or function for the rest of the night. Just before sunrise, he walked back up to Sara's room. He opened the door. Sara sat up in bed to see Hammond standing in the doorway with the memory of her betrayal still replaying in his mind. "I saw why you were sorry. I get it now. I'm sorry too." He walked over to his room and opened his door, shutting it behind him. He lay down on his own bed for the first time since arriving at The Society. "Take away Sara Lehman's access to my living quarters," he said to his PED.

The door locked just as Sara went to open the door. For the next hour and a half, she knocked on the door, pleading for Hammond to open it with tears gushing from her eyes until a security bot asked her to comply with leaving the premises.

9. REGRESSION

CHELSEA WALKED THROUGH the outside garden, headed for the fruit trees. Still upset about how the Grand Welcome Celebration had gone a few days ago, she was in need of a pick-me-up, and a ripe orange sounded like the perfect sweet treat to give a boost in her mood.

Every day, each resident was allowed to pick up to two servings of a fruit or vegetable directly from the outside gardens. The rest of the produce was used for the meals made within the cafeterias. Chelsea took advantage of this benefit almost every day. There was something inherently satisfying about picking fruit directly off the tree and enjoying it in the open air with the light of the sun beating down and the ocean breeze on her face.

Even though it had been several days since the Grand Welcome Celebration, she still had not been back to the dome to do the usual video-related tasks she'd been signing up for. She'd decided that after working there almost every day for months, and after the fiasco at the show the other night, she needed a break.

The last few days, she had signed up to learn how to repair the robotic chef instead. After it broke down the last time, she wanted to make sure she never had to endure the complaints and long lines of a food shortage again. The training was tedious and nonsensical to her though, and she soon realized it might take her many months, or even years, to complete her training if she only worked two hours a day—but she couldn't bring herself to work the extra hours when there was no imminent need or incentive. *Why should I have to work extra? No one else does.*

She scanned some oranges with her bracelet until she found one at its peak ripeness and then sat against the trunk of the tree and began to peel it. Spurts of orange fragrance sprayed out from the peel as she tore at the thick casing. She breathed in deeply and tried to focus on the sweet, refreshing smell and the sound of the waves crashing in the distance. She wondered if she would ever be able to learn the complexities of robotics and silently hoped someone else would master it before her so she wouldn't need to.

She continued to peel the skin of her orange in the midst of her musing until a small girl and her mother came to the tree to pick an orange as well.

"That one!" The girl pointed while the mother lifted her up so she could reach the oranges. The young mother scanned the orange with her wristband and then picked it off the tree. "I want a bite! I want some! Pleea-se."

"I have to peel it first, Tassy. Please be patient," the young mother urged.

Tassy. Chelsea recognized the name. She was the toddler from the childcare center. Tassy scowled slightly while she waited for her mother to slowly peel the orange. Then she saw Chelsea who was still sitting at the foot of the tree and immediately forgot about the orange she was waiting for.

"Hi," she said, getting directly in Chelsea's face and waving hello energetically. "What's you name?" Chelsea smiled and managed to suppress a laugh so she didn't make Tassy feel embarrassed about her small grammatical error.

Tassy's mother turned around and quickly pulled Tassy back away from Chelsea's face. "I'm sorry," she apologized. "She doesn't understand personal space yet."

"It's okay," Chelsea said as she chuckled and looked back to the little girl, still awaiting an answer. "My name is Chelsea. You must be Tassy. I recognize you from a while back at the childcare center."

"Oh, hi," the mother sputtered, now remembering their first encounter. "How are you?"

"I'm fine," Chelsea replied. "Were you able to talk to the government offices about spending more time with Tassy?" Chelsea asked for the sake of conversation.

"Yes, but they said no," she said glumly. "They said the state is in charge of her learning and development, and if I took away from her time at the childcare center, she would be hindered. Said if I didn't allow for essential cultivation, they would have to limit my access to her even more. So I stay out of it and take advantage of what time we do have together."

Chelsea felt sorry for her. She could see her obvious love for her child and her despair at having so little involvement in her life. "That's too bad. It seems unfair."

"It's okay," the mother replied. "I can't think like that. We can't afford to be kicked out of The Society. We just make do with what time we have." She looked down at her wrist to check the time. "Speaking of which, we were going to build a sand castle. We have to get going so we have time before I have to take her back."

"Oh, okay," Chelsea said. "Have fun." She waved vigorously at Tassy as they walked away toward the beach. Tassy's silly expression and awkward waving amused Chelsea until her mother playfully tickled her and lifted her up onto her hip. They seemed so happy to be together. Chelsea thought it was a pity they weren't allowed more time if they wanted it.

Acknowledging she had no control over the situation, she returned her attention back to peeling her orange. She pulled apart each slice and picked the white strings of membrane from the edges. Just as Chelsea took the first succulent bite, a small, repetitive noise interrupted her chewing. There was a constant hum accompanied by three clicks, then a short buzz that sounded like a small child wheezing. She looked down to see one of the small weeding bots just a few feet in front of her struggling to get its wheels over a small mound of dirt—a small mound that it normally had no trouble treading. After struggling for a few seconds, the bot's small struggles piddled out until it came to a complete halt just in front of Chelsea's feet.

She picked it up from the ground to examine it and see if it was jammed or needed some other simple fix. She looked closely but found no signs of jamming. There was plenty of sun for the small solar panel on top of its round body to absorb, so the problem was not a lack of power source. She tried to remember some of the things she had learned in her robotics course from the day before but was not sure how to apply them to the weeding bot.

She felt useless as she set it back on the ground, still very much broken. And as she did, she noticed the unusual amount of weeds surrounding it. This wasn't altogether surprising since the bot had obviously not been performing properly recently, but as she looked out farther, she noticed multiple patches of thick weeds. And somewhere within the weeds, a weeding bot could be seen— broken-down. Consumed in her own mind and focused on reaching the orange tree, she had completely overlooked them when she first walked through the orchard.

"Back off, robot! I'm telling you—one of them is for a friend." Chelsea tuned in suddenly to Tray Wong's voice yelling at the robot blocking his path.

"Mr. Wong, may I reiterate the garden rules to you? Each resident is allotted, *at most,* two servings of fruits or vegetables per day. You have three servings in your hands currently. I must ask you again, please surrender one serving. Do you comply?"

"I'm so sick of dumb robots bossing me around! You can't even understand that I'm getting *this* fruit for a friend," he said, holding up an apple in his left hand. "*These* two are for me," he said, holding up a grapefruit and a pear in the other hand. "The apple doesn't count as my serving. How do I get this to cooom-cooom-pute in those short circuits of yours?" he said as he did an impression of a malfunctioning robot.

Chelsea noticed bold white letters on his shirt that read **SOCIETY RULES** as he turned in her direction. She recognized the unique font and the phrase from the plaque that hung in the welcome area of the ground floor of Tower One. She also recalled that Tray was the same Mr. Wong with dark spiky hair who was in her group when she first toured The Society grounds. The apprehension he had felt then for the way The Society operated had obviously festered into a robust aversion since she last saw him.

"You cannot confirm your claim, sir. Do you comply or not?" the robot persisted.

"Oh my—NO! I *don't* comply! I'm sick of this! I am done complying with a hunk of metal that can't understand anything that's not programmed into its system! This tiny, broken-down island isn't worth having to deal with this anymore. I'm done. I'm out," he said, throwing the fruit to the ground.

"Very well. I will escort you to The Society authorities, and they will terminate your residency if you wish."

"Fine with me. Best to get out of this place before it breaks down completely anyway," Tray muttered, mostly to himself, as he walked past the robot toward the towers. When he walked away, Chelsea read the words **YOUR LIFE** on the back of his shirt. She was confused at first until she pieced together that the shirt was meant to be read as two pieces to a whole. **SOCIETY RULES**

. Tray had made the shirt in one of the shopping kiosks the day before—hoping to catch people's attention and get them thinking.

As Tray disappeared into The Society buildings with the bot, Chelsea sat back and contemplated the words on his shirt and what Tray had said about The Society breaking down. The broken bot at her feet seemed a testament to his words, but as for the words on his shirt, she was less sure where she stood. *Does The Society rule my life?* To the contrary, her days seemed very free and open to her desires. But she was well aware that any of the plans she made or the ideas she came up with could be prohibited at any time with a simple command from a nearby robot. After further thought, she concluded that living at The Societies meant living subject to the two extremes of liberation and subjugation concurrently.

At that same moment, Davin sat in his living quarters on the opposite side of The Society grounds mindlessly twirling his wristband between his fingers. He knew allowing his mind to wander was an uncertain and possibly treacherous risk, but the long, uneventful day, filled with his usual meaningless encounters, left him weary and apathetic. Had he known Chelsea sat quietly in the orchard by herself, he would have eagerly jumped on the chance to speak with her again.

On days that he didn't have a show to perform or a promotion to shoot, he was directed to peruse The Society and internally promote The Society to the residents indirectly in lieu of the required two-hour task. He had just finished a long interaction with a large group in the pool area, reiterating the rote dialogue he had been instructed to use that he had now committed to memory.

Though he sometimes enjoyed an engaging conversation as he learned about the lives of interesting people at The Society, he often found himself stuck in an infomercial about The Society or in shallow conversation about his movies or looks. He had grown tired of people wanting to talk about his films—it was another time, another life. To speak of them when things could never be as they were back then was a sore reminder of things he wished he had not seen and people he would never speak to again. As these memories ran through his mind, his breathing became shallow, and his thoughts morphed into a fog of destructive flashbacks.

A long minute passed where Davin was stuck in the pit of his own mind. Anxiety was overtaking his body. Another minute longer and his wristband would have notified the health center and made an emergency call to his therapist. But before it did, his wristband lit up, indicating he had a phone call coming in. The flashing light and ringing in his ear snapped him out of his flashback of the news reports and panoramas of the earthquake's destruction and back into the present.

"Uh, yes? Hello?" Davin said, trying to breathe through his shallow breaths and get his heart rate back down to a normal level.

"Davin, I have some potentially great news," Lola, his self-appointed agent, said into his ear through the phone. "Go to the dome in ten minutes and meet me in your dressing room."

Davin nodded, still half dazed. "Right. Okay. I'll be there in ten." He hung up with Lola and went to the bathroom to splash his face with some cold water before he left for the dome. In the mirror, he saw a pale face reflected back at him. Beads of sweat streamed down his forehead. The cool water he splashed on his face helped shock his senses back to reality. He dried his face and left for the dome, very grateful to have something to occupy his mind.

Lola sat in Davin's chair examining the latest addition to her tattoo-covered face. She had added some purple highlights to her eyeshadow to match her purple lips and redefined her cheekbones to appear higher. As Davin entered his dressing room, she wondered if he would notice. "Davin, wonderful news," she said as she got up and walked toward him. With the usual unprovoked kiss to his cheek, she said, "I think you'll be really happy to hear—there's a retired director who wants to revive the movie industry, and she plans to use *you* as the star for her first film. I told her that I assumed you would be interested in something like that. Am I right?"

Davin felt instantly rejuvenated and was excited to hear this news. He desperately needed something to do to fill his days and keep his mind occupied. "Yes, I'd love to! That's awesome! When do we start?" he asked, anxious to begin.

"The actual filming won't start for quite some time, Davin. This is just a preliminary assurance that you're interested in something like this. They still need to finish writing the script and get funding. It may be quite a while before they're actually able to begin filming. I need to work something out with your contract here at The Society as well. They will need to approve it, especially if you have to travel off the island to film it." Lola clarified the few details she knew.

Disappointed he could not begin working on the film immediately, Davin tried to remain grateful for the prospect of a new opportunity. "Okay, well, let her know I'm in," he said with a smile.

Lola smiled back, happy to see she had been correct in assuming he would want to participate. "Good. I actually want us to call her together right now. You can let her know yourself."

"Alright. Let's make the call then," he said as Lola flicked her wrist to activate her wristband and call the director. She placed the call on speakerphone and aimed her wristband at their faces so they could both be seen.

"You like my new eye color, Davin? I just added it yesterday," Lola quickly asked as they waited for the call to be answered.

Davin glanced over and quickly examined the color. "Um . . . Yeah—very beautiful. Matches your lips."

Lola was delighted he noticed.

A woman with short curly hair appeared on the screen that was being projected on Lola's forearm. "This is Genevieve Thrope," she said in a raspy voice.

"Genevieve, it's Lola. I just spoke with Davin, and he said he would love to star in your film! He can't wait to begin," Lola reiterated enthusiastically.

"Yes, Genevieve—wonderful to meet you. I can't tell you how happy I was to hear about your proposition," Davin chimed in.

"Glad to hear it, Davin. There've been a few who wondered if you would be up to it, but Lola was certain you would be and that she'd be able to work something out with The Society to make it possible." Addressing Lola now, Genevieve got right to business. "Speaking of which—Lola, I've instructed the screenwriter to set the film in a tropical climate, and I'll have a massive, portable set built that I will bring with me for the indoor and city scenes. That way you won't have to concern yourself with working out a travel clause for Davin's contract."

Lola's face lit up with relief. "That's brilliant. It'll be much easier to convince The Society to allow him to do it if that's the case."

"I hoped so. However, the funding has been harder to collect than I anticipated. It may take longer than I expected. Maybe give me a few months, and I'll follow up with you then," Genevieve said.

"Is the script complete then? Could you send it to me?" Davin asked. In the past, he had been very choosy about what roles he'd agree to play.

"Almost. I think my writer's experiencing some writer's block. He hasn't told me that directly, but he's far less elusive than he believes he is," the old woman said with a smile on her face and the wisdom of her age in her eyes. "It's based on a book by Rogue Blanchet. Feel free to read that if you have the time. I sent you a link with a copy of it. Otherwise, I'll send the script your way as soon as I have it, and you can give me your final answer then. Are you okay with that, Davin?"

"Yes, that's fine. Consider me a tentative yes then," he said.

"I really hope I'm able to pull this off. After losing my sweet husband, Ace, I need something to keep me going, and I'd be very excited to work with you, Davin. Your success and talent are admirable, and I believe there is more to you than the world knows at present. I would push you hard though," she said as she stared directly at him with a stern expression. After a split second that felt like it lasted forever, her gaze softened. "You'll be wonderful. I have no doubt," she said and gave a gentle smile. "Everyone was relieved to hear you were safe during the earthquake—really, that anyone was safe. It was a dreadful tragedy," she remarked. "The world will never be the same, but maybe we can create some hope by bringing a familiar face back to the screen and reviving the American film industry once and for all."

"I would like nothing more," Davin said, hopeful the script would be one of interest and the film would actually happen. "I look forward to reading the book, and I'm excited to see what you're able to come up with. If those things deliver, consider me in."

"Good." Genevieve smiled. "I must be going. Having Davin as a possible lead does make for a good selling point to communicate to potential executive producers."

"Let me know when you have the final word, and I'll begin negotiations with The Society right away," Lola said.

"I will. Have a good day, you two," Genevieve said pleasantly as she waved goodbye and ended the call.

Davin was so happy to have a project to hopefully look forward to, even if it meant waiting a while for it to come to fruition. He pumped his fist in a momentary victory stance before hugging Lola. "I'm so glad you said I would be up for it. You're the best."

Lola gave him a huge grin and melted into his arms. He rarely hugged her, but she cherished every second when he did.

"Come on—I'm going to tell Roy and get the gang together to go celebrate tonight!" Davin said enthusiastically, letting her go and running out of his dressing room. Lola stood motionless for a moment with empty arms, still relishing their short embrace.

10. A LOST FRIEND

"**H**EY, DAVIN—me, Chloe, Kona, Lola, and Roy are going out on the boat today after lunch. You in?" Eli's voice asked on his earpiece the next morning.

"Uh, sure. I can do that," Davin responded sleepily as he stretched out on his bed.

"You can't honestly still be in bed," Eli taunted him.

"Are you kidding me?" Davin said, pretending to be irritated. "Yes, I'm still in bed. I have to stop letting you talk me into staying up all night with you guys."

"Hey, you said we were celebrating!" Eli protested before quickly changing his tone. "Nah, I'm only messing with you. We're still in bed too." He laughed as he gave Chloe a playful smile and twisted a strand of her hair around his finger. "We'll meet you at the docks at one o'clock sharp." There was a small bit of silence. Then Davin heard some shuffling over the phone. "Now, that means we still have an hour and a half for me to figure out what I should do with you, Chloe bear."

"Oh geez, please spare me. You forgot to hang up again."

"Oops, can't have you hearing my lines or you might steal Chloe out from under me," Eli joked.

Davin gave a forced chuckle. "I promise I won't. See you later," he said as he hung up.

Every four months or so, Eli had a new girlfriend, and Chloe was his latest. Davin respected that Eli dated only one woman at a time, though Eli joked that it was only because he couldn't possibly keep track of more than one. But Eli didn't need to concern himself with Davin stealing Chloe away—she wasn't his type. Though she was beautiful, with caramel skin and a body that most men lust after, Davin couldn't stand being around her. She was so agreeable in every conversation that he wasn't sure if she'd ever had an independent thought in her life. He assumed she just wanted to be liked, but he couldn't understand how she could be so . . . *blank?* He wasn't sure how else to describe her. He equated her to a robot—all the hardware was there, but she lacked depth.

Davin wasn't surprised to hear Eli had already invited Kona and Lola to the boat outing as well. They usually spent most of their time wherever Davin was anyway, and Eli prided himself on being surrounded by as many beautiful women and public figures as possible. He was always trying to bring a group together for some activity he had cooked up. Eli was a fun and energetic kind of guy in that way. He had a large build and short dark hair that contrasted starkly with his bright red beard. Davin wouldn't consider Eli his best friend, but he was fun to be around and generally easy to please.

However, Kona was never easy to please. Though things between Davin and Kona were better at this point, most of their initial appearances had been mandatory interactions where Davin had to carefully orchestrate his next action to mend the awkward tension between them. Their partnership was thrown off-kilter from the beginning after Kona fervidly threw herself at Davin during their first few moments together. Kona was surprised by his reluctance and highly offended by his rejection, though he tried to decline her advances as politely as possible. It took some time for their off-stage relationship to relax into the more casual companionship it had become. Oddly enough, most of the world was under the impression they were deeply in love. Davin always chuckled at that thought, knowing that she secretly resented him for his indifference to her. But in reality, Kona and Davin were simply *expected* to attend events and parties side by side, since together they were the public face of the Hawaii Society.

Lola was Davin and Kona's self-appointed talent agent. She made sure they attended important events and briefed them on any messages The Society needed them to communicate at these events. If Lola wasn't drilling Davin with questions on his upcoming appearances, she was with Kona. They had quickly become very close friends as soon as they met—possibly because they both shared an unreciprocated interest in Davin. Though she would never openly admit it to Davin, she was quite in love with him—a fact he was oblivious to.

Roy was Davin's best friend at The Society. They had been acquaintances when they were very young in Oklahoma. Roy's parents came to America from New Zealand to start a large automated cattle ranch. They settled in the town just over from where Davin's family lived. During their childhood, they would bump into each other at public events or the state fair every so often and spend the whole day playing. But after Roy's parents died in a freak accident, their ranch slowly failed until it was forced to close, and Roy had to move in with a distant great aunt.

Roy and Davin didn't get to know each other that well before Roy had to move away, but they coincidentally ended up in the Hawaii Society together and hit it off immediately when they recognized each other from their childhood days. Roy was exactly the kind of friend Davin needed in his life. He was laid-back and playful and kindhearted. He had dealt with the loss of his parents by embracing optimism as his core strength. His cheerful disposition always helped lighten Davin's mood when his anxiety got the better of him. He always appreciated that he could easily talk to Roy about any topic and leave the conversation feeling better.

IT WAS A CALM DAY at sea. After Eli had his fill of racing the boat across the water, he turned off the motor so the boat could float atop the waves. He immediately grabbed Chloe, threw her in the water, and jumped in after her. A pair of dolphins was swimming nearby, and Eli wanted to watch from the water as the dolphins dove deep and then surfaced.

Roy took off his shirt and went to jump in the water to join them before stopping to look at Davin. He could tell Davin was either zoning out or deep in thought, and he always worried when Davin got like that for fear that he would have another anxiety attack. "You comin' in, mate?"

"Nah, I'm just going to take it easy for now. You go ahead."

"I can stay with ya if you'd like." Davin could tell Roy was worried about him again.

"No. Really. I'm fine," he assured him. "Go check out those dolphins."

"'Righty. Well, come join us if you need to get your mind off things," Roy said, trying to remind Davin of his therapist's suggestion to avoid too much downtime. "Kia kaha," Roy called out to Davin with a smile as he jumped in the water. The phrase was one often used by New Zealanders. It meant 'stay strong.' It was an expression Roy's great aunt shared with him as a boy to help him deal with the loss of his parents, and now Roy used it to help encourage Davin whenever he got down.

Davin appreciated Roy's concern, but today he had things to think about to keep his mind from slipping. He had things to be excited about. He put on his sunglasses, lay back on one of the benches of the boat, and soaked in the sunshine as he thought.

He wondered what kind of role he would play in Genevieve's movie and what she could have meant by wanting to push him. *She must have a very difficult character for me to play. I'll start reading the book tomorrow to find out,* he thought to himself.

Lola and Kona had curled up next to each other in one of the corners of the boat and had been discussing whether or not they liked Lola's new pineapple tattoo that she got in addition to her new makeup. " . . . Ultimately, I chose the color scheme to match my sunglasses, and I kind of love that they go together. Besides, I just feel like a pineapple is the perfect symbol for Hawaii, you know?" Lola said, looking at the freshly inked tattoo on her lower right abdomen.

Just then there was a loud pop from the shore that made everyone within fifty yards jump. They looked over to see a pair of men smiling and waving apologetically. One of them had popped a beach ball trying to do a backflip while balancing on it.

"That scared me so bad. I seriously almost peed," Kona confessed to Lola with a guilty smile as she observed the two culprits on shore. To the right of the two men, Kona spotted Chelsea among some friends building a sandcastle. "Hey, isn't that the girl you were gawking at during the Grand Welcome, Davin?" Davin instantly lifted his head and raised his sunglasses to see if it was Chelsea. "You should have seen him, Lola—completely distracted right as we were about to go on stage. She caught him checking her out too," she teased Davin. "The thing is, she really isn't even much to look at," Kona said somewhat softly to Lola but still loud enough for Davin to hear.

Davin spotted Chelsea as she dug a trench to protect the perimeter of the sandcastle. "Could be," he replied to Kona's earlier inquiry, though he knew perfectly well it was Chelsea. He lay his head back down and put his sunglasses on and watched as Chelsea continued to help build the sandcastle with her friends. A small smile grew on his face as he watched her purposefully fling sand at a nearby friend as she dug.

"Which one is she?" Lola asked Kona. Kona pointed her out, and Lola examined her with a smug expression.

"Honestly, Davin, you could do way better. She's not exactly a knockout," Lola commented.

"Maybe not to you," Davin replied. "Doesn't matter much anyway. I'm fairly certain she couldn't care less about me," he said as he sat up and reached for a nearby bottle of water.

Just then Eli began splashing water all over Kona and Lola from the side of the boat. They both protested and headed to the opposite side of the boat near Davin. Eli, Chloe, and Roy pulled themselves up into the boat and sat down to rest.

Roy noticed an awkward lull in the conversation between the girls and Davin as he boarded the boat and was curious about what they could have been discussing. "What have you three been talking about? You really missed out—the dolphins were extra friendly today."

"Oh, just Davin's love life," Lola said as she leaned into Davin.

"What they mean is my *lack* of a love life," Davin clarified while moving away from Lola and lying down on a different bench.

"Well, that's a bloody relief. For a second there, I thought you might have been leaving me out of the loop, Davin," Roy commented. He was sure Davin wouldn't be in a relationship without filling him in on it. "We all know Davin doesn't have time for girls anyway. This is Davin Chapman we're talking about—the bro who's nonstop work, sleep, and parties."

"I'm out here hanging with you, aren't I?" Davin protested.

"Which definitely fits in the partying category," Eli chimed in. "Mostly 'cause I'm here," he said with a wide grin as he took the last sip from his bottle of water and threw it overboard.

"More like the sleeping category—not sure it really counts as party time when he just sits there with his shades on, nodding off," Kona said, somewhat irritated at Davin's lack of involvement.

"Geez, Kona. Don't rock the boat. You're going to make Davin want to leave," Eli said, maliciously smiling before using his weight to force the boat to rock violently back and forth.

"Stop, stop, stop!" all the girls protested at once.

As Eli stopped the rocking, Roy's wristband lit up, and a buzzer went off in his ear to notify him it was time to leave. "It's about that time, mates—got to go. I'm off for some ocean escapading today with my bro. We found a cave the other day, and I've been dying to explore it. Anyone in?" Roy asked the group.

"I'm going to pass. Maybe next time," Davin said. "I'm wiped out from staying up with you buffoons all night," he said jokingly. "I think I'm going to head back to my room in a little for a nap. If it's amazing, let me know, and we'll check it out some other time," he called out as Roy dove into the water with his mask and flippers.

Roy popped out of the water. "'Course it's going to be bloody keen. Would I be going if it wasn't?" Roy challenged after hearing Davin's excuses. Davin shrugged and nodded in acknowledgment of Roy's broad list of adventurous activities, but his mind remained unchanged. Exploring a cave didn't sound at all appealing to him. Roy rolled his eyes and sighed. "No worries, mate. It's all good. But don't say I didn't give you a fair shake. Anyone else?" he inquired.

The rest of the group declined as well, so Roy shrugged and put on his flippers and mask to begin escapading. Escapading was a water sport that was a cross between scuba diving and snorkeling. Escapading masks were made of a thick cloth-like material that covered the entire head except for a translucent front to see through. They were capable of extracting enough oxygen from the water around them for a large male to breathe freely through the mouthpiece inside. This made large, bulky oxygen tanks unnecessary and removed the time limitations associated with a limited oxygen supply. Wearers could either float near the surface to look down on the ocean floor with its world of sea creatures or they could dive down deep to swim among them. An application could be downloaded to the wearers' wristbands to instruct when they needed to allow their body to acclimate to water pressure and warn divers of dangerous conditions and currents.

For about the next hour, everyone but Davin sat on the boat and talked. Though Davin appeared to be sleeping, he was actually watching to see if Chelsea would separate from her friends in order to give him a chance to talk with her alone. Just before a full hour had passed, she finally broke away and started walking toward the towers. Davin bolted up abruptly, making Lola jump in surprise. He headed for the edge of the boat.

"Where are you suddenly off to?" asked Kona.

"The beach," he said as he dove into the water. He knew he had to get there fast if he was going to catch Chelsea before she was out of sight. Just as he was reaching the shallows, he received a phone call in his ear from Branch Willix, the society coordinator. He knew he had to answer, but it meant he would probably lose Chelsea. "Hello?"

"Davin, hi, we need you and Kona and Lola to come in for an emergency meeting this evening with Ms. Waverly and me. Normally, we just communicate our needs to Lola, but this subject needs particular care, and we want to make sure you're fully aware of your role. Will you comply? You can count it as your two hours today," Branch finished.

"Uh, sure, what time?" he asked, trying to keep an eye on Chelsea as he dodged people wading in the shallows around him.

"Six o'clock sharp in the government offices."

"I'll see you then," Davin said as he hung up. He still had a chance to catch up with Chelsea if he hurried. As he started walking on the beach in her direction, he suddenly heard Roy's voice yelling out behind him.

"Davin, Davin, hold up! Davin!" Davin turned around to see where Roy was, then spotted him running right toward him, escapading gear in hand. "We got to talk, eh!" Trying hard to catch up with Davin, Roy bumped into a swimmer who swam into his path. "Buggar! Sorry!" he exclaimed while trying to reclaim his footing. "Slow down, cuz!" he called out to Davin.

Davin looked one more time in Chelsea's direction, but she turned a corner and was out of sight. "What is it?" he asked, irritated he lost his window of opportunity.

"Th-the cave," Roy panted, out of breath. "We went to it. I couldn't fit through the entrance we found, but I saw some really suss stuff." He paused and looked at Davin with a forbidding expression. "And it wasn't really a cave. I mean, it was," he backtracked, "but . . . " He stopped and looked around nervously at all the people surrounding them. Then he grabbed Davin's shoulder to guide him to a less crowded area of the beach.

When he found a spot where no one would be in earshot, Roy turned toward Davin and started to take off his wristband and remove his earpiece—motioning for Davin to do the same. Trusting Roy, Davin reluctantly followed suit, even though he knew it was technically against the rules to do so. Roy's hands were shaky as he grabbed Davin's things and immersed them in the ocean water they stood in. He didn't want anything he was about to say to be understood in their recordings.

His voice quivered as he spoke. "I'm still not exactly sure what it was supposed to be, but I've never heard of something like this on The Society grounds. There were a bunch of underwater garden pods and heaps of boxes and this empty glass room with this Asian-looking guy. At least, I think he was Asian. It was hard to tell. And some other guy in it—just sitting there, all curled up." Davin gave Roy a perplexed look. "I swear I'm being straight with you.

I couldn't make things out all that well, but I think I saw another entrance that should be big enough to fit through if we can find it. My diving mate took one look and bailed on me. So I was wondering if you would come out there with me for a squizz?"

"Right now?" Davin asked as he tried to decide what exactly Roy was insinuating. Roy was not acting at all like himself. "I can't. I have to get ready for a meeting tonight. I still have to get dinner and stuff too. Can we go out tomorrow?"

"You have a meeting tonight?" Roy asked. "You bailing on the hike? I was gonna talk to you more about this up on the mountain where there are fewer people."

Davin forgot he had planned to go on a hike with Roy and Eli that evening. "Oh man, I'm sorry. I can't anymore. I have an official Society meeting tonight. I had to comply and everything. You and Eli can still go though."

"A'right," he said, disappointed. "But can you go check it out with me tomorrow? I don't think I should go it alone. In case, I don't know . . . something happens," Roy said with a concerned look in his eyes.

"Yeah, sure. Tomorrow we'll go together," Davin assured him.

"Thanks, bro. See you tomorrow, six o'clock, at the escapading gear station," Roy said as he ran toward the tower to return his gear and then examine the map of the grounds one more time to see if he had missed the cave when he had looked at it other times.

"Six in the *morning*?" Davin asked under his breath as Roy disappeared. Unfortunately for Davin, Roy was definitely a morning person.

Davin went back to his living quarters and showered and put on some presentable clothes. After he ate dinner, he headed up to the government offices for the meeting. As he walked, he ran into Lola and Kona who were also on their way to the meeting.

"Good evening, ladies," Davin greeted them.

"Davin," Lola said, politely acknowledging him.

"Davin, take my hand," Kona insisted as she extended her arm toward him. "You know how they like it when we present ourselves as a team."

Davin took Kona's hand as instructed and opened the door to the conference room of the government offices where they were supposed to meet. Sandra Waverly and Branch Willix sat at a large white oval-shaped table, waiting for their arrival.

"We need to have a Society-wide mandatory meeting at the end of the month," Ms. Waverly began.

Having worked with Ms. Waverly often, Lola wasn't fazed by her lack of greeting and immediately responded. "Of course. We'll do all we can to make that possible and successful. What will this meeting be about, and what are the objectives Lola and Davin need to communicate?"

"We'll be holding the meeting to encourage those on the island who have specific specialties to use their abilities to better The Society. We also want to encourage more people to take courses to master a specialty of their own if they don't already have one," Ms. Waverly stated.

"After a few months of close observation, I've found we have a number of people with some hidden talents—people who should be using those talents but have instead decided to waste their task work doing only the simplest of tasks or filling their time with coursework and never using what they've learned. It's causing a number of" —Branch paused to contemplate the word he wanted to use to describe the predicament— "complications around The Society that need to be addressed."

The rest of their meeting consisted of the specifics they needed to communicate and the verbiage that would be expected of them to use during the meeting. At the end, Ms. Waverly stood to leave. "You'll receive your copies of the script soon. My portion of the event will have the logistics, but remember, I expect you to sell it.

I will reel the residents back into their place, but you must convince them to be happy about it. Understood?"

Lola assured her they did and encouraged Davin and Kona to nod in agreement.

"I'll escort you out," Branch said as he directed them to the door. They walked down the government hall where there was a large map hanging on the wall that detailed the inner workings of The Society. The girls continued down the hall toward the elevator, but Davin stopped to inspect the map.

"Is there a problem, Davin?" Branch asked.

"I'm just looking for a specific room my friend was telling me about. He said it was a cave-like room that would be underneath The Society. Do you know what that might be? Is it on the map?" Davin inquired.

Branch looked perplexed at first, but then his expression changed, and he quickly called out to the ladies as they approached the elevator. "You ladies go ahead and head back to your rooms. Lola knows the way. Davin will be down shortly." Lola and Kona waved goodnight and pressed the button for the ground floor. Once the elevator doors closed with the girls inside, Branch slowly turned back to look at the map and at Davin. "A cave, you say? No, you won't find any cave on this map. There are no caves on The Society grounds. Who told you about a cave?" Branch asked.

"My friend, Roy. He said he found the cave today, and it seems odd it wouldn't be on the map because he made it sound like it was constructed rather than natural. I was hoping if it wasn't on the map you might know about it."

"Sorry, Davin. Can't say I do. Who is this friend, Roy?" Branch asked. "Where is he now? Maybe he can tell me where exactly he saw it, and we can look into it. Did he tell anyone else anything about it?"

"No, he just wants me to check it out with him tomorrow. And he probably won't be able to see you today—he's hiking on the mountain this evening, and we plan on starting early tomorrow," Davin answered.

"Ah, gotcha. Another time then. Well, I have to go now. Have a good night, Davin. The elevator is just down the hall."

With that, Branch turned and headed quickly for the door that Ms. Waverly had entered just a moment earlier. After confirming there was no cave on the map, Davin turned, boarded the elevator, and went back to his room for the night.

Branch slammed open the door to Ms. Waverly's office. He rushed over to the cabinet and hurriedly unlocked the safe inside. "What do you think you're doing, Branch?" Ms. Waverly asked.

He looked back at her with a crazed look in his eyes. "Someone found the cave today. I don't know how, but he's on the mountain as we speak. I'm gonna take him out with a bolt of lightning before he tells anyone else."

"Who else knows?" asked Ms. Waverly.

"Just Davin, but I told him we don't know about a cave. And unfortunately, pretty boy can't so easily be gotten rid of—we need him around. Anyway, *he* doesn't know the location of the cave yet," Branch answered as he pulled out his PED and connected it to the prototype of the government-issued weather controller.

After a slew of horrific storms hit the world in the late forties, the United States invested billions of dollars to develop new technologies to control and, most importantly, suppress severe weather conditions. Almost twenty years later, it was finally paying off. The prototypes were in their final stages of testing in the States. With the help of specially placed satellites and the technology found at the moon's Astronomy and Meteorology Science Center, the controller could influence the earth's atmosphere by adjusting the pressure and temperature. The technology had already successfully stopped a severe hurricane from wiping out the coast of Florida just three years prior. Now, one of the few top-secret prototypes available had been issued to the Hawaii Society. It was to be used as a last resort to protect the large investment the government had placed in the Hawaii Society should a hurricane threaten its grounds.

"Very well," Ms. Waverly agreed. "I just spoke with the vice president yesterday, and she said people are growing tired of hearing about The Societies eating up tax dollars. To cut down the costs we're incurring, they will no longer advertise after this year. So we may not need Davin's services much longer."

"Good. Maybe I should take him out too while I'm at it," Branch said with a smirk as he searched for Roy from the names in the resident directory.

"Let's not go there unless we absolutely have to. People would eventually start asking questions. Everyone has a soft spot for Davin," Ms. Waverly cautioned.

"Aha! Got him!" Branch exclaimed. "I found this Roy character— only one at The Society! Once I reverse the weather controller algorithm, we'll work up some lightning and shoot it right toward him. Everyone will assume it was an accident, and our problem will be eradicated just like that."

"Fine, fine, just hurry before he decides to tell anyone else. But make sure no one else gets hurt. I don't want a bunch of needless deaths on my hands," Ms. Waverly urged.

"I'll try, but from what I've been told, this weather controller isn't always an exact science." Branch typed furiously as he quickly reprogrammed the weather satellite to generate rather than dissipate. Though Branch did not often apply himself fully, he was extremely intelligent and well-versed in all technical engineering. Using Roy's wristband, he tracked Roy's movement as he programmed the accident. "First, let's introduce a little rain to make it realistic."

Not even seconds after he hit enter, clouds began to form in the clear blue sky outside the large window in Sandra Waverly's office, and rain began to fall. The rain quickly turned into a downpour.

Sudden bouts of rain were not uncommon in the region, but the blankets of rain that poured down at that moment were more severe than normal.

"Now, let's light him up," Branch sneered as he watched Roy and Eli race down the mountain to escape the pouring rain. Then he hit enter once more.

❖

BOOM! DAVIN QUICKLY looked toward the window of his living quarters after hearing the loud noise from outside and witnessing the sudden powerful lightning bolt that struck the side of the mountain out of the corner of his eye. His heart skipped in a panic. *Roy is still out there!* He raced out of his room to locate his friend and make sure he was safe. He tried reaching him by phone, but Roy wasn't picking up and Roy's wristband locator wasn't working for some reason. The elevator seemed to move at a painstakingly slow pace. When it finally reached the ground floor, Davin ran out onto the pathway that led to the bridge. He ran into a crowd of people heading indoors to take shelter from the sudden onset of the heavy rainfall.

Once he was out from under the shelter of the dome's cover, the wind and rain beat down hard on him in the open air. He ran across the bridge and past the waterfall toward the foot of the mountain. Just as he reached the mountain path, two medical bots, carrying a scraped and bleeding Eli on a stretcher, came into view.

"Eli! Eli!" Davin shouted into the treacherous winds.

"Davin?" Eli said as he struggled to sit up and see through the thick sheets of rain coming down. "Davin! He's gone!" Eli yelled out as the bot carried him down the mountain. "Roy! Roy is gone!"

The large white medical bots slowed as they approached Davin. "Please go inside," one said with its eyes firmly fixed on him. Medical bots were among the most human-like bots with full human figures and more emotion ingrained in their expressions.

A glowing red cross symbol shone on each of the robots' chests and a bright headlamp shined bright in Davin's eyes. "The weather conditions are not suitable to be outside at this time."

"What do you mean he's gone?" Davin asked Eli, ignoring the robot's command.

"He's dead! I watched him get struck by lightning and fly off the side of the mountain! It sent me flying too, but I hit a tree. I couldn't even see him after he fell. I looked around as best as I could, but then the bots came and got me. I'm sorry, man. I'm so sorry."

"This man is in distress and in need of immediate medical attention. We need to take him to the hospital facilities. Return indoors immediately. Will you comply?" one of the robots insisted.

Davin reluctantly replied, "Yes." It was almost a sob. He looked up at the mountain and struggled to accept the fact that Roy could be gone. His last true friend—taken from him by tragedy just like the others. He wanted to bound up the mountain and find Roy himself, but he knew he couldn't disobey a direct order to comply, and it would be too dangerous to stay outside in the storm. The medical bots started running toward The Society grounds, and Davin followed close behind.

"I'll stay with you," Davin told Eli solemnly when they reached the elevator to go to the hospital.

Eli sighed. "Thanks, man." He could barely manage a shallow breath of air because of the excruciating pain in his chest.

I can at least make sure Eli will be all right, Davin thought, telling himself to remain calm and ignore the urge to go back into the rain to search for Roy.

After Eli was placed in the body scanner to evaluate his injuries, Davin went to the window of the hospital wing. He watched as the wind and the rain grew stronger and stronger outside. He wept as he imagined his friend's body— struck by the only sign of lightning he had ever witnessed on the island, limp in a puddle of rain on a ledge of the mountain.

11. HURRICANE

THE MEDICAL SCAN SHOWED Eli broke a few ribs and had three deep cuts. The cuts were easily cleaned and mended by a device in the medical bot's finger that shot out a kind of glue that brought the skin together under a UV light, but even after taking the accelerated bone healing serum, his broken ribs would take some time to mend. Once the medical bots were finished attending to his immediate needs, Eli was given a medication inhaler, and they released him. Davin offered to walk him to his room. Grateful for the offer, he accepted, and Davin put Eli's arm around his shoulder for support.

"I was glad to hear it was just the ribs," said Davin as they walked slowly.

"Yeah, me too. But it still kills," Eli said, wincing in pain with each step. "I think the first dose of pain medication is starting to wear off. Every breath I take feels like the bones are breaking again."

"You go ahead and just save your air then. We'll lay you down in your room, and I'll give you the rest of your pain medication to take off the edge and help you sleep."

When they reached Eli's room, Davin tried to lay Eli's massive figure down on the bed without disrupting his chest cavity. Eli still let out a groan of misery but felt a little better once he settled atop the comfortable mattress.

"Breathe deeply," Davin instructed as he placed an inhaler over Eli's mouth that emitted a mist to deliver sleep aid and pain reliever directly into the bloodstream. The pain on Eli's face melted away with each breath he took in. "I called Chloe. She'll be here soon."

"Thanks, Davin." Eli looked over. Davin had never seen him so serious and sincere before—his normally jovial face was now solemn from his suffering. "Thanks for staying with me in the hospital wing. I'm sorry about . . . " Eli paused, and a troubled look appeared on his face. "I swear I tried . . . " His body began to quiver as he held back tears.

"It's okay," Davin said, resting his hand on Eli's arm to calm him. "I know. Just get some rest for now. I'm just glad you're going to be all right."

Just then there was a knock on the door. It opened to a worried Chloe. "Eli, you okay, hun?" she said, running over to his side.

"I'll be okay, Chloe bear. Just some broken ribs and cuts," Eli assured her.

"Oh, good," Chloe said and sighed as she sat down on the bed beside him. "And Roy . . . I just can't believe Roy is gone. What are the odds of being struck—"

Davin gave her a look. "Not now, Chloe. Let him rest," he said while grabbing Chloe's arm and steering her away from Eli. He turned his body away from his friend and whispered to Chloe, "As soon as the storm passes, I'm going to search for Roy. In the meantime, don't bring up anything about Roy to him." Turning back to Eli, he said, "I'm heading back to my room now. You rest easy, okay, buddy?"

"I won't move an inch," Eli said with a sleepy smile.

"I'd better head back to my room as well," Chloe said, making Eli's smile fade to a frown. "Rest well, gumdrop."

Davin could tell that Eli was unhappy Chloe wasn't planning on staying, but Eli couldn't manage an objection as his eyelids began to droop shut from exhaustion. Davin was irritated Chloe wasn't going to stay with him. His opinion of her wasn't the greatest already, and it sank lower as she walked out the door.

"I'll check on you first thing in the morning," Davin said to Eli before he left.

Davin returned to his room just past one in the morning. He lay down on his bed and watched the storm out of the window. The winds raged outside as he wrestled with his own feelings—wondering how he could cope with losing another close friend. He wanted to let his tears stream out until there were none left, but he knew from past experience that his tears would do his friend no good.

He considered putting on a coat and walking into the storm—succumbing to the small hope he still harbored that Roy had somehow survived the lightning strike and the fall—but he knew it would only lead to disappointment or injury. Instead, he focused his energy on trying to block out the hurt and ignore the pain while he waited for the storm to subside. To his surprise, sustaining his apathy proved to be as equally emotionally draining as crying. Soon enough, his exhaustion from the long day and staying up all night the night before overtook him, and his eyes closed shut.

"WHY ISN'T IT DYING DOWN?" Ms. Waverly asked Branch frantically. "It just keeps getting worse. Program it to stop already!"

"I've been trying," Branch spouted through gritted teeth. "Anything I do just seems to stoke the fire. I'm afraid to do anything else. Should we contact the White House? Maybe we can get the people who made this to make it work right."

"Are you kidding me? They'd know we used it. They'd see that you reprogrammed it to *make* the storm! No. No, we're not going to tell anyone about this." He could almost see Ms. Waverly's mind spinning as she formed her plan. "We are going to hunker down and let it pass. Then we'll work to get things back to normal." Ms. Waverly looked out her window into the storm. "Until then, we need to cut communications to the mainland and keep people quiet. Eventually, we'll tell Washington that we experienced some adverse weather conditions, but we're fine, because, at that point, we will be. Then we'll downplay anything that the residents say about the storm. Understood?"

"Okay," Branch agreed, putting the weather controller back into the safe and closing it tightly. "So what do *we* do?"

"Grab some scissors. We'll need to cut the communication line and internet cables first. Then, we'll sound the alarm and head for the dome to wait out the storm with everyone else," Ms. Waverly instructed.

DAVIN'S EYES SHOT OPEN to the sound of harsh sirens ringing throughout The Society halls. He jumped out of bed and opened his door to a whirl of confusion and chaos. The wind from the storm could be heard whipping through the halls of the living quarters. Everyone was headed for the elevator. Davin assumed they would head for the outer circle of the dome since it was the only structure in The Society buildings that did not have any windows. He was hurrying to the elevators when he realized Eli would probably still be stuck in his room!

Davin raced into the crowd of people herding toward the elevator, pushing and shoving anyone in his path. He was heading straight into a section of the living quarters that was ripping with wind. As he got closer to Eli's room, the wind grew fiercer. He rounded the hall and spotted the source of the incredible wind tugging at him. A door to one of the rooms was open. Inside, a window had been smashed open by a fallen tree. Davin ran past it, holding onto door handles to anchor himself against the suction.

Once he safely reached Eli's room, he swung open the door—holding onto the hope that Eli was still safe inside. To his relief, Eli lay motionless on his bed where Davin had left him just hours before. "Eli! Wake up! We have to get out of here!" Eli remained still. Davin ran over to him and shook him hard. "Eli! Get up!"

Eli opened his eyes and saw his friend standing over him, panic on his face.

"We're in a hurricane! We need to get out of here! Help me!"

Eli struggled to sit up with Davin's assistance. His eyelids were heavy with exhaustion, and his chest felt even sorer than when he had initially fallen asleep. But with Davin's support, he was able to move forward slowly.

Eli saw the broken window as they struggled to move past the open door. Furniture and small items were being sucked out into the storm through the hole that used to be a window.

"Keep moving!" Davin urged.

They reached the elevator just as the last group of people crowded on. "Where do we go?" someone shouted.

"Head for the outer circle of the dome. There are no windows there," Davin said.

"Are you crazy? That means we have to walk between buildings to get to the elevator that goes up to the dome!" the person retorted.

"Do you have a better idea?" Eli shouted back. No one responded. "Didn't think so." He reached over and pressed the ground button.

The doors to the elevator opened, and everyone rushed down the hall to the door leading outside. It stood ajar, held in this position from the strong wind. Ankle-deep water was flowing into the building, and even deeper pools formed outside. As they neared the exit, there was a sudden calm in the wind.

"Quick! Now's our chance! Run! Run! Run!" Davin shouted as he pushed people toward the door to make a break for the nearest tower. Everyone struggled to keep a fast pace through the resistance of the deep water. The wind was still strong but bearable in the moment of calm as they waded through.

They reached the door, and Davin struggled to get it open against the weight of the water pooled around it. With the assistance of a nearby woman who quickly jumped in to help, they were able to open the door a crack. Just as that happened, a huge gust of wind forced the door wide open, and a large piece of debris flew past Davin's ear. The door shattered into millions of tiny pieces. The woman who had helped him had been hit by the piece of debris that barely missed him. A few yards out of reach, her motionless body floated, and the current carried her away from the entrance. Davin shivered, knowing he would never be able to rid himself of that image—another death he irrationally felt responsible for.

The winds suddenly came back in full force, and the rain beat down hard on Davin's back. People began to funnel into the entry of the tower, forcing Davin along with them as they ran for the elevator. They quickly reached the elevator and loaded on, riding to the safety of the dome in silence and carefully listening in fear to the sounds of the catastrophic storm outside.

The elevator doors opened, and they made their way to the outer circle of the dome. Groups split off and found shelter in individual rooms. Rooms with no external walls were already crowded with people. Knowing that the rest of The Society buildings were made largely out of huge glass panels, many of the other residents had made their way to the dome as well. There were few safe places on the island for them to hide from a storm of this magnitude. With the natural barrier that the mountain provided to The Society building and the added insurance of the government-issued weather controller, the architects were told there was no need for a hurricane shelter on the island.

Some of the residents tried to contact their families to inform them of what was happening and let them know they were safe. Others tried to reach their friends on the island to make sure they had made it to safety. But no one was able to reach anyone. All communication was down. No internet or phone service was available to anyone. Thankfully, the electricity remained stable.

Suddenly, there was a deafening noise from outside that could be heard throughout the halls of the dome. Screams rang out, and a few people burst into tears, not knowing what the crash was or whether all their friends were safe from the storm. The loud boom was unsettling for everyone.

Friends gripped each other's hands tightly, and couples embraced as they experienced what was—for most of them—the most frightening experience of their lives.

After Davin had situated Eli on the floor of his personal green room, he searched for Chloe, Kona, and Lola. He passed by a room where Chelsea had patched a direct line to a surveillance camera to display on a large screen, and people had crowded around to monitor the storm's progression. Davin breathed a sigh of relief to know that Chelsea had made it to safety. She looked unharmed. He was impressed that she had thought to monitor the storm. He gave her a slight smile as she looked in his direction. She glanced at him and seemed pensive, then looked away as if she hadn't seen him.

But she had seen him—standing there, slightly bloody from the shards of debris that had grazed him and still soaked from the rain—staring at her. But she didn't want him to know that she had seen him—though she couldn't explain why. She hated the extra attention he gave her. She could only guess that he enjoyed taunting her with his affection.

Unsurprised by her indifferent reaction, Davin went to continue his search for Lola and Kona and Chloe. But then, as if watching a mesmerizing time-lapse, the storm suddenly dissipated into nothing. A still night with a soft sunrise approaching on the horizon appeared on the screen as people in the room gasped in both relief and disbelief. An eerie quiet fell over the dome after the noise from the storm disappeared. A few people rushed to the center of the dome to observe the sky for themselves through the glass ceiling above them that was, thankfully, still intact. The same clear sky they observed on the surveillance camera feed looked down at them. Just as quickly as the storm had formed, it was gone, and there was calm again.

More and more people gathered in the center of the dome where the stage and LED wall remained dark in front of them. Many sat in the arena chairs and gazed up toward the sky in dismay. Conversation broke out among the residents.

"Is it okay to go outside?"

"I wonder what that loud noise was."

"What do we do now?"

Then, from the shadows of the stage, an unlit Sandra Waverly appeared from backstage with a microphone in hand. "Greetings, residents. This is Sandra Waverly, your Society Leader. We aren't positive, but we believe the storm has passed. Please take this time to get some rest wherever it's comfortable. Once we are certain the storm has passed, we'll take the rest of the day to assess the damage. Report any damages you find to the government offices. Tonight at eight, we will meet back here for a meeting to go over the actions we need to take to ensure The Society's survival. As you may have already noticed, the internet is completely down. We've already verified that communications with the mainland were utterly destroyed during the storm. Please don't attempt to reach out to your families and friends until we have restored communications. Thank you for your patience as we handle the implications of this devastating tragedy."

After the sun rose high into the sky, and there were a few solid hours of clear, radiant blue skies, people were allowed to exit the dome to investigate the damage to The Society building and grounds. Besides the smashed door and multiple broken windows, a huge portion of the glass on Tower Two was gone where the indoor garden was located. People soon realized that must have been the cause of the loud noise they had heard during the hurricane. Much of the indoor garden equipment had tipped over from the wind that made its way through the cavernous hole in the side of the building. The equipment was salvageable, but a majority of the fruits and vegetables that were growing were lost. The ground floors were knee-deep in water throughout The Society buildings, and toward the shore, the water was neck deep. The outdoor gardens and orchards were flooded as well. The fruit from the trees was blown off and destroyed or lost in the midst of the storm. The livestock was missing. It was clear as everyone walked around that their food sources had suffered a major blow.

Throughout the day, each missing piece of equipment or broken chair or fallen tree was reported to the government offices. That evening everyone sat down to dinner knowing the food that was harvested the day before would dwindle quickly. Portions were smaller than normal. They suspected food was being rationed to keep a stock for the following day. After everyone had eaten and the damages had been assessed, the masses made their way to the dome to hear the decided courses of action.

Promptly at eight, Ms. Waverly again took center stage in front of the unlit LED wall with a microphone in hand. "Evening, everyone. We thank you for all of your work today in gathering the necessary information we needed to determine our forward course of action. After assessing all the damage, we have decided to enact some changes to ensure success in rebuilding after the devastation of the storm. We believe the following solutions will provide us with eventual success. Henceforth, until conditions stabilize, the following rules and requirements are now *mandatory* to live here in the Hawaii Society."

She looked down at her feet for a moment, collecting her thoughts before she began the list of additional requirements. "First, all residents will put in a minimum of six hours of work a day, which may include multiple tasks as opposed to the two-hour, one-task requirement previously enforced. During those task hours, you will perform *assigned* responsibilities. Keep in mind that the six hours required are a minimum," she said sternly. "Residents should constantly be looking for things that need to be done and assisting during every spare hour to restore the grounds and equipment to its original state.

"Second, all food rations will be at a minimum. Additionally, one-third of the residents will be required to abstain from food *entirely* for one meal a day on a rotating basis. Residents who are required to abstain from the upcoming meal will be notified and required to sit out their meal in level two of Tower Four or here in the dome. Entertainment options in both the virtual reality facilities and the theaters will be provided to help ease your hunger. A strict head count of the residents who are supposed to sit out the meal will be taken as you arrive, and the exits will be blocked to ensure proper compliance. You may be wondering if you will be allowed to stay in your room for that time. Unfortunately, until the internet is restored and we are able to track residents' whereabouts once again, we have no way of guaranteeing people will comply with the once-a-day meal fast without a manual headcount. So everyone must report to his or her assigned rooms for the time being. This is a precaution to make sure that *everyone* receives the food allotted to them—in the name of fairness. Our carefully calculated food rations will be essential to ensure everyone's survival until food supplies have been replenished, so please understand these limitations are your insurance to guarantee a subsequent meal—however meager it may be." Whispers broke out across the crowd. Ms. Waverly pressed forward and spoke above the hum until it died down.

"Third, everyone will be required to complete the specific assigned tasks specified by the government offices. You will not get to choose which tasks you perform as you did before so that we ensure that the most vital tasks are attended to first. Fourth, *all* outdoor recreation is henceforth suspended. It will be restored as we are able. Since the internet and communications are down, you should know that residents can still communicate with each other through their wristbands using the two-way radio system. This is an offline feature that is standard in each wristband and the range can reach any part of the island. Government officials will also use this feature each day to communicate your tasks and which meal you will be required to sit out," Ms. Waverly explained.

A reluctant smile came over her face before she continued. "You will be happy to know that besides the network, no other electrical systems were damaged in the storm. That is all for the rule modifications for the time being. As always, *no one* is above these rules. *All* must comply to participate as a resident in The Society. To demonstrate that no one is above these rules, Davin Chapman and I will be among the first group of residents who will sit out tomorrow's breakfast. For those lost in the storm last night, we will pause for a moment of silence on their behalf." Ms. Waverly closed her eyes and stood quietly as silence swept the room.

After a moment, she looked up again. "Please return to your rooms for the night. If your room was damaged in the storm, feel free to find a place to sleep here in the dome or with a friend. Rest well tonight. We have a lot of work to do in the morning to rebuild."

Ms. Waverly then walked off the stage. Her audience remained silent for a moment more, then slowly the crowds dwindled down until everyone had returned to their rooms or found a place to rest somewhere in the dome.

IN THE MORNING, Chelsea shot up in bed as she woke to an alarm reverberating in her earpiece. She looked down at her wristband to see a request to connect over the two-way radio. She hit accept to silence the harsh beeping.

"All residents in buildings A through E will be among the first to abstain from breakfast. By 7 a.m., please report to Tower Four, level two. Afterward, you will be divided into groups by buildings to begin cleanup."

Never before had residents been given a wake-up call. She quickly got dressed and headed for level two of Tower Four as instructed. She and a few others boarded the elevator of Tower Four to go to the virtual reality rooms to sit out breakfast.

As the doors opened, a security bot stood waiting for them. "Please put out your wristband to be scanned," it ordered. All security bots stood at six foot four inches and looked like a metal man without a face. If their orders were repeatedly met with resistance, a large taser was hidden in the chest cavity that was supposed to be very painful. Chelsea did as instructed and extended her arm. As the bot's large mechanical finger touched her bracelet, it said, "Chelsea Coremon. You are confirmed to abstain from food. Please stand in line for room number thirty." Chelsea nodded and walked past the bot to look for her assigned room.

Crowds of people stood around the entrances to each virtual reality room, waiting for their game to begin. Chelsea had not played many games in the virtual reality rooms yet, so she spent some time weaving through people and trying to find room thirty. When she finally found it, the clock struck seven and government officials began to walk around and unlock the doors.

A woman who worked in the legal department soon came to Chelsea's group's door and unlocked it as she explained, "You may now enter your assigned room to play your predetermined game. Enjoy the next two hours of play before beginning your task work. And please remember, with the internet connection down, your scores will not be shared with the global high score records as they normally would be. So please don't ask where you ranked. We won't know until we have connection back. This is merely for your entertainment. Please enjoy." She opened the doors, and everyone shuffled into the large gray room. Each player followed the arrows on the floor that directed them toward the back wall where they grabbed a pair of gaming glasses. Everyone took a seat on one of the three rows of oversized stairs that acted as a bench for players to sit while they were given instructions for the game.

"Welcome to *Leagues of Reprisal*. This game was released in 2043 and quickly became popular among young teenagers. It is a historical combat game set in various times of rebellion in civilization's history. Weapons and vehicles from any time period are available for each level. Today you will be fighting against the reign of the early Egyptian monarch, Seth-Peribsen, in the Set Rebellion—the earliest formal rebellion known to man. Each player will be assigned a role and a position and then have five minutes to choose armor and weapons. Good luck, and remember, 'Rebellion never goes without consequence.'"

I haven't played this game in a long time. I love this one, Chelsea thought to herself, wondering which role she would be assigned.

As the introduction to the game ended, Egyptian monuments and structures suddenly appeared in the room in front of them using holograms and digital effects. The gray walls, which were actually large LED walls, disappeared and transformed into a desert landscape as far as the eye could see. "Please put on your glasses to select your armor and weapon," the game instructed the crowd.

Chelsea put on her glasses, which looked like normal glasses except with large noise-cancelling headphones that covered the ears and a microphone that sat in front of the wearer's lips. By putting her glasses on, the details in the game suddenly appeared. She could see the dust settle under people's feet as they walked to their positions. Individual rays of sunshine were shining down through a hole in a nearby Egyptian monument, and she watched as a fly buzzed past her. Had she not known she was in a game, her eyes could've been convinced she was actually there in 2730 BC preparing to fight for her freedom. Then a screen popped up on her glasses that covered the virtual world before her. "You have been selected to play *the driver*. Please select your armor and your vehicle. Your vehicle will act as your weapon," a voice said through the headphones attached to the gaming glasses.

Chelsea selected a black and teal titanium suit and scrolled past the horse and chariot of the time to a tan jeep. "Your first assignment is to meet up with your partner between the stone pillars found at the marketplace." Suddenly the tan jeep she had selected as her vehicle appeared around her. She pulled up a map of the area to locate the market while she waited for the game to begin. Then she listened for the countdown.

" . . . Ten, nine, eight, seven, six, five, four, three, two, one. Begin."

Chelsea revved her engine and popped the stick into second before zooming off toward the marketplace. She loved the thrill as she drove past Egyptian guards and cursed mummies rising from their tombs to protect their royal bloodline. Purple arrows directed her way to the pillars. Soon she spotted the pillars that were placed in the center of the marketplace, and she slammed on the brakes as she drove up next to them. *My partner better get here quick if we're going to make it*, she thought as she watched some guards start to run toward her.

Suddenly the passenger door swung open and a man holding a shotgun and wearing black armor that resembled a SWAT uniform jumped into the car.

"I call shotgun," she heard a familiar voice say as he cocked his gun and looked over at her with a smile. Davin's heart stopped. "Chelsea. Uh . . ."

Of all people, it had to be Davin Chapman, she thought as she turned her attention away from him and back to the guards running toward them.

" . . . How have you been? You doing okay after the other night?"

"Can we skip the small talk? I don't want to die in the first five minutes of the game," she said, not wishing to discuss her blunders at the Grand Welcome Performance.

"Gotcha. Okay . . . Well, don't worry. If anything goes wrong again, I won't try and console you. Based off the last time I tried, I'm not very good at it anyway," he said as he chuckled and hoped for the best.

Seeing a window of opportunity to turn the conversation around onto Davin, she took it. "You mean the other night when you gave me the up and down?" she asked as she raised an eyebrow.

Chelsea steered away from the guards, and the next mission was announced. "Your next mission is to find the shipment of food supplies and drop it off to the rebels at camp before nightfall."

Davin sighed a sigh of remorse and wondered if he would ever find a way to persuade Chelsea to warm up to him. "I assure you it was completely involuntary, and I meant no disrespect. I was just instinctively appreciating your beauty, you could say."

"I suppose I should take that as quite the compliment coming from *Davin Chapman,*" she said teasingly. She couldn't understand why he insisted on flirting with her. She knew very well he couldn't possibly find *her* beautiful. She could only reason he enjoyed the extra attention, and since they were stuck with each other for the next two hours anyway, she decided to play along. "It's okay. I'll forgive you. But you have to promise to never do it again," she said as she gave him a playful smile.

Is she flirting with me? Davin wondered as he smiled back at her warily. "'Course not. Not without your permission."

"Right," Chelsea said, rolling her eyes slightly. "Look! There's the supplies," she said, pointing to a package at the end of an alley. She pulled over, and they got out of the jeep to haul it to the back of the trunk. As they reached down to grab it, a cursed mummy suddenly came out of a doorway behind Chelsea.

"Duck!" Davin yelled as he raised his shotgun and fired.

Chelsea looked back as the mummy fell to the floor.

"Thanks," she said as she heaved a sigh of relief.

"No problem," he said with a grin. "I got you."

Chelsea remembered Drake saying the same phrase as he hoisted her up on the pool float, but when Davin said it, she couldn't help but smile. They grabbed either side of the package and threw it into the trunk of the jeep. "I did appreciate you trying to console me the other night though," Chelsea said out of the blue when they got back in the jeep. "However horrible you were at it. It was . . . sweet of you," she told him. "I was just too ticked to talk to anyone at the moment."

"I think you had every right to be ticked," he said, quite pleased that the conversation seemed to be going better than usual. Chelsea smiled. She began driving toward the camp, and Davin rolled down the window and kept his eyes open for any more guards or mummies.

As they rode, Davin's stomach grumbled loudly. "Well, clearly, my stomach hasn't forgotten its mealtime, despite Ms. Waverly's best efforts," Davin said as they both chuckled.

Chelsea felt her own stomach ache with hunger as well. "Yeah, I'm a little surprised at how hungry I already am. Makes me a little worried about the next couple months of rationing."

"Me too. It could get really rough," he said. "It doesn't help that after everything that happened, I couldn't bring myself to eat any dinner yesterday." Davin's face turned glum as he thought back on Roy and the lady floating away in the water during the hurricane.

"It does feel really silly to be here messing around after everything that's happened and all we have to do to get things back in order," she said as she drove into camp. The rebels weren't there yet to pick up the package, so she parked and they waited for them to arrive. "I don't know how The Society is going to pull itself up from this. I was already questioning if we were even in a good spot *before* the hurricane happened."

"What do you mean?" he asked.

"A bunch of stuff has been breaking down. Broken bots everywhere, no one knowing how to fix anything. Even before the hurricane, this place wasn't functioning like it's supposed to." In a more hushed tone, Chelsea leaned in toward Davin and continued. "And just a few weeks ago, I saw this Asian guy get taken away for not complying, but the thing is—the transporter pod hasn't come back since it returned to the mainland for maintenance a month ago. Where is this guy? He can't be back on the mainland, that's for sure."

As Chelsea spoke, Davin took in her words and began piecing together an all too clear puzzle he had been oblivious to beforehand.

"And how can we sustain this standard of living when nobody is really inclined to care? Honestly, I've been considering if it would be better to jump ship before it sinks, if you know what I mean." Just then the rebel players arrived to pick up the package. "Oh good. They're here." She got out and helped them unload the package. Davin remained in the jeep.

As she returned to the driver's seat, she continued. "Anyway, I'm probably just being super paranoid. I watched a lot of conspiracy movies in college," she confessed and let out a chuckle. "Every system's got its kinks to work out, right?"

"Your next assignment is to find the vial of poison hidden in King Narmer's tomb," the game instructed them.

"Alrighty. On to Narmer's tomb then?" she asked.

"What if you're right?" Davin questioned, not caring about the game anymore. "Maybe we *should* leave together."

Chelsea laughed, thinking he was teasing her. "Yes, let's just go. Run away with me, Davin," she said with a playful smile.

Davin did not respond. His mind was too overwhelmed to flirt as he considered the gravity of the accusations he was theorizing. A new kind of panic was beginning to creep into his mind— a fear, not of the past, but of the world in which he lived.

He ripped off his glasses, wanting to escape the inconsequential realm of the game and consider his thoughts in reality. The jeep and Chelsea's titanium suit vanished, and he looked out on a room of people wandering around and fighting the air in front of them. One group and two stragglers stood only a few feet away from where they sat, and then he spotted the government official in charge of monitoring the room. She stood with her arms crossed and was staring at him with questioning eyes, wondering why he left the game. When he didn't return, she began walking toward him to see if he was all right. In a panic, Davin pulled his glasses back on.

Chelsea jumped when he suddenly appeared in her passenger seat. "What was that about?" she yelled, trying to mask her fright at his abrupt return. "It's not like I was *seriously* proposing you should leave The Society with me."

Davin grabbed her hand. "Chelsea, we can't keep talking about this right now. We need to just continue the game quietly. There's a government official headed our way. Because of the glasses, you wouldn't even know if she was standing right next to you." His tone was intense and his face serious as he spoke. Chelsea suddenly felt very nervous. "Don't breathe another word. Just keep playing the game."

Is he being serious? she wondered. *Does he really buy into my crazy theories?* She meant to possibly scare him off with her outlandish ideas, but he seemed to be agreeing or at least playing a very convincing card. *He is an actor,* she thought.

They sat in silence as Chelsea drove them toward Narmer's tomb. She kept peeking over at him to see if he would drop the act, but each time she looked over, he was still wearing a stern expression and appeared to be very focused on the game. He sat with his shotgun at the ready at all times and only ever spoke to assist in completing the objectives of the game.

By the time their two hours of gaming were over, they had retrieved the vial, delivered it to their commander, and were on their way to intercept the secret location of Seth-Peribsen's hiding place from an ex-monarch loyalist. They had made excellent progress in the time they were given, and they had made a surprisingly good team. However, Davin's rigid demeanor and their unfinished conversation kept Chelsea on edge.

While returning their glasses, Chelsea watched as Davin's eyes repetitively scanned the room. Multiple times he looked over to the government official and studied her closely before looking away if she ever turned in his direction. Beads of sweat had formed on his brow, and yet they hadn't done much moving to warrant it.

"Davin, are you okay?" Chelsea whispered as they followed the crowds toward the elevator. "I don't *really* know if something is going on. It's just a stupid hunch that's probably wrong."

Davin looked nervously at the people around them and suddenly slipped away from the crowd as he whispered in Chelsea's ear. "Follow me."

He went to an empty theater and surveyed the room. Then he watched to make sure no one followed them. When he felt certain they were alone, he turned to Chelsea.

"Are you at all serious about finding out if you're right and escaping with me if you are?"

Chelsea was taken aback for a moment but then thought seriously about the question. "Um, sure. I mean, yeah. If it's at all true that there's something fishy going on and The Society isn't going to work out like we hoped, then yes. I don't want to stay."

"Then meet me in my room—room A814—tonight at eight, after all your work is done and dinner is over," Davin said, looking at her with his striking blue eyes.

Then, without another word, he left. Chelsea stayed where she was, trying to figure out what was happening and what the true intentions of Davin's invitation to his room were. But she found she was too distracted to think clearly—still engrossed by the memory of his deep blue eyes.

12. HIS ROOM

DAVIN MADE HIS way to his room quickly, completely unaware of his surroundings as his mind raced with concerns and theories. He walked past Kona without even noticing her or stopping to say hello. *Is the Asian man that Chelsea saw taken away the same Asian man Roy saw in the cave? And if it is, why wouldn't they send him home? Could Chelsea be right? Was the system failing without me even noticing?* The concerns Ms. Waverly and Mr. Willix expressed in their meeting did seem to correlate. He hoped Chelsea was wrong and that he could prove that to her. He knew what he had to do to start, but it would take time before he would be able to do it.

As he entered his room, he closed the door behind him. "Davin, I'm sorry you had to go without breakfast. Please understand, we value you for choosing to endorse our Society, and I think your support will be key in recovering from the effects of the hurricane," Ms. Waverly said as she handed him a plate of fruit.

Davin was shocked by the unexpected intrusion. Confused, he looked at the plate of food. "It's really no problem, Ms. Waverly. I expect to be treated the same as anyone else."

"Is there a problem, Davin?" Ms. Waverly asked, keeping the plate extended while looking at him with some disdain.

Feeling a discomforting sense of malice, Davin felt a sudden inclination that he needed to put on a show. "No. No. Glad I don't have to suffer these conditions unnecessarily. Thanks for bringing this. I'm starving," he said, taking the plate and lying across his bed to snack on his food. "Take a seat," he motioned to his desk chair. "What can I do you for?"

"Well," she said as she sat down, pleased he seemed relaxed now, "I have some instructions for you—I need you to physically help out with the other residents as much as you can during the cleanup period of the hurricane. And during the process, you need to communicate a positive outlook on the future of The Society and keep an upbeat attitude. Once things have settled down and there's less physical cleanup to do, I want you to perform a series of shows to keep spirits high. When The Society has returned back to normal and communication with the States is restored, we will perform another show that we will broadcast. In this broadcast, we will not mention the hurricane. There will be no need to worry people once we have everything in repair," she said with a pleasant but uncomfortable smile. "The main objective will be to let them know things are good at The Society—as always. We can't risk losing support, and we have enough resources here to repair the damages we have suffered on our own. We're supposed to be self-sufficient after all, and we don't want people losing faith in the system. You are the face and the voice of The Societies. You must be on board with this to ensure our survival. I spoke with Kona last night, and she is prepared to do the same. Can we count on you, Davin?"

"Of course," he said, popping a blueberry in his mouth with a smile.

"Good," she said. "Finish your meal—you'll need your strength. Then begin the cleanup with the rest of the residents as soon as possible."

"Will do," Davin said, continuing to eat as Ms. Waverly exited his room.

After she left, he put the plate down and drew in a deep breath. He stared at the plate of half-eaten food sitting on his desk. *Clearly, The Societies are not as impartial with their residents as they claim to be*, he thought.

DAVIN WENT TO WORK that day with a smile on his face. He worked hard and efficiently as he removed wreckage from the grounds in preparation for the water to recede to normal levels. He made comments like, "We'll have this place as good as new in no time." People really only smiled during the cleanup when they were close to Davin. He gave hugs to those who needed it and told great stories about his days acting in Hollywood films to anyone working around him. Sincerely hoping to raise people's spirits, he tried to follow Ms. Waverly's instruction, although he also worried she would be monitoring him to make sure he followed through with her request, and he did *not* want her to pay him another private visit.

As much as he wished he could continue living in ignorance as he did before, he knew he could not. His best friend was missing, and he had questions that needed answers. He was still anxious to search for Roy after he finished his work, but his hope that he could find him alive dwindled quickly as the hours passed by. That afternoon would be the first time Davin would be able to go out and look for him. Water levels had receded enough that he could safely wade through more of the grounds.

When his six hours were up, he headed for the mountain to search for Roy. If he could get over the bridge and reach the foot of the mountain, he would be able to easily search on dry ground. He tromped through the mud on the grounds and looked out to the bridge that was still covered by a shallow layer of water flowing over it from the river's high levels. To his relief, he was able to cross the bridge with little difficulty by holding tight to the railing and soon he made it to the dry ground on the mountain path.

He was glad to be on his own and not have to put on a facade—though it made him feel glum to face reality. As he trudged along the path up the mountain, he scoured the ground for any trace of Roy. The longer he walked, the more the loss of his friend weighed on him. He missed talking with Roy. He was the only person at The Society he ever felt he could truly open up to, and Davin knew that if he ever needed anything, Roy would always have his back.

Then he felt a prick of regret as he realized he hadn't been there for Roy. He remembered Roy telling him about the cave and how obviously upset he was about the whole thing. Yet Davin had brushed off his concerns and thought little of it—until he was gone. Now Davin was even more concerned about searching for the cave than Roy had been, but it was too late—he would no longer be able to uncover the truth with his friend by his side.

"I'm sorry. I should have paid more attention to what you were saying," Davin apologized to the wind as he looked up to the sky. "I know I need to find that cave and figure this thing out, but I have no clue where it is." *Ugh! I should have just gone with you to the cave in the first place,* he thought to himself. "You would have known right where it was, and we could've figured this out together."

He continued to walk and talk to his friend as if he were right there beside him. But in verbalizing his regrets, he began to feel his anxiety trigger inside of him. His palms turned sweaty and darkness started to cloak his thoughts. Then he heard Roy's voice inside of his head saying, *"Don't dwell on the negative, mate. Let your fear fade. Kia Kaha."*

Davin quickly changed the subject to something that would keep his mind off the pain. "Things are looking up with Chelsea. That's right, we have a bit of a date tonight." He paused and thought about his conversation with Chelsea from earlier. "Well, I guess it isn't really a date. But I'm pretty sure she was flirting with me."

Just then an alarm went off on his wristband, notifying him to head back for dinner. He sighed, upset that he found no trace of Roy and that his conversation with his friend was nothing more than a conversation with himself.

At dinner, he sat and wondered if Chelsea would decide to show up that night. It had been a long day, and he wondered what she thought of him after he had become so rattled from their conversation that morning. He flicked his wrist to look at the time—only one hour before they were supposed to meet. He needed to go to his room and shower before she came, so he quickly finished his meal to give himself enough time.

MEANWHILE, CHELSEA SAT EATING her dinner with Finley in the opposite tower from Davin. She had spent her day installing limited force fields over broken windows as temporary protection. The force fields were a kind of electrical netting that was usually used for outdoor recreational protection from rain and bugs. Anything with less than a pound in force could not penetrate them. This convenience plus the fact that they were easy to install over the holes of the broken windows made them the perfect temporary fix until they were able to install the self-melding glass pieces that The Society was equipped with in case of broken windows.

The process of installing the self-fusing glass to a broken window could take up to a month depending on the size of the hole. Since The Society had very large windows and multiple windows to repair, Chelsea expected it would take the full month, especially because many people had probably never used self-fusing glass before.

She remembered back to the time her father sat over her shoulder making sure she did everything just right while she repaired a sliding glass door that she had broken in the house when she was fifteen. "Get it lined up right, Chelsea," he had scolded. "You can't just place it any which way. The glass has to line up perfectly if there aren't gonna be any bumps or creases." After observing a few of her insufficient attempts, he snatched the glass piece from her hands and showed her how to line it up correctly, and then he used the heat gun to trigger the bonding agent. She watched carefully so she wouldn't get it wrong again and upset her father further. Using his methods, she was able to master the technique soon enough—her father never said if he was pleased with the end product. But since he didn't have anything to say, she figured she must have done a fair job.

As they ate, Finley spoke rapidly about her task of cleaning up the indoor garden. She had no idea what she was doing when it came to gardening, so she was infuriated that she had been given that task rather than working with Chelsea installing the force fields. "Lighting technicians are well-versed in electricity— I could have been so helpful in your group, but no. I was stuck with plants all day. It's just ridiculous. I need to have a little chat with this Branch guy. He's got me in the wrong task."

Chelsea listened to Finley complain, knowing there was no interjecting until she finished her thought. She could tell Finley felt strongly about this and knew it was pointless to argue with her. "Sounds like you need to go set the record straight with Branch," Chelsea said, repeating what Finley had just said.

Finley nodded. "Yeah, I think I will."

Chelsea quickly finished her last bite of dinner and picked up her plate to leave.

"You out of here? Where you headed?"

"I have some stuff I need to figure out. I'm going to head back to my room and . . . do that." She was trying to be as nonspecific as possible without causing suspicion. She didn't want Finley to know what was going on until she figured out exactly what it was for herself.

"Okay, see you tomorrow to fix those broken windows . . . hopefully," Finley said, thinking nothing of Chelsea's comment. She quietly cursed Branch under her breath one more time for making her deal with plants all day.

Chelsea tried to walk at an even pace as she made her way to her room to get cleaned up. Earlier that day, when she was contemplating whether or not she would meet with Davin that night, she almost instantly came to a decision. Although she had second-guessed herself multiple times during the day, her mind was made up long before she was willing to admit it. Whether or not her decision was wise or justified, her plan was to meet with Davin Chapman that night.

She speculated throughout the day about what things he might know to prove or disprove her theories. However, each time she began thinking of what he may have to say, she found her thoughts drifting from what he might say to thoughts about him—the way his smile slanted every time he looked at her, his blue eyes glancing in her direction.

Each time she caught herself thinking of him, she reminded herself that that kind of naive and foolish thinking would only bring her heartbreak. She couldn't allow herself to lose control over her emotions with him or be distracted by his looks. She had to remain focused. *I am only going so I can find out what information he has about The Society,* she told herself.

She showered and changed into a clean pair of pants and her favorite shirt. Then she put on some lip gloss and took one last look in the mirror just before the alarm on her bracelet notified her it was time to leave. The walk to Davin's room seemed incredibly short, though it wasn't. She arrived a minute early and stood at the door until eight o'clock exactly, then knocked quietly.

Davin opened the door and smiled brightly. "Hey, come in." Though he knew it probably wasn't for the reasons he was hoping for, he was elated that she decided to come. He closed the door behind her and took off his wristband and removed his earpiece. "Do you mind?" he asked, pointing to Chelsea's bracelet. Chelsea took out her earpiece first and then extended her arm toward Davin so he could remove her bracelet. He began carefully removing it from her wrist, and as he did, it felt as though her skin caught fire where his warm fingers touched her. Davin was too busy examining her bracelet to notice her blush slightly at his touch. "I've never seen a bracelet like this before. What's it made out of?"

"Copper," she answered. "I actually made it myself."

"Really? Well, that's neat," he responded. He took one last look at it. He could tell she had put a lot of work into it from the detailed design. "I like it," he said with a grin. He placed both wristbands and the earpieces on top of each other on the bathroom sink and shut the bathroom door.

Chelsea watched the door close—with her bracelet and earpiece inside—and was all too aware that without recorded footage, any wrongdoings that may occur in his room would be invalidated. Davin sat on his bed after shutting the door and motioned to her. "Please, sit down." She sat on the farthest edge of the bed from Davin. Not noticing her guardedness, Davin unconsciously moved closer to her as he began. "Well, I don't even really know where to begin. Maybe we should get to know each other a little to start?"

"I want to know what information you have that is so secretive you couldn't tell me this morning," Chelsea demanded.

"Or we can skip the hellos and jump right into it," Davin said, trying to remain unperturbed. Chelsea remained silent, waiting for his response. "Okay . . . well, here's what I got," Davin began. "So about three days ago, I was out on a boat with some friends while you were building a sandcastle, and my buddy Roy said he was going to go check out a cave. I decided not to go with him."

Reflecting on what she was doing three days ago, Chelsea interrupted his story. "Wait, if you were on a boat, how would you know I was building a sandcastle?"

"I could see you on the shore from the boat," he said quickly, "but that's really not important to the story. Anyway, when I was on the beach later, my buddy came running up to me acting all skittish and secretive and telling me about this cave. He said he saw a bunch of boxes, floating gardens, and a room where an Asian guy was sitting—apparently doing nothing," Davin explained, counting on his fingers as he listed the three things Roy had told him about. "And then you tell me a story about some Asian guy going missing. And I started to think—maybe the guy in the room and the missing guy are the *same* person," Davin said. He studied Chelsea's face, trying to read her reaction to his theory.

"Yeah? Was he wearing a black shirt with big white letters?" Chelsea asked.

"Well, I wasn't there. I don't know," Davin said matter-of-factly.

Chelsea thought briefly. "That could be something—if we could prove it. But maybe there's an explanation."

"I have more though," Davin said. "Sandra Waverly came to my room after we spoke—with a plate full of food," he told her with wide eyes, "even though she announced to everyone that I would be fasting, same as everyone else. She also encouraged me to keep The Society in high spirits throughout the rebuild and then play it off to the public like the hurricane was inconsequential."

"That *is* suspicious," Chelsea said. "Can we ask your friend? He might remember if the Asian guy was wearing a black shirt with bold white letters. If we can prove it's the same guy, then maybe we can prove The Society isn't taking people where they're claiming they are."

"No, we can't," Davin stated glumly, looking away from Chelsea's face reluctantly. "That's the other thing—my friend who told me about the cave, Roy . . . he died during the storm. Lightning hit him—right after I told a government official about the cave." Davin paused and sat quietly for a second. "I know it's probably unrelated. It's not like they can control the weather. But it just seems like such an odd coincidence."

There was a deep sadness in Davin's eyes that pierced Chelsea to the core. She had never lost a friend and could not imagine how hard it would be. It seemed a little overdramatic to blame The Society when his friend was probably just in the wrong place at the wrong time when the storm hit, but she knew it must be hard to be rational during times of grief. She moved closer and grabbed Davin's hand sympathetically. "I am so sorry about your friend, Davin."

Davin looked at her appreciatively. He could sense her sincerity and was moved by her compassion. Before he got too emotional, he cleared his throat and proceeded. "So I thought about it a lot today, and I think the next logical step is to find the cave and figure out if it's the same guy. If it is, and he's not there by choice, I fully intend to leave The Society. I just couldn't see myself living in, let alone endorsing, The Societies anymore."

"Okay. That makes sense to me," Chelsea said. "So how do we find this cave? Do you have any idea where it might be?"

"Well, Roy was escapading when he found the cave. So I figure we wait until we're allowed to go out in the water again and then go out looking for it."

"Seems logical. Though it definitely prolongs things, doesn't it?" Chelsea added as she thought of the flooded grounds outside and the ban on all outside recreation.

"True, but hopefully that's not a huge problem. I've got nowhere to be but here. And honestly, I'm really hoping we can completely disprove all this—The Society is a pretty wonderful place to live for the most part." He stopped to think for a moment. "But I just couldn't live with myself knowing I was endorsing a place like this if we find out any of these speculations are true."

"Agreed." Chelsea admired Davin's resolve to live ethically but also hoped they wouldn't have to leave The Society's breathtaking island. "It feels so wrong to complain about The Society when it's such a beautiful place to live and the facilities are so nice. It's so frustrating and confusing to love this place but feel like it's on a path to collapse at the same time."

Thinking back on how hard it was on the mainland, she wondered if she would eventually come to regret trying to discredit The Societies. A number of memories from her childhood came to her that got her thinking. "You know, growing up, things were always kind of rough. But before my dad moved out, we tried to go on a family vacation every so often—they are some of my best memories. We had so much fun and did some really amazing activities together," Chelsea reflected. "Coming here, I almost thought it would be like living in that same vacation-like bliss every day—and for a little bit, it was. But after a while, the splendor of it all went away," she said, thinking about all the days she fell asleep staring up at the ceiling, wishing she had something meaningful to wake up to. "I used to feel drained all the time before I came here. Now I just feel empty a lot of the time, which is almost worse in some ways. I think I need something I can call my own again—or maybe even that isn't enough. Maybe I need to have someone to share it with—like I did when I had my family on vacation."

"Nothing can replace having the people you care about with you," Davin said, leaning back against the wall and thinking about all the people who had left him that he could never replace. He looked over at Chelsea and smiled. It was comforting to see her sitting next to him. He wasn't alone—at least not for the moment.

Chelsea looked over at Davin, who had so patiently listened to her as she worked through her own feelings. "It seems easy to talk to you. It's nice," she said, giving him a grin.

He smiled back and slowly reached over and took her hand in his, and to his surprise, she didn't pull away from him. She laced her fingers between his and sat silently staring at their hands.

Her nervous heart beat loudly in her head until she couldn't stand it any longer. She said the first thing that came to her mind. "So you're really prepared to run away with me?"

She regretted asking the question the minute it slipped from her mouth. Recognizing how awkwardly forward it was, but not wanting to admit it, she played it cool and raised one eyebrow flirtatiously, like she meant for it to be playful.

That made Davin smile in amusement. "Well, I guess that would depend. We could just as easily run our separate ways if you would like," he said nonchalantly. "I could return to my mother's and figure something out in Oklahoma, and you could go back to your family. Or," he said as he slowly leaned in closer to her, "if you'd rather, we could run off together—that would be entirely up to you." Chelsea could no longer concentrate on her thoughts. She could only feel his hand firmly holding hers, and she began to notice how close he was leaning in toward her. Her cheeks grew warm from his deep gaze. "Personally, I haven't stopped thinking about you since the day we met under the peach tree."

"The peach tree?" Chelsea asked. The unfamiliar story pulled her out of her daze as she tried to recall what he could be referring to.

"Yup." Davin remembered her unconventional approach to picking a peach and reflected aloud. "You told me off like you were so sure of yourself," he said with a chuckle. Chelsea struggled to recollect the exact encounter, but then Davin turned to her with a smile that made Chelsea's heart flutter. "It was completely irresistible."

Then he leaned in close—so close Chelsea could smell his cologne and feel his slow, steady breathing across her face. His lips sat inches away from hers as her stomach twisted with anticipation. She could sense his urge to kiss her, and she felt no reservations inside about wanting to kiss him back. She had never wanted someone to kiss her more in her life.

But he paused and then lingered, refraining—in order to give her one last chance to reject him.

His kissable lips anxiously waited, tempting her. The tension increased until Chelsea finally gave in. She closed her eyes and leaned her body into his warm embrace as their lips met. His lips were soft and gentle but filled with passion. He closed his eyes and enjoyed the flavor of her lips. She showed no signs of stopping, so Davin came at her without reservation. He pushed one hand firmly against her hip while carefully rotating his body on top of hers. His other hand glided up her body to the nape of her neck where he traced the infinity symbol shaved into her undercut. Then his fingers coursed up through her hair and gripped the back of her head, and their kisses grew more and more intense.

The hand that rested on Chelsea's hip began skimming the top of her jeans as Davin whispered into her ear, "Is this mutual?"

Those words snapped Chelsea back into consciousness, and she realized what was about to happen. She stopped kissing him and gently pressed her hands against his chest to stop him. "And that is where I have to stop you," Chelsea said. "I can't do this, Davin."

"Why? What's up?" he asked, perplexed. He had never been so sure about something in his life. He had never liked a woman the way he did Chelsea. Not because he had a particularly deep love for her, but because he had never experienced the kind of draw he felt to her with anyone else. Since he had come to believe that he would never have a chance with her, he was in complete bliss for the split second he thought he'd be able to act on his passions.

"I just can't," Chelsea said.

He was not altogether surprised based on Chelsea's previous dismissals of him, but her zealous kisses had given him hope. He went to apologize for assuming too much, but Chelsea continued before he could say anything.

"I know how this goes—you act like you care about me, get me in bed, and in the morning, you thank me for a wonderful night. Then I go home dreaming about you for the next . . . who knows how many years! I just can't do that again. I promised myself I would never do that again." She turned and lifted her hair to better show the infinity symbol that was shaved into the nape of her neck. "I get this cut to remind myself of that promise. The promise that I will never stop searching until I find someone who will actually respect me enough to love me for more than just a night, with a love that won't end, and the promise that I will still try to love myself even if I never find that." After she explained, she let her hair drop back down and her head drooped. "I'm just not like everyone else. I don't know how to do meaningless. I don't know how to stop loving someone when the morning comes." Chelsea cringed when she realized what she was saying to Davin Chapman. *I probably sound so passé*, she thought.

She sat there on the bed—looking at him tentatively but still firm in her resolve—awaiting his response. She expected him to be irritated and possibly angry that she wouldn't sleep with him, but Davin just ached for her. He could see she had been hurt, and he wished he could somehow make it better.

"You honestly believe I just want you for sex, don't you?" He watched as her determined look turned to befuddlement with his words. "I'm so sorry that you've been used, Chelsea." She remained silent, questioning if he actually meant the words he said and skeptical that his kind understanding might be a trick to get her back in the mood. He paused and thought carefully for a long moment. He thought back to the infinity symbol on her neck, and then he came to a decision. "Chelsea, I want to make you a promise." She sat baffled but curious as she tried to guess what he could be promising her. "I promise you that I'm never going to sleep with you until I am absolutely sure that I want to spend the rest of my life with you by my side."

That was not the promise she had expected to hear.

"I know we don't legally recognize any forms of commitment anymore, but until I tell you I am absolutely certain that I want you, and only you, for the rest of forever, I refuse to do more than kiss those sweet lips as often as possible—if you'll let me." Davin held his breath and earnestly waited for Chelsea's response.

She was rattled at first. Then her expression softened, and she shook her head impatiently. "You're joking. You can't possibly mean that. Who talks like that?"

"I plan to—for the foreseeable future," Davin assured her confidently. Chelsea tried to give him a smile, but her eyes inadvertently narrowed in disbelief. "For now, I think we should both get some rest. We still have a lot of cleanup to do tomorrow, and as soon as we can, we also have a great deal of escapading to do," he said with a smile.

Davin returned Chelsea's bracelet and earpiece and walked her to the door. He gave her one more kiss. It was short and sweet but just intoxicating enough that she found it hard to leave as their lips parted, and he wished her a good night.

13. CLEAN UP

CHELSEA WOKE UP long before her alarm went off for breakfast the next morning. She lay in her bed, encased in her sheets, smiling at nothing in particular. The sunrise seemed particularly beautiful, even just watching a portion of it through her window. She reflected back on the night before, the feeling of Davin's lips pressing firmly against her own as he pushed his body up against hers—a memory that had haunted her all night in her dreams. She grinned in contentment as she thought back on his endearing promise and the sincerity she saw in his clear blue eyes. Only time could tell the true level of his sincerity—though Chelsea stopped to wonder if she wanted him to keep his promise if it took too long for him to choose if he wanted to be with her long term.

Unable to decide, she remembered a portion of her conversation with Davin she had not fully appreciated—due to Davin's distractingly close proximity at the time. Davin was the man she had met under the peach tree her first day at The Society! She laughed out loud, thinking about how their conversation had bothered her. She remembered how indignant she had felt and acted toward him, even though she privately begrudged that she had not thought to look for a stool in the first place once he pointed it out. She recalled finding him attractive initially but not even recognizing him as Davin Chapman—the famous actor!

A knock at the door distracted her from recalling her now humorous first encounter with Davin. Not knowing who it could be, she quickly wrapped her bedsheet around her nightwear before answering.

"Hey," Davin said and greeted her with a smile.

"Uh, hey," Chelsea replied, wishing she had glanced in the mirror before coming to the door. "Um, what are you doing here?"

"I thought we could walk over to the cafeteria and have breakfast together," he said.

"I haven't even gotten ready for the day yet. I probably won't be going for another twenty minutes or so. You go ahead without me. I don't want to slow you down."

"It's no problem," Davin said, working his way around the door into her living quarters. He walked in and made his way to the desk chair where he made himself comfortable. Chelsea stood frozen for a moment before she gathered her composure and shut the door.

She had experienced a similar situation in high school when a boy offered to walk her to the track after she changed into her gym clothes on a day she was running late—only to find that the boy expected to watch her while she changed in exchange for his accompaniment. She remembered the boy's wandering eyes taking in her bare skin like a wolf behind bars staring at a strip of meat. After she declined his invitation to ditch gym with him, he scoffed at her figure and muttered that she wasn't pretty enough anyway.

She assumed Davin's intrusive entrance meant he expected something similar. *Maybe his intentions aren't so noble after all,* she thought with a silent sigh of disappointment.

She knew most other women wouldn't hesitate to undress, even in public. It wasn't considered particularly indecent if one needed to change quickly outside, and many other women would have been more than happy to put on a show for the movie star, Davin Chapman. But Chelsea couldn't bring herself to be comfortable with exposing herself like that again to someone she did not fully trust.

"I'm not going to change in front of you, Davin," she stated impatiently. "I'm not interested in playing games. If you aren't interested in a real, genuine relationship, and just want some hyped up sexual banter—then you might as well just leave now."

Davin gave Chelsea a blank stare for a moment before crossing his legs and leaning back in the chair. "As enticing as that sounds, I'm actually totally okay with you stepping into the bathroom to change," he stated. "I honestly was just hoping to chat with you more over some breakfast—get to know you beyond your crazy conspiracy theories and your kissing abilities." He looked up at her, watching for her reaction, and was, secretly, very entertained.

"Oh," Chelsea said, feeling diffident. "Okay. I'll just be a minute then."

She slowly made her way into the bathroom and shut the door tightly behind her. She silently groaned at her inaccurate conjecture and sank to the bathroom floor in embarrassment. She wanted to be angry with him for his brash entrance that had confused her into thinking his motives were rash, but the unexpected relief that she felt from him being nearby overpowered her frustration. She jumped into the shower and fumbled with the shampoo, almost dropping it multiple times.

Davin sat at her desk studying the photos that displayed on the LED screen attached to her wall. Pictures of her friends and family from back in Las Vegas and Chelsea as a little girl entertained him as Chelsea hurriedly attempted to get ready, despite being completely distracted by his presence in the other room.

As she finished washing her hair, she realized that during her retreat to the bathroom, she had not thought to grab a change of clothes. She groaned inside as she finished her shower and pressed the automatic dry button. After doing her hair, she wrapped her bedsheet around her bare skin, not wanting to put her dirty clothes from the night before on her clean body. Quietly turning the handle and opening the door, she tiptoed over to her closet to retrieve her clothes for the day.

Davin turned then stared in confusion. "Change your mind?" he asked teasingly.

"No," Chelsea said sternly and grabbed her clothes as she quickly turned back around to close the bathroom door.

"I thought not," he said to the empty room with a smile.

After a short minute, Chelsea walked back out fully clothed and ready to go. "Should we head to breakfast?" she asked.

"Definitely," Davin answered and made his way to her side. He gently clasped Chelsea's hand in his own and lifted her chin up with his other hand to give her a drawn-out kiss. His kiss lacked the passion he exuded the night before but was replaced by a gentle, intense warmth. He slowly broke away, looking at her face. "You are quite beautiful, Chelsea," he said and then bit his lip, smiling—pleased with how things were going.

Since the day he met her, he had imagined freely kissing her and wondered what it would be like to be with her. She was just as stubborn and entertaining as he had expected and just as pleasing to look at up close.

Davin strolled past her and opened the door. "After you."

"Thanks," she huffed, giving him a devilish grin as she walked past.

"What was that look for?" he asked.

"Nothing really—I've just never had someone open the door for me before," Chelsea said. "It's sweet, but annoying at the same time."

Having been taught to always hold the door for others, Davin contemplated her comment for only a short second. "Hmm, can't say I see a workaround for that one. Guess you'll just have to get used to it," he said. Chelsea huffed again but smiled in acceptance. She was beginning to realize Davin had his own amount of stubborn. "So you're going to have to tell me who all those pictures are of on your wall back in the room. Pictures of your family back home, I assume?" Davin asked.

"Yes. A few are of my friends back in high school, but they're mostly pictures of my parents and brother and sister."

"Was your brother the little kid always making goofy faces and wearing a long, baggy shirt?" Davin chuckled.

"Yup." Chelsea smiled thinking about her fun-loving younger brother. "He went through a phase when he couldn't manage a proper smile, so he just made funny faces for pictures. And that kid *hated* pants, so my parents made him wear long shirts to cover his underwear around the house. I'm pretty sure he still walks around pant-less whenever he can. He's actually living at the Society in Texas now."

Davin laughed. "Can't say I blame him about the pants. What about your dad and mom? Where are they?"

"They're both in Las Vegas still, though my dad doesn't really live at the house anymore. He pretty much lives in his RV and goes where he pleases. My sister lives nearby to keep my mom company," Chelsea said.

Not understanding why someone would choose to live out of an RV when they owned a house, Davin asked, "So why isn't your dad home much? Does he travel for work?"

Chelsea wasn't particularly fond of talking about the subject, but she recognized it was a valid inquisition. "No. After they deinstitutionalized marriage, my dad kind of stopped wanting to hang around. I guess he felt less responsibility or something, especially since we kids were mostly grown at that point." It made her sad to think about how much her family had changed. "Our family kind of fell apart after that. My mom's been brokenhearted ever since. Anyway, there's not much to say about my family.

They work a lot to stay afloat—same as everyone else outside of The Societies. My dad works in solar, and my mom is an accountant. What about you? I'm sorry to admit, I haven't really researched your life or anything—so I really don't know much about you," Chelsea confessed, trying to change the subject away from her family situation.

"Really?" Davin twisted his tongue, trying to think of how he should tell his story. "Well, that's kind of refreshing for a change. Most people seem to know more about my life than I do. It's incredibly annoying."

"Well, fire away. All I know is you are an actor, and you did not die in the earthquake—obviously."

"Okay, where to start?" Davin thought. "So I grew up in Oklahoma, of all places. My family, the Chapman family, was a very rich and powerful family with a long history in the oil industry. My dad had *everything* riding on the oil business. He fought tooth and nail for its survival for a long time. So after the US banned the use of oil—we pretty much lost everything. A few years later, my dad became very sick, and we lost him to colon cancer. That was about two years before they discovered the cure for cancer." Davin sighed. "It was really hard to think that if he could have just held on for a few more years, he would have made it."

"Oh, Davin, I'm so sorry."

"It's all right," he quickly assured her, having spent many years reconciling the loss of his father through religious assurances. "After my dad was gone, it was just me and my mom. My mom tried to go back to work but could never really get us on our feet again. She suddenly became kind of obsessed with southern manners and made sure I held doors for people and said *sir* and *ma'am* to everyone. I think it was kind of all she had left from her days as a rich higher-up, so she kind of clung to that part of her identity. She's a wonderful lady—very kind and *very* stubborn.

A real southern belle as they used to call it," he said, smiling at Chelsea.

"But you don't say sir or ma'am or have a southern accent or anything," Chelsea said.

"Nope. It didn't test well with audiences when I went to Hollywood, so I trained myself not to speak with an accent—the southern culture is just considered too old-fashioned," Davin explained.

"So what made you decide to move to Hollywood and try acting then?" Chelsea probed.

"Well, for a couple of reasons. One—I figured if I did well, I could support my mom and myself on an actor's income. Two—it was one of the few industries left that was still looking for young faces to break into the market. And three—I'm really good at acting. I took it up as a kind of emotional outlet after my father died, and—I don't know—it just came really naturally."

"Fair enough," Chelsea said with a smile. "You were really good in all the films I saw you in. How did your mother feel about you leaving?"

"Mmm, not happy at first, but I promised her if she let me go, I would take good care of her. And, eventually, I did," Davin said proudly. "I worked like crazy—auditioning for every good role I could find and immersing myself in my role to perfectly execute it on screen. Pretty soon, I got a good reputation in Hollywood and all my films did really well. I had a really great career going, and I made some really close friendships in the movie business along the way. Then the earthquake happened." Davin paused to take a deep breath. "Lucky for me, I was on a small set in Utah when it happened. Once Hollywood was gone, and most of California with it, I tried to go back to see if any of my friends made it," Davin said, trying not to dwell on a few particular memories he wished to forget. "None of them did," Davin said mournfully. "I lost my career, my lifestyle, my house, and my friends all at once—from the worst earthquake this earth has ever seen."

Chelsea wanted to console him, but she felt awkward and didn't really know what would make him feel better. She decided to remain quiet and listen patiently like he had for her the night before.

"After that, I went to live with my mom," he continued, "until she confessed she had blown most of the money I sent her already." He laughed. "We sat down with an accountant, and she calculated out that my mom would barely have enough to live out the rest of her elderly life—assuming inflation rates don't experience another spike. So as soon as I heard about it, I signed up for The Society program." Davin gave a shrug of resolve. "I got my invitation letter really quick, but they said I could only come to Hawaii if I would 'promote Society living.' So I agreed and left my mother in Oklahoma for a second time. And here I am," Davin concluded.

They were not scheduled to sit out a meal until lunch that day, so they proceeded to the breakfast line to grab a plate. "I had no idea," Chelsea began. "Even before the earthquake, it sounds like you had it really rough as a kid with losing your dad and your family fortune."

"Yeah, but I try not to dwell on the sad stuff too much," Davin said. "That's just the short version of my story. A lot of my struggles have helped me learn to value people a lot more, 'cause you never know when you're going to miss them."

Chelsea admired his ability to learn from his hardships. She smiled and quietly listened as Davin went on about all the amazing things about his father that he missed most. Then, as they continued their conversation, they began to discuss arbitrary facts about their lives. They tried to focus on happy memories like what Halloween costume as a kid they remembered best or what kind of pie they preferred during the holiday festivities. Most holidays were not formally recognized in the US anymore and had instead been replaced with generic holiday periods to avoid offending any particular group. But both of them remembered Christmas parties and Easter egg hunts as children with fondness.

"Well, I really have to get back to the grounds to help with cleanup, but I look forward to seeing you later for whatever game they have us doing. Hopefully, we can be partners again," he said with a wink.

"Okay," Chelsea said with a smirk. "I better get going too."

THAT DAY WENT BY slowly for both Chelsea and Davin as they went about their work in separate areas. When lunch finally rolled around, Chelsea quickly placed her last piece of force field before heading to the virtual reality rooms. She had never thought she would be so excited to sit out a meal. But when she arrived, she found Davin was not yet there. She disappointedly got her room assignment. "Which room will Davin Chapman be in? Is he in my group again?" she asked the security bot.

"We're not allowed to divulge others' assignments, but if he was in your group yesterday, he will be in it again. You will rotate rooms, but your group will remain the same for reasons of simplicity."

Chelsea smiled. *Two hours with him every day,* she thought as she walked to room thirty-one.

A few minutes later, Davin came sprinting into the room and immediately walked up to Chelsea. "Sorry. I got tied up trying to finish a project before lunch, but I'll just have to finish it afterward," he said as the introduction of the game began. Their group would be divided into the royal navy and a gang of pirates, and they would fight for the control of a large naval ship. Chelsea and Davin were assigned to the royal navy and were to begin the game tied to the mast.

"Man, I thought I got tied up with the cleanup, and now—I'm *actually* getting tied up," Davin said to Chelsea with a grin as they put their arms around an imaginary mast.

Chelsea laughed. "Nice," she said with a small eye roll and a smile. Davin's quip made her realize she had missed Finley's normal slew of puns at breakfast that morning. *I'll need to find her later and explain why I ate in Tower Two instead,* she thought. *Though maybe I should leave out the part about it being Davin Chapman who I've been with.*

"Was it difficult to install the force fields?" Davin asked as pirates and navy members fought around them. Despite the commotion surrounding the ship, it was hard to keep their minds on the game after surveying the very real damage around The Society that day.

"No. They have an adhesive you can apply to the edges. The hardest part is trying to juggle the roll while cutting it into the right shape to cover the hole."

"Stop chatting and get your head in the game, lady," their teammate said as he cut their ties.

Davin rolled his eyes. He pulled out his sword and made short work of a number of the pirates around him. Chelsea stood back, impressed. "Remember—I've had to train in fencing and swordsmanship for a number of movies," he explained.

"Oh, that's right," she remarked, thinking back on a few of the movies she remembered him sword-fighting in. "I'm sticking with you."

He smiled and protected her for the rest of the game until they had easily secured the stolen treasure and captured all the pirates. After winning, they were honored in a ceremony at port for protecting the royal navy's ship against the most dreaded pirates of the seven seas. Davin was awarded high honors, as he held the high score. As the ceremony ended, the game vanished, and they were left in their vacant room. The government official supervising the room looked up from his wristband in surprise.

"What happened?" he asked.

"It's over. We won," Davin answered.

He looked down at the time. There were still five minutes left until their two hours were up. "There's not enough time to start another round. Just hang out until I tell you it's time to leave."

Everyone shrugged and separated into groups to discuss the game—but most started discussing how odd it seemed that Davin seemed to show particular favoritism to a random girl.

"Do you know who she is?"

"No. I don't recognize her at all," another girl answered.

"Great. Another reason for all the girls to be in love with him," one man grumbled, who was still disgruntled that Davin had defeated him in the final duel.

Davin paid no attention and wiped the sweat from his brow as he walked with Chelsea to their stairs at the back of the room.

"You were amazing! We dominated because of you," Chelsea said as they sat down.

Davin just chuckled in modesty and then his mood became serious. "Hey, I was wondering, would you mind going with me to search the mountain after we're done with our tasks? I could really use some company out there if you're up for it," he said, hopeful she would say yes.

Chelsea thought for a minute and couldn't find a reason why she shouldn't go. "Sure. What exactly are you searching for?"

Davin looked down, unsure how to phrase it, and realized he should have explained his reasons for the hike before she agreed to go. "I want to see if I can find Roy or . . . his body, I guess. You still okay with going? You really don't have to. And we may not find anything anyway," Davin backpedaled, realizing she may not want to go on a search for a body. When Chelsea didn't give an immediate answer, Davin looked down at the floor. "I just don't know if I can handle another two hours searching that mountain and talking to a ghost again."

"I'll go," Chelsea said. "I want to go. We certainly can't just leave him out there."

Davin managed a smile and nodded.

"Times up. Return to your assigned task work," the government official instructed before opening the door so everyone could leave.

AFTER THEIR TASK WORK was complete, Davin and Chelsea met at the base of Tower Three.

"We'll have to make our way through some deeper water before we make it to the dry ground on the mountain. Are you okay with that?" Davin asked.

"Yeah, let's go. I've hiked the mountain many times," Chelsea told him so he wouldn't worry about her.

"Okay, just let me know if you want to turn back."

"I'll be fine. Trust me. Let's get going," Chelsea said as she led the way. Davin was glad she seemed confident to proceed with the search and quickly followed after her.

Once they were through the flooded areas and they reached the foot of the mountain, the trail became dry. Walking became much easier, which allowed them to chat as they hiked the incline. "Before you started working in the dome, what were you doing all that time?" Davin remained focused on searching the trail but was glad to have someone to talk with to keep his mind occupied. "I never really saw you around even though you were one of the first ones to come to The Society."

"I mostly filled my days with a bunch of water activities. I've always loved them, and I finally had the chance to do them."

"I never really got into them, to be honest. I was always too busy working on shows or just hanging around with friends. I like quad skiing just fine, but I've only tried the rest of them maybe once or twice. Which water activities do you like most?"

"My favorite is flyboarding. I've been practicing a lot. It's so exhilarating! I just love it. You used to have to have a jet ski or boat to provide a powerful enough water stream to fly up into the air with your board, but now flyboards are just a board with a tube attached that goes directly in the water and sucks it up from the ocean and sends you shooting into the sky—all by itself!" Chelsea said, her enthusiasm visible on her face.

"I think I've seen them out there on the water before. It's the board that hovers over the ocean and shoots water out the bottom, right?"

"Exactly! It's seriously so much fun. You've never tried it?" Chelsea asked in disbelief.

"No, I just haven't taken the time."

"Once the water has gone down, and this place is back to normal, we've got to take a break from escapading and try it out. It's amazing!" Chelsea struggled to contain her excitement. She was eager to get back on the water for more flyboarding once they were allowed.

"Okay," Davin said as he lightly chuckled at her apparent delight.

When they reached the top of the mountain, Chelsea looked out over the ocean and let out a sigh. "One of my favorite views," she said as she looked over at Davin and smiled.

He looked at her just as she turned and stepped in close to his chest. She wrapped her arms around his neck and slowly made her way closer to his lips. As he waited for her lips to meet his, he was pleased to see that she was initiating, but in the back of his mind, he still felt the urgency to continue the search for Roy. When her lips grazed his, he decided to return her kiss with an extra amount of vigor so she would know he appreciated the gesture. She matched his vim, and the short adoring kiss that Davin had intended quickly grew into a powerful longing for more. But with Roy's absence still weighing heavy on his mind, Davin soon pulled himself away as he resisted the urge to let his hands explore her body further. "We better keep looking," he whispered.

Chelsea quickly agreed and returned her focus back to the path of the mountainside as she felt a small amount of guilt for letting herself get carried away in the moment. They walked for some time, staying alert for any signs of Roy. But as they walked, Chelsea still found herself preoccupied with the memory of Davin's lips. She looked down at her feet, watching each step, and replaying their kiss in her mind when strange black marks on the ground managed to rouse her from her musing. *What are these markings from?* she wondered. She looked farther down the trail and saw a large divot in the soil near the edge of the path up ahead.

"Look at the ground," she called to Davin, who was searching the mountainside elsewhere. "It almost looks like something exploded over there. Do you think it could be from the lightning that hit Roy?"

Davin's eyes widened. He looked at the marks and then climbed a nearby rock to get a higher vantage point. He closely examined the greenery that blanketed the mountain until he saw what he had dreaded he would find. Farther down the mountainside, he could see Roy's limp body concealed in a thicket of vegetation.

14. FUEL FOR THE FIRE

"**W**E MAY BE ABLE TO SAVE HIM!" Davin shouted, struggling to carry Roy up the side of the mountain. "His body's still warm." He gently rested Roy on the path and checked his vitals. He listened for a heartbeat and held his wrist to check for a pulse—nothing. Roy had severe burns on his head and right foot. His wristband was charred and obviously beyond repair. Davin ripped open Roy's frayed shirt and tried performing CPR. Chelsea stood by helplessly.

Red treelike marks stretched across Roy's chest and right arm—as though an artist had decided to create a beautiful sketch across his body. Chelsea recognized them as Lichtenberg markings, a kind of pattern left from electrical charges that rupture capillaries in the human body. She had once studied about them in school and found the phenomenon entrancing. She had even considered getting a tattoo of them across her back but thought better of it.

Davin pumped Roy's chest and performed mouth-to-mouth while Chelsea stood off to the side, brokenhearted for Davin as he tried to resuscitate his friend. After ten minutes, she placed her hand on Davin's shoulder and whispered gently, "He's gone, Davin."

Davin pulled back, panting from his efforts. "I know," he said with a sigh. He sat back and wrapped his arms around his knees like a sulking child. His head slumped down. Chelsea gave him his space as he sat there breathing heavily. After several minutes, he raised his head. "We should take him down the mountain and give him a proper funeral. And the girl who died during the hurricane, we should honor her as well."

Chelsea nodded.

Davin carried Roy's body down the mountain with a stern expression. He and Chelsea walked in solemn silence. She wished she knew what he was feeling and thinking but knew it was not the time to ask.

When they reached the foot of the mountain, Chelsea helped carry Roy through the high waters and thick mud. On Society grounds, she cleared the way and opened doors for Davin as he walked slowly—weighed down from the weight he carried.

"I want to take him to the hospital until the funeral—make sure there's really nothing we can do and clean him up." Chelsea nodded and led the way.

Davin handed Roy's body over to the robotic medical team when the elevator doors opened, and the team rushed over to assist the hurt resident. "He was struck by lightning the night of the hurricane," he explained. "Looks like his wristband took the initial hit, so it's toast. That's why you didn't know he was hurt or where to find him."

They took a scan of his body in the medical scanner. "I am afraid there's nothing we can do for him. He died two and a half hours ago," the medical bot said.

Davin fell to his knees in anguish. "I could have saved him."

Chelsea knelt down beside him. "It's not your fault, Davin. You did everything you could."

"No," he whispered. Shame washed over him. "If I had searched harder yesterday, I would've found him, and he'd still be alive."

The bot turned to Davin. "If it is any consolation, sir, you should know he also suffered major brain damage and his eardrums burst. He would have been deaf and dumb, and he was likely in a coma when he passed."

"You could've fixed him," Davin retorted.

"We could've repaired his hearing, but his brain damage would have likely been irreversible. The human brain is very complex, and we have yet to fully understand how to repair it. He would have led a half-life."

Davin stood and walked to the window. Leaning against it with one hand, he closed his eyes and inhaled deeply. He tried to forgive himself. He tried to tell himself it wasn't his fault, and more importantly, Roy would want him to move forward and be happy. Roy would want him to be strong. But from past experience, he knew he needed time to grieve, and strength would come later. First, he would honor his friend in a proper ceremony, and he prayed forgiveness would follow.

He contacted Eli over his two-way communication to let him know he had found Roy's body. Then he contacted Lola and asked her to meet them in the hospital wing as soon as possible.

"We found Roy's body on the mountainside today," Davin said when she arrived.

"We?" Lola interrupted as she looked over at Chelsea with a raised brow.

"Yes," Davin answered without further addressing her prying reproach. "I'd like to have a funeral service tomorrow morning for him and the girl who died during the hurricane."

"There was another man who died that night as well," Lola said.

"There was?" asked Davin. "I hadn't heard."

"Yes, you seem to be very distracted these days," Lola said, taking one last look at Chelsea before pulling her gaze back to

Davin. "A man named Truman Wells. He was killed when one of the trees fell. It crashed through his window on the same floor as your living quarters."

"Truman Wells? I know him!" Chelsea blurted out. "Knew him," she corrected. "He was there with me on the beach a few days ago when we were building the sandcastle. I met him my second day at The Society. We had become good friends," Chelsea said, her expression softening at the news of his death.

Lola turned to look at her again and recognized Chelsea from the other day on the beach. *She's the girl Davin was interested in.* She quickly turned back to look at Davin. "So what do you want from me, Davin?"

"I want you to organize the logistics of the service. Get the word out. Figure out what we will need to make it happen," Davin explained.

"Another additional service for being your agent, I suppose?" she asked him as she looked back at Chelsea. Chelsea saw Lola's hatred for her in her cold expression.

"I was hoping it would be more like a favor for a friend in honor of our mutual friend's life," Davin snapped. "I'd like to speak at the service, and I wanted the rest of the evening to gather my thoughts and prepare."

Lola realized how petty she was being, and quickly changed her demeanor. "I'm only kidding, Davin. Of course I'll do it. It'll be a one-hour service at 10:30 tomorrow morning. It'll start in the dome, and then finish at the edge of the forest where we will perform the cremations."

"Thank you, Lola. We'll see you in the morning." He then turned and looked in Chelsea's direction. "You ready?" Chelsea nodded, and they walked past Lola and headed back to the elevator.

When they boarded the elevator, Davin said, "I don't think I want any dinner tonight. You go on without me. I need to think about what I'm going to say tomorrow."

"Okay," Chelsea agreed. "Are you sure you'll be all right?"

"Yes, I think so. You go ahead," he affirmed.

AT DINNER, CHELSEA SAT at her normal table in Tower One and picked slowly at her small plate of food.

"There you are!" Finley said as she sat down next to Chelsea. "Where have you been?" Not pausing long enough for Chelsea to answer, she said, "Guess what I did today?" Chelsea shrugged her shoulders, not caring what it could be at the moment. "I set Branch straight! I'm going to be fixing the broken windows with you tomorrow." Finley was beaming with pride. She was in an annoyingly good mood in contrast to Chelsea's sad disposition. "I had to do some convincing with a hardcore make-out session," she said, leaning in and whispering into Chelsea's ear for the last bit. "But I did it! No more gardening for me," she said as she quivered at the thought of touching another plant.

"Good for you," Chelsea said unenthusiastically. "You always have very creative ways of getting what you want."

"He was kind of a jerk about it, but hey, if it means I don't have to garden anymore, I was willing to do just about anything," Finley said.

"Hey, I gotta go. It's been a long day. I'll talk to you later," Chelsea said as she stood up to leave.

"Seriously?" Finley said. "I haven't even heard what you've been up to."

"Next time," Chelsea said over her shoulder as she left. She had lots to tell Finley, but she wasn't ready to tell her yet. As she walked, she suddenly got a request to talk on the two-way radio, but it wasn't Branch's voice telling her what her task was for the following day as she expected.

"Chelsea," Davin's shaky voice whispered, "can you come to my room?"

Her mind filled with worry. "Sure. What's going on?"

"Nothing. Nothing," he said, and then there was an uncomfortable silence. He had a hard time saying it. "I just don't want to be alone tonight."

CHELSEA KNOCKED, and Davin opened his door. He stood there slumped up against the wall. Despite the sadness in his eyes, he smiled the best he could. "Turns out it's pretty rough to write a eulogy for your best friend," he said.

"I bet," Chelsea said, coming in and giving him a hug.

He grabbed her hand and led her to the bed. He lay down, bringing her with him, and then he pulled Chelsea close to his chest and ran his hands through her hair as he held her head close to his own. They stayed in that position for a long while until Davin let the question that was worrying him break the silence. "Will you stay with me?" he whispered, thinking of all the friends and family who had left him too early. He wasn't actually asking her if she would choose to stay. It was a question posed to the universe, wondering if she too was doomed to some tragic ending as so many of his friends had been.

Chelsea didn't realize the true depth of his question. "As long as you will have me," Chelsea replied with a smile.

Davin chuckled, thinking, *That may be longer than you bargained for.* Aloud, he said, "I'm hoping I'll be able to sleep tonight if you do stay. Are you okay with that?"

"Yes," Chelsea said as she reached up and gave him a small kiss. She grabbed the blanket from the edge of the bed and spread it out over him. She ran her fingers through his hair until his muscles relaxed from the strain of the taxing day. He rested his head against her shoulder, and the tangled emotions of despair and nostalgia that strangled him as he wrote his friend's eulogy melted away with each stroke of her hand. His eyes closed, and he thought of nothing—he was done thinking, he was done feeling. He concentrated his focus on the sweet smell of her skin. Taking in long, deep breaths, he soon fell into a deep slumber.

DAVIN WOKE UP just before the sun rose the next morning. Chelsea rested peacefully beside him, curled up in a ball with her back against him. That made him smile, and he leaned back and looked up at the mirror on the ceiling above him. Seeing the two of them lying next to each other seemed right. *We look good together*, he thought, though he had never really doubted they would. He had imagined this moment many times, but he had honestly never thought it was a possibility—not after their initial encounters.

Then he remembered they were holding Roy's funeral that day. It would be a long, hard day. However, somehow he had a strange sense of strength that he'd lacked the night before. He no longer felt the urge to dwell on the tragic loss of his friend. He only wanted to focus on what a wonderful person Roy was. He would strive to honor Roy's friendship and share in his optimism for life.

He silently slipped out of bed, careful not to wake Chelsea, and he grabbed his PED to look over the notes he'd spent several hours scribbling out the night before. He read them over and sighed in disappointment. It did not seem a good enough tribute. Davin was a talented actor, but a writer he was not. However, he wanted his words to be genuine, not some perfected script without an authentic voice behind it. He needed to be the one who wrote it. It wouldn't be perfect, but it would be from the heart.

He looked at the time and realized they should start getting ready so they would have enough time to get breakfast before the service. Setting his PED back down on his desk, he made his way to the side of the bed and sat down beside Chelsea. He moved her hair out of her face and kissed her forehead. When she did not wake, he decided to let her rest. He grabbed a change of clothes and headed to the bathroom to shower.

He stood in front of the mirror, yearning to rehearse some monumental speech prepared for him by an inspired, professional writer. He had become so used to delivering polished speeches written by others that he found it uncomfortable to utter the words he had written himself. Roy was the first true friend that Davin had made after losing his friends to the earthquake. The world had felt so lonely before Roy, and it was starting to feel lonely again without him. However, after he showered and cleaned up for the day, he popped his head out of the bathroom door to spot Chelsea sitting up in bed. When she smiled, the world suddenly felt less lonely again.

"Good morning," he said, pulling his shirt on and running his fingers through his hair to brush it up off his forehead.

"Hi. How you doing?" Chelsea asked with some residual concern from the night before.

"Better," Davin said. "Much better." He sat next to her in bed and put his arm around her shoulder. After giving her a slow, soft kiss, he said, "You'll need to hurry. You slept in."

Then a request came up on both of their wristbands. They accepted the request and listened to the announcement that sounded in the earpieces. "There will be a funeral service for the three members of our Society who we lost to the destruction of the recent hurricane," a recording of Lola's voice gracefully chimed. "Please join us in the dome at 10:30 a.m. as Davin Chapman leads us in a tribute to the lives of Roy Wilson, Truman Wells, and Rose Johnson. Thank you."

Before Chelsea left to get ready, Davin asked her what he could say about her friend Truman.

"He had a quiet sweetness to him. He was humble and unexpectedly witty at times, and he was always up for spending time with a friend. When he spoke to you, he had a way of making you feel like you were the only person in the room. I always liked that about him," Chelsea said, looking into the distance and remembering the face of her friend.

"Thanks. That helps a lot. I'll see you at breakfast," he said. While Davin stayed in his room to prepare his final thoughts on a tribute for Rose and Truman, Chelsea quickly returned to her room to get ready.

In the cafeteria, they ate the last of the supplies of bacon and eggs. They would need a shipment of livestock from the mainland to replace the animals they had lost to the storm soon, but Ms. Waverly was not going to allow outsiders to know the condition of The Society until after they had repaired the majority of the destruction and the water levels were back to normal. Until that time, she planned to keep communications down and hold all shipments.

"Hey, Chelsea. I was wondering if you would be willing to work as the video engineer for the funeral service?" Davin asked. "It would just be a camera shot and scrolling through pictures of Roy, Truman, and Rose as I talk about each of them. Everyone knows you're the best at The Society."

"Of course. I planned on doing it anyway," Chelsea said.

"Great. Thank you so much." He was happy she would be there for both technical and emotional support.

When breakfast was over, they both headed directly to the dome's stage to set up for the funeral service. Chelsea turned on the system and created a simple graphic for each of the deceased residents. Then she handed Davin a microphone.

Davin's heart sank knowing he was about to publicly acknowledge the loss of his friend. Chelsea reached up to give him a supportive kiss before he took the stage, but as her lips hit his, he reciprocated her affection tenfold—his passion acting as an outlet for his pain.

Lola switched on a single spotlight aimed for center stage, and she cued Davin via their open line of two-way communication. "Whenever you're ready, Davin," he heard in his ear.

Breaking away from his kiss with Chelsea, Davin turned and gathered his composure. Chelsea had to gather her composure as well after being surprised by his rather indulgent kiss. She shook off her surprise and returned to her station before switching to Davin's hover camera on the screen as he walked into the light of the spotlight.

As he examined the crowd, he was disappointed to see that only a portion of the residents had come for the ceremony. Standing still in the spotlight for a moment, he let out a sigh before he began. "Today we gather to honor the lives of three of our fellow residents." He paused, and then corrected himself, " . . . three of our friends. Today we remember our friends Rose Johnson, Truman Wells, and Roy Wilson.

"I did not personally know Rose—but I was there when she died. She was helping me open the door to assist in getting others to safety. She didn't have to, but she stepped forward to help without hesitation. She was brave and strong, and she put herself in harm's way without worrying about whether or not she could or should help. I needed her strength that night, but like so much of the grounds of our Society, her life was destroyed by the storm." A picture of Rose smiling on the beach appeared on the wall behind Davin as he finished his tribute. "We honor her life and her bravery—rest in peace, Rose," he said as he bowed his head and allowed for a moment of silence.

"I never met Truman Wells so I didn't think I would do his character justice with my own words. Instead, I will share with you the words of love a friend of his shared with me this morning." With that, Davin shared Chelsea's tribute to Truman word for word. Chelsea's eyes started to fill with tears as she heard her own words honoring her lost friend. She switched to Truman's picture on the screen as Davin spoke. Seeing Truman's wide smile and large puppy dog eyes made Chelsea's heart fill with emotion. She tried to fight back the tears.

She had never lost a close friend before. It was a hurt she had never known. She not only felt the regret of how she might have been a better friend to him, but she also ached for the life he still had yet to live. He was so young. Her guilt swelled inside when she realized how much she had taken him for granted. His quiet disposition often left him forgotten in the background. She wished she had told him how much she appreciated his friendship and had taken time to tell him what a great person he was when she still had the chance. Now her words and compliments rang out to the deaf ears of an audience who was equally guilty of the same neglect. After the moment of silence for Truman, Chelsea cleared her throat and wiped away the few tears that had escaped with her shame.

"I did know Roy Wilson," Davin continued. "He was the best friend I could've ever asked for," he said, struggling to keep his composure. "He was the kind of man who made you want to be a little kinder, a little better, every time you were around him. I knew him as a child, and even then, he had a strong and loyal heart. He cared deeply for others and his optimism throughout life was inspiring. Roy had a longing for adventure, and arguably the best accent you could have in this world." He chuckled as he thought about Roy's mild New Zealand accent and the phrases he used to use. "His upbeat, positive attitude could brighten your day when you needed it most, and his curiosity for life was contagious. I'm a better man for having known Roy. Kia Kaha, my friend." Roy's picture appeared on the screen behind Davin as silence ensued.

After the moment of silence for Roy, Davin raised his head with pursed lips, unsure if he should share the hopes he was feeling. "I know this isn't a popular notion anymore," he began. "But I would like to believe that this is not the end for our friends. My deepest hope is that they are in a better place. A place where they know just how loved they truly are, and where someone with a more perfect love is waiting for them, to show them the way." At this point, people began to stand up and leave the dome to begin their task work, not caring to hear the rest of the fantasy Davin had clearly bought into. He bowed his head in grief at their disregard, but the hope of his words helped him raise his head again and finish the program.

"My lovely cohost, Kona, will now join me in a small musical tribute to our lost friends," said Davin as Kona joined him from backstage with a beautiful ukulele in hand. Together they performed the most beautiful rendition of "Somewhere Over the Rainbow" that Chelsea had ever heard. Kona's voice danced above Davin's low steady tone as she effortlessly strummed a beautiful countermelody that she had composed the night before. At the end of the song, Kona stepped forward, and through thick tears, she invited all to attend the cremation ceremony.

Those who still remained followed the group down to the grounds. The floodwaters had dissipated around the forest and Tower One, and there on the ground rested the bodies of Roy, Rose, and Truman. Davin and a few other close friends moved forward to carry the bodies of their friends to the prepared Bermuda juniper pyres.

As the flames grew over the bodies, Davin stared across them into the face of Ms. Waverly. He studied her blank expression and wondered what secrets she may be hiding behind her cold eyes. Then he looked down into the face of his friend and was reminded of Roy's resolve to uncover the truth concealed within the walls of the cave, and a fire was lit inside him. He said his final goodbye to his friend, and then made a promise to uncover the truth. He closed his eyes as he grabbed Chelsea's hand and squeezed it tight.

Ms. Waverly looked over at Davin—holding the hand of the dome's video engineer—and smiled.

15. BLIND SEARCHING

ONCE THE WATER RECEDED back to normal levels, the grounds slowly began to look recognizable again. A little more than a month had passed since the hurricane, and the best networker at The Society was supposedly working to restore communications with the mainland, but word was that there had still been no headway. All the broken windows had been repaired. That, of course, irritated Finley, because it forced her to work around the grounds. She regretted not prolonging the process.

The number one priority was restoring produce growth before the Society ran out of food storage entirely. After a month of cleanup, no communication with family, and being cooped inside anytime they weren't slogging through the muddy grounds, everyone was acting very anxious.

"Ugh, I don't think I can do it anymore, Chelsea," Finley said as they sat down to dinner one evening.

"I know. Once we get normal food again, I don't think I will ever be able to take another bite of oatmeal again," Chelsea said as she glumly looked at her small portion of plain oatmeal for dinner. The residents had tasted nothing but oatmeal for the past several days, and it was quickly losing its appeal. Thankfully, the first harvest would be soon, and they were promised that variety would be reintroduced into their meals again at that point.

"Not that. Though I'm totally with you there. If I weren't so hungry, there's no way I could stomach another bite," Finley said as she scooped up a spoonful of oatmeal with her spoon and watched it splat back down into her bowl. "But I'm talking about all this gardening we have to do. You think we'll be able to choose our tasks again after the first harvest? I'm going crazy. I'm seriously going to be the next person who loses it at this rate."

"What do you mean 'the next person who loses it'?"

"You didn't hear?" Finley perked up. "Another guy went berserk and had to leave today when he was asked to comply to sitting out his meal for the day."

"Leave?" Chelsea again questioned where they could be sending people without a transporter pod around. "*Another* guy? This has happened before?"

"It happened the first time right after the hurricane hit," Finley explained. "Kind of weird, 'cause it's not like we hadn't been eating well up until that point, but apparently he threw this big tantrum and put up quite the fight."

"How odd." Chelsea knew Davin would want to hear about this. She shoveled the few bites she had of the oatmeal dinner into her mouth and swallowed each spoonful whole to avoid tasting it. Even the texture made her want to gag, but her stomach appreciated the respite to her hunger. "I'm off. I'll see you tomorrow sometime," Chelsea told Finley. Chelsea had asked Davin if she could spend one meal a day with Finley to keep her questions at bay until she was comfortable telling her what was really happening between them.

"What? You just barely got here. Where are you always off to these days?" Finley asked.

"Just . . . helping with the grounds. Saving my energy. Stuff like that," Chelsea replied, trying to sound innocent. Finley gave her a look of skepticism. "Listen, I'll fill you in on the details more later, but in the meantime, someone's got to get stuff done so you don't have to rummage through the dirt forever, right?"

"True that," Finley said while taking her first bite of oatmeal. She knew Chelsea had more to spill, but it was obvious she wasn't going to share at the moment, so she settled for the hope of her gardening days ending sooner than later. Chelsea walked away seeing that Finley was satisfied with her answer for the time being, or at least that she had moved on. She heard her turn to the person sitting beside her and ask, "Do *you* know if we get to pick our own tasks after the harvest?"

Chelsea flicked her wrist and located Davin's contact information to request to talk with him directly over the two-way communication. "Davin, this is Chelsea. You done with dinner?"

"Yeah. I finished a while ago. Doesn't take me to long to finish my tiny bowl of oatmeal," he said, laughing. "I'm in my room."

"Okay. I'll head your way. We need to talk."

Davin was livid when she told him the news. The fact that the list of missing persons was growing was a sure sign of trouble in his mind, and he was certain the Society leaders must have purposefully kept this information from him. Of course, for the time being, he would only share his true feelings with Chelsea. "Doesn't anyone find it odd that people are 'leaving' The Society without *any* trace of a transporter pod?" he asked without waiting for an answer. "Do people not think about this? Or do they just not care?" He took off his dirty shirt from the day and angrily threw it into the hole at the top shelf of his closet to be cleaned and folded by the insta-laundry system found in each resident's room, and then he jumped onto the bed next to Chelsea. Letting out a huge sigh, he said, "I don't know how much longer I can keep playing this charade. I've always been good at pretending, but this role is a never-ending one."

Pretending. The word scared Chelsea. *How will I know if Davin is pretending with me?* Despite her apprehension about The Society and her hungry stomach at night, Chelsea had never been so happy. Each day with Davin was wonderful. But she couldn't help but worry that it was all temporary—or worse, an act. Davin had given her no reason to believe so, but memories from her past hopeful relationships still scared her into believing it could all be a lie. She tried not to entertain the thought. She knew he didn't deserve her mistrust. She silenced her fears and responded to Davin's concerns as soon as she came back to her senses.

"But we can't just assume these people are 'missing.' There might be an explanation. It's all speculation and theory, and someone like you can't just walk away without people noticing," Chelsea pointed out.

"You're right. I need to be patient. We need to stick with the plan and find that cave—figure out what's really going on before getting too worked up," Davin replied.

Davin and Chelsea lay in silence for a moment and gazed up at each other in the mirror on the ceiling. "Why do those words feel *so* good to hear?" Chelsea asked with a mischievous grin.

"What words?" he asked, and then, after a moment, he realized. "'*You're right*'?" Chelsea held back a laugh. "Oh, you're a punk," he growled, rolling on top of her to hold her down with his weight while he tickled her.

He began kissing her neck as she curled up in protest, laughing out loud. His lips made their way up her neck to her earlobe, and he used his teeth to gently tug it. His hands moved her arms up to playfully pin her down, but she unexpectedly twisted and forced his weight under her—leaving him pinned instead as she straddled him.

He lay frozen with wide eyes—he hadn't realized Chelsea's physical strength. He knew she was a particularly toned woman but was still impressed. It turned him on. Catching *her* off guard this time, he sat up, quickly sneaking his hands under the back of her shirt and kissing her intensely. As he ran his hands down her bare back, he had the strongest urge to let them wander around to her front, but he pulled away, realizing he was letting his attraction for her take control of his actions. He was losing his strength to resist. It was getting harder every day to keep his promise to her. He hung his head and took a deep breath.

"It's okay," Chelsea whispered in his ear. Despite the irrational fears that still loomed in the back of her mind, she felt safer with Davin than she had ever felt with anyone. He was slowly convincing her with each day that he really was interested in something long-term. And even more unbelievable—rather than his own self-gratification, his motive was to make *her* happy. That alone made her willing to release Davin from his promise.

"No. No, it's not okay," he said, looking into her dark brown eyes. "It's not good enough—not for you. I really want to keep my promise to you," he said as her arms fell to her side in disappointment. "Listen, I'm falling for you more and more every day—and I'm not even sure how that's possible, because I've never felt such an intense draw to someone right off the bat before. So don't think I don't want you. But I still want to be sure, because I would *never* want to hurt you. I want you to know it will be forever, not just for the night," he said, trying to remind her why he made his promise in the first place. Still finding it hard to resist, he slowly removed his hands from her shirt and moved out from under her straddle. "I need a cold shower."

He was taking a lot of those lately.

Chelsea lay back on the empty bed, silently regretting her initial resistance to Davin's advances, but thankful that when it did happen, she would be more certain than she ever was before. She truly did appreciate Davin's resolve to keep his promise, but she worried it could be years before he could wholeheartedly promise to love her *forever*—that was a big commitment. She hoped it was only a matter of time until he could no longer resist her.

After an irritatingly long shower, Davin stepped out of the bathroom. "I think I need to keep my distance a little more. This is a lot harder than I thought it was going to be. So don't worry if I'm not as physical as I have been lately," he said, somewhat ashamed of his inability to maintain his control. "I just know my limits, and I can't keep pushing them."

"I suppose I should be happy I actually found a guy who *wants* to keep his promises to me," replied Chelsea with an unenthusiastic chuckle.

"Honestly, I'm already having a hard time imagining life without you. I just want to give it some time," he said with a charming smile that made Chelsea's heart flutter. She still couldn't understand what it was that drew him to her. *What about ME could he find so irresistible?* She was so painfully ordinary in her reflection. It was hard to believe the man everyone found so desirable could find her so appealing.

WHISPERS BEGAN TO SPREAD throughout The Society that the ever romantically aloof Davin Chapman seemed to be favoring one girl in particular. Few people knew her name and some believed the whispers to be nothing more than rumor—attributing the story to Davin's usual friendly demeanor. Others whispered sightings of stolen kisses and handholding around the grounds.

When Chelsea finally told Finley about Davin, Finley just about went into hysterics. She was shocked the rumors were true and that Chelsea was the one dating Davin Chapman, and even more shocked Chelsea hadn't slept with him yet. Chelsea was also beginning to struggle with that fact.

❖

The morning of the harvest, Ms. Waverly arranged for a meeting at the dome. She again showed up unexpectedly in Davin's room with a plate of food to personally brief him on what he was to say and do at the meeting.

As people gathered in the dome, Davin took a deep breath to help him get into character and act like he was all right. But in reality, Ms. Waverly's visit had left him on edge—her conduct had seemed almost threatening as she asked him to comply with her demands. He grew more anxious each day to begin the search for the cave, but for now, he had to wait—and play his part.

Standing up straight and grinning wide, he took the stage. "Welcome to the first of a series of celebrations we will host as The Society rises from the ashes of the hurricane's destruction! Let me be the first to communicate an overwhelming thank you to *you*— the fine people of The Hawaii Society who have made that possible! You are the reason we are here today—celebrating and preparing to have our first harvest this afternoon!" The crowd applauded with what energy they could muster and then stopped short to find out what more Davin had to report. "Water levels have returned to normal. Our trees and gardens are beginning to grow at comparable rates to those before the storm. And today, for the harvest only, *everyone* will get to feast on the rewards of your labors." With the word feast, the crowd erupted into a loud cheer. "Now before we start the celebrations and begin the first pick of the harvest, Ms. Waverly would like to address us." Ms. Waverly emerged from the shadows behind the screen.

"Thank you, Davin. Yes, I have some updates for you. As Davin explained, things are progressing well in our quest for normalcy. As of today, residents are still required to sit out one meal and complete a minimum of six hours of work a day, but recreational activities will again be made available to residents at your convenience." The audience stood and cheered in unison with overflowing enthusiasm. It was a day everyone was waiting for—the day in the path to recovery when people would be allowed to enjoy the outdoors again.

Davin was especially ecstatic. He cheered backstage and turned to Chelsea's workstation to shoot her a smile. As soon as they were able, they would each grab a mask and fins and make their way to the turquoise waters to search for the cave.

"I'm glad to hear you're excited about this news. You should also be glad to know that I have been told communications should be restored very soon as well."

The crowd gave a much less enthusiastic cheer—bearing in mind it had been an empty promise that had already been given many times to anyone who inquired about it.

"I'll believe it when I see it," one man in the crowd commented to the person next to him.

"When communications are restored, we'll be able to order a shipment of livestock and supplies from the mainland. That will be a crucial shipment, necessary to fully restore our former way of life, but for today, please join me in celebrating our first harvest."

As she exited the stage, everyone cheered, relieved to finally be participating in a high-spirited activity. A band made up of a few musically inclined residents entered the stage and performed a series of songs about rising up and overcoming. The crowd cheered and bounced up and down to the music. Finley sat at her lighting console, working her magic to provide the best concert atmosphere she had ever designed. She cheered with elation as the band played, simply happy that she was not working in the gardens for the time being.

After the band performed their last song, Davin returned to the stage with Kona. "We will now make our way to the gardens and orchards to pick the first spoils of the harvest. Everyone is welcome to enjoy eating his or her first pick. After that, please continue harvesting all the ripe fruit, and bring it all to the harvest bins that the ground bots will be carrying so they can bring our harvest to the kitchens," Kona explained.

"Then maybe, just maybe," Davin said with a smile, "we can all get some time out on the water to enjoy ourselves!" The audience stood and cheered as they all raced for the exits—excited to begin the harvest and get out on the water.

No one had to sit out the first pick of the harvest. For the first time in over a month, everyone ate together and happily enjoyed an item of produce. Davin and Chelsea both made their way to the trunk of the peach tree where Chelsea picked a ripe peach for herself, and Davin picked a peach using a nearby stepstool. They smiled at each other, thinking back to their first encounter. The sunshine was bright on the outstretched ocean, and its warm rays made everyone feel joyful again. The taste of freshly picked fruit and the prospect of more to come brought everyone some much-needed relief.

After picking three baskets of fruit, Davin and Chelsea headed straight for the escapading gear. "It's finally time. We can start escapading!" Chelsea ran excitedly to the gear and handed Davin a set of fins and a mask. Anyone passing by wouldn't have guessed that her enthusiasm was more from the possibility of her questions being answered than from the amusement of floating in the water among colorful tropical fish with The Society's most eligible bachelor.

"Yeah, let's get out there! We only have an hour or two before we need to get back to do more cleanup, and I only have a general direction of where we should look," Davin said.

They ran for the shore and jumped in, pulling their masks and fins on after getting a few feet deep into the cool, clear water.

"Let's do this," Davin said, smiling while taking Chelsea's hand in his.

In two hours' time, they returned to shore having seen the kind of beautiful tropical fish and coral reefs that most people only dream to behold, but neither of them was happy about it. They had seen no trace of a cave at all. They weren't sure where to look, and as they arbitrarily searched, they realized they would need a strategy if they were going to avoid looking in the same places repeatedly.

They each still had three hours of task work to complete that day. Branch informed Davin he was assigned to pump water out of various parts of The Society grounds. He was told to start at the pool covers so that the pools could be reopened for use as soon as possible. After people had used the gear that day, a number of complaints were given about the gear being dirty from being scattered all over during the hurricane. Consequently, Chelsea was tasked with cleaning the gear in the Outdoor Recreation Supply Room and then reorganizing it. They went their separate ways and got to work.

The three hours went by quickly. There was still so much to do to make the grounds as clean and kempt as they originally were. The work to restore things to the way they used to be sometimes felt endless, especially while trying to maintain the essential tasks of gardening and repairs. No one had the option of training or education classes within the six-hour work shifts anymore.

After an enjoyable game of virtual golfing as they sat out dinner, Chelsea and Davin went back to Chelsea's room to chart out an escapading route. They used a large piece of very thin bark to draw out a map and mark possible locations of the cave entrance. Davin had found the piece of bark during his task that afternoon and thought it could be used for this purpose since paper and pencils were very hard to come by. Typically, everything was digital, but digital could be traced, and Davin felt strongly that it was not a good idea to use their PEDs for what they were doing. They used charcoal Davin had gathered from the bonfire pits for a pencil. It was incredibly difficult and messy to write with charcoal though, so Chelsea and Davin agreed to make the map as simple as possible to keep frustrations down.

They began by drawing a simple outline of the island and all the possible areas in the water used for escapading where one might find a cave entrance. Then they created seven different zones and prioritized the zones for the search based on what geographical information they knew and the direction in which Davin saw Roy go to explore the cave. There was only a small portion of zone one that they felt comfortable marking off as searched from the escapading they had completed that day.

"I think it's a really good idea we did this. It'll track our progress and keep us moving so we won't give up if we don't find it initially," Davin said, looking down at the map as Chelsea finished drawing the last section.

"I wouldn't give up," Chelsea told him, somewhat baffled Davin even considered that a possibility. "Though I agree this map will be very helpful in tracking our progress," she said, drawing a key in the corner that only she would know how to interpret.

"Not intentionally give up—just maybe forgetting why we're doing this as things get back to normal around here and life becomes enjoyable again," he said.

"Once I've decided to do something—and I'm serious about it—I just don't have it in me to forget." She paused to think more about why she operated that way. "I may give up eventually, I suppose—but I could never forget." Her face turned serious as her words came out and she reflected on some past experiences in her life. "I suppose that's why it's so hard for me to get over someone—I can't bring myself to forget about them once I let them in."

"So if I left, would you be able to get over me?" Davin asked with a mischievous smile, trying to figure out how serious she was about their relationship. He slowly worked his body between

Chelsea and the map to divert her attention to him. She stood up straight, facing Davin, since she now had little access to the map.

"Maybe," she said playfully, "but I'm pretty sure every girl has a hard time getting you out of their mind."

"I don't care about every girl," Davin said softly but with fervor. "Just you." Davin's soft, deep voice made Chelsea weak at the knees.

She tried to comprehend how Davin could care for her. It wasn't long ago she was certain he was like all the other men who had pursued her—who cared little about anything other than themselves and their ability to get women. She had always figured when he took note of her, it was merely because he viewed her as forbidden fruit who was playing hard to get. She had never dreamed that he actually liked her.

She had been let down by so many men in the past—including her father when he abandoned her mother. Her father's indifference toward her mother after so many years together had convinced her that an everlasting relationship was a fable from the past. She admitted to herself that it was partially because she didn't see herself as particularly attractive, but Davin did not seem to feel that way. She could see it in his eyes and taste it in his kiss—he wanted her, and she wanted him.

Davin was still waiting as she thought. He raised his eyebrows. "So? Could you get over me?"

Chelsea knew the answer, but instead of answering him directly, she began to kiss him—hoping it would communicate what she was somehow unable to put into words.

There was no getting over him. She was in love with him—and always would be.

She could only hope that what they had would be never-ending. Despite all her fears telling her that nothing good could ever last, she wanted to believe in her heart that together they could prove that sentiment wrong.

Not to say that there weren't plenty of times that Chelsea worried they weren't entirely compatible. From experience, Chelsea knew her hardheaded ways and blunt tongue always threatened her personal life. And there were things about Davin that infuriated her, like the way his cool confidence came across as cocky at times or the fact that he was clearly under his mother's finger by the way he spoke about their interactions. But, every time she found herself frustrated or annoyed with him, she chose him anyway. It was as though she had no choice in the matter—like her love for him was a reflex and only he had the ability to break her of her stubborn and guarded disposition.

As they kissed, Chelsea's mind reeled with all these feelings. Then her thoughts suddenly went silent, and all she could focus on were Davin's hands that were now tracing the front of her body. Before she could react, he pulled away and put his hands behind his back. Still smiling, but more solemn, he announced, "I'm going to head back to my room now."

Chelsea surmised a number of depressing reasons why he would retract from her body so suddenly. *I bet he was disappointed.*

"In the morning, we should wake up early and do some more escapading. We'll start back in zone one and get as far as we can. Does that sound good to you?"

"Yeah," Chelsea replied quietly, lowering her glance and pushing her bangs back from her face.

"Don't go reading into this," Davin said, sensing Chelsea's change in demeanor. "I told you I need some more space—for me—not because of you. I mean, kind of because of you . . . on account of the fact I can't keep my hands off you," he explained, chuckling. That made Chelsea happy, and she put her worries to rest. "I need you to believe I mean that." Davin looked into Chelsea's eyes.

"Okay," Chelsea said, unable to hold back a satisfied grin as she answered.

THE NEXT MORNING, DAVIN woke Chelsea at six. They crept down to the escapading gear and gathered their things before beginning their second attempt to find the cave. They made sure to thoroughly search every rock and crevasse they encountered, but they again returned with no luck.

Chelsea marked off zone one with the charcoal when she got back to her room and sighed as she looked over the remaining six zones. They were much larger areas, and for the next week, Chelsea and Davin continued to search the turquoise waters as often as they could during their free time. They were able to mark off zone two and part of three but still had the majority of the map left. As much as Chelsea liked escapading, it was beginning to lose its appeal quickly.

ONE AFTERNOON, WHEN they had planned to go out on another escapading route, Davin ran up to Chelsea. "I know we said we were going out escapading, but I think we need a little break," he said, smiling. Chelsea was tentative at first, but the sound of something other than escapading did sound enticing. Seeing her soften to the idea, Davin continued, "How about you show me how to flyboard today?"

Chelsea's face lit up. "Seriously? Yes! That would be so much fun. You're right, we do need a break," she submitted eagerly.

Davin swung his arm around Chelsea's shoulders, and they began walking toward the flyboard station. He was thrilled she was happy with the idea. He leaned in playfully and whispered, "Those words *are* nice to hear from you," referring to Chelsea saying that he was right. She instantly knew exactly what he was referring to and rolled her eyes with a small laugh at his playful banter.

To begin, Chelsea read through the instructions and safety warnings with Davin. He patiently listened to her read as she added her own commentary to each rule and instruction.

Then Chelsea grabbed a flyboard, and they hopped on a quad ski to get out on open water so she could demonstrate. Davin thoroughly enjoyed seeing her so excited. She threw out the flyboard and turned toward him to show him how to properly strap the board to his feet. He watched intently, hoping he would remember her instruction when it came his turn. She showed him all the controls and what each one did.

"It's really simple once you get the feel of it. The trick is to keep your balance." And with that, she shot into the air with a massive rush of water streaming out from under the board. She weaved back and forth and circled around Davin on the quad ski. Then she rushed forward and dove headfirst into the water, only to emerge twenty feet away as she spun in a circle in the air. Davin smiled, impressed but not surprised. She slowly released the power to the jet stream and gently sunk back into the water. He applauded as she swam toward him.

"That was awesome!" he exclaimed.

"You're up," Chelsea said with a smile, excited for him to try.

"Okay," Davin said and dismounted the quad ski.

Chelsea stayed in the water and walked him through how to strap the board on one more time. After getting the board properly attached, he was feeling ready to try it out. Chelsea returned to the quad ski to watch from above water.

With some coaxing from Chelsea, he hesitantly put his finger on the trigger and braced himself as he pushed down slowly. He began rising up above the water. He felt the adrenaline pulsing throughout his veins. He smiled wide—feeling he was doing pretty well for his first try. He was about four feet above the water when he thought to try turning. He angled his foot up slightly as Chelsea had instructed beforehand, and with that, he plummeted headfirst into the water.

Thankfully, he remembered Chelsea had told him to pull his finger off the trigger if that were to happen, and with the help of his lifejacket, he popped to the top of the water soon after falling. Chelsea struggled not to laugh at his shocked expression as she swam toward him.

"You all right?" she asked him as he lay flat floating atop the water.

"Yeah, pretty sure it's just my pride that's bruised," he joked in a tense voice, still jittery from the fall.

"You were doing great. I think you just lifted your foot a little too abruptly," she said. "You want to head back and call it a day?"

"One more time," Davin said with determination.

"Okay." She gave him a quick kiss and swam back to the quad ski.

This time he rose out of the water much quicker and almost lost his balance at the top of his ascent. He re-centered himself just in time and even moved forward a little before falling back into the ocean—this time swallowing a decent amount of salt water. After that, they returned to the equipment room to bring back the quad ski and hang up the flyboard for the day.

They spent the rest of their free time simply lying on the sandy beach, talking and laughing about nothing in particular, until someone nearby walked up to them.

"So Davin, what *is* this exactly?" he asked, motioning to the two of them. The man maintained eye contact with Davin and acted as if Chelsea did not exist.

Davin's brow furrowed at first, then his expression lightened as he answered. "Well, we're together if that's what you're referring to. And who are you?" Davin asked. He could never understand how complete strangers felt they could approach him and involve themselves in his life without actually knowing him—but he was used to it.

"Just a longtime fan—asking the same thing everyone's been wondering. Trying to figure out how someone like you got whipped by her," the man replied in disgust, pointing to Chelsea.

Davin wanted to punch the man squarely on the chin for being so rude. The fact that he had no regard for how this comment would affect Chelsea made him furious. It was one thing when people insulted him, but it was far more difficult to hear someone belittle Chelsea. However, he thought better of his initial reaction and hoped he would be able to fix any damage the man had inflicted on Chelsea later.

Trying to maintain his composure the best he could, Davin said the only courteous thing he could think to say. "And I can't figure out how you can't see it." Then Davin grabbed Chelsea's hand and pulled her up with him. They walked past the man while Davin gave the man a sorry pat on the back.

There was silence for a short moment as they walked. Then Chelsea spoke before Davin had been able to come up with a way to communicate all the things he wanted to say. "He's right, you know. You could do a lot better than me," she said matter-of-factly.

"If you really believe that, then I don't think you see you how *I* see you," Davin said. "I find you extremely attractive."

Chelsea gave him a reluctant half-smile before continuing her denial of her supposed good looks. "Even so, there are girls out there with the kind of beauty no man can deny—with much better bodies than mine."

"That's not how I see it," he said, a look of bewilderment on his face. "You have to understand that every guy has his type. Granted, some guys will settle for any girl with a heartbeat, and it's true that a lot of men want a girl with the kind of body the world has told him he should like. But usually every guy has something different he looks for in a woman, and I've been looking for you my whole life."

"Come on—that's not true. Everyone can pick out the most beautiful girl in a crowd," Chelsea said. "There's no mystery to what beauty is."

Davin stopped walking and pulled her around to look at him. His voice was soft but intense. "Beauty isn't limited to an exact definition. Beauty is simply the lure that draws each person in—and you've pulled me in, Chelsea Coremon," he said lovingly, his lips lingering inches from hers and the soft hum of his deep voice still echoing in her ear.

She couldn't help but be smitten by his charm as he spoke.

He traced her face with his fingers as he continued. "Just like some people prefer the mountains over the plains or the sand to the snow, I'm drawn to you like a sailor is drawn to the waves of the sea," Davin said, smiling. "So as long as you don't mind that you aren't some *other* guy's type, I would appreciate it if you wouldn't insult *my* type and believe me when I say—I think you're *gorgeous*."

Then Davin kissed her without shame on the banks of the crowded shore as onlookers stared in shock. His kiss contained a passion that brought truth to his words. And despite the man's rude comments toward her, it had been a good day—her favorite yet. Beyond their enjoyable time together, it was the day she would come to remember as the day Davin helped her believe that she could be beautiful—even if it was only to him. He was the only one that mattered.

16. STARS ALIGN

AT THE NEXT CELEBRATION meeting, Ms. Waverly took the stage to make a big announcement. "Thank you all for coming. I have very good news this morning. I am pleased to announce we were able to temporarily make contact with the mainland." There were some claps heard throughout the dome, but the news of a temporary connection was underwhelming considering how long it took to get to that point. "During our communication, we were able to request a part that we need from the mainland in order to restore communications permanently. The transporter pod is on its way to deliver that part as soon as possible!" The audience joined together in applause at the news. Some even cheered and whistled at the thought of real progress toward a viable solution.

"I would also like to inform you that once the transporter pod has arrived with the part and communication has been restored, the four former residents who have chosen to leave us will be taking the transporter pod back home." Davin breathed a sigh of relief and joined the crowd in clapping their approval. Though it was still disconcerting to think they had been hidden away, at least Waverly was openly addressing it, and this wrong would soon be righted. "I know a few of their friends have been concerned for them, but I assure you they were taken care of while waiting for their ride home."

Davin walked over to Chelsea at the video switcher and knelt down beside her. "Maybe there's a good explanation after all," he said with a smile. Chelsea nodded with hope in her eyes. The prospect of staying at The Society and knowing their concerns were unfounded was a pleasant notion.

After making those important announcements, Ms. Waverly invited Kona to the stage to perform a fire dance. Kona masterfully spun and tossed her fire rod as the hot flames swirled around her in a mesmerizing display. The roaring of the flames was enchanting. Chelsea was constantly amazed by Kona's skill set. There seemed to be no end to her talents as she took the stage each show and surprised everyone with another skillful performance. Her talent and beauty were unmatched on the island—she was truly The Society's native Hawaiian gem. Chelsea pondered in disbelief how Davin had not fallen in love with her from the beginning.

As Chelsea sat at her station, entranced by the swirling fire, Davin came up behind her, giddy and excited with a spontaneous idea. "Let's ditch this and go downstairs to the pool together. My act is all done," he said with a huge grin and wide eyes. "We can lay out on the pool chairs and look up at the stars, and no one will be around to bother us—no one staring or asking nosey questions. Just you and me and the night sky."

"I can't, Davin. I have to finish my part of the show," Chelsea replied.

"Oh, come on. It's electronics—you can program it to do the rest of it or something, right?"

"Well, technically, but the automatic camera switching isn't always accurate on its own. As soon as someone else enters the stage, it could get mixed up without me."

"Kona is the last one on stage. As soon as her act ends, the lights go to blackout, and everyone can leave," Davin told her, hoping she would give in.

Chelsea thought for a minute as to how she could program the remaining time in the show. Once she solidified in her head that she *could* program it with little to no risk to the show, she thought about whether she *should* leave mid-show. It was against everything in her. She never had left a show early before. But, as she looked up into Davin's anxious and excited eyes and imagined a quiet evening alone with him outside, she couldn't help but love the idea—and she liked that Davin had thought of it. She turned to face the switcher and tried to hide her smile as she worked to program the rest of the show so the cameras would follow Kona and the system would shut down five minutes after Kona exited the stage.

"Yes!" Davin exclaimed quietly, concluding Chelsea had decided to come.

After Chelsea had finished the programming, she stood and grabbed Davin's hand. Smiling at one another, they found a moment when no one was looking and bolted for the door to the elevators.

When they arrived at the pool, Davin laid out two chairs beside each other to face what could be seen of the vast starry sky shining over the mountaintop. It was a beautiful view. The stars shone bright in the night sky, and the sound of the ocean waves and a small breeze created a soothing calm. Chelsea and Davin sat together holding hands and looking up into the abyss.

After some time of quiet, Chelsea turned to Davin with a serious expression. She had decided to finally ask the question that had been weighing on her mind for some time. She was reminded of it as they looked up toward the heavens. "So from your remarks at the funeral service, I gather you believe there is a God?" she asked, genuinely curious to hear his response.

Davin, still looking at the stars, answered, "I do." Then he looked back at her. "Why? Do you?"

"I guess you could say I'm undecided. It seems like everyone thinks that people who still do are stuck in a fantasy. All our advances in technology are considered proof that science is the universal ruler, but I just can't help but hope there's a reason for all this beyond living and dying. It's comforting to know on really hard or lonely days, there's always someone looking down who cares—even if no one else does." Chelsea fell quiet for a moment. When Davin did not respond, she continued. "When I start talking like that, though, all I hear in my head are people telling me that believers are just daydreamers who can't face the hard facts of reality. And they point out a number of reasons why the world has been better off since the government took away churches' tax exemption so that most of them had to close their doors. And that if I'm going to buy into such a silly illusion, it's best I keep to myself."

"Sounds like your mind and your heart are telling you two different things," Davin said. "But maybe if you would let go of what everyone else thinks, you'd find your mind and your heart see eye to eye more than you think."

"And why do you think that?"

"Well, everything you just said that makes God a fantasy comes from the opinions of others and from the belief that science is real."

"Which it is," Chelsea stubbornly interrupted.

"Right," Davin agreed. "But what we know of science now was at one point fantasy for those who lived a hundred years before us. So really, science is just our way of trying to understand God and learning to control and understand the elements—as God already does." Davin looked at Chelsea, who was quietly contemplating his words. "Think about it—a known law of science is the rule of entropy. Everyone knows that as soon as you leave something without work, it falls apart. And yet we have a complex and integrated world that operates without our assistance. They always say *nature finds a way*, but I think God really just provides a way."

"I suppose that could make sense," Chelsea thought out loud. "I just feel like a crazy person when I talk about a man in the sky looking out for us and an eventual heaven in order to soften the harsh realities of life and death."

"Well, I really hope I can see my dad and all my friends again one day," said Davin. "I've had so many friends leave without having a chance to say goodbye, without having a chance to tell them how much I really care, and with so little time for them to have a life for themselves. I just can't imagine a world where I never saw them again."

Chelsea felt so bad for him as she thought about how hard it would be to cope with the amount of loss he had already experienced in his short lifetime. She moved over to his chair and grabbed his hand as she sat on his lap. "I can understand that. I would be really sad if, when I die, I never got to see you again."

"Not possible. I'll be there to bug you some more," Davin said with a smile. "It wouldn't be heaven without you."

The line was almost too corny for Chelsea to tolerate, but his playful eyes held her gaze, and she found that she couldn't help but smile back at his good nature. She loved how sweet he was to her.

Staring at his smiling eyes, she couldn't deny she wanted him. The more Davin distanced himself from her, the more she craved his kiss, his touch. How she wished she could take advantage of his physical impulses and convince him he no longer had to keep his promise. As much as she knew his feelings on the matter, she couldn't help but try.

Chelsea ran her fingernails up his familiar hairline—giving him goose bumps down his neck and arms. She rotated her body toward him and brought her leg around in order to straddle the chair with Davin underneath her. As she slowly leaned in, she let her hands trail down his chest to the ends of his shirt and lifted it up over his head. When his shirt came up over his face, she immediately placed her lips on his, and they kissed in slow, passionate strokes. She allowed her tongue to slowly slip across his lower lip in a tantalizing fashion—and then he suddenly stood. With his hands wrapped around her waist, they continued to kiss, and Chelsea wrapped her legs around him and pulled her body close to his.

Davin managed to pull his lips away to speak as Chelsea continued kissing his jawline. She jumped down from his waist and let her hands trail down the ripples of his abs. "I know what you're doing, Chelsea Coremon," he said, "and it won't work." Grabbing her waist and lifting her into the air, Davin threw her into the pool with a splash. The force of the water hitting against her and soaking her clothes disarmed her advances. Her determination dissipated, and she emerged out of the water completely riled.

Davin had followed her into the water and emerged from the air bubbles surrounding them shortly after Chelsea did. He had a wide grin on his face and immediately gave her a short, hard kiss on her pursed lips. "Don't be mad," he pleaded. "I don't know what I would've done to stop you if there wasn't a pool nearby," he said, smiling and affording her some of her confidence back. She splashed at him in playful defeat.

Just then, a bright light lit up their faces. It was a grounds bot. "Swimming in the pool facilities without proper swimwear is not allowed. Please exit the pool immediately. Do you comply?" Chelsea and Davin shielded their eyes from the bright light as they made their way to the edge of the pool.

"Yes, yes. We will get out," Davin replied to the bot. The bot left as soon as it was given assurance of their compliance. "Stupid bot, killing all the fun. Sometimes I wish I could just have my own pool back, and we could jump in with all our clothes on whenever we wanted," he said with a scowl as they climbed out of the pool, and he picked up his shirt and put it back on.

Chelsea was about to agree when she saw the light of the transporter pod approaching the docking station in the dark. "Look, it's the transporter pod," she said, pointing to it.

"Wow," Davin said, "that was quick." They watched as four men in black exited the pod. They quickly ran for the nearest tower. "That's funny, I thought we were getting a piece of equipment, not visitors."

Soon after the four men entered the building, a few residents who were just coming from the end of the meeting to enjoy some late-night fun exited Tower One. Chelsea and Davin hid behind some plants. They watched as some of the residents made their way to the pool and others broke off to walk the grounds. Chelsea and Davin's focus remained fixed on the transporter pod and the tower where the four men had entered. Not thirty minutes after they arrived, the same four men exited the tower wearing baseball caps—walking in a row and escorted by two security bots. They were headed back toward the transporter pod.

Chelsea jumped out from behind the plant where they were hiding and raced toward the transporter pod. Davin was caught off guard, but he followed her lead and ran after her.

To Davin's surprise, Chelsea walked directly up to one of the men and turned him around. "You were the man wearing pineapple shorts that I met on the beach months ago," she said with certainty. The man stood frozen with a stunned expression. "What are you doing here? Why do you keep coming here?"

Suddenly her bracelet lit up and informed her that their internet connection had returned. Multiple notifications from months of no internet started to populate on both Chelsea's and Davin's wrist displays. She looked down at her bracelet and then realized what had happened. "You came to fix the internet, didn't you? Just like last time."

The man looked nervously toward the security bot.

"Stand back," the security bot said. "These residents have chosen to return to the mainland. You will stand down and allow them to enter the transporter pod. Do you comply?"

Chelsea looked at the bot in horror, realizing that these men were supposed to look as though they were the residents who had chosen to leave The Society. But she knew very well that the man in front of her was no resident of The Society. She looked at the other men and did not find Tray among them—it was a cover. Snapping out of her moment of understanding, she stepped aside as she was ordered to, not knowing what other option she had.

Without another word, the four men boarded the transporter pod. As soon they were inside, the door shut, and the transporter lifted from the ground before zooming toward the ocean. Chelsea stood motionless, watching the pod leave. When it was out of sight, she turned to run to her room to get changed. She wasn't sure what she was going to do about it yet, but she knew one thing for sure. "The Society is—"

Davin rushed in front of her, grabbed her, and covered her mouth with his hand. Her eyes widened in surprise from his unexpected seize. He slowly let go of her mouth and directed her attention to her bracelet that was now lit with the thirty-five notifications she had received since the internet went out. Realizing that the return of internet connection meant the return of recorded footage and active monitoring of each resident, she did not say another word as the two of them made their way back to her room.

Closing the door tightly behind them, Davin spoke first. "Meet me at the waterfall tomorrow morning at six."

She was shocked he didn't want to immediately talk about what had just happened. Davin walked toward the door and put his finger to his lips to remind her to be careful what she said aloud.

She sighed and nodded, recognizing they needed to be more cautious than ever.

He walked back to his room, deep in thought about how they should proceed with their plans now that communication and personal surveillance were restored. He knew they would have to be far more secretive, especially now knowing that they were, in fact, being lied to. He wasn't sure to what extent the government tracked what people were saying at The Society, but he knew he was someone who was watched more closely than the average resident. As he opened the door to his room, a hand brushed up against his shoulder.

"Davin," Ms. Waverly said with a forced grin. "Glad I caught you alone. Mind if we have a word," she said, coaxing him into his room. Terrified of the reason for her presence, Davin reluctantly followed her.

As she entered the room, she turned to face him. "As you have probably noticed, the internet has been restored. The part we needed came on the transporter, and our great networkers have got it fixed already," she said with a smile. "Our four former residents are headed home on the transporter pod as we speak. Understand?" she said and waited for him to acknowledge and confirm the story she was feeding him. He nodded silently, realizing she was already aware that he knew something.

"Great. You will also find that in your email you have a proposal to film a movie. You will be accepting that offer and will begin preparing immediately. We will proceed with the last two celebration meetings, and you will continue to have a positive, upbeat attitude about The Society—same as before. You will film this movie on the grounds, and everyone will see for themselves that the island is in good repair. And if you want to keep dating that girlfriend of yours, I suggest you keep her happy and quiet. Do you comply?"

"Yes," Davin managed to reply.

"Good. Have a nice evening, Davin." Ms. Waverly left his room, and he sank to his bed—horrified as he thought about what had just happened and what he knew he had to do.

IN THE MORNING, Davin met Chelsea at the waterfall as he'd instructed. "What should we do now, Davin?" she asked.

Davin removed his earpiece and put it in the stream of the waterfall. Then he used his other hand to cover the camera of his wristband. He motioned for her to do the same. As soon as she did, he leaned in close to her and whispered into her ear, speaking as quickly as he could manage. "We are being watched—*closely*. We can't openly discuss things without being in a controlled environment, and we can't have these discussions very often. I think we should continue to look for the cave, but we won't use any verbal communication as we search, and we'll *especially* avoid discussing what we're searching for and why. As soon as we verify where those people are and figure out why they aren't letting them leave, we'll come up with a way to inform the other residents and plot an escape. Starting as soon as possible, I'm being forced to film a movie here on the island. We'll have to work around that schedule and act completely normal and content in the meantime. After I'm finished filming, we'll escape. I don't think we'll be safe here after that. Are you okay with all that?"

She tried to process everything he was saying. "Yes, I think so," she said while working to commit his suggestions to memory, but she could tell he was withholding something. "What are you not telling me?" Chelsea whispered.

"Just know we can't risk being caught plotting."

Seeing her unsatisfied expression at his vague response, he knew she wasn't going to leave it at that. He breathed a hesitant sigh, then looked around anxiously before giving in. "Last night, Waverly intercepted me on my way to my room. She was threatening and on edge. I'm more certain than ever that we aren't going to like what we find in that cave, but we need to learn more and let the other the residents know. Now, what do you know about those men who got on the transporter pod last night?" he asked Chelsea.

"I recognized only one of them. He was here a few months ago when the internet was down last time before the storm. He's too old to be a resident, and he left as soon as the problem was fixed. I think they're bringing him in to repair things that we can't repair ourselves, but they're trying to keep that a secret for some reason. I didn't recognize the other men," she said.

Davin's forehead wrinkled with concern as he considered her words. "I think your theory makes sense. Be thinking about ways we can prove that and what we should do with the information we collect," Davin said. "Now let's kiss and make it look like we came out here to make out and watch the sunrise."

Chelsea nodded and kissed Davin hard, her heart racing with the prospect of escaping and the looming consequences of uncovering a conspiracy within The Society. She knew she should do the right thing no matter the penalty, but the warning in the game *Leagues of Reprisal* suddenly came to her mind and caused a shiver to run down her spine. *Remember 'Rebellion never goes without consequence.'* Then she wondered, *at what cost will our rebellion come?*

17. ON SET

THE NEXT DAY, Genevieve Thrope showed up on the transporter pod, ready to begin filming. With her were three crewman and four other actors who would play older roles in the film.

One of the crewmen brought with him a large crate that barely fit through the transporter pod's large doors. He slowly walked down the center of the ramp, and the crate automatically followed behind him. Invisible to the eye, a self-driven dolly sat under the crate and followed the man wherever he led it by tracking the GPS in the man's wristband. He brought it to the far end of the trees where he pulled up the controls on his wristband and set the box down in a spot far away from the grounds of The Society. Then, like Bumblebee from the old *Transformers* movies, the crate popped open and expanded into a small house alongside a large building that housed another large set inside it. The man looked up at his creation, pleased that it had traveled safety, and then walked inside to check that the internal components were still intact. For the next three weeks, he would be busy finishing the insides of these sets, and once filming began, he would be responsible for positioning the props and furniture for each scene.

Bringing only a collapsible chair and large bag, the next crewman walked off the pod with a smile beaming brightly across her face. Lynn brought her lucky collapsible chair with her wherever she worked so she could sit in it to control her lighting drones, microphone drops, and cameras all from the convenience of her PED. She was elated to escape the sets of small independent films that too often left her with meager compensation and instead be working on a fully funded feature film.

The other crewman walked wearily off the transporter pod with a suitcase that was programmed to follow two feet behind him. He wore sunglasses to shade his eyes and followed closely behind Genevieve. His name was Jon Dunn. He was the scriptwriter for the film, and Genevieve had asked him to come as her assistant director as well. Like Genevieve, he also had a long history in filmmaking but had transitioned into news writing after the earthquake occurred. The poor man had not had a decent vacation in over fifteen years, and the wear on his spirits was obvious. He rubbed his scruffy face and yawned as he walked. Looking around the island with his tired eyes, he took in the splendid scenery and smiled. *This is as good any vacation,* he thought, content to be at such a beautiful location.

Genevieve brought a huge crate with her as well. Smaller than the set manager's but still massive compared to the usual luggage one would expect for an extended stay. Inside was food to last the visiting cast and crew for the next two months. With food shortage still a concern at The Society, Ms. Waverly had requested they provide their own meals. Five rooms were available for them to sleep in, and the rest of the visitors would be living inside the set house they transported with them whenever it wasn't being used for filming.

With a bounce in her step, Genevieve led the group toward Davin, Lola, Kona, and Ms. Waverly who stood waiting to greet them as they arrived.

Though Genevieve was old in years, she had the energy of a much younger woman. She could hardly contain her enthusiasm knowing they were going to begin filming soon. After not hearing back from Davin or Lola for weeks when she informed them that she had acquired the funding for the film, she worried the project would lose its footing without the commitment of the main star. But once she received an urgent email back from Lola explaining that their internet had been down, she quickly made arrangements to travel to The Society with a small crew to begin filming.

Genevieve placed her suitcase down at her feet and threw her arms out wide. "We're here!" she exclaimed with a smile.

"Welcome to the Hawaii Society. I'm Sandra Waverly, the Head Society Leader," Ms. Waverly said. "All your requests to accommodate for filming should have been taken care of. I have much to attend to, so I'll leave you to your work. Please speak with Lola if you have any questions or additional needs." She nodded her head and bid the newcomers farewell.

Genevieve watched her walk away, slightly offended by Ms. Waverly's short and unfriendly demeanor, and then shrugged as she turned to greet the others. They hugged and made each other's acquaintance.

"I'm so excited this film is coming to fruition, and I thank each one of you for the role you have played or will play in bringing it to life. Now that we've all met, let's get going. We have lots to do to be ready to film in three weeks' time."

GENEVIEVE CAME TO THE SOCIETY with a fraction of the crew she would normally have for a large-scale production. Operating under the assumption that she would be able to persuade a number of Society residents to participate in the film, she arrived hoping she would be able to secure a strong supporting cast and find a crew that would be helpful in assisting the few crewmen she was allowed to bring along—a gamble that had kept her up at nights.

She went to work right away by sending out a mass invitation to The Society residents calling all wishful actors to audition for a part. Even though their time on the set would be in addition to their task work, a line of hopefuls still circled the dome during auditions to take their chances on an opportunity to star in a movie with Davin Chapman.

Davin and Chelsea had already decided that Chelsea would not audition in order to reserve her time to search for the cave. Chelsea wasn't too upset, since she hadn't done much acting in her lifetime, but Davin was disappointed not to have the opportunity to work with her in what could be their only chance to act in a film together. And though she would've made an excellent addition to the crew, Chelsea insisted it was most important that she remained focused on finding the cave.

Davin was instructed to spend every spare minute during the three weeks before filming studying the script and rehearsing his lines, working to master the characters of the seven different roles he was to portray. In addition to any work he had to manage for the film, he would still be required to complete his six hours of task work each day. Between his film preparation and his task work, there would be little time left to spend with Chelsea or to search for the cave.

One night Chelsea came to his room after dark when she couldn't search for the cave any longer. She quietly observed as he went over each line until he felt it was just right. "What is your problem?" was one line he rehearsed. Then he tried it again with different inflections on each word. "What is *your* problem? No, no, what is your *problem? What* is your problem?" He looked up from the script and snapped out of character. "What do you think? Would he say it irritated or would he say it more matter-of-factly?" he asked Chelsea.

"Who's your character at this point again?"

"Joel," Davin replied. "He's very self-centered and has a hard time being empathetic to his girlfriend—or anyone for that matter."

"Right. Hmm, I'd probably say matter-of-factly then. Like he hasn't even considered there's something the matter since he hasn't really been listening, but she won't drop the subject, so he finally feels like he has to address her."

"That was my thought too, though Genevieve could totally interpret it differently once we're on set. So we'll see," Davin said with a shrug. "Want to run the lines with me so I know my cues?"

She lifted one shoulder. "Sure."

Davin hopped on the bed next to Chelsea and angled his PED screen so that she could see the script as well. "Just read Louisa's part until the end of the scene."

"Okay." Chelsea looked at the screen until she found her start, then read. "Joel, I'm home. Joel? Where are you at?"

"I'm in the kitchen," Davin said as Joel, getting back into character.

"Oh, hi. How's it going?"

"Good. Just ordering in some food. One second . . . Alright, done."

"Oh, great. I'm starving. You won't believe my day."

"Oh, I didn't get anything for you."

"What? Why not? You knew I would be home by five," Chelsea said, trying to sound like she imagined Louisa would sound.

"Yeah, but you hate sushi, and I really wanted sushi tonight."

"Okay. Well, I'll just order something else for me, I guess." Chelsea tried to sound irritated. She went on to read Louisa's lines, doing her best to play the part. In his responses, Davin effortlessly displayed the appropriate emotions and remembered each line precisely as it was written. Even as they casually read through lines, Chelsea realized how naturally gifted Davin really was. He had barely begun memorizing the scene when Chelsea came in, and he already had it completely memorized and thought out.

"Mind running through it one more time?" Davin asked her at the end of the scene.

"I'm not sure you need to. You literally said every line perfectly," Chelsea replied in amazement.

"Still. It helps to cement it in my mind if I run through it perfectly a few times," he explained.

She agreed and began saying the lines to him over again until he reached the line where he again asked, "*What* is your problem?"

Only this time Chelsea didn't answer as Louisa. "My problem? I miss you, Davin. We've hardly said a word to each other lately, and I'm afraid it's only going to get worse when you start filming."

He fell out of character and sighed. He had been so busy he hadn't realized how Chelsea would be feeling during their separation. "I know. It sucks. I think that's just how it's going to have to be for a while though." He put his arm around her and kissed the top of her head.

Chelsea sighed in disappointment. *He's never going to decide he wants to be with me if we don't get to spend more time together.*

Davin could tell she was upset, and he hated to disappoint her. "I'll tell you what—one of the days I'm filming, you should come to visit me. Take a break from escapading and be on set with me the whole afternoon, and any mealtimes I have off, we'll spend together. If Finley wants to join, she'll just have to deal with me bumming in. And every night, you're welcome to come read lines with me before you go to bed. That way we at least get to see each other each meal and before we go to bed for the next two weeks before filming begins." He waited for her response and tried to read the lines of her face as she contemplated his offer.

"Alright," she finally agreed. "It'll be fun to spend some time on set, and I'll need some breaks from escapading. But how about we just sleep in your room at nights, so we get to be together all night too—even if we are just sleeping."

Davin laughed. "No way. I'm going to miss you all day long. There's no way I'll be able to handle having you right up next to me all night. It would drive me crazy, Chels. I wouldn't get any sleep."

'Chels'—he'd never called her that before. She wasn't sure she liked it.

"I wouldn't mind losing some sleep with you," she teased.

He turned and glared at her with a little smile slowly appearing on his face. *She's trying to tempt me again.* He contemplated whether he should break his promise and give her what she wanted, but he wanted to see something first. "The first time I came onto you, you demanded respect, and yet you don't respect yourself enough to wait for the kind of commitment you demanded. Now what kind of man would I be if I didn't give you the kind of respect you deserve?"

"Maybe I don't want that kind of respect anymore. Maybe I just want to be loved." Saying that went against everything in her heart and the promises she made herself after being used by too many men in the past, but she didn't want to fight her feelings for him any longer.

Davin thought for a moment. "Fine," he said. Then he pushed her down and forced his way on top of her. He used his legs to hold her down. He kissed her, but his lips weren't full of passion like they normally were. They were full of rage. This wasn't the scene she had imagined. It was all wrong. He went to lift her shirt over her head.

"Stop, Davin!"

He immediately stopped, and his grip loosened on her wrists. He rolled off of her, and his demeanor completely changed.

"What was that?" she yelled as she got up off the bed and away from him.

"You want me to be selfish? I can be selfish, Chelsea," Davin said.

"Yeah? Well, that was selfish!"

"I've been *trying* not to be selfish! But how do you expect me to keep my promise to you when you keep throwing yourself at me? I want to know you're the one too," he said. "If that's not what you really want, then I want to know. 'Cause that's not who I am."

She thought for a moment, and then she realized. "That was an act, wasn't it?"

"Yeah," he confessed. "I just wanted to remind you what I *know* you don't want. So that hopefully, one day, we can have the night that leads to the kind of love you *really* want—the kind that lasts."

She wanted to be mad, but she also wanted to cry and beg his forgiveness. She could see his earnest desire to keep his promise in his eyes, and she realized he was truly determined to respect her on a level she'd never thought she was even worthy of.

"I'm sorry, Davin," she barely managed to whisper. Tears were beginning to form in her eyes.

He quickly jumped out of bed and wrapped her in a soft hug. "Don't cry, Chels. You deserve the best, and I just want to give that to you." He looked at her sorry-filled eyes and smiled. "Let me love you right." He kissed her tenderly as she nodded, and then he walked her to her room for the evening.

She went to bed alone that night and each night following, looking up at the mirror and dreaming of the day that Davin might sleep beside her, but no longer in a rush for that day to come too soon—finally grateful for the kind of respect he wanted to give her.

LONG DAYS OF FILMING began shortly after casting finished. Davin smiled and laughed through each day, being careful to play his part and put on a mask of gratification to appease Ms. Waverly. With

Davin so occupied in his work, Ms. Waverly soon observed that he had no time left to investigate the night with the four men on the transporter pod, even if he did have suspicions. He went to bed exhausted each night and woke up early in the morning to complete his task work before filming began. Ms. Waverly eventually stopped monitoring Chelsea as well since she only seemed to fill her abundant spare time with escapading and her time in the evenings with Finley.

Time on set for Davin was marked with long, hard days. Genevieve had a very particular vision for each scene. Sometimes she was able to communicate her demands articulately enough that Davin was able to translate her words into action within a few takes. Other times, they shot a scene over and over until she finally signaled the cast to move to the next scene—to the relief of the whole crew.

Although Davin had experience with similar directing tactics, he felt Genevieve was particularly picky in her art. And though this could have made Davin cross with her, he only gained respect for her during their time together. She was endlessly patient with the cast as they worked to portray the feelings behind each character. When someone wasn't able to deliver the performance she had anticipated, she would work with them to explain how they could change their approach.

For new actors who needed extra guidance, Genevieve paired the older, more experienced actors from the mainland with them for mentorship on their days off. Despite being warned ahead of time, there were those who got frustrated with the taxing days on set that they had to manage between their task work and decided to leave the cast altogether. Some scenes had to be reshot. Words were exchanged, but ultimately, without a paycheck to incentivize people, there was nothing to keep them there. Money was no good to them in The Society anyway.

Chelsea and Davin tried hard to make the most of their short time together while Davin filmed. During the meals they were required to sit out, they enjoyed some of their best conversations and they learned how to work together as they tried to win each game they were assigned to for the day. They learned each other's minds in that time and began to understand the why of who they were themselves. Their time spent in the virtual reality games was the reason their relationship continued to blossom during their busy days apart.

And when they did sit down for a meal together, they were inseparable. Davin kept one soft hand on Chelsea whenever they were together. He would play with a strand of her hair or trace her palm with his finger under the table as they ate their food or spoke with friends. Chelsea enjoyed the constant presence of his gentle touch. It reassured her his heart still belonged to her despite their separation.

For Davin, there was only one day on set that did not fade into the blur of the weeks of filming. That was the day he had arranged for Chelsea to visit him on set. Chelsea was excited to see him at work, and he was equally excited to have her close by. Any time he had with her was treasured time.

The same day Chelsea was supposed to visit him, Davin found out his scene would be shot with Chloe. She had been cast as Davin's love interest in the scene. He was supposed to have been madly in love with her for many years, while her character considered their relationship platonic. The scene was meant to depict how it feels when love is one-sided and off-balance—a feeling that Davin's character had never had to experience before that moment. Genevieve reminded Davin multiple times that she had to see the love in his eyes when he set eyes on Chloe. He had starred in a number of romantic films in the past, so he felt confident he could capture the moment Genevieve was looking for.

Chloe had just finished with makeup and hair when Davin went up to her to say hello before they began filming.

"How have you been, Chloe?" Davin asked as he gave her a friendly side hug.

"Fine. Thanks," she said with a bright smile, nervously pushing her long curls back from her face. The thought of being in her first film had her terrified.

"Congratulations on getting the part! We should have a fun day today—nothing too difficult. It's a short scene," he said, hoping to make her feel at ease. He knew how nerve-racking it was for most people to be on set, especially for their first time. "How is Eli doing?"

"His ribs should be healed up by now," replied Chloe, "but honestly, I wouldn't know. He's with someone else now."

Davin shouldn't have been surprised to hear that, but he still couldn't believe how short-lived people's relationships were. "Oh, sorry to hear," Davin sympathized. "You doing okay?"

"I'll be fine," she said. "I'm glad you and I still get to spend some time together," she said, flashing him a brilliant smile. "Just like before that awful hurricane hit." Chloe put her hand on his arm and squeezed it.

"Yeah," he said uncomfortably. "My girlfriend should be here in a little bit. It'll be fun to introduce you two."

Chloe maintained her smile, but her disappointment was apparent in her body language. She took her hand off his arm and turned away ever so slightly. "Great—that will be great."

Just then a production assistant came running up. "Davin, Genevieve told me to tell you that they're ready for the next scene and for you to bring the other lady who's supposed to be in the shot too."

Davin could always tell if someone had a background in film by the way they spoke to him. This particular production assistant was especially new to film. "Great! Thank you, Lilliana. Chloe and I will be there right away." He motioned the way to Chloe. "Shall we?"

Chloe walked ahead and didn't make eye contact with the production assistant who obviously did not know her name or that she was "the other lady who's supposed to be in the shot too." Davin chuckled to himself that, with her potential five minutes of screen time, she was already showing signs of becoming a pretentious leading lady.

Davin looked at the time and knew Chelsea should be arriving just in time for the scene to wrap up. He smiled—excited to see her.

"Thanks again, Lilliana," Davin said as he patted her lightly on the back and walked toward the set. Lilliana, happy that Davin Chapman even remembered her name, breathed a sigh of relief that she was able to communicate the message.

Genevieve had the scene set up precisely as she wanted it. A microphone for each speaking role floated silently in place, waiting for the actors to take their positions, and camera lights hovered at just the right angles around the large indoor set.

Genevieve and Lynn, along with three other technical support crewmembers selected from among The Society residents, wore outsized goggles over their eyes. The goggles default display showed them a large image of all the cameras' perspectives, as well as the sound levels for the audio recordings. Custom-tailored settings allowed each camera operator to see full theater-sized images of their camera shot if needed or whatever settings people wished to have displayed.

"Positions, please," Genevieve called out as Chloe and Davin approached. "Chloe, you'll find your purple marks at your starting and finishing positions. And Davin, yours are green, as usual.

Extras—just stay in your spots, as you are, and do what I told you to do as soon as you hear the word *action*."

Walking up to Chloe, Genevieve grasped her by the shoulder and examined her. "Lovely, you look lovely. Now, remember what I told you. You think of Davin fondly, but nothing more. Deliver your lines casually as you rehearsed. No matter what handsome faces he shoots your way, I don't want to see any longing in your eyes, understand?"

"Yes, Ms. Thrope," Chloe responded in a shaky voice.

"Call me Genevieve," she replied before turning to speak with Davin. "Now, Davin, I know I have already told you a million times—but sell it. Make me believe you love her and would do anything in the world for this woman. She's gorgeous. She's kind. She's smart. You want only her."

"Got it, Gen," Davin said confidently. Davin liked to give people nicknames and had become comfortable enough with Genevieve to call her by his shortened nickname. Genevieve didn't mind. She felt mutually comfortable with Davin.

"Excellent," Genevieve replied as she walked back to her position out of the camera shot. "Now, quiet on set!" she called.

"Cameras are rolling and records are speeding. Files 0145," Lynn called out from her PED station.

"Actors in character," Genevieve yelled, then waited. "Clapper," Genevieve called out when the man in charge of the clapper did not call out his part.

"Oh," he said, jumping up, distracted by Chloe's good looks. He raised the clapper and shouted out, "Scene fourteen. Drew sees Penny. Take one." He dropped the clapper down forcefully to provide an audible marker of the beginning of the scene.

"Action!" Genevieve yelled.

Davin turned and saw Chloe. He donned his best lovestruck face.

"Cut!" Genevieve yelled. "Again."

Davin looked at Genevieve. He thought the take went well and hoped for more direction if it wasn't what she was looking for. *Maybe it's Chloe who needs to change something?* he thought to himself. Before he could probe for more guidance, Genevieve cued the crew to restart the scene.

"Re-rack. Quiet on set!" she called.

"Cameras rolling. Records are speeding. File 0146."

"Actors in character."

"Scene fourteen. Drew sees Penny. Take two."

Clap.

"ACTION."

Davin turned again to look at Chloe. He gave his best lovestruck look again and tried to show longing in his eyes.

"Stop!" Genevieve called. She turned to the crew and muttered, "Just keep it rolling."

"What is it?" Davin asked.

Genevieve thought for a moment and then raised her hands in the air. "I don't know exactly, but *that* wasn't it. Make me believe you *love* her—*really* love her. Do it again. Try something else. We'll just keep going until we get it."

"Do I need to change something?" Chloe asked.

"No, you're doing fine," Genevieve replied after quickly looking at the footage of Chloe's camera angle. "Keep doing what you're doing. Re-rack." Chloe gave Davin a smug expression and then turned back to her initial position. Davin let Chloe's haughty look slide. He took a deep breath and repositioned himself for another take.

"Everything's still rolling," Genevieve called. "Actors in character."

"Scene fourteen. Drew sees Penny. Take three."

Clap.

"AND ACTION."

He turned. He saw Chloe. He gave her a look of longing and allowed a slight smile to appear on his face. He stared at her face and breathed a quiet sigh.

"No," Genevieve said. "I'm sorry—that's not it. It needs something. Again."

He had to do the look five more times before Genevieve even let them finish to the end of the scene. When they finally got through the whole thing without any mess-up and at every angle Genevieve needed, Davin froze in place and looked toward his director, waiting for some feedback or a cue to move to the next scene. But she was quiet.

"It still wasn't right," she huffed quietly. "The look was still off. Davin, try it again."

"What am I missing, Gen?" Davin asked, trying to get instruction on what she wanted. It wasn't like her to not have a suggestion or an explanation for her disapproval.

Genevieve turned to Jon Dunn, who sat in a nearby chair sipping water from a bottle. They whispered between themselves while reviewing the footage.

Davin sighed and ran his fingers through his hair in frustration. He wasn't sure what else to try. If she didn't give him any more instruction, he planned to do the same thing he did originally. That tactic had worked in the past with other directors—after multiple takes, if he tried his first approach again, they suddenly thought it was great and moved on to the next scene. It was the oldest trick in the book for stubborn directors who weren't sure what they were looking for and didn't recognize it the first time they saw it. With his mind made up, he took in a few deep breaths to get back into character and prepare himself to try his first approach once more. He centered his mind and let his frustrations leave him. Repositioning himself, he waited for Genevieve's feedback or for her to call action—whichever came first.

But Genevieve continued to discuss with Jon. Davin finally gave up and turned around to wait until they were finished. As he did, Chelsea quietly sneaked up beside Lola, who was nearby observing the set. Careful to not distract the actors, Chelsea gently hugged Lola and pulled up a chair beside her. Davin watched her with a half-smile on his face and a proud look in his eye as he saw her try to break Lola's unfounded disdain for her and try to earn her friendship. He loved Chelsea's way with people. The way she tried to please them, even if she ended up intimidating them with an overly honest comment or an unexpectedly strong opinion. He adored the way she carried herself so confidently, despite her insecurities.

Genevieve suddenly perked up. "Are the cameras still rolling?" Lynn looked over at Genevieve nervously and nodded, worried that she had done something wrong. "That was it! We got it!" Genevieve said, jumping up out of the chair next to Jon. She did a little victory dance while Davin stood in complete confusion. He looked at Genevieve celebrating, then back to Chelsea.

After Lola pointed Davin out and gave Chelsea the okay to get his attention, Chelsea waved. He waved back slowly—still confused as to how Genevieve thought he had managed the correct look as he casually looked at Chelsea—until he understood, and he smiled.

Genevieve looked over the footage one more time and then announced to the crew with a big smile, "That's a wrap! Next scene!"

Genevieve ran up to Davin after she directed the crew to set up the subsequent scene at their next location. "I'm sorry to hang you out to dry like that, Davin. You weren't doing a bad job. It just wasn't quite right. Although you ended up getting it without my help—I guess that's why you're so good at your craft," she said with a smile.

"Don't be fooled," Lola said as she walked up to Genevieve and Davin, with Chelsea following closely behind her. "Davin wasn't acting," she explained. "That was genuine." She looked at Chelsea as she walked up beside her. Lola crossed her arms and gave a reluctant grin—she liked Chelsea more than she cared to admit, considering she had stolen *all* of Davin's attention.

An impish smiled crossed Davin's face. He chuckled softly as he reached for Chelsea's hand and grabbed it. "Gen, this is Chelsea," he said while rubbing the back of his neck. "My girlfriend."

Genevieve looked at Davin, then to Lola to verify. "Oh," she said. A smile grew on her face, and her eyes lit up. "I see. Well, it's nice to meet you, Chelsea. I'm *very* glad you came." Chelsea didn't fully realize why Genevieve seemed so pleased to meet her, but she was happy she was welcome on set just the same.

18. RECONCILIATION

THERE WAS ONLY one more week of filming left. After Chelsea had lunch and her task hours were completed, she went out to the beach to begin her escapading for the day. It was the first day since the hurricane that no one was required to skip a meal. The night before, The Society had held another meeting where Ms. Waverly happily announced the good news that the mandatory meal fast would be permanently lifted. The shipment of supplies and livestock had arrived the week before, and the gardens and orchards were now producing consistent quantities. Everyone was pleased to know they would be provided three meals a day instead of two, especially since the portions were still scanty, but Chelsea missed her time with Davin more than she enjoyed the extra food.

Chelsea walked across the beach, headed for the next zone on the map that she needed to search. As she looked up from watching her feet march through the sand, she saw Hammond strolling along, his arms around two women, one on either side of him. He was smiling wide and his sunglasses covered his eyes. But as soon as his eyes met Chelsea's, he raised his glasses to look at her, and his smile faded away entirely. He looked unwell.

"Hammond?" Chelsea questioned, confused by the scene she was witnessing.

"Hey, Chelsea," Hammond said as he took his arms off the girls' shoulders and brought them to his sides.

"What's going on? Where's Sara?" Chelsea asked, trying to keep away any judgment from her tone.

Hammond shifted his weight as he considered what exactly he wanted to tell her. Then he turned to the women standing impatiently by his side. "I need to have a chat with my friend here. You ladies have a nice day. Maybe we'll spend some time together some other night," he said, trying to smile.

The two girls looked at each other and shrugged, then they turned away to inspect the beach for the next lonely man. Chelsea overheard them whispering as they left. "Isn't that the girl who dated Davin Chapman?" She had learned to ignore people's comments, though she did feel a small amount of sadness that people no longer could tell they were together.

"No, I think they're just friends. There's no way he would be into her."

Though Chelsea was curious to hear what Hammond had to say, sitting down for a long chat had her worried. She knew she still had a lot of escapading to do and that time was running short. Each day Davin finished filming was one day closer to an unsure future. But Chelsea could tell Hammond wasn't doing well, even though he was trying to mask it under a smile. She tried to quiet her nerves, sensing there was a long story behind Hammond's troubled eyes.

"Mind if we sit down?" Hammond asked her. She nodded her head, already accepting that her afternoon of escapading may not happen. They sat under the shade of a nearby beach umbrella on the warm sand. "It's been a while," Hammond said, trying to make small talk to ease into the conversation. Seeing Chelsea's impatience and her raised eyebrow, he gathered that he was better off not mincing words. "I know you're wondering what I was doing with those girls and why Sara isn't dragging me around everywhere like usual. If you must know, I broke up with her a few months ago."

Chelsea's jaw dropped. She couldn't picture Sara without Hammond, or Hammond without Sara. She sat dumbfounded, trying to understand why he would leave Sara when they had always been so unmistakably happy together. Chelsea's heart sank, and a little hope left her heart—the part of her heart that still believed a happily-ever-after was really possible. She could not help but fear that if it was not possible for Hammond and Sara, it was not probable for anyone.

"Why?" Chelsea managed to get out.

"Long story short—she cheated on me and then made up some bogus lie about being raped to try and feel better about it," Hammond said, the anger growing on his face.

Chelsea was shocked. She couldn't imagine Sara doing something like that to him. "That doesn't sound like something Sara would do. She's always been so in love with you. Why would she *claim* to be raped? And how do you know it's not true?" she asked, trying to unravel the details behind the story so she could better understand or disprove Hammond's story.

"Well," Hammond said and took a deep breath, not really wanting to relive the experience. "She came to me, super upset, after the Grand Welcome Celebration, but she wouldn't tell me what the problem was. Then when I finally got something out of her, she said she was raped."

"And you don't believe her?" Chelsea asked, surprised.

"I did," Hammond responded defensively. "But after she told me, she kept saying sorry all the time. I couldn't figure out why she would need to be so sorry. And, of course, I was angry with the guy who supposedly did it, so . . . I confronted him—which I know could have ended really badly," Hammond remarked. "But it ended up being the best thing I could have done. He has access to all the surveillance system footage. After the worst five minutes of my life, watching the woman I thought was the love of my life openly getting it on with another man—that was that. I figured out why she was so sorry. She just had a guilty conscience. The rape story was just her way of trying to get away with it." Hammond tossed some sand out in front of him in frustration.

Chelsea sat stunned for a moment. "I'm so sorry, Hammond. I can't believe it. How have you been holding up?"

"Well, I was sad, super sad—for about a month. Then I was just mad—for a long time. Now—now I've just decided to do my own thing, whatever I want. I'm my own man for the first time in my life," he said, trying to smile even though the furrow on his brow still remained.

"I guess that explains the girls," Chelsea said. "Have you seen much of Sara since? Is she still with that guy? Who was it?" Chelsea asked, trying to remember the last time she spoke with Sara. She recalled briefly speaking with her during the hurricane to make sure she was safe. Sara was particularly distressed and upset, but Chelsea had attributed that to the effects of the hurricane. Clearly, that wasn't the whole story.

"Don't think so. Maybe it was a one-time thing. He's supposedly a bit of a hot item among the women, so I guess she just couldn't help herself. Or maybe she's been with lots of guys that I just never found out about," he said, shrugging his shoulders. "Honestly, I've been avoiding her. It's just too painful," he sat still, looking out on the waves crashing down and trying not to get emotional. Then he had a thought that irritated him every time it came to mind. "And whenever I see Branch, he gives me this wave and stupid face like we shared something. It makes me sick to my stomach. I really thought Sara and I had something special—something different. And if I'm being honest, I *don't* like being my own man. I *liked* who we were together—or rather, who I thought we were."

"Branch Willix? The government guy?" Chelsea asked. "Isn't that the guy who's always making awkward comments—assuming everyone wants him? I think because he's a government guy, people just don't press the issue. But if he *raped* her, that's a totally different thing, Hammond—"

"Chelsea, I saw the whole thing—on video, from multiple angles!" Hammond cringed at the memory of the footage replaying in his mind.

"Okay. I'm sorry," Chelsea said, realizing the proof was indisputable in his mind. She put her hand on his shoulder. "Well, if you ever need a friend, I'll always be here for you."

"Thanks, Chelsea," Hammond replied sullenly. He sat quietly, attempting to regain his poise, but after their conversation, all he wanted to do was get away from the outside world. "I think I'm going to head to my room and catch a nap. I'll see you around, Chelsea." He stood without another word and left for his room. His room was no longer next to Sara's but in a different building entirely—a favor that Branch had made happen for him.

Chelsea watched him as he walked away. His shoulders were slumped, and he walked at a slow pace. Chelsea could not understand why Sara would have cheated on him when she had always been so outspoken about their love. She wondered what Sara's perspective was.

Chelsea looked toward the ocean and debated if she could afford to skip escapading altogether that day. She still had so much ground to cover in the search for the cave. Especially considering that searching took twice as long without Davin, and the searchable area seemed endless in the larger zones. But with the heartbreak in her friend's eyes weighing heavy on her mind, she decided the search could wait if there was even the slightest possibility of helping her friends to reconcile. She walked back to the equipment room to return her things and then went looking for Sara.

She had not seen a trace of Sara in months. Recognizing how concerning that was now that she knew the situation, Chelsea used her locator to find her friend so she wouldn't waste time. She didn't usually use this PED feature out of respect for people's privacy, but she felt a sudden urgency to locate Sara after realizing how odd her absence was. She looked down at the map on her arm that revealed Sara could be found in her living quarters. Chelsea immediately left to hear her side of the story.

WHEN SARA HEARD A KNOCK at the door, she had every intention of not answering it. She continued to sit in her chair and look out her window toward the sun—trying not to feel. Chelsea knocked again, harder. "Sara, it's me, Chelsea. I know you're in there, so open up. I want to talk."

Sara hadn't heard from Chelsea for a long time. She assumed it was probably due to Chelsea being too wrapped up in her blooming romance with Davin Chapman—she had heard the rumors. Although talking anything romance made her physically ill, Sara's fondness toward Chelsea was still present, and despite her reservations, she opened the door for her to come in.

Chelsea stood and stared at a completely unrecognizable Sara. Her long blonde hair was pulled back into a loose, sloppy ponytail, and her normally colorful attire was replaced with a gray hooded T-shirt and black leggings. Her eyes seemed permanently swollen, and her dimples could not be seen because her face lacked her ever-present smile. The usual glint in her eyes was gone. She avoided Chelsea's gaze as she walked into the room.

"Sara, are you all right?" Chelsea asked with concern. "I just finished talking to Hammond, and to be honest, I'm really confused right now."

"You did?" Sara asked, perking up ever so slightly at the sound of Hammond's name. "What did he say? How is he?"

"He seems . . . " Chelsea paused trying to think of how to describe him, "rough, I guess you could say." She said it with uncertainty—not knowing if that was the best word she could have used, but it was the only word that came to mind.

"He does?" Sara said, both concerned and somewhat relieved. "But I've seen him a few times on the beach lately, and he seems just fine—more than fine," she said, thinking of all the women she had seen Hammond walking with through her window. "He isn't in a relationship, is he?"

"No," Chelsea replied, "I don't think he's ready for any real relationship right now."

"Okay, good." Sara sighed. Relieved Hammond had not completely moved on and not wanting to discuss the handful of women she had seen him with any further, she decided to change the subject and put her curiosity to rest. "Speaking of relationships—you and Davin Chapman. Is it true? Are you dating him?"

"Yeah, it's kind of crazy," Chelsea said with a small smile as her cheeks flushed with color. Then she remembered she hadn't come to discuss her relationship with Davin. "But I'm not here to talk about that. I want to know what happened between you and Hammond."

Sara was relieved to hear that Chelsea didn't come to elaborate on her relationship with Davin, but she was equally averse to the idea of sharing what had happened to her. She sat staring blankly at the floor with slumped shoulders, but she knew Chelsea wouldn't leave without some answers. "I've tried so many times to talk to him. He's completely shut me out. He even changed rooms and took away my ability to track him. Lately, I've just resigned myself to staying in my room. I've realized there's no point in trying to reach out to him anymore," Sara said with sad eyes. "Seems like he's moved on. Even if he hasn't, he won't talk to me."

"But what happened?" Chelsea insisted.

Sara was silent for a moment before she finally spoke. "Branch." Sara managed to get out his name but then broke out into sobs. "I was raped by Branch Willix the night of the Grand Welcome Celebration in a dirty bathroom stall!" she cried before calming down enough to elaborate. "At first Hammond believed me and was so supportive and sweet about the whole thing, but then the morning after I told him, he just suddenly shut me out." Chelsea got up and handed Sara a tissue from the bathroom as she continued to cry. "He hasn't said a full sentence to me since," she sobbed, trying unsuccessfully to calm down.

Chelsea sat and thought for a moment as she analyzed the two stories. After thinking about it for a moment, Chelsea decided that Sara deserved to know why Hammond was shutting her out. "It's because he knows, Sara. Hammond went to Branch, and Branch showed him the footage of the whole thing. It really tore him up to see you guys together. I think he would handle things better if you would just admit to the truth," Chelsea told her.

"See us together? The truth?" Sara's tears turned to rage. "You mean he got mad at me when he saw Branch force himself on me? Because he saw how I tried to beat him off, and every move I made he came back at me with twice as much force?"

Chelsea was confused. *How can Sara and Hammond both seem so adamant about their stories?* "That's not what he saw, Sara."

"Well, that's what happened—what *really* happened! I don't know what he thinks he saw, but I swear to you, what *I* told you is exactly what happened." Sara sat on her bed, sinking back into her sullen mood as her temper deescalated.

"Well, if he raped you, why didn't you turn him in, Sara?" Chelsea asked as she sat down next to Sara on the bed.

"I couldn't bring myself to do it. I feel so weak and broken." She shrugged. "Besides, what's the use? I couldn't even get Hammond to listen to me. I'm probably going to get removed from The Society soon anyway. I've missed a few days of task work, and I was already given a warning. I got the message today," Sara admitted. "Some days, I just have a hard time getting myself out of bed."

Sara was in worse shape than Chelsea had realized, and with an eviction looming, she knew she needed to do something fast if there was any chance of getting Hammond and Sara back together. It broke her heart to see her friends both so miserable. Sara looked especially emotionally broken, possibly because her current depressed state contrasted so starkly to her normally high-spirited self. But worst of all, Chelsea could tell Sara was being sincere when she told her story. Either she did not realize she wasn't telling the truth, or what Hammond saw on the video was inaccurate. Chelsea reached over to her and gave her a gentle hug. "I'm going to talk with Hammond again. We're going to sort this out."

DAVIN AND CHELSEA had planned to meet for dinner and spend the rest of the evening together before he had to go back to filming and work through the night. Chelsea was very excited to finally spend some time with him but nervous to report that she hadn't done any escapading that afternoon. Nonetheless, she felt she had done the right thing. She wanted to do anything she could possibly do to help her friends reconcile their love.

"Hey, Chels." Her heart sang to hear his voice. She smiled, and he gave her a quick peck on the cheek. "How was your day? Run into anything of interest while you were out?" This was the phrase that they had decided on as code to inquire about the search for the cave.

"I actually didn't get out today," she reluctantly confessed.

"No?" Davin asked. "That's okay. What did you end up doing?"

Chelsea was surprised he didn't seem to mind and relieved he wasn't upset with her. "I ran into my friend Hammond on the beach. Then I went and spoke with Sara, my other friend. I haven't had a chance to introduce you guys yet, but they're really awesome. They were the first people I met on my way to The Society in the transporter pod. I think you would really like them."

Then she told him their story. He quietly sat, listening to Chelsea speak and asking very few questions as he ate his dinner. Hearing about Sara and Hammond's relationship made him reflect on his own relationship with Chelsea. As she wrapped up the story, Davin thought for a moment, then looked up from his plate of rice and vegetables. "We should go tonight and talk to Hammond together," he suggested. "It sounds like this is really important to you, and maybe I can help."

Chelsea was appreciative he wanted to help and anxious to speak with Hammond again, but she was worried that Hammond may find it off-putting to have Davin around for such a sensitive conversation. "I don't know, Davin. He may not want to open up if there's someone he doesn't really know around."

"Come on, Chels. I'll be good, I promise. Besides, it's the only time I'll get to see you for a few days." He knew that would convince her.

HAMMOND WAS STILL sleeping when they arrived at his living quarters. Chelsea knocked on the door. Davin grabbed her hand and smiled supportively as they waited for him to answer.

Hammond opened the door, still dazed from sleep. "We need to talk, Hammond," Chelsea said as the door opened.

"Chelsea?" Hammond asked, still trying to gather his senses. As Chelsea and Davin came into focus, he decided to invite them in—curious as to why Davin Chapman would be paying him a visit as well. "Sure. Come on in."

Davin and Chelsea walked in together and sat on the unmade bed, and Hammond sat on the chair at his desk.

"Oh, I'm so sorry," Chelsea began, "This is Dav—"

"I know who he is," Hammond said as he reached out to shake Davin's hand. "It's nice to meet you. Looks like our girl Chelsea's got you wrapped around her finger, doesn't she?"

Davin laughed and looked at her. "Yeah, she does."

"So what are you two doing coming to talk to me?" Hammond asked.

"It's about Sara," Chelsea began. Hammond huffed and turned his gaze to the window, unsure if he wanted to have another conversation about Sara. "I just spoke with her before dinner. She's miserable, Hammond. I just don't believe she cheated on you."

"Of course she's miserable. How many times do I have to tell you—I saw it with my own eyes? Lying little—"

"Hammond," Davin interrupted. "I can understand why you're upset, and we haven't been dating that long, so maybe I have no right to say anything. But I've already started to see that the more I believe in Chelsea's goodness over my own perceived notions, the more she surprises me and the more I can't help but love her."

Chelsea was confused by his seemingly unrelated comment. She didn't understand how it was applicable to the situation or even true. She began to wonder if she should've come alone. But Hammond understood, and like the turn of tides, his mood lightened as he allowed himself to remember Sara for who he knew she really was. He pondered on all the times that he had put his trust in her and never regretted it, and he realized he had allowed himself to be blinded by jealousy.

He looked up at Chelsea. "You really believe her, don't you?"

"Yes," Chelsea replied, feeling surprised that Davin's comment had somehow helped. "I don't know what actually happened. But after talking to her, I can tell she fervently believes her story. I know that doesn't make much sense—"

"So you honestly think she's not just trying to cover up a mistake. You believe she really was hurt."

"I do," said Chelsea. "I didn't at first, but she seemed so sincere, and she is completely miserable right now. She's not acting like herself. She doesn't look like herself. They're going to kick her out of The Society because she's not been completing her tasks. She can't even function she is so miserable, Hammond."

As Chelsea spoke, Davin took out his earpiece and motioned for Chelsea to do the same. After she did so, he motioned to Hammond as well. "Would you mind?" He placed them in the bathroom along with their wristbands and shut the door. Davin returned to the bed and leaned in close as he whispered to Hammond. "The man who supposedly raped Sara, Branch Willix—I work with him fairly often. *I* don't trust him. Though I could be wrong, I consider myself a good judge of character. He's important to The Society's operations and has privileges that he could easily abuse. If you have any faith in Sara, I would trust her—not him—even if it doesn't make sense. There are ways to deceive the eye, but the heart can only hide behind malice."

Hammond sat in silence with his head down, contemplating Davin's words. Then Davin stood and retrieved their earpieces and wristbands, and as Davin returned Hammond's things, Chelsea walked over to Hammond and knelt down beside him. "You're a good guy, Hammond. I just want to see you happy again." Then Chelsea and Davin grabbed hands and walked to the door in silence.

After they left the room, Hammond sat in the chair by his desk and continued to think about Sara. It felt good to think of her again. The emotional walls he had secured against any thoughts of her were easily broken down. He contemplated her every detail. He was still very much in love with her, and the more he allowed himself to think about her, the more he found he didn't care either way. Even if it was true, he realized that as long as she still loved him and wanted to move forward from this awful experience, he could forgive her.

An hour later, Sara's door flung open. Hammond stood in the doorway, panting from running down the halls. Sara jumped up and looked in Hammond's direction—startled by the abrupt entrance. He was the only person she had allowed direct access to her room. Sara looked at him, confused, but hope rose inside her for the first time in months.

He stood and stared at her for a few heart-stopping seconds. Then Hammond caught his breath. "I love you, Sara. I'm so sorry."

She jumped up to run toward him, and he met her halfway. They embraced and held each other close in the middle of the room. Bliss overcame them as they hugged each other in a familiar embrace.

"Will you still have me?" he asked. Sara laughed as uncontrollable tears streamed down her face. She found it strange that he would ask that question when she felt like she was the one who was unworthy of their love, but she nodded in assurance just the same.

"Will you still have *me* though?" she asked, her voice quivering with emotion.

"Yes. Yes, of course," Hammond said, holding her close to his chest and kissing the top of her head. He sensed the same heartbreaking anguish he had seen on her face the day she told him about the rape. He ached with sorrow for not believing her, despite the evidence against her. "The day I married you, I told you for better or worse. It was the happiest day of my life. The day I thought you lied and cheated on me was the worst." Hammond took a deep breath and let his tears fall freely now as he spoke. "But, baby girl, I loved you on both of those days." He smiled through his tears. "So whether or not the state still recognizes our marriage as binding or not, I am going to put my pride aside and entrust you with my heart again like I promised you I would— if you'll take me."

Sara nodded, and they cried tears of joy together. Then they shared a kiss that turned into an all-night affair as they rekindled their undeniable love for one another. And afterward, for the first time in months, Sara slept peacefully—wrapped in Hammond's arms.

19. A NEW PROMISE

THE NEXT TIME Chelsea and Davin saw Hammond, he stood tall—smiling and holding Sara's hand. Sara was wearing her brightest pink sundress and had orange hair-ties holding four tight buns on the top of her head. She was smiling from ear to ear as she tugged at Hammond's arm to encourage him to sit next to Davin and Chelsea for dinner.

"Nice to see you two again," Chelsea said, overjoyed for her friends' happiness.

"Hammond tells me much of that is due to you two," Sara said.

"I can't begin to express how indebted I am to you for helping me realize what I already knew," Hammond said, looking at Davin directly. Chelsea smiled, pleased that bringing Davin that night ended up being a good decision. She was impressed with Davin's deep insight into what Hammond needed to hear. She could not help but be proud of him.

"No problem at all," Davin said with a smile. "I know how easy it is to not take full advantage of your happiness—even when it's right in front of you." He looked at Chelsea with a message in his eyes that she couldn't decipher.

"Well, I hope we never have to go through something like that again, but I think we're going to come out stronger for it," Hammond said, putting his arm around Sara in support. "We've never felt closer."

Sara smiled and looked up at him lovingly. "Hammond even made up some of the task hours I missed, and he got The Society leaders to pardon my absences."

Hammond merely smiled, and Sara went on. He did not elaborate about these additional favors Branch had granted him for his continued complacency, and for the rest of dinner, the four of them talked and laughed, grateful they were sitting next to the people they loved most.

THE FOLLOWING DAY marked Davin's last day of filming. For Chelsea, it came with feelings of both relief and concern. She was excited at the possibility of spending more time with Davin but nervous as to what plans Ms. Waverly had in store for him next. Davin was also worried. He wondered if Waverly still suspected he knew too much. If nothing else, it was clear she had been trying to keep him busy.

Thankfully, as far as they knew, no one was aware of the depths of their suspicions or the lengths they were willing to go to should their fears be confirmed. And since Chelsea assumed they'd want Davin around for the opening debut of the film, she felt confident he would be in no danger before then. This gave her peace of mind whenever she worried about his uncertain future. Just the same, having a boyfriend at the mercy of his elaborate Society contract that could be changed at any minute was often unnerving.

The process of searching for the cave was still slow, and so far, no sign of the entrance had been discovered. However, they only had two zones left to search, and now that filming was over,

Chelsea hoped that with Davin's help, they could search the remaining area more quickly.

That night also marked the last of The Society's scheduled gatherings that were meant to entertain and update the residents on the status of the hurricane relief. For the first time since the hurricane, the meeting would also be broadcast back to the mainland for the public to view.

Just a week before, the news hit the general public that a storm had been what had caused the communications with the Hawaii Society to go down, but despite this unfortunate event, the Society members had repaired the damages themselves without assistance from the government and had even been busy filming a new movie with a beloved, retired director. Millions around the US were tuning in to hear from The Hawaii Society again, and to learn more about the soon-to-be-released film by well-known director, Genevieve Thrope, featuring Davin Chapman as the star. Everyone was excited about this movie. It restored a sense of hope and joy for the entire nation that felt lost after the earthquake on the California coast when the US had lost most of its other Hollywood stars and directors. No other studios or actors had been able to capture the hearts quite like the well-known names of Hollywood yet.

Davin was instructed to keep the meeting as lighthearted as possible and downplay the destruction the hurricane had caused to The Society. "Only mention the *success* of our recovery from the storm," Ms. Waverly had told Davin in his room the night before. "Besides that, your speech will focus on the movie."

Davin was prepared with his memorized lines, and Chelsea sat at her workstation ready for the show to begin. As Davin entered the stage, the crowd erupted into cheers. An atmosphere of comfort and delight was back in the air as The Society returned to normalcy, little by little, and the enthusiasm for the film grew.

When the applause finally died down, Davin began his speech. "Aloha everyone, and welcome to the last of a series of updates and celebrations as we commemorate The Hawaii Society in all of its success and beauty," he said. "I tell you what—we have some exciting news to discuss today! But first I would like to invite to the stage my lovely cohost, Kona, the Hawaiian beauty."

The crowd cheered loudly when Davin kissed her hand as she entered just before he exited the stage. Then Kona introduced a new promotional video for The Societies. The video showed beautiful flybys of the towering mountain and the majestic waterfall splashing down into the river and out to the ocean. It featured shots of people enjoying their time back on the water—paddleboarding and sailing on the ocean. Multiple B-roll shots showed the beauty in the details of the island, like shots of honeybees crawling on a brilliant hibiscus and toes running through the sand. Images of The Society buildings were showcased showing the large towering dome and the high-tech facilities throughout. A shot of Kona and Davin waving at the camera from a speeding boat ended the video as the crowd applauded in approval of the facility and the lifestyle they had originally come to The Society to enjoy.

"Isn't this a wonderful place to live?" Kona prompted the crowd.

Davin reentered stage as the audience whooped and hollered in agreement. "That's right, Kona. We're all very blessed here at The Society to be amid the beauty of Hawaii. Additionally, I know The Societies Program has blessed Society members across the US. And after seeing our residents pull together to *completely* recover from the tropical storm that hit our island, we're happy to inform the world that the Hawaii Society will continue to benefit this generation. We should all be very proud. Our recovery serves as a tribute to our strength and a testament to the system in which we live."

"And not only have we recovered from a storm, but we've also been very busy with an exciting project underway. Haven't we, Davin?"

"I've certainly been busy, Kona," Davin said with a chuckle. "For everyone in the States watching this broadcast, the stories are true! We've been working tirelessly to bring back a little movie magic! Director Genevieve Thrope is here with us on the island. Back from retirement, she's at it again, and I tell you what, that woman has the artistic vision to match her reputation."

"She's truly one of the greatest directors of her time and remembered fondly for her work on her previous films."

"Absolutely, Kona. I've been so fortunate to have worked with her and can't wait for you all to see the debut of our new film, *A Mile in Their Shoes.* Now, what you've all been waiting for, let's take a look at the first trailer!"

Chelsea began the clip of the trailer and brought it to full screen on the LED wall. Everyone watched in anticipation as the trailer teased their interest. People cheered over the crowd when they saw themselves or their friends featured, and the reality of being in a film became palpable. Chelsea became absorbed in the clip as she watched Davin in the trailer and almost missed her cue to bring back the camera shot of Kona and Davin as it finished.

"Doesn't it look like it's going to be amazing?" Kona squealed. Cheers and applause filled the room.

"I can't wait to see the end product with all of you at the film's debut right here on June 26th. That's only a few short months away! And we invite everyone outside of our Society to join us through our network to view it remotely that night as well. It will be a film premiere unlike any the world has ever seen!" Davin said as he threw his hands in the air. He waited until the cheers quieted, then continued. "Now our Head Society Leader has a message for our residents. We look forward to seeing you all back here for the premiere, but until then, Ms. Sandra Waverly . . ."

"Thank you all for coming," Ms. Waverly began as she walked on stage following Davin's introduction. "We truly live in a wonderful place, and we are very grateful for the life provided to those who weren't able to make a life for themselves due to circumstances beyond their own control." She waited as the crowd applauded in agreement. "Now that the storm has been overcome, we will restore all previous rules and requirements of The Society." Ms. Waverly tried to be as nonspecific as possible for the viewing public abroad, but the residents knew her statement meant the workload requirement was going back to two hours a day. The majority of the audience, happy to have a shorter workday again, began clapping. Others were less enthusiastic, as they had come to enjoy the productivity of their time. "Now we can all return to life as normal, and we look forward to the day that Davin Chapman's new film is released—where we will get to see our very own Society grounds featured in the film." People erupted into applause. "Please also enjoy an added treat tonight as we will be providing a dessert."

No one had tasted a dessert since before the hurricane struck. They were rarely made, even before the storm, since anything with processed sugar was not permitted because of health concerns. Fresh fruit was the usual treat that satisfied people's sweet tooth, but that night a scoop of coconut ice cream with a raspberry on top was available to everyone in large coolers near the exits of the dome.

As people began to clear the room, Davin ran up to Chelsea as she was finishing turning off the video system. "Can you believe it? I'm done with filming, and no more six hours of work every day! It's going to be amazing—I get to spend way more time with you now," he said, smiling and resisting the urge to lift her in the air and spin her around. He knew how much she would hate that.

"Yup! And tomorrow we can go escapading together," Chelsea replied.

Davin nodded half-heartedly, as he had his hopes set on a different plan. "Yeah, but I was also thinking we could go for a hike or something like that in the morning. Would you be up for that?"

"I suppose so," Chelsea said, not wanting to say no and disappoint him, "but we really should make escapading our priority now that you're done filming. Between the two of us, I would think we still have at least two weeks left," she estimated, referring to the two zones they still had left to search. "But what we should really figure out is what we are doing tonight to celebrate the end of filming! Any ideas?"

"I have some," Davin said, unable to hold back a smile. "Let's head to my room and figure it out. I need to grab something."

After indulging in some delicious creamy coconut ice cream, they began walking to Davin's living quarters. Davin laced his fingers with Chelsea's. She could tell from his smiling eyes that he was in a particularly good mood that evening. He was looking at her the way he did on occasions when he was especially enraptured. She used to grow shy when he looked at her that way, but she had become used to it. He didn't turn his gaze, even when she looked away with a charmed smile. As they approached his room, he felt confident in his plans for the evening.

Inside his room, he slowed his step—breaking Chelsea's forward momentum. He gently coaxed her back into his arms and looked at her lovingly. She held his gaze as he pushed her hair back behind her ear. Instead of kissing her as she had anticipated, he reached for her earpiece and removed it and then slipped off her woven copper band. He walked to the bathroom, placed them on the counter, and then removed his own.

Perplexed, she wondered if he wanted to recalibrate their approach on investigating The Society. She knew it was probably a wise move, but she had hoped to go do something fun to celebrate the end of filming, especially since there were supposed to be lots of fun activities available on the grounds that night.

He closed the bathroom door and casually leaned up against it. He breathed a sigh and rubbed his left hand. "I've come to a decision," he said thoughtfully, looking at the floor. After a lingering pause, he looked up at her with an intense but charming rapture. "I've wanted you since the day I met you, Chelsea Coremon, but tonight," he said more quietly as his gaze softened and he moved closer, "I need you to know that I will *choose* to want you *forever*."

Chelsea instinctively moved a step closer to him. Her eyes widened as she realized what he might be saying.

"When you first came to my room, you stopped me from making the mistake of toying with your emotions when I hadn't even decided what I wanted this to be. You gave me the desire to put our relationship before my desire for you—something I've never had to do before. I made a promise to you that night." He paused, and a crooked grin appeared on his face. "And it proved to be much harder than I had anticipated, but I want to thank you for giving me that opportunity." He became serious, his tone laced with sincerity. "It's made me learn to love you beyond my physical attraction for you. It started me on the path of loving you for who you are instead of for how I feel toward you in the moment. It's taught me that I really do just, well . . . I love you, Chels, and I love to be around you. So I want to make a new promise to you."

Davin took a step closer, and she stepped closer to him. As they were about to meet in the middle of the room, Chelsea's heart raced with anticipation. She yearned to touch him. But then he stopped and cocked his head to the side ever so slightly.

"But before I do, *I* need to know something." He spoke these words as he reached up to grab something from the shelf, but what he grabbed was too small for Chelsea to see. She could not fathom how it could relate to what he was proposing. Then he turned and looked at her with a profound intensity. "I need to know if *you* choose *me*."

He revealed a small ring made from the shell of a coconut. "I know a lot of people think of a ring as a sort of branding of ownership, and I know that no one will even recognize it as anything of importance, but that isn't what matters to me. I want to use this ring to serve as a reminder to us of our commitment to each other." Davin paused for a moment and studied her expression. "You have to realize that *your* heart is not the only one at stake here." Chelsea couldn't understand how he could think she didn't love him. She went to respond, but he cut her off before she could speak. "Take your time to decide—I want you to feel as confident about us as I do. I will wait—as long as it takes."

"That's the thing," she responded immediately. "I don't need more time." She smiled as she reached out to hold his hand that held the ring. "I know you think I'm blinded by your looks or your fame, but I don't think you realize that I have constantly questioned your intentions and your character *so* many times over the past few months." From Davin's expression, she realized he wasn't sure how he should feel about her statement, so she added, "But you've proven to be so much more than just the handsome face I suspected you to be. You're sweet and funny and patient. You're a good friend who really cares. You put up with all my annoying antics, which are only present because I'm so comfortable being myself when I'm around you." She looked down and shrugged. "I've never had that with anyone. I feel so comfortable to be me when I'm around you. So beyond your good looks and fame, and the fact that you're insightful, and you're kind—I choose you because, for the first time in my life, I feel so happy to just be me when I am around you. I love you for that." And without reservations, she said, "I choose you too, Davin."

Davin had stood, quietly smiling, until she finished. Then he looked down and opened his hand to offer her the ring. He had spent every spare moment he had over the last month carving it out of a coconut shell with any sharp rocks he could find around the grounds. Upon closer inspection, she noticed a small design etched into the ring that formed a simple flower-like design. Chelsea ran her finger over it. "Is it a hibiscus?"

"It's actually supposed to be two connected infinity symbols," he said. "One represents you and the other is me." Davin inspected his design more closely. "It does look kind of look like a flower though, huh?" He laughed. "I just thought the infinity symbols would be fitting since I'd like to have the forever kind of love you promised yourself you'd find," he said as he ran his fingers through the hair on the back of Chelsea's head and traced the infinity symbol there.

Chelsea continued to look down at the infinity symbols. "That . . . That's *really* sweet, Davin." It was perfect. She almost wanted to cry, thinking back to the promises she had made her brokenhearted self, but then she realized she had no reason to cry any longer. She had found her forever love, and he was more wonderful than she could have ever imagined.

"I plan to have my ring tattooed on in the morning," Davin explained. "I don't do well with jewelry, and besides, I won't ever need to take it off."

Chelsea smiled. "I like that idea. Maybe I'll get one too." As she spoke, she slid the ring on her ring finger, but it was too large and would've easily slipped off if she left it there.

Davin frowned. "Uh, I'm sorry. I was trying to surprise you, so I didn't take exact measurements. Clearly, I haven't sized you up as well as I thought I had," he joked.

Chelsea laughed and tried it on her other fingers and found it only fit her thumb. She held out her hand to look at it. The ring was simple and elemental, but she was pleased to find that she loved everything about it. She had never asked herself what she would want in a ring before. Very few people wore commitment rings anymore, and even fewer wore diamond rings after the truth about the blood diamond scandals spread. But the more she looked at the ring on her thumb, the more she felt it belonged there. She hadn't known it before she saw it, but it was everything she could have ever wanted—she even loved the way it looked on her thumb.

"So do you like it?"

"I do," she said, grinning and eventually looking up from it. "I love it!"

Davin smiled, happy to see she was still pleased with a thumb ring. "Well then, now that we are certain we want to love each other forever, I propose a new promise—a promise that we will put each other before anyone else, a promise that we will choose to love each other no matter what, a promise to work together despite our differences, a promise to spend the rest of forever lovin' on each other with complete fidelity, respect, and every ounce of passion we possess. Even if God is the only one to witness it, I promise to keep all these commitments and more if you promise me the same," Davin said tenderly and then waited for her response.

"I promise," Chelsea replied.

Before she could take in a full breath, Davin moved in quickly, wrapping his hands around her waist and pulling her close. He kissed her with the same passion he'd shown the first night she visited his room—holding nothing back, but with a gentle care that he lacked the last time he acted on his desires.

The force of his body pressing against hers gently moved her toward the bed. "I guess I just have one more question to ask you then." He pulled back a little and playfully smiled as he kissed her more softly and whispered, "Is this mutual?"

His deep and alluring voice saying those words to her when she actually had a definitive answer made her heart skip. She smiled. "Yes," she said confidently.

Knowing he had her commitment and her permission, he kissed her and held nothing back. Her calves met the back of his mattress, and she sat down on the bed. He made his way from her lips to the nape of her neck. Chills ran down her spine, and the aroma of Davin's cologne encircled her as he ran his hands over her body.

Chelsea removed Davin's shirt, feeling a complete sense of peace knowing that in the morning, she would wake up with Davin still by her side, and every day after that, she would go to bed kissing those same intoxicating lips that were making their way down her body. Every concern about scandal and the cave and The Society went forgotten as they finally indulged in their desires for each other—intensified by their commitments to one another.

IN THE MORNING, Davin traced his finger down Chelsea's bare back—smiling at his sleeping would-be-wife. *If only I could be so lucky,* he thought, wishing he still had the option. As a boy, he had often watched as his parents danced in the living room. His dad would tell him, "One day when you have a wife of your own, make sure you let the world know you love her—at every opportunity." His father would pause and press his forehead against his mom's. "And kiss her like you mean it," he would say before planting a long, sweet kiss on his mother's lips. Though he found it embarrassing as a child, Davin grew to admire his parent's relationship, and he was now forever grateful to have witnessed such a love every day before his father passed.

Davin looked at the ring he had put so much care into that now rested on Chelsea's thumb. The world would know his love for her, even if they did not recognize it. But more importantly, she would know it, because he would make sure of it every day.

After the sun rose, Chelsea awoke to the feel of Davin's bare skin still pressed against her. She smiled—pleased that her belief that he would still be there in the morning light had turned into a reality in that moment. Her confidence that he would continue to be there in the years to follow grew as well. And even though her fear that it was all a fantasy still haunted her, she was content knowing they were one day closer to forever.

Grinning at her sleepy smile as she woke, he greeted her. "Good morning." He beamed with fulfillment and kissed her lips. Then pulling back to look at her again, he whispered, "You're gorgeous." Chelsea gave him a grin before letting out a subtle laugh—she still could not fathom how *he* could possibly find her gorgeous.

"So . . . I know we want to get a jump on searching the last two zones, but I was wondering if we could spend today together—just enjoying each other." Davin evaluated her facial expression as she contemplated the wisdom of prolonging the search again. "Come on, Chels. We'll make it up later, but just for today, let's go out and have some fun," he pleaded.

As he spoke, Chelsea got lost in the calm blue of his enchanting eyes, and suddenly the urgency to search for the cave was gone. She gave him a reluctant half-smile, wondering if she would ever be able to resist his radiant smile or pleading eyes. "Alright," she said, excitedly jumping up and grabbing her clothes.

After breakfast, Davin turned to her. "First things first, we need to even out." He raised his left hand and pointed to his ring finger. Then he took her by the hand, and they eagerly raced to the elevator.

At the tattoo station, Davin uploaded his drawing of the infinity symbols that he had inscribed into Chelsea's coconut ring. She looked down at her coconut ring and smiled as he placed his hand under the calibration machine. Davin selected where he wanted his tattoo to be located and then rotated the orientation of the design to where he liked it. The mounted tattoo pen shifted and rotated to begin precisely etching the image exactly where Davin had specified. Davin grimaced playfully at Chelsea as the needle worked its way across the skin on his left ring finger.

After a short while, his tattooed ring was complete. He removed his hand and held it out to look at the finished product—mimicking Chelsea from the night before.

"Like it?" Chelsea asked.

"I do," Davin rehearsed back to her. They both laughed at each other as they thought back to the night before.

"My turn," Chelsea said as she moved into the seat where Davin had been. She got the same tattoo on the same finger. When it was done, she looked at it. "It looks so good!"

"You don't have to keep the coconut ring," Davin said, unsure of the merit of his workmanship and feeling bad it had turned into a thumb ring. "I figured it would be more like a placeholder, so I could give you a chance to say no before getting it permanently etched on your skin." Davin laughed.

"My coconut ring?" Chelsea asked, playfully offended. "Nope—it stays on. I just got the tattoo so we would match and so even if I take the ring off, I'll never be without my reminder of how much I love you." She paused for a moment before an impish grin grew on her face. "Even during those times when I am completely annoyed with you." Chelsea smiled and studied his reaction. She couldn't help but immediately revert to teasing him when she was open about her feelings. She knew it was just an unfledged attempt to mask how vulnerable she felt, but for some reason, she felt comfortable teasing him.

He shook his head and chuckled. It was somewhat refreshing to him that she was not constantly trying to impress and compliment him—like most women did. Plus, he liked it anytime Chelsea said I love you. He could always see it in her eyes, but she infrequently said those words out loud. It was as though she was afraid to utter them, but Davin knew she was actually afraid there would be a day that he wouldn't love her back. *Such a silly notion.* He looked down at his newly-formed infinity tattoo, still slightly red from the needle, thinking about how much he loved her—how he would always love her.

"So what's next?" Chelsea asked anxiously.

After the long days away from each other because of filming, they felt an overwhelming sense of joy to be in each other's presence. They filled their day doing the things they liked most and simply enjoying being together. Davin tried flyboarding again and vastly improved his performance after applying some more techniques Chelsea taught him. And with some instruction from Davin, Chelsea broke open a coconut and drank from it directly for the first time in her life. After their two hours of task work, they relaxed on the beach and then hiked the mountain.

Davin enjoyed their day together, but secretly he couldn't wait until the day ended and the night came. He grabbed Chelsea's hand when darkness fully enveloped the night sky and pulled her back to the sandy shores of the island without explanation. "What are we doing?" Chelsea asked.

Davin turned to her with a mischievous grin. "I've been dying to take you here forever—indulge me."

Chelsea relinquished control as Davin began to lead her. However, when they reached the bridge that traveled over the river to the base of the mountain, she couldn't help but stop him for a short kiss.

Putting his own intentions aside for the moment, he leaned up against the bridge's railing and gladly kissed her back. It was an unusually still and quiet night. Their lips parted, and Chelsea leaned back with her eyes still closed and whispered, "Thank you."

"For what?" Davin asked.

"For making a daydream of mine come true," she said. "Ever since I arrived and saw a couple kissing on this bridge, I've always wanted to share a kiss here."

Davin smiled. "I was actually hoping you would do something similar for me tonight—if you're up for it."

Chelsea smiled, intrigued. "What exactly did you have in mind?"

He took her to the far side of the mountain, and then he walked her through thick foliage until they reached a small beach. The tall palm trees reached out over the ocean, and the wild plants that grew around the outskirts of the seashore formed a picturesque silhouette around them. It was clear the beach was unknown to most and very much deserted that night.

"Look at the stars with me?" asked Davin while enjoying her enchanted expression.

They sat down in the soft, white sand, still warm from the sun, and looked up toward the heavens. The night sky was clear, and the stars were shining brightly, providing a perfect backdrop to the tropical canvas that surrounded them. Nothing but the sound of the waves crashing around them was there to interrupt. They turned off the flashlights of their wristbands and snuggled up close to one another. Besides the multitude of satellites circling around and the light from the moon, no other lights could be seen.

"How did you find this place?" she asked.

"Roy and I found it." Davin smiled as he thought back to his adventures with Roy. "I never thought I'd want to come back when he died, but I couldn't think of a more perfect place to share this evening with you. Plus, I think he would have wanted me to share it with someone as special as you."

Chelsea smiled, and Davin hugged her close. Then he sat back and looked up to enjoy the view of the starry picture that blanketed them overhead.

In what light there was from the night sky, Chelsea studied Davin closely. His strong jawline angled up toward the sky, and his wide eyes seldom blinked as he tried to identify different constellations. Strands of his sun-dyed hair spurted out in all directions, framing his tanned face. She felt so small sitting next to him. His muscular physique and height difference almost made her feel like a child, and she found herself wishing she were just a few inches taller.

But as the thought crossed her mind, she reminded herself that she was *his* type—whether she understood it or not, he wanted her just the way she was. Her self-deprecating thoughts silenced as she stared at him, and the recollection of his deep soothing voice filled her mind—reminding her she was perfect the way she was.

The corners of Davin's lips turned up and the slight crow's feet at the ends of his smiling eyes appeared when he noticed Chelsea's intense gaze. "It's *so* beautiful out tonight. What an incredible view," he said, still looking at the stars. He then turned to look at her in the moonlight as a wave brushed up against her legs and soaked the bottom of her sundress. There was a glimmer in Chelsea's eyes as she looked at him that made Davin want to burst. "But I find it even more incredible how I can barely know you, and yet, every time I look in your eyes, I feel like I know your soul, and everything in me tells me to love you. I really do love you, Chelsea."

"I love you too," she said as her heart warmed to his words. She watched as his smile widened at hearing her say those words for the second time that day. Then she found herself transfixed on the lower lip of his smile, compelling her to come closer. She leaned in toward him and kissed it softly, then pulled back, knowing that if she continued, she wouldn't want to stop.

He had so gracefully allowed her to live out a small daydream of her own on the bridge that she felt it'd be self-indulgent to dismiss his stargazing. But as much as she tried to ignore it, she was finding it hard to keep her mind on the sky when his skin was pressing up against her, tempting her with his touch—until she could finally stand it no more.

She moved herself a few inches away and forced her gaze away from him.

Davin chuckled to himself to see her restraint. Then he turned to her and whispered, "You know, I didn't bring you out here just to look at some stars."

20. THE FRIEND

AFTER A FUN-FILLED day and a passionate evening, Chelsea and Davin returned to Chelsea's room tired and ready to turn in for the night. Though neither of them regretted their decision to put off the search and enjoy the day together, they knew their leisure couldn't last. They showered to wash away the sand and sweat from a long day of activities, but even during their soft, wet kisses and lighthearted laughter in the shower, they both began to think about the following day and what they needed to do to refocus on the search.

Weary from the day, they went to bed and held each other close—but neither of them could sleep. Davin lay on the bed and stroked Chelsea's hairline, thinking of the loss of his friend. He relished how happy and certain he was in his relationship with Chelsea, but he still felt a void in his life that Roy had once filled. He wanted to tell him about Chelsea—her stubborn disposition under the peach tree, the first time Chelsea flirted with him as they played *Leagues of Reprisal* together. If Roy still had the chance to meet Chelsea, he would undoubtedly laugh as she recounted how Davin landed flat-faced in the water during his first attempt at flyboarding. *Roy would approve of her*, he thought—he was sure of that.

Besides the longing to tell his friend about Chelsea, the memory of Roy telling him about the cave was replaying in the back of his mind for some reason. The concern on Roy's face and his trembling hands haunted him, and guilt began to bubble up inside him for not having found the cave yet. He knew there was little more he could have done with all the obligations Ms. Waverly had placed on him and the demands from filming, but he still wished he could've contributed more instead of leaving it all up to Chelsea. He wondered if perhaps he shouldn't have spent the *whole* day enjoying himself. *Tomorrow will be different,* he told himself, and he swore from that day forward he would remain focused and diligent in finding the cave until he had answers.

Chelsea lay with her eyes closed, feeling Davin's hand stroking her head and thinking about the man in the pineapple shorts. With the evidence she had to prove The Society was sneaking him on the island to fix problems, she contemplated what the motive behind hiding his visits could be. *Maybe he's an illegal immigrant and doing the job at a discounted price?* she wondered. Given how difficult it was to immigrate to the United States illegally now, she doubted that was the reason. *Or maybe he has a history riddled with crime and the government is overlooking it.* But there were plenty of repairmen with a clean record they could have hired if that were true. Then she remembered Tray Wong's argument with the grounds bot that she overheard at the orange tree. "The Society is breaking down" . . . *I wonder if they are keeping it secret to hide the fact there are inefficiencies in the system?*

She guessed there could be a swarm of complications that would accompany the discrepancy of having to hire a high-cost specialist to visit a supposedly *self-sufficient* facility on a regular basis. But without the means of proving her theory, there was no way of really knowing.

Then Chelsea stumbled back on the question she had been asking herself the past several days of escapading. "What we are going to do if we decide to leave?" she asked Davin.

He jumped, thinking she was asleep but now realizing she must have been deep in thought as well. "That's a good question," he said. Though he had wondered the same thing, they had never really discussed the matter further than wanting to leave. This was mainly because neither of them *really* wanted to leave their beautiful island, and since they could not yet prove The Society's corruption with certainty, they didn't need to decide yet. But since they had already stored their earpieces and wristbands in Chelsea's bathroom for the night, Davin concluded it was probably as good a time as ever to discuss it. Plus, he felt more comfortable discussing things in Chelsea's room than his own.

"What would *you* like to do?"

"I'm not sure. I don't really think we can go back to our parents if we want to live on our own terms," Chelsea thought out loud.

"As much as I would love to be with my mother, she really doesn't have the money to support us. After all, I left her every penny she has, and I'm not sure it will even last her to the end of her life."

"Yeah—I'm not sure I want to compete with your mom for your affections anyway," Chelsea teased, knowing how much he cared for his mother. "And I can't say I really want to live with my mom either. I was already enough of a burden to her when I lived there, and she is still having to pay Glenn's deposit fee each month since he didn't have as much money saved up as I did. She definitely wouldn't be happy to have me returning with another dependent," she said with a sigh. "And even though I would love to meet your mother, what I really want is to be on our own. I've never felt like I've lived an independent life. I thought I would get that here—living alone at The Society. But somehow it feels like I might as well be living at my parents'."

Davin pondered her words. Being the face of The Society came with its own set of challenges. Though he also wanted the sense of independence that comes from providing for himself, more than that he wanted to escape the feeling of being trapped and controlled. He wanted to be somewhere where he could make his own choices, with Chelsea by his side. He wanted to be somewhere where he could be himself without having to conform to someone else's agenda. "I agree. I don't want to live with either of our parents," he decided.

"But if not with our parents, where do we go? We'll still run into the same problems we faced before. There won't be steady, good-paying jobs for me, and without an established film industry, you may not have a job, even with your reputation," she replied.

"Maybe—although the movie business may pick up again if our movie takes off. Some studio will set itself up as the hub, and the movie business will finally revive itself," Davin said confidently as he thought about the implications of a new and successful movie being released with a familiar Hollywood name and celebrated director behind it. *The anguish of the earthquake's destruction will fade with the excitement,* he thought.

According to Genevieve, this movie was meant to spark a new era of film. She had pushed the grounds of creativity and made Davin work harder than ever before, but he didn't mind. He loved acting and felt at ease behind the camera—though he did often wonder if he would enjoy doing something more challenging and purposeful if he had the opportunity.

"Did you like living in California?" Chelsea randomly asked.

"Yeah. It was beautiful. California had great weather and nice scenery," he answered. "Why?"

"Why doesn't anyone live there now?"

"Mostly because, after such a massive earthquake, there really wasn't much left to go home to. All the main cities are under water now. It's not even considered a state anymore. Puerto Rico is now the fiftieth state."

"I know that, but what about the small towns that were deep inland and still unclaimed?" Chelsea said—trying not to be irritated by his obvious answer.

"Well, for one, there was still quite a bit of damage to those towns, and, for two, I think a lot of people were spooked. Staying there would have continually reminded them of the horror they experienced during the earthquake—almost like PTSD." He had spent some time after the earthquake exploring what was left of the state. For some reason, he thought that time would help him heal or he would miraculously find a friend who had escaped the disaster—even though he knew that was next to impossible. Unfortunately, all he found were tragic stories and mass destruction.

"Do you know if any of the cities that are still unclaimed are at all livable? We could try and live somewhere around there," Chelsea suggested, thinking aloud.

"That may not be a bad idea," Davin said. "Supposedly the parts of California that haven't been claimed by neighboring states are basically ghost towns, so that could be a good option for us if we want to escape the system altogether. But it could also be dangerous, and we'd probably have to do a lot of cleanup and repairs to make it livable."

"Do you feel like we could manage something like that?"

Davin shrugged. "I think so," he said. "Assuming it's not too dangerous, and if we're okay with living very basically. Or maybe we could see if there are others who would like to escape with us that could help us rebuild?"

"Maybe," she replied. "But that might be risky as well. If word got out to the wrong people that we plan to leave, who knows what they'll do to us." Davin looked up at her in surprise, so Chelsea expounded. "If The Society is not allowing people to leave like we think, then they certainly aren't going to let us go quietly—especially not you, Davin. Are you sure you want to do this?" she whispered reluctantly as she thought about the millions of ways an escape could end poorly. "Maybe we should just stay and be content with the life we have. I can't say I'm entirely unhappy, especially now that I have you."

"There are lots of fun things to do at The Society, and I do like it here a lot of the time," he said as he ran his fingers up her neck and through her hair. "But you're the best thing about this place, so I think I could be happy anywhere as long as you're there with me," he said. He paused and smiled at her. Then his smile faded, and he continued. "Plus, if we confirm they're keeping people here against their will, I can't stay and advocate for a place that's trying to hide contempt for its own people. And if The Society had *anything* to do with Roy's death, I will *not* overlook that." He took a deep breath and thought more about the implications of leaving. "You are right though. I would be breaking my contract by leaving, so they will definitely try to stop me," he said. "But legally that should only mean I won't be allowed the benefits and accommodations of The Society. They shouldn't be able to physically stop me."

Chelsea gave him an impatient glare. "We are toying with the idea that The Society has a hidden cave where they are secretly hiding people. And your friend, who happened to be the *only* person who knew the location of the cave, is now dead," she whispered sternly. She stopped for a moment to let that statement sink in. "Legal or not, if any of that is true, I don't—"

"That's it!" As Chelsea spoke, Davin suddenly remembered something he had overlooked. "He *isn't* the only one who knows where it is!" He looked up at Chelsea with wide eyes. "I completely forgot—Roy said he went with a friend to the cave!"

A swarm of questions rushed into Chelsea's mind. "Who was it? Where can we find him?"

"I don't actually know," Davin said. "He just said a friend."

"Is there a way we can find out?"

Davin thought hard, knowing that if he could come up with a solution, they would easily find the cave and get the answers they needed to decide their future. "What if we were able to see footage from Roy's wristband? We could figure out who the friend was or maybe even see right where the cave is," he said, full of hope. "I never thought about it before because, honestly, I thought we would have found the cave by now. But we're almost to the last zone and have found zero signs of a cave." Then he shrugged his shoulders in defeat. "But they aren't going to let us see the security footage if they're trying to hide something. We'd have to break into the security room or something, and I'm not sure we're equipped to pull that kind of thing off. At least . . . I'm not." Then he looked toward Chelsea inquisitively.

She looked back. "Don't look at me. I don't know how to break into a security room."

"Hey, you never know. It was worth a shot," Davin said, smiling.

She laughed. "I don't have a secret life of crime if that's what you're asking." Then a thought came to mind. "But there may be another way . . . " she said as a smile grew on her face. "I have a friend who supposedly has quite an affinity for cyber-hacking."

"Do you trust him?"

"Her. And yes," she replied. "If nothing else, she can keep a secret."

As he considered the option, Davin returned her smile. "If you trust her, I say it's worth a shot."

"So will you do it?" Chelsea asked after she and Davin had explained the situation to Finley the next morning after breakfast at a remote spot on the island.

"First off, I just want to clear the air by saying I'm not buying this whole conspiracy you guys have conjured up. That's crazy talk. Second, I could get kicked out of The Society or worse for doing this. So I'm out," Finley said and started to leave.

Chelsea quickly grabbed the airtight box she had borrowed from one of the edit bays and removed Finley's earpiece and wristband from it. "Wait, Finley," she said, extending her things. As Finley walked back and reached out to retrieve them, Chelsea decided to try one last time. "Come on—I know you can do it. You've told me all about how amazing you are. If anyone on at The Society can do it, you can."

"I never said I *couldn't* do it," Finley said defensively.

"Please," Chelsea pleaded.

Finley looked at Chelsea, then at Davin, then back to Chelsea. "Fine. I'll do it for you. I appreciate your friendship, Chelsea, and I'm awesome like that. You won't be able to do it without me. Meet me in my room tomorrow morning at 6 a.m. sharp." Looking at Davin, she said, "Bring him along. He's nice to look at." Then she walked off.

Chelsea rolled her eyes and tried to remind herself to be grateful that Finley was going to help.

Davin looked at Chelsea's expression and smiled. "Don't worry, Chels. Not my type," he said reassuringly. Chelsea smiled knowingly, and Davin shot her a flirtatious wink. "Though I do think we should still go out searching one last time while we have the time—if we find it, we can avoid having to use Finley's help altogether."

Chelsea agreed, and they went to pick up their gear and investigate the waters once more. They searched meticulously with an added sense of urgency. They finished searching the second to last zone on the map and continued on to the final zone—feeling closer to success than ever before. *It has to be in this last zone,* Chelsea thought to herself as she swam faster to try and finish the zone before dinner.

Chelsea's legs and arms were stronger than ever from the many hours of escapading she had completed each day for weeks on end. She'd developed methods of efficiency to search areas quickly without having to retrace her steps. Davin had split off from Chelsea to be as productive as possible, and they searched with tangible hope that this was the zone the cave would be in.

Chelsea turned the corner of a reef, and then she saw something. A hole. An opening to something. *The cave?* She swam toward it and without thought she plunged in, headfirst. It curved around, and she saw a glimmer of light at the end. But as she swam the hole became smaller and soon she could swim no farther. She looked up toward the light—so close, but so far away. She couldn't see much of anything at the end of the tunnel, so she turned on the light on her mask. Besides being able to see more of the details of the walls and a few nervous fish scurrying away, she still couldn't see anything at the end of the tunnel. *How did Roy see so much detail?* Chelsea wondered. *I can't make anything out.* Then a face popped up and peered down at her! She jumped back and froze in terror. Then a light came on and shone down on her still body. The figure gave a friendly wave, and then Chelsea realized it was Davin looking down at her through the other end of the hole.

Chelsea carefully backed out of the hole, completely let down. They continued searching until they could search no more, but unfortunately, they once again ended their search without having found the whereabouts of the cave.

After eating dinner and finishing their task work for the day, Chelsea and Davin sat down on Chelsea's bed to further discuss their plans if they were to leave The Society. " . . . And once we're in

California, we'll find a place we can salvage and set ourselves up there. We'll make it our own, live the simple life, start our family, and who knows from there," Chelsea said with a smile.

"Start a family?" Davin said, looking over at her.

Realizing what she had said, she blurted out, "Maybe. We don't have to. Really I was just saying 'family' as a general term."

Davin chuckled at her nervousness. "It's okay—I'm not against it. It's just good to know," Davin simply stated.

Chelsea was relieved he wasn't offended by her assumption, and then her heart warmed at the thought of Davin as a father. She hadn't considered it before that moment, but she somehow knew he'd be great at it.

"I'm sorry again for scaring you in the hole, by the way," Davin said. "You seriously jumped a mile."

"I know. I totally freaked, but once I figured out it was you I was fine. In fact, I was relieved it was just you. Although I was convinced I'd finally found the entrance, so it was a bit of a bummer."

"Sorry to be such a letdown," he teased. "But hopefully tomorrow will finally bring some answers—if Finley's as good as she thinks she is." He laughed.

"If her stories are true, she is."

"Good. Then tomorrow's the day. Now let's get some sleep."

IN FINLEY'S ROOM the next morning, each of them carefully removed their wristbands and earpieces and placed them in the bathroom. Finley turned off the lights and ran the shower as an extra precaution that nothing would be heard. She closed the door to the bathroom behind her and shut the blind. Sitting at her desk, she expanded her PED to its full length and began hastily typing. "We will need to be in and out of the system in less than five minutes to not be detected—that's really hard to do by the way.

But not impossible—not for me at least," she said with a smirk while looking over at Davin—who, to Finley's disappointment, was smiling at Chelsea in anticipation that the hack would work. She turned back to her screen, less than enthusiastic but more focused.

Finley inserted a small flash drive that contained all her hacking tools. She had hacked files many times before without being caught. Her first attempt at hacking was to help her grandma, who lived in another state, to protect her information against some sophisticated hackers. Then she continued to perform similar practices for some grateful friends and colleagues until it became a bit of a hobby. She appreciated the challenge and began testing her abilities. It became an addiction, an adrenaline rush. Soon she found she was able to infiltrate a number of highly protected servers. But after breaching the CIA's server, undetected, she decided to kick the habit before her luck ran out and never spoke of it again—except to Chelsea.

"I spent most of last night decrypting the nearby server names, and I think I've found the right one," Finley told them over her shoulder. There weren't many within a mile's radius, so she was feeling confident. "I imagine the server we want is the one labeled *Hawaii Society Security*. It seems obvious, but if I'm wrong, that would be bad."

"How bad?" Chelsea asked.

"I only have five minutes—I don't have time to crack multiple server's codes, so that'd be the end of it," Finley explained. "I think it's a safe bet though. There's tons of data on this server, and a server with lots of video footage is going to have a ton of storage used up."

There was a long pause before Chelsea spoke again. "I think we should do it. I trust you if you think it's our best option."

"If it's the wrong one, get out, and we'll find another way," added Davin. "We don't want to risk you getting in trouble."

With that, Finley nodded and took a deep breath. As she clicked on the server, a password box popped up for verification. Finley then began a program that could run through a trillion unique passwords every ten seconds. "As soon as the correct password goes through, and I enter Branch's security clearances, then the five minutes will begin. The sooner we get out, the better."

"How do you know Branch's security clearances?" Chelsea asked.

Finley smirked. "I said I spent *most* of the night decrypting the servers," she said as she lifted one brow. Chelsea shook her head and tried not to imagine what she had to do to get his login information.

Soon enough, the server information popped up, and a login was required. Finley immediately entered Branch's username and clearance code before using a projected video of his face to get past the facial recognition.

"That actually works?" Davin asked.

"If you do it right," Finley explained. "Thankfully, Branch wasn't too camera shy last night," she said, still smiling. "*And* he had to change his password right in front of me when some unknown security breach happened while I was there," she said, and then gave them a wink.

Finley and Chelsea were so different that Davin wasn't sure how they had become friends, but before he could come to any certain conclusion, a screen with all the video footage from the wristbands and cameras across The Society appeared. Finley quickly started a five-minute timer.

"Find Roy Wilson's wristband footage from the day of the hurricane just after noon," Davin urged.

Within seconds, Finley found Roy's file, and since his wristband footage stopped recording immediately when the lightning struck, it didn't take long to find the footage they were after. It was only a few hours before he was hit by the lightning that he was swimming with his friend in search of the cave. "Can you do some sort of face recognition to figure out who that guy is?" Chelsea asked as they saw the unfamiliar face of Roy's friend for the first time.

Finley took a screenshot of the friend's face. "With the screenshot I just took, I can run a face recognition program I have and then cross-reference The Society's directory after we're out of the server."

"Great. Keep scrubbing through the footage, and let's see if we can figure out where the cave is," Davin prompted.

Unfortunately, as they quickly ran through the footage, there were few recognizable landmarks or clues as to where he was. Roy's wristband was either engulfed in water bubbles from his swimming strokes, facing the wrong direction, or the image was pitch black.

"Anything else you want to look at while we're here?" Finley asked. "We're only a minute into our time."

"Yes. Bring up Ms. Waverly and Branch's wristband footage right before the hurricane," Davin quickly responded.

Finley found the files and pulled up the exact spot. Now that she had seen the inside of the system, she was able to rapidly navigate the files. She sped through the footage, and they watched Branch as he left his conversation with Davin that night. They saw Branch run to Ms. Waverly's office and immediately go to the cabinet behind her desk and unlock a safe that was inside. Davin tapped Finley's shoulder to stop her. "Play it here. I want to hear this."

"What do you think you're doing, Branch?" they heard Ms. Waverly asked.

"Someone found the cave today. I don't know how, but he's on the mountain as we speak. I'm gonna take him out with a bolt of lightning before he tells anyone else."

Davin's heart stopped when he heard Branch's words. His worst fear was realized—his friend's death had happened because *he* had mentioned Roy finding the cave to Branch. Suddenly, his lungs felt paralyzed.

Finley bumped the playback into double time, allowing them to witness Branch threaten to kill Davin as well and then program the lightning. Later on, they heard him admit he was unable to stop the storm's growth, and they all watched in horror as they realized the true cause of the abrupt and massive storm that had hit The Society.

As unnatural as it seemed at the time, thinking back, they'd never considered the possibility that the hurricane could've been artificially conjured. No one knew it was even scientifically possible. Only one man at The Society recognized the storm could *not* have been a natural phenomenon.

Seeing the corrupt plot unfold and listening to Branch collaborate with Ms. Waverly to cover it up triggered a question in Chelsea's mind.

"Stay on Branch's feed and go to the night of The Grand Welcome Celebrations. I need to see something," Chelsea told Finley.

"We're running out of time. We have less than a minute—" Finley began.

"Just do it!" Chelsea demanded.

Despite feeling uneasy with the lack of time remaining, Finley jumped back to the footage of the Grand Welcome. It wasn't hard for Chelsea to spot the exact scene she was looking for. Seeing the contrast of the glaring white background of the empty bathroom compared to the dark, crowded room with the well-lit stage in the distance was an obvious indicator.

"Right there." Chelsea stopped Finley when she saw Branch in one of the bathrooms of the dome as Sara had mentioned. Chelsea could only watch for a few seconds after she saw Branch and Sara come together in an intense carnal greeting. "That's enough."

Finley immediately disconnected from the server and closed out every application. After each program was closed and inactive, she opened a special program and arranged for the past twenty-four hours' activities to be wiped from her PED's operations history. The five-minute timer rang just as she clicked the *Clear History* button, and Finley jumped in her seat in anticipation. "That was way too close," she huffed. "But we should be fine. I think I made it out in time."

"Thank you, Finley," Chelsea said as she gave her a hug. "We really appreciate you going out on a limb like this. Obviously, you can see we're dealing with some pretty serious stuff."

"Don't mention it," Finley said. "Seriously though, I want no part in this. Never tell anyone I helped you."

Davin and Chelsea looked at each other in dismay and then turned back to Finley. They both nodded, agreeing to respect her wishes.

After seeing confirmation, Finley spun back in her chair to face her PED again. She pulled up the screenshot of Roy's friend that she had captured from the video footage. She began a facial recognition process to match the face to residents at The Society. Chelsea bit her lip in anticipation, hoping they would be able to find a match so that Roy's friend could once and for all divulge the secret location of the cave and end their unsuccessful hunt.

"I can't believe it's true," Davin said, staring off in the distance. He was blind with anger knowing his friend had been murdered.

"Yeah, pretty heavy stuff," Finley remarked. She exhaled, trying to forget everything she had just seen. She knew if she wanted to remain neutral and uninvolved in the future, she must not allow herself to linger on the judgments that were forming in her mind. She forced herself to think about anything other than her newfound knowledge about The Society, and instead focused on a minute detail she noticed on the footage that she would have otherwise discounted. "And I don't know what that little encounter we witnessed at the end had to do with anything, but whatever it was, it wasn't supposed to be there."

"How do you mean?" asked Chelsea.

"Like, the whole bathroom scene was somehow spliced into the footage or maybe written over the real footage or something. I could just see the clip wasn't part of the original timeline," Finley said.

"But if the footage was spliced in, wouldn't that mess up the timecode so that Branch's PED would have been out of sync for the footage in Ms. Waverly's office?" Chelsea asked.

"That's true—which it wasn't. So it must have been written over the footage that was already there," concluded Finley. "But why? Why cover something up with an intimate moment in the bathroom?"

"Because that's not what *really* happened!" Chelsea's eyes lit up. "The girl in the bathroom is my friend Sara that I've told you about."

"The Sara who's been going steady with the same guy for thirteen years?" she asked. "With the guy you thought was hot on the transporter pod?"

Davin looked over at Chelsea.

"I said I thought he was cute *at first*," Chelsea corrected Finley, trying to ignore Davin.

"You making note of the competition?" Finley asked Davin.

"No competition," Chelsea said before Davin could reply. "That thought ended as soon as I met Sara. Now can we please focus on the issue at hand?"

"I'm just saying, their steady relationship obviously didn't keep Sara locked down," Finley said, grinning with the intent to aggravate Chelsea for amusement. "So you may want to look out," she said, teasingly eyeing Davin.

Finley often made these kinds of provoking remarks to try and get a rise out of anyone she could, so Chelsea discounted her comments easily. Plus, Chelsea had no qualms about the matter—she had already decided to whom her heart belonged. And thankfully her comments didn't faze Davin either—not because he knew Finley to be flippant, but because it was not an uncommon opinion that relationships should be open. However, Davin knew his relationship with Chelsea was beyond such things.

"That's the thing though—Sara told Hammond she had been raped that night," Chelsea clarified.

Finley's smile quickly faded. In spite of her promiscuous viewpoints, she had no respect for nonconsensual sex—though, personally, she never thought twice about consenting to Branch. She found him quite alluring.

"It's easy enough to digitally manipulate what a person does in a video clip with advanced CGI. It happens all the time in movies when a scene didn't go the way the director thought it did on set. That would explain the discrepancy between the truth and what Hammond saw," Davin explained. "Branch must have deleted the real footage and replaced it with a fabricated scene to cover up the rape."

"That's possible," Finley attested. "Or I'm wrong, and Sara is just lying to save face," she said with a smirk.

"Sara was telling the truth," Chelsea said defensively. "I could see it in her eyes. People don't hurt like that for a lie."

With that, Finley sat back in her chair, knowing when to quit. Plus, it seemed logical enough that Branch would want to cover up a rape, so she found no reason to dispute it anyway.

Just then, Finley's PED made a dinging noise to notify her that a match had been found. "We got it—looks like your guy's name is Wane Tracy." The Society's picture and the image Finley captured from Roy's wristband were obvious matches. The two images showed a slender and lanky man with tight black curls nested on top of his head. His vivid green eyes carried a sense of curiosity or madness—Chelsea couldn't decide which.

Chelsea and Davin looked at each other with determination. Chelsea ran to the bathroom and turned off the shower before grabbing their things. She put her bracelet back on and handed Davin his before flicking her wrist to activate her bracelet screen. "Locate Wane Tracy," she said into her earpiece. A pin on the map of The Society appeared on Chelsea's arm with a description of where Wane was. Chelsea looked up with a smile and put her earpiece back in. "I knew you could do it," Chelsea told Finley with a glint in her eye. Finley rolled her eyes and folded her arms with a smile—recognizing that she was trying to play to her ego. It was working.

Davin had already jumped up and was headed for the door. "Thanks, Finley," Davin said as he waited for Chelsea to catch up.

As they ran for the door, Chelsea and Davin heard Finley remind them in a serious tone, "Just don't mention it!"

Then they headed in the direction of the river.

21. INSIDE THE CAVE

DAVIN AND CHELSEA came to the river and ran upstream in hopes that they would intercept Wane before he reached The Society buildings. Now knowing that Branch had murdered Roy for merely having knowledge of the cave, Davin wanted to make sure there were no witnesses to the conversation they were about to have.

When they came to the thicket of trees at the edge of the forest, they spotted a lone kayak drifting toward them in the distance. Wane could be seen skillfully maneuvering through the water. Davin and Chelsea took off their wristbands and removed their earpieces, and Davin put them in the pockets of his shorts and waded into a still portion of the river. With his waistline submerged in the water, no discernible video or audio could be recorded from his pocket, and as long as Davin was able to get Wane's wristband in the water and remove his earpiece before mentioning anything about the cave, he hoped they would be invisible to The Society's watchful eye. Chelsea began following him into the water. "You should stay on shore. I don't know how willing he will be to talk. This could get ugly."

"No," Chelsea replied sternly. She kept her feet in the water but did not wade in any deeper. Davin rolled his eyes and sighed—not surprised by her willful response.

As Wane spotted them standing in the river, he lifted his paddle out of the water and rested it across his lap. His expression turned from one of tranquil concentration as he enjoyed his peaceful journey down the river to one of concerned apprehension. Wane recognized Davin but had no previous connection to him. He only knew that Davin was good friends with his former escapading partner, Roy Wilson.

"What do you want?" he called out to them.

"We need to talk," Davin yelled.

"We need your help," Chelsea added.

"What about?" Wane asked as he placed his paddle back in the water to slow his progression toward them.

"I need you to get out of the kayak first," Davin instructed.

Wane's eyes shifted from the shore to them, then back to the shore. He bolted for the shore—paddling as fast as he could. Chelsea sprinted toward him and plunged into the water to intercept him.

"Take your hands off my kayak," he demanded.

"Okay," Chelsea said with a smile and then jumped on Wane's paddle and angled it so that he wouldn't be able to brace his fall. Completely caught off guard by her sudden maneuver, he tipped into the water.

Davin reached the side of the kayak just as Wane splashed into the river. After quickly fishing him out, Davin grabbed his wrists and pulled them behind his back, being careful to keep his wristband below the surface of the water. "Get his earpiece, Chels."

Completely drenched, Chelsea's hair partially draped over her face. She flipped her hair back and walked up to Wane's side to reach for his earpiece. Wane examined her closely and smiled. "Chels? Is that short for Chelsea?"

Davin's grip on Wane tightened. Chelsea sneered without an answer and grabbed the earpiece out of Wane's ear. She placed it in Davin's pocket then wiped her hand off on her shirt, making sure Wane saw her do so.

Wane redirected his attention to Davin. "What do you want from me?"

"I'm only holding you back for your own safety. If you keep your wristband in the water while we talk, I'll let you go, and you should be safe," Davin tried to explain.

"And if I don't want to talk?" asked Wane.

Davin looked down and tried not to let his frustration with Wane show in his voice. "Then we will let you go. I know that's what Roy would want," he said with resolve. "But I also know Roy died for this secret, and I think the truth needs to come out. We need your help for that to happen though. You don't have to get involved. I just need you to talk."

Wane's angered face turned to one of thoughtfulness as he contemplated the implications of talking. "Don't say another word," he instructed firmly. "I'll *show* you where it is. Then I'm gone. You won't be able to find it if I just tell you where it is. Understand?" Davin let go, and Wane turned to face them with a stern expression, taking care to keep his wristband below water. "This is my only offer, and I'm *only* doing it because of Roy. He was a good guy, and we both knew there was something odd going on. But I'm not putting my butt on the line for this. If you ever come after me again, I will turn you both into the government offices without batting an eye."

Chelsea nodded. "We won't. We promise. Just show us where the ca—" Wane jumped forward and covered her mouth with the hand that didn't have his wristband on it. Davin jumped forward instinctively to protect her.

"Get off her," he yelled, throwing Wane's arm back.

"Don't ever say that word—ever," Wane demanded as he pointed at Chelsea and glared. "In fact, don't say anything. Meet me at the reef with your escapading gear in twenty minutes. Tell no one. Once you see me—start following. Make sure you keep up. If you don't show up or you don't *keep* up, then I'm gone. Now give me my earpiece. It won't matter once we're under the water. I'll cover my wristband camera with the sleeve of my rash guard." Wane held his hand out to Davin who slowly reached for his earpiece and reluctantly handed it over—knowing that was his last leverage over Wane and that they still didn't have any solid information about the location of the cave.

Wane placed it back in his ear and hopped back into the kayak. Chelsea and Davin parted in separate directions so he could glide past them. He immediately began to paddle back to the boat docks in Tower Four, looking straight ahead with intensity.

Once he was out of earshot, Chelsea turned to Davin. "Do you think he's actually going to help us?" she asked.

"We can only hope," he replied. "We better head back now and change so we'll be ready in time to meet him."

"Okay," she said. "Let's meet at the equipment room as soon as we can."

Davin replaced their earpieces and wristbands, and they both sprinted toward their separate living quarters without another word.

DAVIN ARRIVED at the escapading station wearing his long-sleeved rash guard just before Chelsea. As she approached him, Chelsea looked at his covered arms and then down to her short-sleeves. "Do you think it will be okay if I don't have long sleeves?" she asked.

"I'll just carry your bracelet in my pocket once we get out there. I wouldn't worry about it," he assured her. They gathered their gear and then quickly ran to the reef to look for Wane.

As they stepped into the water, they started putting on their fins and masks. Then they spotted Wane in the distance, standing waist deep in the water and wearing a bright orange rash guard. He immediately pulled his mask over his face and dove into the water when they saw him. Realizing he was leaving without them, they struggled to get their gear on while stumbling into the water. "Hurry. We have to catch up," Chelsea said as they fumbled over their fins.

Once they were submerged in the water, they were able to quickly finish adjusting their gear and began swimming in the direction Wane had headed. Frantically inspecting the waters, their heads scanned left to right—searching for any sign of Wane—while their legs kicked vigorously behind them. Davin began to panic inside, thinking they had lost their chance.

Then Chelsea suddenly jolted out in front of him, pointing at the orange figure in the distance. As she did, a glint of sunshine reflecting off her copper bracelet caught Davin's eye. In the rush to get into the water, they had forgotten to take it off!

Swimming forward as fast as he could to catch up to her, Davin grabbed her wrist, pulled off her bracelet, and stuffed it in his pocket. Not knowing Davin's true intentions, Chelsea was furious he slowed her down with his unexpected reach, and the pull on her wrist came with an unpleasant sting.

She was tempted to confront him about hurting her, but then she realized what he had actually done. *Of course,* she thought. *How could I have forgotten?* Having had a wristband as a perpetual extension to her wrist since before she could remember, she was often numb to its presence. *I'll have to remember to thank him later.*

Relieved to have Chelsea's wristband safely stored away, Davin looked up to continue the chase, but then realized he had completely lost sight of Wane. A fog of fear began to swallow him up as he wondered if he had made a mistake that would ultimately result in missing their window of opportunity. But before his mind became flooded with regret, he noticed Chelsea's pursuit had not wavered through his disturbance. She was still actively swimming with a purposeful stroke. He could only hope that she still had Wane in her sights, and he followed her tail blindly.

Thankfully, Chelsea had made sure to keep her sights on the glimpse of orange still visible in the distance throughout the commotion, and as soon as she was able to free herself from Davin's grasp, she had swum forward and left him behind without a second thought. After so many hours of searching, she was determined to not let this opportunity to finally discover the location of the cave and uncover its secrets slip through her fingers.

Like ducks in a row, the three swam out of the common escapading areas and into an area on the outer ridge of zone three on their map. Wane, Chelsea, and Davin all neared the cave with Wane swiftly gliding through the water at the front, followed by Chelsea's frantic quest to catch up, and Davin's sightless pursuit at the rear—closely mimicking Chelsea's every move in hopes that she knew where she was going.

Chelsea could feel her leg muscles aching with fatigue and her lungs stinging with lactic acid from the strain of such a strenuous pace. She was suddenly glad she had been escapading daily— it had prepared her physically to keep up with Wane's brisk speed. Thankfully, the orange of Wane's rash guard eventually grew more visible as Chelsea narrowed the distance between them. He had stopped. He was treading water peacefully in the deep while she zeroed in on his location. Seeing that it was in fact Wane, Chelsea breathed a sigh of relief that she had been pursuing the correct person.

The underwater section of the island that stood behind Wane was one that Chelsea had searched before. She still saw no cave entrance as she scanned the rock behind him, and she began to wonder if he had led them to the wrong place. With Wane's obvious reluctance to help them, she worried this was no accident. *Was his true intention to take us away from the crowds and into the murky deep?* Her heartbeat grew faster. Pushing her terrifying thought aside, she continued on toward him, praying that she was wrong. *Please—if you are there, keep us safe,* she pleaded in her heart.

She reached Wane shortly after finishing her first short, silent prayer. She heard nothing but the soft treading of their legs while they floated in the water. Chelsea looked for some sort of signal or form of communication from Wane, but he just stared at her with a blank expression.

Only a short moment passed, but in her fearful mindset, the moment felt like an eternity. The terror in her rose—imagining what horrible things Wane could be plotting. She heard something large approaching her on her left. She twisted to defend herself— only to be surprised by a figure at her side. So engrossed in her chase, she had forgotten how close behind Davin would be. After the initial shock wore off, she was relieved to have Davin by her side and thankful he was not a shark or a malicious accomplice to a dastardly plan.

Once Davin had joined them, Wane turned on the flashlight that was affixed to the top of his mask. Davin and Chelsea did the same. He then swam a little lower—keeping his hands pressed up against the rock wall and feeling its surface like a blind man searching for his fallen cane. Under an inconspicuous ledge, there was a small gap in the rocks. Wane pointed inside the gap and shifted a loose rock to the side. He then swam away in a different direction from where they had come—leaving them alone.

Davin and Chelsea looked at each other then back to the gap. It would be a tight fit for both of them to swim through. Davin took Chelsea's hand and squeezed it tight as they swam forward into the cave. He had been dreading this part of the discovery, but now was the time to earn his forgiveness for having failed Roy. He braced himself and tried to block out any fear so his mild claustrophobia would not get the better of him. Inside, the crevice was dark and inconsequential, but as they went farther in, Davin's breaths began to shorten as he felt the tight walls slowly closing in on him.

Thankfully, a small amount of light came into view a few feet in. Seeing that bit of light gave Davin enough sanity to remain calm if he kept his focus on its hopeful rays. As they approached it, they discovered the light was coming from a small opening that looked up into a vast cavern full of all the things Roy had described. The hole was situated on a slant that sat at the base of the farthest wall of the naturally formed cave. Some stairs and a ramp led down to a large concrete pad where a huge glass room was built. They spotted the piles of boxes and the floating gardens Roy had mentioned. It appeared that most of the boxes had been opened and emptied. They could see people standing in the empty glass room, and Chelsea spotted the man she guessed was Tray, but it was hard to decipher details because the top of the hole was below the surface of the water, causing the details to blur into a murky haze.

Davin looked up the hole to the open air and was able to find his breath again. The walls stopped feeling so close as he envisioned himself escaping the cramped fissure and emerging into the large, open room. Seeing that no one was in the cave except the people in the empty room, Davin started to make his way through the hole to investigate the inside, but as he pushed his head through, he found himself stuck at the shoulders. The hole was too small to fit his whole body through. The top of his head breached the water, but to his dismay, that was the only part of him that would be reaching the surface of the cave that day.

Beginning to feel even more claustrophobic from being stuck in the hole, Davin pulled out as fast as he could. He again focused on the light and slowed his breathing—devastated he could not escape his torment. Chelsea looked at his face and concern washed over her as she saw his pale color and panicked eyes. She put her hand on his shoulder and looked up at the light, then back to Davin. She squeezed his shoulder with a look that begged for his forgiveness before letting go and swimming up through the hole. Being smaller than both Davin and Roy, she was able to fit through the hole, but just barely.

She wiggled through the entrance and rose out of the water. An eerie feeling loomed within the cave. The water dripping from her hair echoed throughout and interrupted the shrill silence. The people sitting inside the glass room turned and looked toward the source of the noise that disturbed their quiet existence.

They watched as she pulled herself out of the hole and swam past the underwater gardens toward them. As quietly as she could manage, she pulled herself out of the water and onto the concrete floor of the cave. Removing her gear, she made her way toward the people who were still gaping in bewilderment at the stranger emerging from the always-tranquil water.

She made mental note of every detail around her. She noticed the underwater gardens appeared to be moderately depleted. Wrappings from some of the open boxes were sprawled out. She spotted empty boxes that were labeled as having Ethernet cable, glass doors, and outside furniture. The majority of the other empty boxes were labeled as emergency food supplies.

As Chelsea got closer to the room, she noticed it was not entirely empty. Against the back wall were large empty storage shelves that had been made into makeshift beds—one for each of the five people found in the room. All five of the entrapped residents gathered around the glass door, observing Chelsea's approach while keeping a nervous eye on the stairway in the distance. Chelsea could now tell the Asian man was in fact Tray Wong as she suspected—still sporting his **SOCIETY RULES YOUR LIFE** shirt. The other residents she didn't know or only knew in passing and was not familiar with their names. Each of them looked weak and malnourished. Tray was especially feeble looking, but his eyes filled with hope the closer Chelsea stepped toward their glass tomb.

When she reached the door, she tried to pull it open, but unsurprisingly found that it was locked. Not wanting to waste any time, Chelsea immediately began asking questions. "Why do they have you guys down here?"

"We thought we were going to be taken back to the mainland, but they took us down here instead. They said no one was supposed to *want* to leave The Society," Tray explained.

"When I protested, they told me that we were sent to The Societies to be out of the way until we were either dead or we became useful to the world," a girl added.

Chelsea wanted to say she was shocked, but after searching so long for the cave and learning Roy had been murdered to keep the cave secret, she felt very little surprise to hear this information. It only solidified in her mind that the system that was supposed to bring relief had transformed into a penitentiary primed for corruption to fester, and she didn't want to be a part of it anymore, but she knew they needed to somehow let everyone know what was going on before they left. At the very least, the other residents deserved to know people weren't being allowed to leave. "Do they feed you at all?" she asked, unable to not stare at their bony limbs.

"Sometimes. We do have access to water," Tray said, pointing to a faucet at the corner of the room. "But Branch only brings food sporadically—it's like he only comes when he remembers we're still down here."

"Branch, huh? Why am I not surprised?" Chelsea huffed.

"Who are you anyway?" someone interjected from the other side. "Are you going to help us or not?"

"Yes. We're going to get you out of here. We're planning an escape," Chelsea assured them.

"Great! Let's go. The keys are over there," someone pointed.

Chelsea looked over in disbelief at the keys that were in plain view nearby. "They just leave the keys out like that?" Chelsea walked over to examine them.

"Yeah, this wasn't really built to be a prison. This is just a storage room. Branch had to move all the boxes of supplies out so I wouldn't get to the food or the tools to bust out of here. I guess they just figured it'd be safe since there's only one way in, and you need a special security clearance to get in and out," Tray told her. "Speaking of which, how exactly did you get in here?"

"There's a hidden entrance underwater from the outside. It's really small though. I'm not sure any of you would fit through it," she said, looking at each of them with apprehension. They were all built larger than she was. Chelsea walked over to where the key tag was hanging and slowly lifted it off of the hook, then stopped and placed it back.

"What are you doing? Get us out of here!" said the man who had pointed the keys out.

"I can't," Chelsea explained. "I don't have a way to get you out of here yet. I don't have any more masks or anything. I want to. I just don't have a safe way for you to leave."

"Just let us out, and we will fig—" Suddenly there was a noise from the top of the stairs that echoed through the cave. The door to the cave was opening as they spoke. Chelsea jumped and began to panic inside. She whirled around to face the five people who were desperately staring out at her, their first glimpse of hope in months.

"I'll come back for you," Chelsea promised earnestly and then quietly ran back toward the hidden entrance she had come from. "No! Don't!" she heard someone say. She slipped into the water, hearing more of the prisoners calling after her as Tray and another one of the men tried to quiet them. She hoped she could earn their forgiveness and free them soon—*but not today.*

Knowing that whoever was entering the cave would hear the discourse, Chelsea began to feel anxious that they would disclose the details of her visit. Unable to control whether they did or not, she pulled her mask and flippers on before slipping into the concealed hole and back into the crevasse to find Davin so she could tell him the information she knew, and they could begin devising a thorough plan of escape as soon as possible.

Two beeps rang throughout the cave, indicating that the video recording on Branch's wristband had stopped, and he could speak freely without fear of evidence. "What are you people complaining about now?" asked Branch as he walked down the stairs just as Chelsea slipped through the hole and out of sight. He held a bag of fruit in one hand and a gun in the other. He walked at a leisurely pace toward his hungry captives.

"Do you have food for us?" Tray yelled out as he clasped his hand tightly over the mouth of one of the men who was about to curse Chelsea for leaving them. "Whoever that girl was, she may be our only hope of getting out of here. Unless you want to ruin that chance, keep your mouth shut, got it?" Tray whispered in the man's ear before letting go and pushing him aside.

"Only because I'm a nice guy," Branch said as he approached the door with a greasy grin. "Now, back up and line up if you want any," Branch said as he held up the bag of fruit and raised the gun.

Guns had been banned and confiscated twenty years prior to stop the spread of gun violence. There were only government-issued guns from that point on.

"I can't wait until my father knows you for who you really are instead of the lovable politician he thinks you are," one of the prisoners said to him as he lined up and glared at Branch.

"Oh, Semaj." Branch shook his head at Semaj's comment as he grabbed the key tag off the hook. "Don't be ignorant. Your dad is a congressman. You think he doesn't have some skeletons in the closet? You can find dirt on anyone." Holding the key tag in his hand, Branch placed his hand near the handle of the door, and the door unlocked.

"I know he isn't locking people up to hide his failures."

"Failures? *My* failures?" he asked, placing the key tag in his pocket. "These are *your* generation's failures we're dealing with, not mine. I may look young, but *my* generation has actually contributed to the world. I can't even get you people to keep this little Society afloat."

Being one of the youngest successful names in the political world, Branch was handpicked to help run The Society program because it was believed his younger age would help him relate to The Society's young residents. But the amount of power and freedom allotted him at The Society had morphed his hunger for success and control into an unquenchable thirst for supremacy over his ignorant subjects.

"The Societies don't account for human inclination—there's no incentive to be more than the freeloaders you've made us out to be."

"Oh, stop sounding like such a lawyer. You gave up your chance for that life when you came here. We're not on trial here, Semaj. Your sentence has already been determined—by me," he said with a smile. Then he cocked the gun. "And unless you want that sentence to come sooner than later, I suggest you shut up."

Semaj stayed quiet.

"Very good," he said. Then he walked to the end of the line where Tray stood waiting for his ration of food. "Now, say please," he taunted. He knew Tray had a particular animosity toward authority, so he liked to torment him into submission before giving him his food.

"Please," Tray said without missing a beat and without any restraint.

Irritated Tray didn't fight his request before toiling into obedience as he usually did, Branch threw the bag of fruit on the floor and left the room. After shutting the door, he turned and started to leave the cave without thinking to return the key tag from his pocket back to the hook.

Realizing he was forgetting to return the key tag, Tray ran past the pile of fruit on the ground and slammed his fists into the glass door. "Get back here and face me like a man, Branch," Tray yelled, hoping to provoke his return so Branch would hopefully remember to hang the key tag back up on the hook.

Satisfied that Tray broke into hysterics after all, Branch just turned and smiled at him before turning back around to leave the cave.

"No! Get back here, you coward! Get back here!"

22. DEVISING A PLAN

AFTER THE BUBBLES settled, Chelsea turned on her headlight to find Davin. She looked one way but saw nothing. She looked the other—nothing. Imagining a myriad of worst-case scenarios, she wrestled with what she should do. Davin had her wristband, and without it, she would not be able to locate him until she got back to her room, where she had left her PED. She couldn't bring herself to leave him if he was lost somewhere—or worse. She searched the small cavern one more time before swimming out into the open water.

To her dismay, there was no sign of Davin outside of the cavity either. She looked down and searched the ocean floor. *No, no, no! Davin! Where are you? Please be okay!* Chelsea screamed in her mind as she scanned the area.

Then she looked up to see Davin swimming toward her from the surface of the water. The terror clutching her heart released its grip, and she began swimming in his direction. They met in the middle, and he grabbed her hand to swim up toward the surface. About halfway to the surface, Davin's wristband vibrated and they stopped their ascent to follow diving protocol and allow their bodies to acclimate to the pressure. As they lingered, they hugged each other close.

This small ritual had become a tradition when they used to dive together before Davin began filming the movie, but this time their embrace was embodied by an overpowering sense of relief and gratitude to be back in the safety of each other's arms. Their need for each other was fortified in each of their minds as they realized how devastated they would be to lose each other. Their absolute love had no uncertainties anymore.

Davin entangled his hands in Chelsea's floating hair and pulled her head close into his chest. She wrapped her arms tight around his core and rested her body against his. In a beautiful, still embrace, they cherished a moment of peace before rising to the top of the water, anxious to hear each other's stories.

"Where did you go? I was worried!" Chelsea started immediately after she removed her mask and before Davin could speak.

"I had to get out of there and come up for air," Davin admitted. "I should've told you before, but I was hoping it wouldn't be a problem." He sighed. "I'm slightly claustrophobic. I couldn't handle being in that crevasse after a while."

Chelsea thought for a moment. "That makes so much sense now."

"Sorry to freak you out. I just couldn't do it anymore." Now that he had come to his senses, Davin felt awful that he had left her down there by herself.

"It's okay," she said. "I'm just glad you're all right, and The Society didn't carry you away or something horrible like that."

"So what did you find out?" Davin asked, impatient to hear what had happened inside the cave. "I was so nervous you were going to get caught or something."

Chelsea divulged the details of what had happened while they floated in the open waters far from shore, away from listening ears.

"It's settled then. We're leaving," Davin said in disgust.

"Yes, but first we need to solidify an escape plan. And somehow we've got to come up with a method to reveal The Society's exploitation without placing ourselves in danger."

"Be thinking of ways to get the word out and how we can set them free without getting caught," Davin said. "But right now, we need to get back and get our tasks done to avoid suspicion. At dinner—don't say a word. We act completely normal. Then tonight, after everyone is asleep, we'll go to our secret beach without our wristbands or earpieces and come up with a plan. We'll need to work out *every* detail if we're going to pull this off."

"Got it," she said with a nod. "Let's go."

DAVIN AND CHELSEA BOTH completed their tasks while racking their brains with ideas for a suitable plan. By the end of the day, neither of them had come up with any grand ideas, which made dinner feel excruciatingly long as they both pretended they had enjoyed another typical day escapading and completing their usual routines.

"You guys seem to really like escapading," Eli commented at dinner.

"It's fun," Davin replied effortlessly as Chelsea worked to maintain a nonchalant demeanor. "It was a particularly gorgeous out there today," Davin said as he smiled toward Chelsea and took a bite from his plate of salad.

Chelsea often let Davin do the talking when it came to concealing their covert undertakings. He'd had many opportunities to practice when dealing with Society officials, and he could always put on a show at a moment's notice. This particular talent often made Chelsea wonder if he could easily lie to her, but whenever the thought ran through her mind, she always forced herself to think better of him and hoped he would never have reason to.

"Yeah, it was," Eli agreed. "Now that my rib is all healed, I actually made it out there myself. I even did some kayaking this afternoon out on the river."

Chelsea's eyes rose from her plate, and she glanced awkwardly toward Eli as he spoke about kayaking on the river. *Had he seen us intercept Wane? Does he know something?* Chelsea wondered.

As Davin continued the conversation, it became clear that Eli was merely commenting on his activities during the day, and the fact that he had gone kayaking on the river that same day was mere coincidence, but it was hard for Chelsea to not feel paranoid after seeing the five hostages stored away in the secret cavern beneath them. Every person, every encounter had her wondering if anyone else knew the secrets woven within The Society.

The magnificent facilities and alluring splendor of The Society grounds lost their appeal with their newfound knowledge of what lay beneath its foundation. No longer was Chelsea concerned about leaving the beautiful scenery and amenities found at The Society. The haunting memory etched in her mind of the captives failing bodies made her want to flee without thought.

And though she felt naked without it, she found herself wanting to rip off and disassemble her bracelet and be free of her earpiece entirely to avoid being monitored any further. She wanted to speak openly with Davin without wondering who could be listening. She wanted to kiss his body without wondering if someone else was also enjoying the view. She didn't want to live in fear that removing them would invalidate her rights. She wanted to be free.

"It's been a long day. I think we're going to turn in for the night," Davin said to Eli, grabbing his empty plate and standing to leave the table. "We'll catch you later." Davin and Eli clasped their right hands and pulled into each other's chests.

Chelsea's wandering mind was pulled out of its deliberation, and she grabbed her plate and stood silently. Eli waved to Chelsea as they departed. "Err, see you later, Chelsea." She managed a smile and wave as they walked away. She could tell her detachment from the conversation was noted, but her emotions had kept her mind on the cave.

"You doing all right?" Davin asked, trying to appear conversational.

"Yes. I'm sorry," Chelsea muttered quietly. "It all just feels so *real* now, and I'm feeling overwhelmed. I don't know if that makes sense, but—"

"No, it does," Davin assured her. He felt equally uneasy, but he had become accustomed to masking it well when he needed to. "I'm going to grab a change of clothes from my room. You should go ahead and get ready for bed. I'll meet you in your room. I think we should get some sleep before heading out tonight. It will be a while before everyone else is in bed and we can leave."

"Okay," Chelsea agreed. "That sounds like a good idea."

Exhaustion was quickly beginning to overcome her busy mind. Despite her determination to find solutions to their impending dilemmas, her body felt as though it could collapse from the physical and emotional strain of the day.

Davin ran toward his room. Knowing he wouldn't get much sleep that night, he was eager to get in bed. He opened the door to the ever familiar and alarming sight of Ms. Waverly's silhouette standing in front of the window looking out over the ocean view. However, this time, with the information Chelsea and he had uncovered that day, her presence was particularly frightening.

"Davin," Ms. Waverly greeted him as she spun around with a pernicious smile. "Been enjoying your free time since you finished filming?"

"It has been nice to have some time to myself—yes," Davin replied as innocently as he could manage.

"Any particularly notable activities today?" she asked. Davin's mouth went dry. Her question suggested she knew something, but he had also grown accustomed to her visits being a conglomeration of prying questions and acquisitions. She was trying to get him to admit to something, but he knew better.

"Just another beautiful day in paradise," Davin managed to get out without sounding too perturbed, but he still feared he wouldn't be able to pull off the performance needed to mask his utter scorn for both her and The Society. "Enjoyed some great escapading, but other than that, nothing of note."

Ms. Waverly gave a slight smile and nodded in acknowledgment of Davin's response—though she was clearly unimpressed. Then she quickly redirected the conversation. "I'm so looking forward to the debut of your film. I hear you delivered an inspiring performance."

"Well, thank you," he said, confused by her conversational tone. "Filming did go well. I have high hopes that it will be successful. Our director was incredibly insightful."

"Wonderful to hear," Ms. Waverly remarked. "It will be great exposure for The Society as well, which, as you know, I'm always happy about."

They both stood silent for a moment, waiting to hear what the other would say. Ms. Waverly's conversations were usually so forthright that Davin was caught off guard by her seemingly social visit. Trying to keep the conversation as natural as possible, Davin decided to break the silence before it became suspicious. "Did you have a meeting or promotional video you'd like to discuss? I'm happy to do whatever you require of me."

"Oh, no. Not this time," Ms. Waverly said. "Although I was hoping to discuss a different matter with you."

"And what matter is that?" asked Davin.

"For the movie premiere, I presume you intend to have someone accompany you?" Ms. Waverly asked.

"I hadn't really thought about it, but yeah—I think I might," he said smiling, thinking about Chelsea by his side at opening night.

"Yes. Well, a while back it was brought to my attention that you're exclusively involved with one girl." Davin's eyes shot up involuntarily as he knew she must have been referring to Chelsea. "Since that is your own personal business, I decided not to get involved. But, as you are well aware, you were sent here to promote The Society, and in order to live here, your number one priority is to do just that. Now, I've been flexible at times, for example allowing your absence to visit your ailing mother and accommodating you to film a movie you will profit greatly from. However, you must keep in mind that the world wants to see Davin Chapman with a particular Hawaiian beauty at his side, not an unknown, dreary nobody." Davin wasn't able to hide his disgust any longer. Ignoring the abhorrence in his eyes, she continued, "So—what you do in your personal time I will leave up to your own devices, but in front of a world audience, I would ask that you come accompanied by Kona, as the world expects, or no one at all."

"I'm sorry—I didn't realize my contract has control over my love life too!" Davin exploded, unable to suppress his exasperation that The Society's control was now trying to seep into his personal affairs as well. "Who I choose to be with is my decision."

Ms. Waverly's expression shifted from a friendly smile to her usual somber and unexpressive visage. "My, my, you do love her, don't you? Even *you* can't hide that," Ms. Waverly said as she flicked her wrist and made a note. "It was only a suggestion to keep up appearances. And though you are welcome to love whomever you would like, I still insist you go stag if you do not wish for Kona to accompany you." Ms. Waverly walked toward the door to leave the room. "Goodbye, Davin, until next time," she said, dodging Davin's stance and exiting the room.

Ms. Waverly left his room feeling quite pleased with her visit. She had finally gained the insight she had hoped for. Knowing the depth for which Davin cared for Chelsea gave her a sense of genuine leverage over him should his income from the film tempt him to abandon The Society. Given that he was a gifted actor, she could never say for certain that his allegiance truly aligned with her own. But that evening she had finally exposed an involuntary response—a perception of his true feelings.

Inside his room, Davin was still fuming that Waverly felt she had control over who he could be seen with, but he also regretted losing his composure. He knew the facade he had worked so hard to maintain throughout their visits was very possibly compromised by his outburst. He leaned back against his door and wondered if she suspected or somehow already knew about his dissent with The Society. Then he deliberated if he could call off the escape altogether and find a way to make The Society release the hostages peaceably.

He spent the next hour in his room thinking of ways to alter The Society's structure to rid it of its corrupt footing—speculating that he could spur some kind of reform, and they could all stay. But with each solution he thought of, he couldn't guarantee a diplomatic change would ever happen with a determined Ms. Waverly at the head of The Society and an armed Branch at her side. So he changed his clothes and left for Chelsea's room.

When he walked in, Chelsea was already asleep on her bed, still in her clothes from the day. He could tell she must have crumpled onto the bed from exhaustion without thought of changing or pulling back the sheets. Her arms and legs were sprawled out in every direction, and she breathed in and out heavily. He smiled and pushed back her bangs from her face. He could hardly fathom the natural love he had for her—it was so involuntary, so sincere.

He quickly set an alarm on his wristband for when he thought they should wake up. Pulling a blanket over them both, he lay down next to Chelsea for the night. She naturally shifted her weight against his body into a snug cocoon as he wrapped his arms around her. The smell from her perfume had worn off and her natural aroma became more noticeable for the first time. As he breathed it in, he was surprised to find that he was oddly drawn to it. It seemed familiar and soothing. It smelled like *her* somehow. He closed his eyes and took in deep breaths, and before long, he was sound asleep.

DAVIN WOKE UP. He looked at his wristband and saw that he still had an hour before his alarm would go off. Repositioning himself to go back to sleep, he reached over to hold Chelsea but found an empty bed. He sat up and looked toward the bathroom, but there were no lights on. There was stillness throughout the room. Complete silence pounded on Davin's eardrums as he called out for Chelsea with no reply. She was gone.

He ran out of the door and began sprinting down the halls of the living quarters, but she was still nowhere in sight. He flicked his wrist. "Find Chelsea Coremon." The map popped up on his wrist and pinpointed her location in one of the virtual reality rooms. He ran to Tower Four and selected the number two in the elevator.

He burst through the doors of room twenty-one where the map showed her. There at the end of the room stood Sandra Waverly and Branch Willix. Between them, Chelsea sat completely motionless in a chair facing the opposite direction. He could not tell if she was tied up or not. All he could see was the unique color and cut of her hair from the back of her head.

"Glad you could join us, Davin," Ms. Waverly said with a smile. "Did you really think you could get away with this? We were just telling Chelsea here all about the plans we have in store for you."

Branch smirked beside her, holding a gun in each hand. "Yes, and I was just about to tell her all the things *I* have in mind for her as well."

"If you even look at her the wrong way, I'll—"

"You'll what? You couldn't even get to us if you wanted to," Branch said as Ms. Waverly pressed a button on her PED.

As she did, the walls quickly closed in on Davin's head. He fell to the floor to avoid getting hit, and when he opened his eyes, all the walls were pressed up against him. At the end of a long, narrow tunnel, Branch and Ms. Waverly still stood—looking at him with satisfied expressions.

"Do you ever feel like the walls are just . . . closing in around you? Tight spaces—they're just the worst, don't you think, Davin?" Branch sneered as he taunted Davin.

"The worse thing is—that's all that stands between you and your lover," added Waverly.

"No! The worst part is, it's all just an illusion—and he *still* can't save her!" Branch burst out laughing.

Davin's breathing quickened. He could feel his heartbeat in his hands. His eyes shifted back and forth rapidly—completely absorbed in the vision of the walls that were urging him to retreat into his own mind. He curled into a fetal position and tried to look out from the tunnel that was engulfing him. He fought to change his focus to Chelsea and gain the motivation to overcome the pull, but it was still too much. In a complete panic, he closed his eyes tight and everything went black.

A few minutes later, he regained his consciousness and opened his eyes to discover an open room. The walls pressing against him were gone, and his senses were centered on reality again. He quickly stood—finally ready to attack and free Chelsea, but Branch and Ms. Waverly were gone. Chelsea still sat in the chair about fifty feet ahead of him. She now faced him. Her mouth was taped shut, and her wrists and feet were tied to the chair. She looked at him with desperation in her eyes.

He started to sprint toward her, but as he did, the ground began to shake, and pieces of the ceiling started to crumble to the floor. He stood frozen for a moment as he took in the scene. *It's just an illusion*, he said to himself as he tried not to let images of the footage from the California earthquake sink him into another panic attack. He advanced toward her. He was almost there. Then a huge chunk of the floor fell out from underneath her chair! Tears rolled down her cheeks as she sank down into the abyss. He jumped over the ledge to follow her into the pit—and then he was jolted awake from the buzzer that was sounding in his ear.

The alarm he had set saved him from his descent into despair, but panic still coursed through his veins. Streams of sweat dripped from his brow, and he struggled to catch his breath. He looked to his side to see Chelsea still peacefully sleeping. He jumped out of bed and paced the room, trying to settle down before he had to wake her up to leave for the beach.

But as he paced, he began to wonder if he could go through with the demands of a treacherous escape plan when his weaknesses and fears were so evident after his torturous nightmare. The thought terrified him, but then the realization that he was *more* afraid that a version of that dream could actually occur made his weaknesses irrelevant. They had to free those people, and they had to escape.

They needed a plan and had to implement it with careful execution. He reached up toward the top shelf of the desk where they had hidden the roll of thin bark that Chelsea had inscribed with the search zones. He grabbed it and woke Chelsea. "It's time," he told her.

They left their wristbands and earpieces and discreetly made their way to the banks of their hidden beach. Gathering pieces of wood and an old coconut as they walked, Davin was able to make a fire in the sand with what materials he had gathered.

"Aren't you handy?" Chelsea commented, impressed that he could build a fire without a match.

"I had to learn for one of my films," he explained with a lack of emotion as he threw the map of the zones on top of the fire. Chelsea looked at the map as the flames engulfed it, and then back to Davin. He could tell from her expression that she didn't understand his motives. "I don't want any evidence that we were looking for the cave laying around anymore."

"Ha—my scribbles on the map were so hard to decipher, I'm not sure anyone would have been able to make sense of them, even if they did find it." Chelsea laughed.

"I didn't think we should take any chances," grumbled Davin.

Davin's irritated response was not what Chelsea had expected to her playful teasing. Looking at his enraged expression, she couldn't understand why he was acting so cross. Irritated with him now, she asked, "What's your problem?"

The muscles in his face tensed, and she could tell he was trying to suppress his anger. She waited to see if he returned her impatience with an equally rude response and began preparing a number of arguments in her defense.

And then she realized she was making whatever was bothering him worse. "Sorry," she said. "It's really not a bad idea. It's smart to be cautious."

Davin's expression softened. "No—I'm sorry, Chels," he said. "I'm all out of sorts right now. I had this horrible dream while we were sleeping, and I'm just on edge because of it."

"What was it about?" Chelsea asked—both curious as to what his dream was about and hoping that talking about it would help him move past the emotions it had surfaced.

He looked down into the flames of the fire that lit his somber face. "They took you," he said with regret. "I tried to free you, but they used my fears against me, and I couldn't save you." Davin looked intently at the fire as he reimagined his dream.

Chelsea could see the shame in his eyes as he admitted the terrors of his nightmare. She sat down next to him in the sand and put her arm around him as she leaned her head on his shoulder. Though Chelsea was pleased to hear that she appeared to be his inner psyche's most prized possession, she could tell his dream was less about her and more about the limitation that came from his fears.

"You know—I don't always expect you to be my knight in shining armor," she said with a smile. "As romantic as that notion is, I want to feel equally yoked to you—recognizing that we both have our weaknesses and strengths, and that, together, we can somehow get out of here and help free those people. But that doesn't mean you have to go back in the cave again if you don't think you can handle it." Davin looked down at the sand under his feet. He remained silent—unable to confess that he didn't think he could go back. But his silence spoke for him. "Well that settles it then," Chelsea said, slapping her knees in resolve. "You won't have to go back in the cave."

"I can't expect you to go down there alone. It is not fair to put that on you."

"It doesn't matter if it's fair," Chelsea retorted. "I'm not claustrophobic. Anyway, if you can't help by physically being down there with me, we'll just have to find another way you can help," she said, determined to lift his spirits. "Now let's think— if you can't be down there *with* me, how can you help from above water?" She contemplated for a short second before a thought sprang into her mind. "I got it! I definitely don't want anyone coming down there again like they did last time so maybe you could serve as a distraction. You could keep people preoccupied. Then I can sneak in and out without worry of having another visitor. We need something that will hold *everyone's* attention though." She pondered. "Maybe you could call another meeting?"

"I think it'd seem suspicious if I suddenly called another meeting, especially because I don't even know what it would be about. And since you normally tech my events, it would seem odd if you weren't there working it, don't you think?" Davin pointed out.

"What if you just openly announce what's going on to the whole Society at the next mandatory meeting?" she wondered. "Though I would worry they wouldn't allow us to leave after that if you did," Chelsea said, feeling her inspiration piddle out.

"Yeah," Davin agreed. He threw a small stick he had been fiddling with into the fire. "However," he said, suddenly perking up, "At the premiere of the movie, everyone will already be occupied with the viewing. We could use the movie as the distraction!"

"That's perfect!" Chelsea looked at Davin excitedly, but then a thought crossed her mind that stole her enthusiasm. "But I would still be expected to work it."

"Nah—I'll insist you get to watch it from the audience with me, and we'll get someone else to do it," Davin assured her. "They can't blame you for wanting to support me. Then you can sneak out when they dim the lights."

The smiles on their faces grew wider the more confident they felt about the plan. "I think this could work," Chelsea said enthusiastically. "But we still need to figure out a way to let the others know what has been going on without putting you in danger."

Davin agreed. They both stared at the fire, trying to think of a way to accomplish it. "What if I broadcast a video explaining everything once we're in California?" Davin suggested.

"After they discover you've left, I worry that they'll stop any broadcasts that come from you. And if we did a broadcast, it'd probably need to go out to the mainland and The Society residents at the same time to ensure that Society members don't get secretly shut out from the rest of world," Chelsea pointed out.

"Maybe they wouldn't think to block *your* PED?" Davin wondered.

"Mmm, maybe, but I wouldn't bet on it," Chelsea said. "They'll find out quickly that I went with you, I'm sure. It'd probably be best if they saw the message before they even realized we were gone."

Davin's expression lit up. "Do you know how to do any video editing?"

"Yes," Chelsea replied, trying to understand why that would matter. "I can't do any really advanced editing, but I know the basics."

"I think some basic editing is all we would need," Davin assured her before fully divulging his plan. "They're still in the process of editing the film in the edit bay of the dome, but they're supposed to have the final cut done soon. Once they have it finalized, all we have to do is sneak in and add a clip explaining everything. The final cut will go out to everyone, plus the viewing is supposed to be broadcast to the States at the same time that we watch it here."

Chelsea thought for a moment, trying to decide if it was a plausible solution. "It might work," she said. "After we're safely out of reach, we could always try and do another broadcast as well, just in case they try to block the broadcast to the mainland at the video engineering workstation."

Davin nodded, jumped up to grab a stick, and began scribbling in the sand. They spent the rest of the night filling in every detail they could to solidify their escape plan. They discussed and contemplated each decision until they both felt comfortable. They knew there would still be risk involved, but they both agreed wholeheartedly to continue.

"Okay, so as soon as they are done with the editing, we need to sneak into the edit bay and add a clip explaining everything. And beginning today, we need to start collecting extra food," Chelsea reiterated.

"Yes, and you need to start looking for the second entrance of the cave that Roy told me about, and hopefully it's big enough to get the others out," Davin added.

"And you will need to make sure you sign up for tasks that have access to the tools so we can borrow an ultrasonic chisel drill and begin widening the entrance of the existing hole just in case I can't find the larger entrance."

"Right," Davin noted. The fire was dying out at this point, and they knew it was time to wrap up. Davin shifted his feet in the sand to erase the logistics of their proposed strategies, while Chelsea buried the fire in preparation to leave. As they did, the rising sun hit the water's edge and lit the morning sky with the glimmer of first light. They both looked out over the water to watch.

"I'm going to miss this," Chelsea said, trying not to get emotional as she considered the possible consequences of following through with their plan.

"Don't worry," Davin said with a reassuring smile as he wrapped his arm around her. "California has breathtaking sunsets."

They took one last look then turned and began the walk back to Chelsea's room before the rest of the residents woke up for breakfast.

❖

"HEY, CHELSEA! DAVIN! Wait up!" Sara called out as Davin and Chelsea approached Chelsea's door. "You guys comin' to breakfast? Come on. Let's go together." Sara let go of Hammond's hand to grab Chelsea's wrist and urge her along.

"Well, we are . . . we . . . " Chelsea had never been good at lying. They needed to retrieve their wristbands and earpieces, but she tried to quickly think of a reasonable excuse to not raise suspicion. "We just need to wash up real quick before breakfast."

"Hey, you aren't wearing your bracelet," Sara said as she inspected Chelsea's wrist inquisitively. Sara and Hammond both examined their bare wrists with concern. Chelsea stumbled to come up with a viable reason as to why they would have removed their wristbands—until she finally broke.

"Come into my room. Quick!" she said as she pulled them both in and immediately began taking off their wristbands and removing their earpieces as well. "Don't say anything," she said as she worked. Sara began to protest at first but quickly fell quiet when instructed—choosing to trust Chelsea instead of resisting. Hammond followed suit.

Once their wristbands and earpieces were safely stowed away with Chelsea and Davin's, Chelsea turned to face her two friends. Davin looked nervously between them, wondering what Chelsea was planning.

"Davin and I are—"

"Pregnant!" Sara exclaimed over Chelsea.

"What? No," Chelsea stopped, feeling rattled by Sara's conjecture. "We're leaving The Society."

Sara's face turned from enthusiastic anticipation to unsettled surprise. "What do you mean, 'you're leaving'?" Sara asked.

"Why did you think I was pregnant?" Chelsea asked back.

"I don't know. You've been acting all weird and secretive lately, and I thought it was maybe from all the hormones," Sara said. "I just got excited, okay? We haven't been able to get pregnant. So when I thought that might be what was going on—I guess I kind of liked the idea."

"I told you she was just hungry," Hammond commented from the background, referring to Sara's remarks about how fast Chelsea ate at dinner lately.

"Hey," Sara said as she gave him a playful glare. "You're supposed to be on *my* side." Turning away from Hammond's guilty grin, she turned back to Chelsea with a serious expression. "So what's this about leaving?"

Chelsea went on to briefly explain the disturbing happenings in The Society and their general plan. She also divulged the information Finley helped them discover about the night of the Welcome Celebration and Branch overwriting the footage. Hammond's hatred for Branch resurfaced as he realized Sara had been telling the truth the whole time. He regretted ever doubting her and became determined to find a way to still prosecute him. Sara was just happy that Hammond no longer had to rely on her word alone to know she was telling the truth.

Davin paced back and forth, listening to Chelsea quietly whisper their plans. He didn't like the idea of sharing this information with others. He tried to hold back his irritation that Chelsea had decided to do so without consulting him first, and he knew there was no reversing what had already been said—so he remained silent.

"Well, this is fortuitous!" Sara exclaimed after quietly pondering the information Chelsea had told them. "If you want to get to the movie timeline—I'm your girl! I'm the new editor! The guy who was doing it broke his arms on the quad ski the other day, and they needed a replacement. I started working on it with the director yesterday. If you need to add a clip to the end to let everyone know all the horrible stuff going on, I want to help," she said with a smile.

"If it means Branch may be held accountable for what he did to Sara—I'm in," Hammond told them. "How can I help?"

Davin's hesitation to tell Hammond and Sara faded away after hearing their support. The idea of having other people to help carry out the plan was instantly reassuring, and an overwhelming sense of gratitude replaced his irritation. "If you could keep an eye on Chelsea when she gets the people out, I would feel so much better about the plan," Davin chimed into the conversation for the first time. "Since I should probably stay until the end of the premiere, I would be forever grateful if you could take her out there, keep an eye on the boat, and make sure she comes back up unharmed—if you're willing."

"We can do that," Hammond replied. "We'll watch your movie some other time," he said jokingly.

"Yeah," Sara agreed. "We wouldn't let Chelsea go out there by herself." Davin held back a scowl. He didn't want Chelsea to go out there by herself either.

"If you could also help us collect any extra food rations each day as well, we're going to need all the food we can get to get us and the others to California," Chelsea added.

"Done," Hammond told them. "You can have the bags we brought with us, and we'll fill them up with whatever food we can collect along with any other supplies you may need."

"And I'll let you know when the editing is finalized, and then we can edit in the clip of Davin at the end," Sara said. "Though I'm worried we won't be able to sneak it past Genevieve," she added warily. "She's very detailed-oriented and specific about how I edit things together. I'll have to be very careful about doing it after she has given the final go-ahead."

"No," Davin interrupted. "Genevieve has become a friend to me. I don't want to do something behind her back. I'm going to go to her and hope she understands."

"Are you sure, Davin? She could turn us in," Chelsea reminded him.

"You chose to trust your friends, and it may end up being the difference in our success or failure," Davin told Chelsea. "Now I am choosing to trust my friend."

Chelsea nodded in resignation, recognizing her error in telling Hammond and Sara without speaking to Davin about it first. Personally, she felt uneasy about telling Genevieve, but she knew she needed to believe in Davin's trust as he had done for her.

❖

THE NEXT DAY, Chelsea and Hammond went out on a boat together to locate the cave and search for the larger entrance that Roy had mentioned.

When nearing the end of the allotted editing time that Sara had scheduled with Genevieve that day, Davin walked up to the edit bay to interject before they were through. Before he opened the door, he took a deep breath and pleaded in his heart that Genevieve would listen and support his proposal. He cracked the door open and stepped in.

The music swelled in the room as the scene cut from a close-up shot of Davin's sullen face to a wide shot of the ocean. The light from the open door and the distraction from the outside noise pulled Genevieve's attention away from editing. "What in the blazes?" Genevieve said as she turned around to see who was intruding. "Who's there? We're in the middle of editing!"

"I'm sorry, Gen. It's just me," Davin said as he stood at the door. Genevieve's petulant look remained, but she excused Davin's interruption and invited him in.

"Did you need something, Davin, or did you want to be here for the editing process? We're about done for the day," Genevieve told him.

"I know. I was hoping to talk to you about something," Davin began. "I need your permission to do something. Will you hear me out?"

Genevieve looked confused but intrigued. "What would you need *my* permission for, Davin? You're a big boy. I can't think why you would need my approval."

"It's about the final cut," Davin explained.

A perturbed look crossed Genevieve's face as she wondered if he wanted to hijack her creative flow for the final cut, but she decided to inquire before jumping to conclusions. "And what did you have in mind for the final cut?" she asked.

❖320❖

Davin and Sara simultaneously took off their wristbands and earpieces and placed them in a box. Genevieve watched in bewilderment, wondering why they would be removing their wristbands. Sara then played loud static in the background to drown out what Davin was about to say.

"I'm going to ask you to not speak or ask questions. I'm going to explain what things I *can* tell you, and then you'll either agree to help me or decide not to," Davin stated as he stared sincerely in Genevieve's eyes and knelt down to gently clasp her hand, hoping to reassure her that his intentions were pure. "I will not begrudge your decision if you choose not to help, but I plead with you to consider my proposition—many wrongs will come to light if you do."

Genevieve nodded her head hesitantly and braced herself to hear Davin's proposition.

"There are things going on within The Society that I cannot continue to condone—heinous and immoral crimes. My life could very well be in danger just by speaking ill of The Society. For these reasons, I will be leaving by boat immediately after the premiere to begin a new life in what is left of California. But I need your help spreading the word about what has been going on—so people are aware of it and can then choose for themselves if they want to continue to support it." Davin paused to analyze Genevieve's expression but saw no signs of either acceptance or distrust. "I want to add a video during the credits of the movie—explaining in exact detail what has been going on to ensure that everyone in The Society hears the message and to be sure those on the mainland know as well. To guarantee your safety in case The Society retaliates against our efforts, I don't expect you to get overly involved. All I ask is that you sign off on the final cut of the film with the added clip in the credits."

Genevieve thought for a moment and then looked at Davin. She looked at Sara and studied her too as she realized she was clearly involved in this setup as well. She then pulled out her earpiece and removed her wristband as well before handing them to Sara without pause. Sara looked at them momentarily before realizing that she was supposed to add it to the box. Sara swiftly shut it up in the box, and then Genevieve looked back at Davin. "I commend you for doing what you think is right—no matter the consequences. This quality alone makes you more worthy of your fame than can be said for most stars. I will help you. This movie will make history in more than one way," she added with a twinkle in her eye as she smiled at Davin. "Now, how did you say you were getting to California?" she asked.

"We were going to . . . *borrow* a boat from The Society," Davin sheepishly admitted.

Genevieve smiled and then leaned back in her chair. "Leave it. I'll do you one better."

THAT NIGHT, after Chelsea finished getting dressed for bed, she anxiously ran over to Davin to take off his wristband and earpiece and placed it beside her own in the bathroom. She slammed the door behind her. "Finally! Tell me how it went," Chelsea said as she sat down beside him.

Davin smiled as the words that were welling up inside were finally able to leave him. "She said yes! Better yet, she's going to help us get to California!"

He explained Genevieve's take on things and how she was planning to help them. Chelsea's eyes lit up with hope and relief to know that Genevieve was also willing to help. The successful outcome of their plan felt more plausible than ever before.

"That's amazing!" Chelsea said when he finished. "We will be set. It seems so unreal. I can't believe she is so willing to help us."

"I think she's secretly hoping to make her mark in social justice history," Davin said with a chuckle. "But she seems to really believe in us. You made quite the impression on her the few times you met. So how did it go with finding the other entrance?"

"I never found it," Chelsea told him, feeling sorry that her news was dampening the excitement. "After searching everywhere, I finally had to give up. It was the oddest feeling being in there—knowing those poor people were right above me, waiting for me to come back. It's going to take some time to widen that hole so it's big enough."

"Speaking of which, I'll try and get one for you tomorrow so you can start."

"That would be great," Chelsea said. "I think I figured out what Roy was seeing from the cave entrance that made him think there was another larger entrance though," she stated, proud that she figured it out. "As I left, I looked back in and realized that he probably was seeing the large light blue tank at the other side of the cave that converts salt water to fresh water for The Society. From far away, it looks kind of like a large opening to the ocean, but it's really just the color of the tank creating an illusion."

"Well, at least we know what you have to do next to make sure you're able to get them out of there once we can," Davin said with a smile, feeling renewed by their progress that day.

ONCE DAVIN MANAGED to acquire a drill, Hammond or Chelsea began visiting the cave every day to widen the hole, bit-by-bit. Using the chisel bit it was equipped with, the small drill could easily break away chunks of rock because of its design that was invented by NASA in the early 2000s to produce more power while needing less force. But because of the small surface area of the bit, progress was slow, and they knew they would have to be diligent in their efforts if they were to ensure the hole would be wide enough in time for the premiere.

Sara, Davin, and Genevieve also worked hard to lay their part of the groundwork for the plan to be successful. Sara worked long hours editing the film to make sure it came together according to Genevieve's vision and still met the optimistic deadlines Genevieve had in place for the premiere. Davin made arrangements for the minute details of the escape so that they would be ready for their journey to California, and he continually mulled over his speech that would reveal the secrets of The Society until he felt confident it communicated everything necessary for people to comprehend exactly what was happening. Genevieve made her arrangements for Chelsea and Davin and worked overtime to promote the film on an even larger scale. She settled the final details of the film in the States with the producers—and then, finally, the day of the premiere had arrived. Everything was in place.

23. MOVIE PREMIERE

EVERYONE ON THE ISLAND was abuzz the day of the premiere. Most had visited the shopping kiosks and printed out new formal outfits for the evening's celebration. It was a night the whole nation had been looking forward to. Everyone missed the excitement behind the release of a new full-length film featuring a favorite star.

"Are you *sure* you'll be okay?" Davin asked Chelsea as he finished putting on his tuxedo for the evening and then sat down next to her on his bed.

"Everything will be all right, Davin. It will all work out." Chelsea had been secretly racked with nerves for the past several days, but she woke up that morning feeling calm and confident. "Have a little faith," she said with a smile.

"Faith, huh?" He chuckled. "Never thought I'd hear you say that."

Chelsea came up behind him and kissed him on the neck. "What can I say, you've been rubbing off on me."

Davin smiled for a moment, but then his smile faded. "I just can't help but feel like I'm leaving you to do all the work. Maybe I need to cut out early and help."

"I think we should stick to the plan," Chelsea replied. "You do your part, and I'll do mine."

"But what if something happens and I'm not there? I'd never forgive myself if something happened to you," Davin replied earnestly as he turned around to face her.

"I'm going to be fine. This is going to work," Chelsea said and kissed him softly on the lips. "You look quite dashing in a tux, by the way."

"I'm being serious, Chels."

Her smile faded, and as Davin wished, she became serious. "I think we're doing the right thing," she said. "And we've done our best to come up with a strategy that will hopefully work. All we can do now is pray it all happens according to plan."

"And if it doesn't?" Davin asked. He knew it wasn't a helpful question, but he still wanted to hear her answer just the same.

"I don't think either of us can continue to go on pretending like there's nothing wrong here," she stated firmly. "We *have* to try and help those people—and if something goes wrong, just know that I *wanted* to do this," Chelsea said, trying to soothe Davin's anxious mind. "I would do it with or without you."

Davin looked at her willful expression and couldn't help but smile. "Have I ever told you how adorable you are when you take charge like that?" He laughed, finally letting go of some the panic that had been building up inside him that morning. He sighed and then took her hand in his. "K, we can do this. We'll stick to the plan."

"Just remember—we're in this together. You just keep them distracted, and I'll be fine. Together—we can make this work."

Davin nodded. Looking out the window, he saw the sun was getting low. It was almost time. He suddenly tackled Chelsea to the bed to steal as many kisses as he could manage before he had to leave for his meeting. Her body tingled as his hand traced up and down her side. Davin's alarm sounded through the bathroom door, alerting him that it was time to depart, just in time for him to keep his tuxedo intact and his hair only mildly tousled.

"I'll see you soon. I love you, Chels," he said as he ran for the door, keeping his eyes fixed on her as long as possible before he had to go.

"Too," she said with a smile.

After Davin left, she fell back on the bed and held her breath. *Today's the day.*

WHILE CHELSEA GOT DRESSED and ready for the premiere event, Davin rushed to his meeting where the schedule for the evening and the role he would play in each event would be communicated. He walked into the meeting room just before it was supposed to begin. Everyone else was already seated and ready to start.

"Do join us, Davin," Ms. Waverly insisted, directing him to the chair next to her. "Let's begin. Tonight we have a chance for heavy exposure to the public. Everyone is very anxious to see the film, and we want to keep the focus on just that. The Society is merely the backdrop for the premiere. We will *not* be discussing The Society or its residents, and we want to take special care to not mention the storm. It's in the past. We have recovered, and it's time to move on. Even if the press asks directly, avoid the topic. Tonight is about the movie. Now, this evening we will start out by welcoming our special visitors from the mainland on the red carpet. After they exit the transporter pod, and we greet them, I will lead them to the dining area for dinner. Each of you will follow suit behind us. This will give the press a chance to see the grounds and photograph the event. So be sure to take your time, keep your heads high, and smile bright.

"After dinner, everyone will meet in the dome for the viewing of the film. Kona will open the viewing and introduce the director, who will say a few words, after which Davin will come out and deliver his speech, which will transition directly into the movie. After which, you can locate the seats you picked out for the viewing. When the film ends, you and your director are all invited to go on stage and take a bow. When the applause dies down, Davin will direct everyone to the after party.

"At the after party, you are all expected to divide your attention between as many residents and visitors as possible. Make it a party people will not soon forget."

Everyone will remember tonight—but not for the reasons you want them to, Davin thought to himself.

"You're there so they can mingle with *you*—The Society's film stars. You will attend and participate for the entirety of the after party, which will likely last into the early morning hours." Ms. Waverly turned her attention directly toward Davin. "Please be sure you do not show favoritism to any particular resident. Should they want to spend time with our local stars, our residents should feel you are at their disposal—one of the many perks of living here in our Society," she said. "Now, are there any questions?" She scanned the table for any raised hands or indications of confusion.

After Ms. Waverly answered a few questions, they proceeded to the transporter pod's landing dock to stand ready for when it arrived. The press, who had arrived in person for this event, was already gathered and began snapping photos as soon as they spotted Davin along with the supporting cast. Ms. Waverly escorted each of the stars to a designated position where security bots stood with projected barriers to block them off from the crowd. After a few minutes, the transporter pod arrived and hovered over to the landing pad before it gently touched the ground. From inside came a small group of prominent people, accompanied by a number of security bots.

"Pleasure to have you back with us here at the beautiful Hawaii Society, Madam Vice President," Davin greeted the vice president as he shook her hand once again. He'd had a wonderful conversation with her the first time she visited The Society at the Grand Welcome Celebration where they had first met.

"The pleasure is mine, Davin. The whole nation is wild with excitement for your latest achievement. I can't wait to see it myself."

Just wait 'til you see the surprise ending, Davin thought to himself. "I hope you enjoy it," he said as the vice president moved on to greet Kona.

The next man approached Davin and gave him a strong handshake. "Mr. Chapman, I hope we have a real winner here. I'd love to make my money back," he said with a smile as he leaned in toward Davin.

"Mr. Crawford," Davin said with a smile, returning his handshake with an equally firm grip. "Thank you for funding this great film. I hope you're very pleased."

"Oh, I'm sure I will be. With all this hype, we are bound for success," he said as he patted Davin on the back.

The next woman to exit the pod walked up to Davin and then stopped abruptly to inspect him. "You're not as tall in person as you look on screen," she commented. "You don't quite fit the description of the main character either, but I suppose they had few options to pick from, and you do good work."

"You must be Rogue Blanchet," Davin said. "It's truly a unique story you conjured up. Your book was wonderful. I only hope we did it justice, and you're pleased with the outcome."

"Well, you know what they say, the book is always better than the movie," Rogue said with a polite smile.

Davin continued to welcome the last few people off the pod, including the writer Jon Dunn and the older actors from the mainland. Then Genevieve Thrope walked out and greeted him with a warm embrace.

"It's all set, Davin," she whispered, her crackly voice a bit harsh in his ear. "And the movie turned out lovely," she said with a grin. "One of your best performances—in my opinion."

Davin had truly enjoyed working with Genevieve. He hoped to keep in contact with her when they reached California. She was already mentioning directing another film with him in the future. "Thanks to you." Davin smiled warmly. "You pushed me for my best. I hope we can work together again soon."

"I'm sure we will," Genevieve replied happily.

"And thank you—thank you for helping us," Davin said with sincerity. "I hope it comes at no cost to you—financial or otherwise. We will find a way to repay you."

"Oh, don't worry about me," she replied. "Just keep making movies with me—I'd forgotten how much I love it. Besides, no one will have anything on me. I know how to play things close to the chest. I'll be gone before they think to question me. And I'm old. There's nothing they can do to me that won't end soon enough anyway," she said with a chuckle before moving on to greet Kona.

The remaining security bots exited the pod. As instructed, Davin followed behind the group of visitors toward the dining hall. He stopped occasionally to be interviewed and to sign autographs along the way. Then he saw *her*.

Chelsea stepped out from the crowd. She wore a black dress with a shallow laced-up V-neck, and her copper hair blew in the light breeze from the ocean. Her radiant smile made Davin beam with pride. He reached for her sun-kissed hand as he continued to look her over. "You're stunning."

"Glad you like it," Chelsea said, looking down at her dress and happy to see that he approved.

"Not it—*you*." He reached for Chelsea's chin, tilted her head up, and gave her a soft kiss on the lips.

Cameras flashed quickly, and anyone not focused on Davin already suddenly shifted their attention.

"Walk with me," he whispered. He didn't care that Ms. Waverly didn't want him to be seen with Chelsea. He didn't care if she thought he would be more likable if he appeared to be available. He didn't care if people in the States thought he was with Kona. He was finally going to get away from The Society and away from Ms. Waverly's puppet strings, and he wanted to follow his father's advice. He wanted to let the world know how much he loved Chelsea.

They began to walk hand in hand. Davin kept his gaze on Chelsea. Only a few steps in, a crowd of people stopped them and showered them with a multitude of questions.

"Who's the girl, Davin?"

"How does Kona feel about this relationship?"

"How long have you been together?"

"What's your name? Are you in the movie with Davin?"

"Is this the girl there have been rumors about?"

Davin stopped and turned toward the cameras to provide them with some answers. He spoke up above the crowd to quiet their mounting list of questions. "Since you are all so curious—this is Chelsea Coremon. I am completely in love with her," he said with a smile. He then turned toward her and lowered his voice to a gentle deep lull. "And I always will be."

Chelsea tried to remain collected, though she could feel her face warming and her palms beginning to sweat. With that short speech, Davin led her past the crowd that continued to ask more questions, and the cameras continued to flash. He put his arm around her waist and pulled her close to his side.

"*This* wasn't part of the plan," Chelsea whispered into his ear.

"No, but I don't care what they want anymore. I want the world to know you," Davin said. He smirked in satisfaction as he noticed Ms. Waverly's disapproving looks farther down the red carpet. His small act of revolt was the taste of freedom he had been craving as he felt the promise of escape ticking closer to fruition.

He also felt particularly grateful that he had someone who could be at his side at these events. He had walked his premieres alone so many times and hadn't realized the peaceful assurance that came with having a supportive companion nearby.

Seeing that there was still concern on Chelsea's face, Davin teased her. "Don't worry. It will all work out. Have a little faith." He smiled as he repeated her words from earlier that day, and she glared back at him with a reluctant grin. "Relax and enjoy the moment," he told her.

Enjoy the moment? Chelsea thought. She looked around at all the smiling people and Davin's fans waving frantically in their direction. They didn't seem to care he was with her anymore. The residents at The Society had grown accustomed to seeing Chelsea by his side. Some even looked happy to see them walking together. So eventually Chelsea conceded and decided to take advantage of the time she had with him at the premiere to celebrate his success. She smiled wide and waved for the cameras. She unapologetically held his hand and kissed him without restraint. Chelsea's proud eyes did not leave his smiling face as they finished the long walk down the red carpet to The Society towers.

In the dining area, each table was lined with linen, specially ordered to cover the usual array of long white tables, along with small, elegant centerpieces. Low lighting and soft background music added to the charming ambiance. Davin recognized the melody as the score from the ending credits of the film.

Davin motioned for Chelsea to take a seat as they reached their table, and he held out a hand to assist her. Though she would normally protest such behavior, she welcomed it and let go of her need to do things for herself. He smiled in satisfaction at her acceptance of his small act of chivalry.

Dinner was a decadent meal of cheese stuffed peppers, pesto chicken, and an epicurean salad, accompanied by a tropical smoothie. It was the first gourmet-inspired meal served since the hurricane. The basic cooking the residents had become accustomed to after the storm contrasted sharply with the exquisite tastes of the meal that night. The chicken was moist with a seared crust that complemented the nutty flavor of the freshly made pesto sauce on top. The cheese inside the peppers oozed out as they were cut and the flavor pairing between the aged cheese and its sweet encasement was perfection. The salad was a mix of obscure fruits and vegetables that combined harmoniously with the unique dressing. And the tropical smoothie was a sweet, indulgent blend of the most delicious native fruits grown on the grounds.

"I feel like we're at the last supper," Davin commented quietly to Chelsea.

"It's so good," Chelsea said while enjoying her last bit of stuffed pepper. "Did the food always taste this good before? Or are we just so used to eating plain oatmeal now that anything tastes good?"

"Chelsea, is it?" Ms. Waverly asked as she walked up behind them.

"Oh, yes," Chelsea managed to say after quickly swallowing her food and hiding her dread. "Nice to meet you, Ms. Waverly," she said and offered her hand. Though Chelsea had been around Ms. Waverly many times during events in the dome, they hadn't spoken or been formally introduced before.

"Likewise," Ms. Waverly said, ignoring Chelsea's extended hand. "I assume you will be running the program tonight in the dome. I wanted to personally make sure you have everything prepared and you know the agenda—"

"Actually, I completed a different task this morning," Chelsea interrupted her. "But not to worry, I trained Roland on everything he needs to know for today, and I have complete confidence in him." Chelsea managed a smile in spite of Ms. Waverly's apparent dissatisfaction.

"That's my fault, actually," Davin announced before Ms. Waverly had time to respond. "I insisted that she have the night off so she could accompany me this evening," Davin said even though he knew perfectly well that was not the reason Chelsea had taken that night off. Ms. Waverly's look of condemnation grew more apparent. "Nothing to worry about though. Roland does great work, and Chelsea can be there to help at a moment's notice should a problem arise."

With pursed lips, Ms. Waverly replied, "I suppose I should speak with Roland then. Let's hope he is as confident in his abilities as you two seem to be. Goodbye." She turned around, her eyes still burning with anger that Davin had once again gone against her explicit demands. She activated her wristband to pinpoint Roland's location.

"That did not go well," Chelsea remarked.

Davin's smile grew wider. "Who cares?" he said, relishing in the fact that he soon wouldn't have to comply with Sandra Waverly's every order. "We do need to get going though. It's about time," Davin said. "Are you ready for this?"

"Yes," Chelsea replied with a deep breath.

They walked to the dome together, giving small greetings to those who passed by. Though they had smiles on their faces, both of them felt the pressure of what was about to transpire.

When they reached the dome, Chelsea stopped by the video workstation to make sure Roland was prepared with the proper version of the movie and ready with each graphic, cue, and camera shot. She greeted him warmly and thanked him for stepping in for her. Though she originally disliked Roland, the past few weeks had changed her mind.

It had begun when he had reluctantly confessed that he was the one who had ruined the settings on the switcher the night before The Grand Welcome Celebrations. Initially, Chelsea had wanted to be irate—until he said with his head hung low, "Watching you work made me want to really learn the equipment, but I was too proud to admit that I didn't know what I was doing. I'm sorry. I tried to go through and learn the system myself, but I accidentally reset the whole thing while I was trying to undo some of the settings I had changed."

As he confessed, Chelsea suddenly had a thought that would benefit both of them. Roland wanted to be trained, and she needed someone to replace her at the premiere. She offered to teach him about video engineering and, to her surprise, the more he learned, the more his demeanor changed. He no longer heckled the others who worked in the dome. He signed up for classes and worked hard to learn from Chelsea whenever she had the time to teach him. Even Finley started to like him. He was one of the few people at The Society who had actually taken the time to genuinely learn the video system. Even if something did go wrong, Chelsea had full confidence in his ability to fix it.

Chelsea wished Roland good luck and then turned to look out over the backstage area. Kona stood at the ready just offstage, ready with her memorized speech to introduce the event and the director of the film. Genevieve Thrope stood next to Davin, her hand holding on to his politely extended arm as she spoke casually to him about the evening's events. Chelsea checked one last time to make sure the broadcast to the mainland was working and then started walking over to Davin to give him the go-ahead.

Davin watched as Chelsea approached him. "You'll have to excuse me, Gen. I need a minute."

Genevieve followed Davin's line of sight to see Chelsea. "She's very beautiful. You two are lucky to have each other, Davin," Genevieve said with a grin. "Go."

Davin excused himself and walked to Chelsea. He immediately pulled her in for a close embrace. His hand stroked the side of her face, and he took in a deep breath of her perfume. Chelsea, who was focused on the logistics of the plan, was caught off guard by his casual intimacy.

"Everything is set," she whispered to him as she went over the plan in her mind to make sure she hadn't forgotten anything. The lights in the audience went dim and the stage lights came on. In the background, they could hear booming applause as Kona walked out on stage.

"Great. Just be safe," he said with loving concern. "You only have two hours—so be fast." Chelsea nodded, though her mind flooded with anxiety at the thought of going through with the plan. "I'll meet you at the dock before the video plays."

"You still want this, right?" she asked, suddenly afraid their plan could be more dangerous than she could have ever imagined.

"You can do this," he said, staring directly into her concerned eyes. "And don't worry. We'll be gone before anyone expects a thing."

Genevieve Thrope was now walking out on stage. Davin wasn't certain how long her speech would be, but he wanted to use what time he had left to hold Chelsea behind the privacy of the backstage curtain before she had to leave him for their daring escape. He held her—hoping to communicate his love and desperately praying for her safety. He kissed her.

The voice in Chelsea's head that always returned to remind her that he couldn't possibly love *her* was finally gone. He *did* love her—she could feel it in his kiss as his lips pressed eagerly against her own and in the way his hands held onto her—forever wanting more. But beyond *feeling* his love, she also decided they were good for each other. He understood her at a level no one else ever had. She never felt like an outsider in his presence. And unlike her past relationships, when she walked into the room, his eyes followed only her. They laughed at each other's humor when others did not. Behind closed doors, they laughed even harder. They teased each other relentlessly, but it somehow brought them closer. She could tell him anything without shame. It was a freedom she had never felt with anyone else before—a bond that grew stronger each day. She was convinced that he was the only person she had ever met who she would dare to take this journey of vulnerability and trust with—the journey that the world calls love.

As Davin clasped the sides of her face, he took one last stroke before Genevieve finished her generous introduction of him. " . . . So it is my pleasure to introduce my friend and tonight's star, Davin Chapman!"

Davin reluctantly pulled away from Chelsea just in time to run on stage. The crowd exploded into shouts and cheers. The anticipation for the movie to begin brought an energy that hung thick in the air.

"Good evening, Hawaii Society members!" The crowd continued to cheer in the background. "Are you excited?" he prodded in spite of their obvious enthusiasm. Even louder cheers burst from the attendees. "Let's give one more round of applause to the lovely Genevieve Thrope, whom we have to thank for the creation of this new film!"

Applause followed her as she exited the stage. She mouthed small thank yous and blew kisses in the crowd's direction as she left—milking the zest that comes from a live audience that she had long since forgotten.

"What an evening it has been—and it's only the beginning!" Davin said, extracting even more energy from the already vigorous group. Davin smiled at their zeal—he had their attention, just as he wanted. "I can't tell you how excited I am to see the end product of all your hard work on this film. I believe it will be one that won't soon be forgotten. It's a masterpiece filled with complex emotion and an unexpected ending. Please enjoy and contemplate on what you are about to see. I also invite you to take action in your life and community on the things you learn tonight," Davin added. His spontaneous changes to the scripted introduction caused

Ms. Waverly's eyes to rise from her copy of the script on her PED. It was unlike him to not follow her instructions, and that made three strikes that day. Unable to reprimand him in public, she determined that she'd have to deal with his rebellion later—even if it meant using her leverage against him.

"Now, without any further ado, let the show begin!" Davin announced as he ran off stage and the lights dimmed to black. He reached for Chelsea's hand as he walked off stage, bringing her along as they quickly took their seats. He had been careful to reserve seating for them that would allow Chelsea to leave easily without being seen. They sat down and waited for the opening scene to begin where there would be a blackout on the screen just before the title appeared, which would give Chelsea the chance to quickly exit with as few people noticing as possible.

Just before the blackout, Davin leaned over to her. "Come back to me," he whispered.

The room went dark, and he let go of her hand—praying it wouldn't be the last time he saw her beautiful face. Chelsea leaned over to quickly kiss his cheek silently in the dark, and when the light from the title screen shone over the crowd, she was already out of sight.

24. ESCAPE

THERE WERE VERY few people in the halls. Everyone was already seated for the beginning of the film. Chelsea walked at a brisk but casual pace to avoid attracting attention from the few people she crossed paths with as they hurriedly ran toward the restroom, hoping to get back to their seats before they missed too much of the film. Once she was safely alone in the elevator, she took in a calming breath. She knew she needed to maintain her equanimity and work fast for the plan to succeed.

When the elevator doors opened, she broke out into a sprint toward the dock, grabbing some escapading equipment and the bag of things she had hidden earlier that day. Then she jumped into the boat closest to her, where Hammond and Sara were waiting. Hammond started the engine. He slowly made his way out onto the river and toward the ocean. Chelsea rummaged through her bag and pulled out her rash guard and board shorts. She took off her evening gown, changed her clothes, and removed her earpiece and wristband. Then she placed them in her bag, alongside some pieces of fruit and her PED.

As soon as the boat hit the ocean waves, Hammond revved the engine to full power and headed in the direction of the cave. Beads

of sweat began to form at the crown of Chelsea's forehead—
a combination of the hot summer evening and the nerves that had
built up as she ventured off on her own to do the most daring act of
upheaval she had ever committed.

Once they neared the entrance to the cave, Hammond slowed
the boat to a stop and set anchor before killing the engine. Chelsea
grabbed her mask and flippers in preparation to dive. She readied
herself at the edge of the boat as Hammond handed her a large bag,
and then Sara wrapped her in a hug. Sara struggled to conceal her
look of trepidation as she loosened her grip and pulled away. To
maintain her own fortitude, Chelsea quickly pushed Sara's face out
of her mind, pulled on her gear, sat back, and dropped off the side
of the boat into the cool, clear water.

Chelsea slowly swam down into the calm of the blue sea. The
weight of the bag that Hammond gave her helped her sink faster
than normal, though she struggled to resist its pull each time she
had to change course. As she went deeper and the light from the
setting sun dimmed, she turned on her headlamp and scanned the
land's edge for the camouflaged entrance. She soon spotted it.
Having visited the location multiple times, she had become adept
at spotting the landmarks that indicated the subtle lip that
concealed the small cavern. She hurriedly shimmied her way in,
hugging the bag tightly to her body to keep it from snagging on any
obstructions.

As she swam deeper into the crevasse, she spotted the entrance
to the cave. She had spent hours chipping away at the narrow
access to make it wide enough for those inside to exit with ease.
Looking at the widened gap, she now wondered if it would be large
enough for the bag to pass through. She tried not to worry too
much, knowing she'd packed the waterproof chisel drill in case she
had to expand it further, but with her two hours quickly ticking by,
she knew any significant lapse of time could be detrimental to the
plan.

It was clear when she reached the opening that she and the bag wouldn't be able to pass through at the same time. She considered emptying the bag one component at a time, but knowing that very few of the items would naturally float, she felt the risk was too great that one of the objects would sink to a mysterious, watery nook. She reasoned she would first try to push the bag up in front of her before pulling out the drill to widen the hole.

Pushing as hard as she could, she struggled to fit the cumbersome bag through the hole. It was so close to fitting, but the objects inside managed to topple into positions that hindered her progression. She grappled with the items—hoping to maneuver them into a position where she could manage the bag's entry. But after a few wasted minutes, she began to worry she was losing too much time and would eventually have to pull it out and begin hastily drilling after all. In a desperate frenzy to avoid that situation, she bore down with the last of her strength.

With a sudden shift of its contents, the bag abruptly emerged on the other side of the hole.

The sudden give sent Chelsea's arms shooting through with the bag. Her left forearm scrapped hard against the side of the hole. She barely managed to keep her right hand on the bag as she shuddered in pain from the large scrape across the top of her left arm. The sting was worse than the cut, but the pain was still momentarily crippling.

The noise from the bag splashing out of the water immediately alerted the five captives inside the cave to Chelsea's arrival. She pulled herself up through the hole and removed her mask. Looking around, she examined the cave. After confirming there was no one there but the five captives looking hopelessly in her direction, she swam to the concrete floor's ledge and lugged herself and the bag out of the water. She rushed over to retrieve the key tag so she could free them, but it wasn't there.

"It's gone," Tray called out to her in despair. "Branch forgot to put it back."

Chelsea ran over to the door in bewilderment. "What do you mean, it's gone? I'm here to free you. You said it was *always* there." Chelsea's frustration built up inside her. She was all too conscious that this was her only chance to free them. "It can't be gone!" She looked in on the five people wistfully staring out at her from their glass prison. One man suddenly gave up on the hope that had surfaced with Chelsea's return and sat back down against the wall in defeat, having already decided that whatever Chelsea's plan was, it obviously hadn't accounted for the missing key tag and was doomed to failure.

Their frail bodies were withered to the bone. "When was the last time you ate something?" Chelsea asked, unable to believe the condition they were all in.

"When you were here last. You barely made it out before Branch brought us our meal—a single piece of fruit," Tray answered, still in disgust of the memory. "Can you come back and check on us every so often until he returns the key?"

Chelsea's heart swelled with guilt. Their elaborate plan depended on the assumption that the key tag would still be there waiting. And to make matters worse, they had placed themselves in a position where they couldn't return after the video played. She regretted not trying to free them beforehand. She knew that regret was irrational, given that she would've had to take the time to drill the entrance hole wider either way, but that didn't stop her from punishing herself just the same. Chelsea's head drooped in anguish. "No. I won't be able to."

"No?" Tray questioned in disbelief. "What do you mean, no? Why not? I thought you were going to help us!"

"I'm sorry," Chelsea stammered over Tray's accusations. "My safety will be compromised after the viewing. I have to leave The Society *tonight*. Maybe the government will come for you guys after everyone knows what's going on." Chelsea's explanation fell on deaf ears, and they glared out at her with looks of betrayal. "I thought the key would be here! I would have come earlier, but I had to drill—" Chelsea stopped mid-sentence. She had an idea.

Tray continued to try to guilt her into coming back later, but she ignored him and opened the bag to pull out the ultrasonic drill. She traded out the chisel bit for a twist drill bit and went to work. She pressed the bit hard against the metal near the door handle and began drilling.

"You know how to drill out a lock like this?" Tray asked, somewhat impressed.

Chelsea had no idea how to drill out a lock, but she tried not to let her uncertainty show. She continued to drill without answering. She pulled the drill out a number of times and tried other parts of the metal casing, hoping she would eventually hit the deadbolt's fixture. But as the minutes ticked on, she knew she was wasting too much time. Her arms dropped to her sides. "This is taking too long." She instead took the drill and placed it directly on the glass itself and began drilling again.

Like most recently made doors, the glass was made from multi-layered composite panels. Though the glass around the drill began to crack and chip away, each layer she drilled through seemed to distend without penetration. But with persistence, the small but powerful ultrasonic drill finally pushed through. The five captives looked at each other with a dribble of hope. They could feel the outside air coming in—taunting them with their freedom. Chelsea smiled and continued to drill along the edges of the small hole.

Unfortunately, their small bit of hope began to fizzle out as the time passed by with little progress. The glass was resilient, and the small drill was making too little headway with the time Chelsea had remaining. She began kicking at the door, hoping a greater surface area would chip off. Then she heard the terrifying sound of a door opening.

Chelsea stopped kicking and froze in place to listen. The door at the top of the stairs was slowly and quietly being closed, but the acoustics of the hollow cave reverberated the small noise across the room. Slow and steady footprints began walking down the steps as Chelsea frantically contemplated what she could do. Looking at the thin faces of the five people inside the glass room, she made her decision.

She got up and quickly hid behind some stacked boxes nearby. Branch emerged from the shadows with his gun in hand. His eyes widened in disbelief as he examined the cracked glass and the holes in the door. The holes in the door fixture explained the alert to his PED, but he wasn't certain if the holes had been made from the inside or the outside until he noticed the large bag left in the middle of the floor. He raised his gun and walked slowly toward the door, then cautiously bent down to inspect the bag's contents.

Seeing his attention diverted, Chelsea seized her opportunity. She threw the drill at his head—disorienting his focus and knocking him to the ground. She rushed over and stepped on his wrist as she ripped the gun out of his hands. He rolled on the floor in pain from the impact of the drill on his skull and put up no fight to maintain his grip on the gun as the stinging from his wound grew more intense.

Having never used a gun before, Chelsea fumbled it into a position that mimicked what Branch had been doing. "Give me the key tag, Branch. I'm freeing them," Chelsea said with all the determination she could muster. Branch looked up from his agony and managed to examine Chelsea's small stature, despite his double vision. He could easily guess her lack of experience with a gun from her stance and could not help but let out a menacing chuckle. "This isn't funny, Branch. These people deserve their freedom," Chelsea said.

"Does your boyfriend know you're missing his movie to break these leeches out?" Branch asked with a smile as blood dripped down his face from the wound on his head. It was obvious from his slurred speech that Branch had gotten his hands on more than the one glass of wine allotted to each resident at the premiere that night. Chelsea glared back without an answer. "I'm sure he's noticed the empty seat next to him—so he would have to, I suppose," Branch thought aloud. "How long have you been planning this? It must have been for some time now in order for you to be able to get in here without me noticing. And that would explain your blatant disregard for wearing your wristbands at night," he reasoned, trying to stall so he could recover from his injury. "And all this time, I just thought you were shy in bed," Branch said with a shrug and a conniving smile.

"The key! Now!" Chelsea yelled.

"The key?" Branch continued, now unable to contain his laughter. "What is this, the '20s? There is no key! I just saw those empty hooks over there and thought how hilarious it would be if they all thought the key to their freedom was sitting just on the other side of the door. After I forgot to put it back on the hook last time, I decided to give up the joke, and I threw it away. I'm the only one who can get in and out of that room."

Branch struggled to stand. He wiped the blood from his face with his sleeve and waited for her next move. Chelsea couldn't tell if he was lying, but she wanted his taunting to end. She looked down at Branch's wristband. "Fine. Then it's a good thing you're here," Chelsea concluded. "Let them out. Or I'll shoot."

"Here's the thing though," Branch replied. "No one can know that they want to leave The Society, and honestly, where are they going to go?" he asked with an exasperated expression. The pain in his head was beginning to subside, and he could feel his strength returning. "None of you people could cut it in the real world before, and if you refuse to be part of the solution, then none of you have a place in this world," Branch said in disgust to the five who were watching intently through the glass. "And if you don't like it, you can join 'em," he said as he turned back to look at Chelsea.

Expecting to call her bluff, he suddenly sprang forward to disarm her. Chelsea pulled the trigger. Branch's hand was able to redirect the barrel of the gun, but he quickly recoiled from the shock of the Glock slide pinching down on the skin between his thumb and index finger near the ejection port.

The bullet hit the glass door—causing the entire outside layer to shatter into tiny pieces. Tray quickly stood and kicked the door with what strength he had, but the remaining layers remained intact against his feeble blows.

Branch quickly recovered and charged at her again. Unsure if she needed to do anything to fire the gun again and afraid that Branch would be successful in disarming her this time, Chelsea threw the gun toward the water—gambling that she would be more successful without it.

But her throw fell short, and she watched in agony as the gun slid across the floor, coming to a stop just before the water's edge. Branch immediately changed his focus to the gun and redirected his course. Chelsea ran for the gun as well, in hopes that she could kick it into the water before Branch could reach it. But realizing he would reach it before she did, she quickly pulled on the escapading mask that she had been holding and prepared for impact. She sprinted toward him and leaned forward—aiming for his upper half.

Branch triumphantly reached down to retrieve the gun just as Chelsea tackled him. They tumbled over each other into the water—leaving the gun behind. As they splashed down under the water, Branch struggled to reach the surface to get a breath of air after the wind had been knocked out of him from the collision. Chelsea grabbed for his tuxedo collar and wrapped her legs around his waist to weigh him down, but his strength and will to survive brought him closer to the surface with each kick.

Chelsea knew she had an advantage underwater because of her mask, so she wanted to keep Branch there if she could. But it was clear she could not stop his force with her meager weight. She would have to change her approach if she was going to survive. Remembering that the elbow is one of the hardest parts of the body, she geared up to make her move. Just before Branch breached the surface of the water, Chelsea pushed against his shoulders to lift herself above him, and then came down hard on his face with her elbow.

From inside the glass room, the five watched as Chelsea briefly emerged from the water and then dove back down. Branch was barely able to take a small gasp of air before taking her blow to the face. Mind-numbing pain coursed through his already sore head, only to be added to as Chelsea began vigorously kicking at him, pushing him down deeper into the water.

Fueled by his pain, Branch's anger boiled inside of him. He opened his eyes to aim his counterattack. The unpleasant sting from the salt water passed after a moment, and he made his move. He grabbed Chelsea's foot and pulled her down. The force pulled him up toward her, and he punched her in the stomach as they met. Chelsea curled into a ball of hurt. Having never been punched before, she struggled to refocus her attention from the pain back to the fight. Forcing herself to act fast in order to avoid another blow, she rapidly lifted her head, and it collided with Branch's jaw. His vision blurred. Chelsea grabbed his shoulders and lifted her knee into his groin. He wailed in pain—letting out a large reserve of his remaining air.

As fast as she could, Chelsea swam around to Branch's back and tightened her arm around his throat while wrapping her legs around his stomach. They sank lower as Branch thrashed back and forth. Chelsea held fast and tried to ignore the torment of his crushing clasp on her arm. Then his grasp steadily loosened. The last bit of his air supply bubbled out of his mouth and rose to the surface, and he floated motionless in the water.

In a frantic scurry to escape the looming presence of his still body, Chelsea ripped off his wristband and swam to the water's edge without looking back to see the haunting results of their altercation. Despite all the horrible wrongs she knew Branch had committed, she could not bear the thought that she was responsible for someone's death.

She reached the edge of the cave's floor and pulled herself up out of the water. The five onlookers pressed up against the glass to see which of the two had come up—Chelsea or Branch. They let out a joyful sigh of relief as they saw Chelsea remove her mask and lay on the floor, taking in long, slow breaths.

Suddenly, she bolted up. Not knowing if there was any time left, she picked up the gun and ran for the glass door. She immediately scanned Branch's wristband against the handle. The door unlocked, and she swung it open, causing a small chunk of glass to fall to the floor when it came to a stop. "Now it breaks," Chelsea grumbled as the five elated prisoners relished their first steps to freedom.

Chelsea grabbed the large bag she brought with her and threw Branch's wristband and the gun inside. Then she pulled out a pair of flippers and a mask for each of the five. "Hurry and put these on. I don't know how much time we have, but I don't imagine we have much," Chelsea said while secretly worrying that time had already run out. "Follow my lead. I have food waiting for you on the boat," Chelsea said as she too put her flippers and mask back on and then entered the water.

Chelsea swam fast. The other five struggled to keep up with her pace. She wasn't sure if her motivation was to get back in time or to get out of the water where Branch's body lay still at the bottom.

To Chelsea's relief, each of the five slipped through the hole into the cavern with ease. They all turned on their headlamps when they entered the dark cavity, and Chelsea motioned for them to follow her. As they exited the hole into the open ocean, they looked up to see the light from dusk was nearly gone. Knowing that meant that time was nearly out, Chelsea swam quickly toward the murky outline of the boat still waiting for them. The others swam behind her—following their heroine with the hope of freedom in their hearts and gratitude for the woman who had risked her life to bring them to it.

As THE LAST SCENE of the movie was about to begin, Davin quickly glanced down at the time before looking back at the screen to watch for his signal. Sara had shown him the scene a number of times so he knew what to look for, and since the scene's opening shot was one that Genevieve had made him reshoot many times before she was fully satisfied, he was especially familiar with his cue.

The sweat that had been accumulating on his forehead throughout the night was now dripping down in droves as he fretted over Chelsea's well-being. His heart rate increased when he witnessed the scene appear on the screen that he had been watching for all night—it was finally time. He leaned over to Kona. "I'm going to run to the restroom before I have to go back up. See you at the after party."

Kona nodded in response to his lie without pulling her attention from the screen. Enthralled by Davin's performance, she watched the last scene with intent.

Though Davin would normally be pleased to see an audience member so captivation with his film, he was too distracted to notice or care. He quickly sprang up and made his way to the hall, but instead of turning down the hall for the restroom, he waited until no one was around and then boarded the elevator that ran down Tower Four. When the doors shut, he opened the clasp to his wristband and hit the off button for the first time in twenty years before reaching into his pocket to turn off his PED as well.

The doors to the elevator opened, and he sneaked quietly to the boat docks. To his horror, there was no boat waiting for him. Chelsea wasn't back. The sun had set, yet there was no boat waiting for him as they had planned. Panic festered in his mind. *Something went wrong.*

He scanned the room, hoping to find something that would inspire his next course of action. But he stood paralyzed, unable to decide if it would be better to go after them or stick to the plan. He habitually flicked his wrist to check the time—forgetting that he had already turned off his wristband. In a panic, he decided it was too risky to wait. He ran for one of the quad skis and hopped on, but just as he did, he heard the low hum of an engine approaching the docks.

Davin looked over to see Chelsea, Hammond, Sara, and five others looking out toward him from the boat. Sara was smiling wide. Hammond kept a focused eye on the dock as he moved the boat into position, and he could see the five rescues eating small bites of what food their starved stomachs could handle. Chelsea kept a steady watch on Davin as they approached. His panic subsided when he saw her. *She's all right*, he thought, and he ran toward the boat to get in. But as he studied her face, he could tell something was wrong. She was smiling, but there was a distress in her eyes that few others would have recognized.

"You did it!" he whispered as he got into the boat and went to kiss her on the head. "Are you all right? Did everything go okay?" he asked, examining her body as best as he could in the dark.

"I'm okay," she said quietly. She gave him a quick but inordinately tight hug. "We should get going," she whispered, wanting to escape the haunting presence she now felt at The Society.

Davin nodded and sat next to Chelsea as he cued Hammond to cast off. Everyone remained silent as they rode out onto the ocean. When they were far enough out, Davin looked over at the five liberated residents and felt a gratifying sense of disbelief. "I can't tell you how happy I am to see all of you safely here."

The five of them stopped eating and looked up from their food. "Are you Davin Chapman?" the woman asked.

"Yes," answered Davin.

"I thought you were The Society's number one fan," Tray commented. "What are you doing helping a bunch of deserters? I thought you would detest people like us."

"Davin is leaving with us," Chelsea told them.

"We've been planning this escape for months," Davin added as the boat navigated around the backside of the mountain. "We've been slowly uncovering The Society's corruption and some cover-ups in the government offices, and I couldn't continue supporting it. And when we found out about you guys, we had to make sure you escaped too. But you can't exactly just walk out when you're . . . " Davin struggled to piece together an explanation.

"When you're Davin Chapman?" the women finished for him. "Yeah—I imagine people would notice if you went missing. Well, thank you for helping us."

"Don't thank me," Davin countered. "Chelsea was the one who convinced me something was wrong, and she did all the work," he said as he motioned to her.

Chelsea looked over at Davin impatiently—feeling that he exaggerated her contribution in persuading him to go when she always felt he was the more adamant defender against the injustices. But before she could respond, one of the rescued residents excitedly joined the conversation. "Man, you should have seen her down in the cave! Watching you tackle Branch was so satisfying. I wish we could have fought him with you. Not only to level the playing field, but because I've wanted to punch that guy for so long." He sighed. "Now I'll never get the chance."

"Tackle Branch?" Davin asked in bewilderment. "Why was Branch down there? I thought you said there was a key," he said, looking at Chelsea as she looked away. "And what do you mean 'Now you'll never get the chance'? Wait—so who was fighting Branch?"

"Chelsea," Tray answered. "Branch came down while she was trying to bust us out. Ended up being a good thing actually—turns out his wristband was actually the key. Stupid prick, giving us false hope with that fake key." Tray scowled just thinking about it.

"You had to fight Branch?" Davin asked Chelsea, horrified he hadn't been there to protect her. "I'm so sorry. I should've been watching him more closely. I knew I should have gone with you. Are you okay?"

"Considering he came with a gun, and she left with it, I'd say she did all right on her own," another rescue said with an engaging smile in Chelsea's direction.

Davin struggled to fathom the thought of Chelsea having to face Branch in a gunfight. Then he saw the scrape on her arm. "You're hurt!" he exclaimed as he examined her wound.

"I'm fine," she said. "I got that from scraping against a rock. It's not bad."

"I'm so sorry, Chels. I should have been—" Davin started to say again before Hammond interrupted.

"Everyone is all right, Davin. Calm down. Just be impressed," he said with a smile. He couldn't conceal the vindication he felt from Branch's fate. The justice he craved for what Branch did to Sara had finally been served. The fact that Chelsea managed to accomplish it while coming out generally unscathed made the victory that much more welcome.

"Don't be impressed. I'm not proud of what happened," Chelsea interjected.

"And what exactly happened?" Davin asked.

Chelsea looked down. "I drowned him," she whispered as she choked back some tears. Davin's eyes widened, and he wrapped an arm around her as he looked out in disbelief to get confirmation from the others.

"You did what you had to do to survive," the girl said in her defense.

"And we're all very grateful you got us out of there," Tray added. The other rescues nodded. "I think they would've eventually let us starve to death. According to Branch, they told our families we were sent back, and then they made up different stories for each of us about how we went missing or were killed. They destroyed our PEDs and wristbands so no one could find us. We were completely expendable in their minds. Ultimately, the good of The Society was more important than any of us."

"And Branch was the worst of it. He was a wolf in sheep's clothing. To the public, he's a likable and handsome administrative genius. But to his victims, he was vicious—using every ounce of power to exploit and demean," Semaj told Chelsea. "You wouldn't believe the horrible things he bragged to us about in the cave."

"Or the things he did," another added, giving the girl of the group a gentle side hug.

"Don't feel bad about what happened, Chelsea," Semaj continued. "It was the only way Branch could be brought to justice. Trust me, I know. My father works in the government, and he's seen it before. Branch has so many connections—even if he was put on trial he would've never been convicted." Semaj was the first resident to be sent to the cave and the son of a congressman. "You would've been locked up in there with us if you hadn't done what you did."

"Or worse," Tray added.

After hearing everyone's assurances, Chelsea did feel some reconciliation about the situation—although the curdling in her stomach persisted as she contended with her feelings.

Tray now turned toward Davin. "So what are you going to do when people find out you left The Society? Don't you think The Society will come after you?"

"No, I don't think so," Davin replied. "If they do, they will have all my fans to answer to for it."

"How's that?" Tray asked.

Davin looked up to check the night sky then back to Tray. "Right about now, I would imagine, everyone is about to find out what has been really happening at The Hawaii Society. And after that, I'm pretty sure The Society won't *want* me back."

AND DAVIN WAS RIGHT—just moments before he explained the situation to Tray, the credits in the movie were interrupted by a brief moment of darkness. Then a steady, straight shot on Davin's face appeared on the screen.

"This is Davin Chapman. This isn't what you think it is. This isn't part of the movie or some promotion or a teaser. It's just me, and I think the world needs to know what has really been happening behind closed doors at the Hawaii Society . . . "

The clip of Davin went on to explain the false notions presented about Society living—that The Society was not as self-sufficient as the government had promised. That their fairness was still subject to favoritism and status. That corruption eroded the leadership of The Society—at a minimum in Branch Willix and Sandra Waverly. He explained that there were members of The Society who were secretly held captive to avoid allowing the outside world any knowledge of the dissension within The Society. And worst of all, his best friend had been killed for the mere knowledge of such secrets.

"So, now that you know the truth, I want you to know this—I do *not* endorse the Hawaii Society as it is currently run and under its existing administration. I was a pawn in their game—with leverage over me to compel me to play. But I am done. I'm leaving—and I'm taking The Society's hostages with me. Now it is up to you to decide what *you* will do. I hope you can see why I had to do what I have done. And if I make it out of here alive, be on the lookout for an update from me soon, because I will no longer be silenced. I will *not* comply."

The screen went black again for a moment and then returned to the scrolling names of the credits. There was a lapse of response while people struggled to process what Davin had so plainly exposed. Then, in a mass exodus, people stood and rushed for the recently locked doors.

25. THE RETURN

"THERE IT IS!" Sara jumped up and pointed to the partially lit yacht in the distance. Hearing Sara say those words again sent Chelsea into a flashback of when she had first arrived at The Society. She remembered coming with a sense of hope that she was walking into a better life. Now, having barely walked away with her life, she questioned whether she was headed for the better life she was imagining or merely another world of problems.

However, as she looked over at Davin, she remembered all the wonderful things she had gained from her experience at The Society. Most importantly that she had found Davin. His companionship brought her the happiness she had always dreamed of. He believed in her, and life felt so tranquil by his side, even amid the uncertainties. Every risk and every fear had been worth facing to bring him into her life.

And as she looked at the five rescued around her, who were huddled in a tight circle, she felt pride in the part she had played in freeing them. Helping restore their freedom had been a privilege. Occasionally, she caught one of them looking up at her and smiling in gratitude, and from their appreciation, she felt an inner strength grow inside her that helped her to feel she could face whatever trials may lay ahead in their unpredictable future.

Looking over at Hammond and Sara, she appreciated all her new friends and the memories and lessons she had gained from each of them. To trust your partner. That progress is the root of happiness. To reach out for help when you need it. And to love yourself for who you are.

The regrets she harbored for coming to live at The Society left her as she realized that her mind had opened to a new world of possibilities because of it. Her heart felt open to a life of greater meaning—beyond simply having her needs met. This time she *knew* she was headed for a better life, because her world would consist of whatever she and Davin made of it.

As they rounded the back of the yacht, Chelsea noticed the word "Ace" painted in large blue letters on its side. She wondered what it meant as Hammond pulled the boat next to the swimming platform where they boarded the yacht to begin their new life. Once everyone was safely on the platform and the boat had been securely attached, they walked up the stairs to the deck to find it was adorned with exotic decorations and pieces of elegant outdoor furniture. "Wow. It's beautiful," someone commented.

Everyone split up and began exploring the deck to see what lay inside the cabin. As Chelsea and Davin ventured off to investigate, they first discovered a fully stocked kitchen. The refrigerator was brimming with food and a list of all the items and their expiration dates shone brightly on its front display. A freezer with plenty of room to spare had a few items frozen to keep fresh longer, and cabinet after cabinet was full of ingredients to make a wide range of foods. Beautiful granite countertops and different appliances speckled the kitchen including a dishwasher that could unload itself directly into the shelves beside it. A long blue resin dining table sat beside a large kitchen island that had a variety of different griddles for cooking and an electric stovetop on top. Pots and pans hung from the ceiling above the island and a large vertical garden hung in the corner of the room. The vertical garden consisted of trays of dirt that hung stacked in a row from a chain on the ceiling like shelves and had pink UV lights and small water sprinklers to help grow small plants to provide them with fresh fruits, vegetables, and herbs. Below deck, there were four rooms and a private bathroom. One of the rooms had a white sheet with lighting equipment set up in a corner, along with a small broadcast camera—just as Davin had requested. As Davin and Chelsea went upstairs and entered the cockpit area, the lights came on, and a video began to play on the large monitor of the control panel.

Genevieve's face beamed at them in the prerecorded video. "Good evening. I'm very happy you've made it here tonight. Let's hope the viewing went well, though I'm sure you caused quite an uproar with your announcement," she said. "Oh well—I'll be glad to finally know the details of this supposed scandal." She chuckled softly at her blind involvement in their mysterious plot. "I hope you find the yacht pleasant. It's about time someone got some use out of this thing again." She smiled. "Ever since Ace died I haven't been back on it, but I'll always be grateful for that boat. Had we not been on it exploring the Caribbean when the earthquake hit, we would've been among the many who lost their lives. I owe my life to that little boat. We lived on it until we were able to move in with my daughter in a cute little 'grandmother' home she built for us just before my husband passed." Chelsea smiled to know their escape vessel was named after Genevieve's husband and felt an overwhelming sense of gratitude for all that Genevieve had done to help them in their quest for freedom.

"I left you detailed instructions on how to live and survive on the yacht with nothing more than the supplies I have left you . . . I hope you like fish," Genevieve said with a smile. "I have no need for it anymore—it's yours. I am quite happy being near my family and living in my small home. Hopefully, you enjoy it while you rebuild a new life. Consider it a down payment on our next film, Davin," Genevieve said with a quick wink. "I'm serious—I'm already working on finding the next film we will make together, so be ready. And since I'm old and I now have your attention, I want to leave you and Chelsea with my two cents—not that you have to listen or that it's worth much. But here it is—hold on to each other. Don't waste a minute regretting the past or holding out for the future. Too many people are holding out and living lives of selfishness. Own your decisions, work hard, and rely on each other." Having returned home between finishing the editing and coming back to The Society for the premiere, it was evident that Genevieve had filmed this clip in the privacy of her own home. A small child ran up to her and jumped in her lap. "Don't listen to the world—hard work and family are the only two things that have ever brought me any *real* joy in all my years. I hope you get the chance to experience both." The video cut out, and Davin slammed his hand against the dash of the cockpit.

Chelsea jumped back, startled by Davin's sudden outburst. "What was that about?"

"All my preparation—and I completely forgot it! Ugh!" Davin grimaced as he berated himself.

"Forgot what?" Chelsea insisted.

Davin hesitated before looking at Chelsea. He didn't know what to say. It was a conversation he hadn't planned on having for a long while, but in his predicament, he felt he had no choice. "The antidote."

Chelsea knew immediately what he was referring to. Davin waited uncomfortably for a response—not knowing how she might respond.

"I think we need to get settled in California before we even consider starting a family," Chelsea finally said.

Davin breathed a sigh of relief that she reacted as calmly as she did. He took her hand and hoped as he tried to persuade her that he could still communicate his support. "I completely agree, and of course it's up to you. But for all we know, it could be *years* before we have access to the antidote again." He wondered how serious Chelsea had been about starting a family when she let the idea slip, but, personally, he had become quite attached to the idea—though he had hoped to quietly secure the antidote and have this discussion when things were more certain. "We don't know what kind of situation we're walking into in California. And after hearing Genevieve's advice, I just can't imagine not having the option."

"I'm not against it," she explained. "I just think it's too dangerous to go back to The Society at this point."

Just then Enzo, one of the rescued, bolted through the open doors. "Sorry," he said. He paused awkwardly before confessing. "I overheard you talking. I need to go back to The Society too. My little brother is still there. I want to get him out."

Chelsea and Davin looked at each other and tried to hide their discomfort that Enzo had been listening to their private conversation. Chelsea considered the proposition, however, and a million apprehensions crossed her mind. *It'll be even more dangerous now,* she thought.

But seeing Davin's pleading eyes and hearing Enzo's concern for his brother had already made up her mind. "We'll go when Hammond and Sara go back—after everyone's hopefully gone to bed—and we'll leave before anyone wakes up." Davin smiled and called Hammond and Sara in to discuss the logistics.

After hours of deliberation, everyone knew their part. Still feeling shaken from the confrontation in the cave, Chelsea decided to man the boat and be prepared to pick up Davin and Enzo when they returned. Hammond would help Enzo find his brother before returning to his life at the Society with Sara. And Sara agreed to help Davin get the antidote using her identification at the pharmacy dispenser. Hammond and Sara had always planned to go back to The Society to be the eyes and ears on the inside.

They planned to contact Davin and Chelsea every few months, or as needed, with any developments there. If things did not improve, they would eventually join Chelsea and Davin in California.

Davin and Enzo would have thirty minutes to return to the boat, with or without their spoils. If anything went wrong, they were to return to the boat immediately. Everyone agreed it was more important that they made it back to the yacht unharmed than to get the antidote. However, Enzo swore he would only leave if his brother was by his side. And Chelsea swore she would leave him if he wasn't back in thirty minutes—though she knew in her heart it was an empty threat.

The whole Society would already be aware of Davin and Chelsea's absence. Davin wore a baseball cap to hide his face and replaced his tuxedo with an outfit Genevieve had left him in the closet that wouldn't call attention. The others had the benefit of being less recognizable—a fact they planned to utilize to sneak back onto Society grounds without notice. But fortunately, Davin and Enzo would at least have an advantage if anything went terribly wrong in that they could not be traced because their PEDs were no longer activated.

By the time they had settled on specifics, it was late into the night, but no one slept the few hours they had before they needed to leave. An hour before sunrise, they boarded the speedboat to return to The Society. Soon enough, they rounded the island's edge and spotted the private beach Davin and Chelsea had kept secret. Chelsea brought the boat as close as she could to shore so everyone could get out with ease.

Before Davin jumped into the water, Chelsea pulled him in for a kiss. "You better come back, or I'll never forgive you," she threatened. He could tell she was being pretentious. Davin just smiled and then hugged her goodbye before jumping out of the boat onto the beach.

"Follow me close through the woods. Once we have Hammond and Sara's wristbands, we'll split up," Davin reminded everyone. Then he looked to Enzo. "When you have your brother, meet us on the bridge, and we'll head back here."

Enzo nodded.

They sprinted through the woods back toward The Society. They made it to the bridge quickly, then headed for Hammond and Sara's living quarters. The Society grounds were very still—it almost felt abandoned.

Hammond and Sara stood in the front of the elevator as it opened, while Davin and Enzo crouched behind them to avoid being seen by anyone in the halls once the door opened. But when the elevator opened, they looked down the halls to find them empty. They all ran for Sara's room and swung open the door. Sara grabbed her wristband and earpiece. She put them on, and she and Davin left immediately for the hospital. Hammond grabbed his wristband and earpiece and spoke, "Locate Jax Gibson." The map showed Jax in his room—in the next building over, three floors up. Enzo's eyes lit up, and they ran for the elevator to get his brother.

DAVIN AND SARA walked out of the elevator and onto the hospital floor. Only one medical bot could be seen stationed by the reception desk. Davin kept the brim of his hat low and quickly turned in the opposite direction of the bot toward the nearby pharmacy booth. They walked quickly, but their presence had not gone unnoticed. "May I help you fill a prescription?" the hospital bot asked as it approached them at the booth.

Not knowing if the bot had voice or face recognition, Davin kept his head low. He leaned up against the pharmacy wall and spoke in the deepest voice he could manage. "No, thank you. Just want to make a baby."

Sara shot him a look of surprise as she tried to withhold a laugh.

"All right. Let me know if you are in need of assistance. I'd be happy to help," the robot relayed its script before turning to leave.

Sara almost burst out laughing, and tears streamed down Davin's face through his silent snickering. "What was that about? It's a robot—you could have just said no," Sara said. She scanned her wristband and began scrolling through the selection of available drugs.

"It was just the first thing that popped into my head," he explained. He smiled. "Never had a robot offer to help me with my love life before."

They laughed to themselves, and Sara searched for the antidote among the list of fertility drugs. She quickly found it, but when she selected it, a message popped up across the screen. *This one-time prescription has already been filled for Sara Lehman. Further dosage is unnecessary. Please select another drug or enter your symptoms or ask for assistance.* The text remained for a few seconds and then minimized to show the previous screen with the selection of available drugs.

Sara's heart sank. She didn't realize that she would only be allowed to fill the prescription once. Davin began stumbling through ideas in his mind of how they could fill the prescription, but all of his options would take too long to accomplish. His only viable thought was to smash the glass, grab the antidote, and make a run for it.

Just before he lifted his elbow to break the glass, Sara shouted out toward the hospital bot, "Wait! We actually do need some assistance. I filled my birth control antidote prescription a few years ago on the mainland, but I accidentally . . . dropped the pill . . . down the sink. And then I decided I wasn't really ready to have a baby after all. But now I am!" Sara blurted out. "I need you to give me clearance so I can finally fill my antidote prescription . . . Please," she said with a smile.

"If you lost your prescription, you should have contacted your doctor so the hospital could record your *ability to conceive* status accurately," the robot replied. Davin looked up at Sara with his back still turned to the bot. He prepared to break the glass once more. Sara looked at Davin warily and then back to the robot. She tried to think of something creative to say to convince the robot to help them.

"I see that extra dosage of this prescription would do you no harm. I will locate your file and give you clearance so you can fill your prescription and the records will be accurate," the bot said. The bot was silent for a moment, and then it popped back to life. "You now have clearance. Fill your prescription, and please notify us if you lose it this time so that the records will be accurate. Let me know if there is anything else I can do to assist you," the robot said as it turned away.

"Thank you!" Sara called out. She selected the antidote for a second time, and a small red pill in wrapping popped out from the dispenser. She handed it discreetly to Davin with a beaming smile. They were both giddy from their success as they ran to the elevator and selected the ground floor to meet up with the others at the bridge.

MEANWHILE, HAMMOND AND ENZO sprinted to Jax's room. Enzo knocked hard on the door, but Jax did not answer. There was a long pause. Then Enzo kicked against the door to produce a loud thud.

"Is he a heavy sleeper?" Hammond asked. "Should I call his PED?"

Then someone answered the door, but it was not Jax.

"Can I help you?" asked a man with tight, blond curls who popped his head out through the door.

"I need to talk to Jax," Enzo said.

"He's busy," the man replied. "Come back another time." The man went to shut the door, but as he did, Hammond caught a glimpse inside the room. On the bed sat a young man who resembled Enzo facing a woman seated in a chair in front of him. Hammond immediately recognized the back of the women's head as Ms. Waverly's.

Before the man could shut the door completely, Hammond lunged forward and hurled his body against the door. The door slammed up against the man's face, and he flew to the floor from the blow. Ms. Waverly whirled around to face the disruption.

Enzo sprinted past the man and toward Ms. Waverly. "Jax—run!" Enzo yelled as he shoved Ms. Waverly against the wall. Seeing his missing brother for the first time in months and noticing his brother's skeletal figure left Jax frozen in shock. "Now, Jax!" Enzo demanded before pushing Waverly to the floor and grabbing his brother's hand to sprint out of the room. Hammond followed close behind.

Ms. Waverly rose to her feet and straightened out her blouse—a look of animosity on her face. "All available security bots, report to the elevator of building H in the living quarters," Hammond heard Ms. Waverly say over his shoulder. As the doors to the elevator shut, Ms. Waverly and the man with the curly hair stomped toward them.

"What is going on?" Jax struggled to say while he tried to catch his breath. "I was told you went missing somewhere in Utah. They found your PED all smashed up. I was worried you went crazy after you freaked out in the cafeteria that one day. But then . . . then Davin Chapman told everyone you've been locked up and you were going to escape, and today, The Society lady comes asking me about you, and then you show up out of nowhere! What is going on?"

"Enzo, there will probably be security bots when we get to the ground level," Hammond told Enzo. "We'll need to make a run for it. Their tasers can't reach us if we keep our distance, but I'm sure they'll be fast."

Enzo nodded at Hammond then turned to his brother. "Long story. Stop asking questions and run like your life depends on it."

A disturbed expression crossed Jax's face as the doors to the elevator opened to reveal three of the security bots zeroing in on them. Sara and Davin stood on the bridge waiting and immediately knew they were in trouble as they watched Enzo, Jax, and Hammond begin to sprint toward them with the bots close behind.

Enzo led the group on the path toward the bridge with Jax following closely behind. Their natural agility and speed carried them out in front of the security bots. Hammond trailed behind them. His long legs gave him a wide stride, but his clumsy coordination left him lagging in their wake. Davin observed as a security bot approached Hammond from the side with his taser at the ready.

"Go to the boat," Davin ordered Sara. "*Make* Chelsea leave." Sara looked at him with fear in her eyes. Davin picked up a large rock that was nearby and bolted toward Hammond.

One of the security bots was about to intercept Hammond's pathway and discharge its taser. Sara screamed out in terror, "Hammond! No!"

Davin threw the rock, and it struck the side of the security bot just in time to redirect the taser. The bot stumbled to recover its balance. "Go! Go!" Davin yelled at Hammond as Davin ran past him in the opposite direction. "I'll draw them off!"

Just then, the elevator opened to Ms. Waverly and the man with the curly hair. Ms. Waverly's eyes met Davin's, and her eyes narrowed into slits. "Security bots—redirect your pursuit to Davin Chapman."

The security bots, which were still following their original orders, stopped and scanned the area. Unable to pick up any signal from Davin's wristband to locate him, they stood frozen—giving Davin time to slip into the Outdoor Recreation Supply Room.

"What are you doing?" Ms. Waverly yelled at the bots. "I told you to get him!"

"We cannot locate Davin Chapman's wristband, Ms. Waverly. His wristband and PED have been turned off," one of the robots informed her as it approached.

"He ran right past you!"

"Our facial recognition was not able to compute, as the man who ran past used the brim of his hat to hide his face, Ms. Waverly."

Aggravated by their ineptness, she ran after Davin herself. "Follow me," she yelled after the bots.

Hammond, Enzo, and Jax ran up to Sara as Ms. Waverly and the bots entered the Outdoor Recreation Supply Room. "What—is—Davin—doing?" Hammond asked as he gasped for air.

Sara grabbed Hammond's hand and pulled him toward the trees. "He said to go to the boat," she explained, purposefully leaving out that Davin hadn't mentioned any plans to meet back up with them. Seeing Hammond chased down by security bots and almost tranquilized filled her with fear. She knew they had to leave The Society now too, but she did not want to do anything else that would put them in danger—even if that meant leaving Davin behind.

"What's his plan?"

Fearing that Hammond would want to go back for him, Sara simply replied, "Keep running! We need to get back to the boat." They ran through the trees toward the beach.

A few minutes behind schedule, they returned. Chelsea stood in the boat anxiously waiting. As they neared the shoreline, she could tell they were running in a panic. She scanned their faces, trying to examine the situation. The rising sun crept over their worried expressions. She noticed Enzo had his brother by his side and no one seemed hurt. She wondered what had happened. Then as they boarded the boat, she realized the problem. "Where's Davin?"

"We don't know," Hammond said. "He ran off in the opposite direction after he stopped a security bot from nicking me."

"He said to leave when we got back to the boat," Sara finally confessed.

"Leave?" Chelsea hissed. Her heart burned with anger and her expression turned cold.

"The bots were right on our tail, Chelsea. If Davin hadn't drawn them away, we wouldn't have made it," Sara tried to explain. Hammond looked at Sara, dismayed at the prospect of leaving Davin when he had just saved him from getting caught by the security bots.

"Where did he go?" Chelsea demanded.

"The outdoor supply room," Hammond told her.

"He said to *make* her leave," Sara said as she turned to Hammond. Sara felt guilt start to seep into her veins—she knew she had let her fear get the better of her.

"I'm not leaving him," Chelsea sternly vowed as she whipped the boat around. The force pushed her passengers to the floor, and she sped toward the docks of the supply room.

DAVIN RAN into the Outdoor Recreation Supply Room. His heart raced, knowing he had no plan to escape. After seeing the look of pure hatred on Waverly's face, he guessed they would be coming after him. He grabbed the closest thing to him and jumped into the water.

There was a chilling silence for a moment while Davin hid under the water waiting for the door to open. He strapped his feet in and then looked up just in time to see the door swing open, breaking the silence in the room.

"Davin!" Ms. Waverly yelled as she entered the room. "You know it's illegal to turn off your PED. Show yourself, and we can make amends over this mess you've gotten yourself into. You will be in far more trouble if you don't." She waited for a moment, hoping for a response, but quickly concluded that fear would not persuade him. "You don't know all the pressure I get from Washington to make this place successful. You *need* this place! Your generation has nothing without it! Don't ruin it for everyone else. We can fix this. I will prosecute Branch. He is the vile carp polluting the system."

The security bots entered the room, and Ms. Waverly continued to search. Unable to find Davin, she turned toward the bots. "You three go out to the beach and search for the man in the baseball cap, Davin Chapman. If you find him, notify me and bring him to me by whatever means necessary. You two, stay with me and search this whole room—every nook. We *must* find him."

The three bots immediately ran toward the beach and the other two split up to search the room. Ms. Waverly moved toward the water and noticed an empty boat dock. She wondered if it were possible that Davin could have quickly left with the boat before she walked in. "Where's this boat?" Ms. Waverly asked the man with the curly hair, who was filling in for Branch.

Branch, she thought. *Good-for-nothing coward conveniently goes missing after Davin's video exposes everything.*

"Looks like a Mr. Hammond Steeply checked it out yesterday evening," the man replied. Ms. Waverly looked at him in confusion. Everyone was supposed to be attending the premiere at that time. "Looks like he's one of the men who burst into Jax's room as well," he added as he studied the picture of Hammond that he had pulled up for reference.

As the gears turned in Waverly's mind, her scorn for Davin grew. "Davin led this man and the others to abandon us," she said, glaring at the empty slot. "Find him. He has completely betrayed his contract!"

Below the surface of the water, Davin's last reserve of air was quickly dwindling as he waited for Ms. Waverly to leave. Finally, he could bear it no longer. He checked his straps one last time and pressed down on the button. He shot out of the water, gasping for air. Ms. Waverly stood in shock as she watched Davin hover over the water in front of her on a flyboard.

Using the techniques Chelsea had taught him, Davin tilted his feet and maneuvered out of the boat docks and into the river's current. The water shooting out from the bottom of his flyboard jetted out as he left—completely drenching Ms. Waverly and her henchman.

The sun was barely peeking out over the water as Davin fled the scene. He could feel the control of the board beneath his feet for the first time. Finally confident that he could maintain his stability, he leaned forward slightly and pressed the power button down harder. This increased his speed substantially, and he wriggled back and forth slightly to retain his balance. He could see the security bots on the shore, looking out at him, and then running back in the direction of the equipment room where he had left Ms. Waverly dripping wet.

Keeping his speed, he headed toward the secluded beach where he had left Chelsea—hoping the others would be there and he wouldn't be followed. But the closer he got to the opposite side of the mountain, the louder a looming noise grew. He did not dare look behind him for fear of compromising his balance. The noise intensified like a swarm of angry wasps approaching him. The alarming noise made it hard for him to concentrate on his control, causing him to sway back and forth as he tried to stay above water. But then, as he looked out in front of him, he realized the noise was not a chase from behind, but a boat advancing toward him with Chelsea at the wheel. As they came into each other's view, he urgently motioned for her to turn around and head back the other way.

Relieved to see Davin safe, Chelsea quickly did as instructed and spun the boat around—circling around Davin's tail. Jax looked out toward The Society one last time, only to see two security bots exiting the equipment room on quad skis and heading in their direction. "They're headed our way," he yelled out to Chelsea. "Go faster!"

Chelsea looked behind the boat. Determined to outrun them, she pushed the boat to full throttle. With the light of the rising sun now glaring out at them, the solar panels across the boat's exterior propelled the boat much faster over the water than the quad skis were able to go. The boat eventually pushed out in front of Davin as well, and he could tell he would not be able to keep up with its pace. He pushed the flyboard to full power and lunged forward just in time to land on the edge of the boat.

Chelsea saw Davin crash against the side of the boat out of the corner of her eye and gasped. Hammond and Enzo pulled him in and sat him down to catch his breath. He struggled to ignore the pain from his rough landing, but regardless, he was happy he had made it.

He detached the flyboard from his feet and stretched out on the floor of the boat. "Are you okay?" Chelsea shouted over the noise of the boat speeding through the water. "I didn't know you were going to jump into the boat! I could've slowed down—you almost got yourself killed!"

"I'll be fine," he replied. He sat up and smiled at her. Despite the fact they were still running from the bots, Davin somehow felt a calming reassurance, like somehow everything would be all right. He reached into his pocket and pulled out the small red pill and showed it to Chelsea as he stood. She looked at it briefly.

After the long wait in the boat, feeling helpless, Chelsea regretted making the trip back. And when Davin didn't return with the others, her regret had morphed into rage. She was livid—angry with herself for agreeing to come back when she felt so fortunate to escape without harm in the first place. But now, seeing Enzo's brother, having the antidote in hand, and having Davin by her side, she began to believe that their trip back might have been worth it after all. However, with the bots still tailing them, she knew there was still time for things to go terribly wrong.

She grabbed Davin's hand and pulled him close to her as she drove. He kissed the side of her face and put the pill back in his pocket for safekeeping. The yacht came into view. Davin looked back toward the bots. Chelsea had put a good distance between them, but they would still need to hurry to lose them. Davin looked back at her as she pulled her sunglasses on over her eyes to avoid the glare from the rising sun. "Nice flyboarding by the way," she said as a smile crept over her face.

"Well, I was taught by the best," he said with a smile before moving to the back of the boat in preparation to jump off onto the yacht's swim platform. Chelsea steered the boat up close to the yacht, and Davin leaped for the nearby platform. Then he pulled the boat closer to allow the others to climb aboard with ease. "Hurry," he reminded them as he saw the quad skis in the distance. "Let's go, Chels. Don't bother throwing out the anchor. Let's make the bots chase after it."

Chelsea put down the anchor and jumped off the boat onto the yacht. They gave their escape vessel a shove and let it drift away. Then the yacht's engine roared to life, and Chelsea and Davin held hands as they ran up the stairs toward the cockpit.

"Let's get moving, Tray! The bots are on our tail. You think you can get us out of here before they reach us?" Davin asked Tray, who stood in front of the controls.

"In theory," he replied. "I've been over all of Genevieve's instructions and studied up on how to drive a yacht using its microblasters, but it's one thing to read it and another to do it.

I won't be able to steer much when the microblasters are on, so if I don't read the sonar system just right we could crash into something if I pick the wrong path."

"Pick any path leading away from The Society that doesn't have any obstructions," Davin told him. "We'll worry about redirecting our course to California after we lose the bots."

"Okay," Tray said as he studied the sonar's suggested paths and picked a direction that looked clearest of obstacles. Then Tray disabled the GPS system so that they could not be tracked. As he manually turned the boat in the proper direction, they heard the quad skis nearby.

"The bots are here!" Sara called out as she looked out over the deck.

"Let's go!" Enzo cried.

Lines formed across Tray's forehead as he concentrated. He knew if they were going to get out of there safely, he had to focus on the yacht being perfectly positioned and ignore the panic that was spreading around him.

The microblasters installed in larger boats were derived from the same technology used on flyboards but applied on a much larger scale. The yacht had a similar engine to the transporter pod and was also made for extraordinary speeds when the microblasters were activated, which allowed the yacht to hover a few inches over the waves and avoid the friction of the water. However, to ensure there were no collisions with other boats, this technology was only supposed to be used in congruence with a GPS. Landmarks and large debris were continually mapped as well to avoid crashes. But since they didn't want to be tracked, Tray had to steer them to safety without the use of the GPS.

Had they decided not to return to The Society or if their plans had gone without a hitch, they could have left at a prudent pace and evaded the use of the microblasters. However, with the bots on their tail, everyone knew that was no longer an option.

Tray aligned the yacht where he wanted it. "Everyone sit down and buckle up," he yelled out. He sat in the captain's chair and lifted the latch to the microblasters controls. Bright red warnings about the dangers of overriding the autopilot while using microblasters popped up across the control panel. Tray looked back on his passengers to make sure everyone was buckled in before reaching down to latch his own buckle across his lap, and then went to perform the necessary override of the system's warnings.

Just then one of the engines of the quad skis went quiet, and a loud thud was heard from the swim platform. Everyone fell silent and looked toward the stairs that led to the platform until a security bot appeared, walking toward them. "Davin Chapman—you and the rest of your group have been ordered to return to the Hawaii Society's grounds. Please come with me. Will you comply?"

Chelsea unbuckled and stood defensively between the bot and Davin. "We're not going anywhere."

Tray looked over at Chelsea, wishing she had stayed buckled so he could try and use the force from the microblasters to knock the bot off the deck now that the override was complete, but he knew it would be too risky when she wasn't secure. Catching a glimpse of the bag Chelsea had left in the cockpit from earlier, Tray quietly reached inside.

"If you do not comply you will be forced to leave The Society. Please step aside," the bot ordered.

"We *want* to leave!" Enzo cried out. "Let us go!"

"I have been ordered to return each of you to The Society. If you do not wish to comply with Society rules, then you can return to the mainland via the transporter pod."

"That's a lie!" shouted Semaj.

"This is your last chance to comply," the security bot stated as a taser extended from its metal chest cavity.

Chelsea stood firm. "Chels," Davin said gently. "Move." Chelsea looked back at him in distress. She sat next to him to protest, but he was already reaching to unlatch his buckle.

Before Davin could unfasten his seatbelt, Tray pulled the gun that Chelsea had obtained from Branch out of the bag and shot into the open chest cavity of the security bot. The bullet hit the taser and smashed its way through the internal wiring—damaging the cables that controlled its lower extremities.

"Davin, hold Chelsea tight!" Tray yelled. Davin instantly wrapped his arms around Chelsea, and Tray flipped the switch on to the microblasters. Water blasted out of the bottom of the yacht, making a loud *hiss* as it began to levitate, and then an even louder noise erupted as the hydrogen jets shot water out of the back to propel it forward with a hard jerk. The injured bot flew back into the wind, knocking against the railing of the boat before flying off into the water. The massive stream of seawater that shot out of the yacht doused the other security bot, which had collected the drifting Society boat and was waiting for its counterpart to come with the residents.

Davin's grip around Chelsea tightened. He held onto her with all his strength as the yacht zoomed out over the ocean waves with ease. The thunderous wind ripped across their skin, and the salty air stung the wound on Chelsea's forearm. She leaned into Davin, forced to rely on his strength to keep her from falling off her seat, but after the night's events, it came as a relief to let her body relax and rely on his strength to keep her safe.

With time the sudden acceleration wore off, and everyone adapted to the speed of the yacht. Davin's hold on Chelsea loosened, and they looked out toward the Pacific. When it seemed they were out of harm's way, Enzo let out a boisterous cheer over the noise of the jet streams, happy to know the threats of The Society were sailing farther and farther away with each second.

26. A PLEA TO BE HEARD

TRAY TURNED OFF the microblasters, and the yacht steadily slowed to a halt. A serene moment passed as everyone collected their bearings and looked out with rapture over the empty ocean. No bots or cavern walls encircled them now.

Their expressions toggled from tears to smiles as they tried to process everything that had happened over the last twenty-four hours. Sara and Hammond embraced while Semaj burst into laughter to mask the few tears that had managed to escape. Davin finally let go of Chelsea, and they smiled at each other as a sense of liberation washed over them. They were free.

Tray unbuckled and jumped up with one fist in the air. "We did it!" He ran over to Chelsea and Davin and hugged them simultaneously. "We didn't wreck! Somehow we didn't wreck," he said with a huge grin. Chelsea and Davin looked at each other—happy to be safe, but only then realizing how fortunate they really were.

Tray redirected their course toward the coast of California, and everyone convened in the kitchen to relax over a warm meal. Hammond and Semaj, who both enjoyed cooking, went to work on an Italian dish while the rest of the group gathered around to discuss their stories.

"I'm so sorry, Enzo," Jax sympathized after hearing his brother's story. "I really had no idea you were still at The Society or I would have been looking for you."

"It's not your fault, bro," Enzo replied. "We were all lied to."

"I just don't get why they wouldn't let people leave," Sara commented. "Why do they care so much?"

"Well, they couldn't very well have people knowing that their brilliant idea to 'aid' our generation didn't really get us anywhere in life," Semaj replied sarcastically. He tasted a small sample of his pasta sauce before adding more oregano and then continued to stir it over the heat of the stove. "That's just politics for you. They sent us to The Societies to get us out of the way. They provided us with everything—they had complete control. When you pair that kind of ideology with a secluded population, it's a recipe for corruption." Everyone took a moment to contemplate that thought as Semaj continued sharing his conclusions. "Don't get me wrong, at first, I was all for The Societies. The idea came as a relief to some very real problems we've been facing, but as I started researching a lot of histories in my free time at The Society, I realized this kind of thing has happened countless times throughout civilization. And it always starts with optimistic beginnings, but it never ends well. It's ultimately what made me decide I wanted to leave, and I think Waverly especially didn't like the idea of a politician's kid leaving."

Semaj's comments left Sara and Hammond contemplative. The rest of the group had already come to their own conclusions and had no qualms with the idea that certain fallacies existed in The Societies—especially since the majority of the group had spent the last several months locked up for their divergence from the system.

"So what was Ms. Waverly talking to you about when we came for you?" Hammond asked Jax.

"She wanted to know if I knew where Enzo was or if he had contacted me recently," Jax explained. "I thought she was trying to help locate you, but I'm starting to think she just suspected that I had something to do with his escape."

Chelsea suddenly jumped into the conversation. "I want to know what happened after the premiere," she said.

Davin listened intently, also wondering how people had reacted.

"Everyone just went silent for a while. Then a few people started running toward the doors, but they were locked so no one could get out. They were just banging and banging—screaming '*Let us out*!' in a panic," Jax explained as he pretended to bang on a door. "Then Waverly went on stage real calm-like and told everyone that she would look into your claims," he said, looking toward Davin. "Then she told everyone to go to the after party and enjoy themselves." He shrugged.

"That's it? That's all she said?" Sara asked in disbelief.

"Did you go to the party?" Enzo questioned Jax.

"Yeah, I did," Jax admitted sheepishly. "A lot of people decided not to go though. They were ushered back to their rooms. And everyone who did go to the party just talked about the clip the whole time—we all wondered if it was some sort of prank or something," recalled Jax. "I was hoping it was. I didn't want to believe that Enzo had been locked up all this time. And when Waverly showed up at my door asking about you, I was really hoping she'd have a different story to tell."

"What about Genevieve? The vice president? Everyone visiting The Society?" Chelsea asked.

"I'm not sure," Jax responded. "I think they left right when the movie ended, but I wasn't really paying that much attention to them."

Davin looked up from the counter he had been transfixed on while deep in thought. "As soon as we finish with lunch, we need to film the next clip."

"The *next* clip?" Tray asked.

"Before anyone figures out where we are, we're going to broadcast another clip so people see you guys and can hear your stories," Chelsea expounded.

"Well, the food's hot now, so let's eat before you get to it," Hammond said as he placed a steaming pot of spaghetti pomodoro in the middle of the table. Everyone made their way to the table with a plate to dish themselves up some of the pasta that was filling the kitchen cabin with the aroma of garlic and basil. "I haven't cooked in so long," Hammond recollected. "I forgot how much I enjoy it," he said with a smile.

"And you always make the most delicious dishes, baby. I'm so excited to eat your food again," Sara said as she made herself a plate.

After a long day, a hot meal was the respite they all needed. Following the preliminary silence that accompanied the clinking of forks, each of the rescues took turns summarizing their stories and discussing what things they felt were important to share with the world during the broadcast.

As Davin listened, he became more anxious to begin filming. He wanted people to know his message had been sincere, especially with Waverly immediately modulating his validity. And the fact that Jax had heard people questioning the nature of what he had said only solidified that people weren't taking the problem seriously. He feared that without follow-up, the issue would soon be forgotten in the long list of world problems that already flooded people's minds.

Davin kept a steadfast eye on Chelsea as she ate, and as soon as she finished her last bite, he invited her to come with him. "Let's get things ready for the broadcast," he told her. Chelsea stood to follow him, and he turned to the others. "When you're done with your meals, meet us below deck. We'll go over the film sequence and begin our broadcast as soon as possible," he instructed. Enzo and Tray nodded in confirmation, and he and Chelsea left the room to prepare. The others rushed to finish the food on their plates.

Walking into their room where the camera waited, Chelsea stopped Davin so she could address the concern she'd been holding inside. "Davin—" She paused, wondering if maybe she shouldn't mention it. "I'm worried you still feel responsible for the success of The Society like you were trained to do."

Davin paused to consider her words. He couldn't deny her conjecture held some validity. "What if our actions weren't enough to incite reform?" Davin replied. "What if the problem is ignored, and the corruption continues? Maybe we shouldn't have left."

"We did what we could with what influence we have. But I think, at some point, we have to let it go. And we had to go— we don't know what they would've done to you if we had stayed. We have to move forward with our lives and shift our focus away from The Society," Chelsea said. "Especially if you're serious about wanting to raise a family. Eventually, that will have to be our focus."

"But what about all those people?" Davin asked, unsure how he could simply move on with his life after all he had invested into The Society.

"Most of them are happy to stay there and are purposefully ignoring their problems," Chelsea replied. "I'm not even sure they will care now that they know, as long as they aren't personally affected—think of Finley." Chelsea shuddered as she uttered her name. She struggled to openly denounce Finley's intentional ignorance. It felt as though she was somehow betraying her in the process.

Davin heaved a sigh—he knew there was truth to her words, even if he didn't want to believe it. "Listen—I promise when we get to California and start our new life there, I will focus on making it everything you could hope for. But until then, I'm going to keep trying to get the word out about The Societies. Even if there are those who would turn a blind eye to its corruption, someone has to stand by those who want reform."

As Chelsea listened to him speak, she couldn't help but yield to his sincere concern for the people of The Societies. She smiled. "You're a good guy." Her sudden change in tone took Davin by surprise. Chelsea removed the distance between them and wrapped her arms around his neck.

"So you'll keep fighting for them with me?"

"I'll always fight beside you, Davin," she said as she pressed her forehead against his.

He smiled and was able to relax again for the first time since the beginning of the premiere. Feeling Chelsea's support helped keep things in perspective. "I'm not sure I've given you a proper greeting since our near-death encounters," he teased as he pressed his lips to hers.

"A definite oversight," she said through their kisses, enjoying their first tranquil moment following such a nightmarish day. They both stared into each other's eyes for a short moment until Chelsea broke the silence. "We should get to filming, huh?"

Davin pretended to think for a moment, and then smiled as he reluctantly agreed. "You're probably right."

Chelsea gave him one last kiss and then went to work. She focused the lights and positioned the camera to a good angle. Davin began discussing the different points they needed to hit and the sequence of the broadcast. He had placed a chair in front of the white backdrop for each of the rescued residents to sit in, and then he placed a chair for himself to the left of them. The others came down soon after Davin and Chelsea had finished setting up, and

Davin promptly began explaining the details of his vision for the clip.

❖

RILEY ARRIVED AT WORK and stood at his desk. He began scouring the internet as he did each morning, looking for any leads on a story for his uncle's small news station that he had been working at for the last several years.

He was in charge of finding any trending stories on social media and going through the long list of emails from people claiming to have a story worth sharing. Some days he spent all day going through trivial videos that had gone viral, ranging from an elephant bouncing a ball to a hundred-year-old senior break dancing to oldies like "Party Rock Anthem." Other days, he easily found a viral story that was newsworthy, and he would pass it along to his uncle, Jackson Overman.

That morning, Riley stood at his standing desk reading the subject lines to each of the emails that were already flooding his inbox. As he scanned them, a new email popped up in his box. *Davin Chapman Reveals ALL About His Hawaii Society Escape*. Riley recognized Davin Chapman's name and thought the story must be related to the premiere of his latest movie. Riley clicked on the email and opened the broadcast link. A simple shot of Davin Chapman in front of a white background with five people sitting behind him popped up on his window. Riley began recording his screen.

"I am Davin Chapman. I am sitting here with five other *former* Hawaii Society residents. During the premiere of my new film, *A Mile in Their Shoes*, I, along with the five people you see behind me and a small group of friends, escaped the Hawaii Society . . ."

Riley flicked his wrist. "Contact Uncle Jack," he said. "Hey, I'm getting a live feed from somewhere. I can't track where, but it's

❖382❖

that movie star in Hawaii, Davin Chapman. He says he left The Society."

"Are you recording it?" Jackson asked Riley.

"Yeah, you think it could be a good story?" he asked. There was no response. Riley stood waiting in silence until his door suddenly swung open.

Jackson ran over to his desk, forcing Riley to jump back out of the way to avoid getting trampled. He looked down at Riley's extended PED and watched intently. Seeing his uncle's obvious interest in the story, he began researching it more on his wristband. "It looks like it's also broadcasting live on a number of social media platforms. It already has a couple hundred thousand people viewing it there." Riley slid his finger over the image that was being projected on his wrist in the direction of his desk to transfer his screen from his wrist to his PED and then spaced out the different websites that were broadcasting the story live across the screen for his uncle to see.

"That's not surprising," Jackson remarked as he watched the number of people viewing the clip continue to rise. Riley gave his uncle a look of confused apprehension. "Did you not see the broadcast of Davin's new movie last night?" Jackson asked, stunned that Riley didn't recognize the significance of the story.

"No," Riley admitted. "I had a late-night gaming session. Was it good?"

"Good?" Jackson asked, focusing more on what Davin was saying rather than on Riley's questions. "The movie? Yeah, it was phenomenal, but I'm talking about the video in the credits. Keep quiet. I want to hear this. You'll have to watch it afterward."

"You've already heard from me, and I shared with you what I discovered while living in the Hawaii Society. Now I'm here to prove to you the validity of my claims," Davin said. "I want to introduce the five residents who suffered some of the worst of The Society's offenses and give them a voice to share their stories with the world." Davin took a step aside and motioned to Semaj. "The first person I want to introduce is someone you may recognize. If not him, possibly his father, Congressman Drake Lester. Semaj, the time is yours."

As Semaj started to speak, the live feeds on social media unexpectedly dropped out. "What happened?" Riley questioned as he tried to refresh the page. "I don't get it. The broadcast is still sending on the direct link they sent."

"They're filtering it out," Jackson said. "Look—it says, 'this broadcast has been removed because it contains unsafe content.'" Riley looked at the message. Then he looked at his uncle with wide eyes. Jackson smiled. "I don't know about you, but I'm that much more interested. Start writing up a script. You're going on air with this story as soon as the broadcast ends." Jackson beamed with delight as he split the PED screen into two separate windows so he could continue viewing the broadcast in full screen while Riley worked on a script.

"I grew up learning the value of hard work from my father," Semaj began. "He is a good man and works tirelessly serving as a congressman for the people of Nebraska and the American people. In my many years of college, I worked hard to become valuable. But after completing my law degree, no job—not even a thankless internship—awaited me. Advanced AI had completely replaced my skill set within the few years it took me to finish my doctorate, and no employer would hire an inexperienced lawyer over the programming that lacks the human error that accompanies us all." Semaj thought back to when he realized the traditional routes that a budding lawyer used to take would no longer apply. "Years of fruitless job hunting led me to apply to The Societies Program when it was introduced—a program my father and I supported, mind you, with high hopes for its success."

Reflecting back to his time at The Society, he summarized briefly. "My time in The Society was pleasant enough overall—

but it was not the life for me. Even though I appreciated the stability, I wanted opportunities for growth and learning outside of The Society where I could somehow use my professional skills. And as I studied the histories of civilizations that detailed similar approaches to fighting poverty, I quickly discovered that in the end, it always led to a population captive to its government," he stated. "So I decided to opt out of the program and head back to the States where I hoped to raise funds and begin an innovated approach to my own law firm," Semaj explained.

"But when I told The Society offices of my intention to leave, and after they found out who my father was, instead of requesting the transporter pod, as I expected, they left me in a quiet room for over an hour before the Society Leader, Sandra Waverly, came in. She sat down and asked me why I wanted to leave. I told her, and then she asked me if I was *absolutely certain* I wanted to leave. To which I replied 'yes.' After trying to convince me otherwise, she conceded and opened the door to where Branch Willix, the Society Coordinator, stood.

"She said 'Semaj would like to leave, Branch. Please assist him as we discussed.' Branch led me to the elevator—where I thought he would take me to the ground level to board a transporter pod or to pack my things. Instead, he scanned his wristband and took me to an unknown basement level below The Society grounds. He led me to a secret storage facility that was built in the inside of an underwater cave, where he knocked me to the ground and tied me to a post before sputtering the words 'no one leaves The Society' in my face. I spent months alone in that cave with little food and an occasional unpleasant visit from Branch. I was on the brink of losing my sanity before I was joined by Tray," Semaj said as he put his hand on Tray, who was sitting beside him. "His company and his fighting spirit were what gave me hope enough to keep going through some long, awful months."

"Tell us why you were forced to join Semaj in the cave, Tray," Davin prompted.

Still proudly wearing his **Society Rules Your Life** T-shirt, Tray explained the reasons he felt the rules at The Society gave it too much power over the lives of its residents. "Imagine a place where at any moment a law could be enacted that made what you were doing illegal. The worst part is so many people believed the lie that there were only seven rules you had to abide by if you wanted to live at The Society. From the beginning, I wondered what kind of liberties they would take to enforce their agendas, but I've always been one to question authority," he said, proud of himself for seeing past the false image The Societies presented. "And the belief that The Societies were all self-sustaining was optimistic at best. Things on the island were constantly breaking down and no one knew how to fix them or cared to learn how. I tried to learn how to repair a milking station at the cow pastures when a unit lost suction, but then I couldn't even get the part we needed to fully repair it. I found out it was because Washington had cut back funds. Having an MBA under my belt, I offered to open up an exports department so we could make the money, but no, they told me all the resources on the island were for the residents only. I just couldn't believe the lack of imagination in finding ways to improve upon obvious flaws. And ultimately, they were so obsessed about control and so fearful of failing to deliver on their promises that they were willing to lock us up—simply to hide our plight from the world."

As Tray finished, Davin stepped in again to continue the conversation. "And Lizzie, tell us your story," he requested, motioning to the only girl of the group.

"My initial desire to leave had less to do with The Society and more to do with my life choices," she explained. "I wanted to leave in order to escape a bad relationship I had formed during my time in The Society. Things took off and went wrong quickly, as they always do in my life, and I needed some distance. And after surviving that deadly hurricane that completely destroyed the grounds, I didn't feel safe there anyway. So I decided I would put in a request to transfer to a different Society—the storm was far worse than they made it out to be on the news from what my family told me, by the way," Lizzie added, and then she turned and looked at Semaj. "I had a similar experience to you, in that I went to tell the government offices that I would be leaving and was led to the cave instead. But they never asked me why or allowed me to clarify that I merely wanted to transfer to another Society. However, after this experience, I won't be returning to *any* Society," she said definitively. "After being held against my will—when I didn't even have a complaint against them—I won't trust them again." She became more and more riled as she spoke. "These guys had been down there for months! We were nearly starved to death! And I thought the food rationing was hard after the hurricane!" She huffed at how oblivious to true hunger she had been. "And every time Branch came down with food for us, I couldn't decide if I should be excited to finally eat or dread the inevitable . . . " Lizzie said before breaking into tears. She leaned against Gregory, who was sitting next to her, and he put his arm around her shoulder.

"Branch assaulted her multiple times while we were locked up in the cave," Gregory explained while Lizzie wept on his shoulder. He had acted as her constant emotional support through the difficult times in the cave, and using his compassion, he masked his secret love for her in hopes that she would one day overlook his shabby appearance and win her affection. "We tried to tell him to back off whenever he came onto her, but the minute we said anything, we'd get a gun pressed to our forehead," Gregory added as he grabbed Lizzie's hand sympathetically.

"Just so everyone knows, Branch Willix was the Society Coordinator at the Hawaii Society," Davin interrupted momentarily. "His main job was supposed to be to make sure all the tasks, which ensure The Society runs smoothly, are taken care of each day."

"Yeah. You may know Branch Willix as very likable, and for his successful political career," Semaj clarified, "but I can tell you, behind locked doors, he's a snake. He boasted about how he got away with raping women, and he's the same man who killed Davin's friend when his friend found out about the cave we were in. Being slightly older and more successful, he looked down on us as if we were vermin. At the core of it, Branch was just an unmonitored henchman to Waverly, but he exploited what power he had to the greatest extent possible."

There was a moment of silence as Branch's unsavory memory haunted the room until Davin interrupted it to move on with the conversation.

"Gregory, how about you tell us your story," Davin gently suggested.

Gregory nodded. "Okay. Well . . . honestly, I had no idea that anything was going on behind our backs. I was just having a good time. But after the hurricane, I thought it was stupid they were having us play games when we were starving. We had no food supply and the place was in shambles, and yet they wanted us to run around playing games on an empty stomach. Some people were okay with that, but when I refused to play along and started pointing out how ridiculous it was to other people, Branch Willix came to my virtual reality room and asked me to follow him. When he got me alone, he beat me up and took me down to the cave. Called me 'an ungrateful lowlife' and locked me up with the rest of these guys."

Enzo jumped into the conversation. "Thankfully, some justice was served when our liberator took on Branch in a fight for our freedom. You'd never guess it, but the real person we have to thank for our freedom is the girl behind the camera. Chelsea is the one who came back for us in the cave and had to wrestle the key to our freedom from Branch in a struggle for her life."

Davin winced. He had hoped to keep that information quiet to protect Chelsea. Though he knew it might have to come out eventually, he wanted to keep the focus on The Society—obviously, Enzo felt differently.

Enzo continued his speech without prompting. "Thank you, Chelsea. If it weren't for you, who knows how long we would've been down there." He then redirected his line of sight directly into the camera to tell his story. "My name is Enzo. I was sent to the cave just before Gregory. I studied meteorology in school before coming to The Society. As I watched the hurricane form, I knew it couldn't have formed naturally, but when I spoke up about it, I was sent to the government offices to be 'educated.' I called them out on their BS, and that night I was quietly collected and sent to the cave. Apparently, they told my family that I refused to sit out a meal, and I was sent back to the mainland where I destroyed my wristband and ran off. None of which is true."

Chelsea suddenly walked away from the camera and stepped into frame. "The Society even went to the trouble of making it appear to us residents that they had sent them home by having decoys leave on the transporter pod. The decoys were, in fact, visitors who secretly came to The Society to fix technical problems that we were unable to fix ourselves," Chelsea said. "All in an effort to conceal the inefficacies that existed in The Society."

She sat casually on Davin's lap as he hung his head and reluctantly wrapped his arm around her waist. Before recording, Davin had fervently expressed his hopes that she remained anonymous, but since Enzo had already exposed her involvement, she decided there was no value in remaining silent any longer.

Davin accepted her wishes and added his insight. "And from all of my meetings behind the scenes, it was clear that The Society officials were under intense pressure to ensure The Society operated without inefficiencies. Success was imperative—to the point that moral lines became blurred, and any problems with the system were ignored instead of addressed."

"And every issue, every cover-up was hidden in a smokescreen of lies," added Enzo. "When I told my friends that the hurricane could not have been naturally caused, they told me that the government officials had confirmed it was caused by a rare atmospheric phenomenon called exponential storm combustion, which is a completely made-up term and not something used by any scientist to date."

"The Society did do me one favor though," Tray interrupted with a smile. "I don't miss having to wear my wristband anymore. It's nice to know that every minute of my life and every conversation I have isn't being recorded."

"Except I wish I could contact my family," Lizzie contradicted. "As freeing as it is, I want to be connected to my loved ones again."

"Considering most of our families think we're missing or dead, hopefully, they see this message and we can get in contact with them soon," Enzo said, looking sympathetically toward Lizzie. "Most of us haven't seen or heard from our family in months. I'm fortunate to have my brother Jax with me now, who we went back to The Society for and managed to narrowly escape with. But I know we're all hoping to make contact with the rest of our families as soon as possible."

"The Society wasn't exactly what we were promised. There were flaws in its execution, but that alone would have been okay. Sometimes solutions are not as obvious as we think, and in theory, it was great," Davin reflected. "But all the comfort and all the ease you can imagine isn't worth your freedom. We've learned the hard way that there is a stark difference between being free from responsibility and free to choose your own fate," he concluded.

Then Davin and Chelsea stood, and Davin stared into the camera with firm resolve. "Thanks for listening to our broadcast.

This is Davin Chapman with the rescued Society members from Hawaii. Let it be known—we are done complying with The Society, and, currently, we are free, and we are safe. Now we are asking our country to do its job and keep it that way."

– END OF BOOK 1 –

To review *Hidden Contempt,* go to amazon.com.

To get a **FREE** sneak peek of Book Two go to:
http://www.celesteshirecliffe.com/books-hcbook2-sneakpeek/
for access to Chapter One of *Hidden Contempt*'s sequel!

To learn more about the writing of *Hidden Contempt*
and author Celeste Shirecliffe, go to
http://www.celesteshirecliffe.com/books/.

ACKNOWLEDGMENTS

A huge thank you to:

My husband, for encouraging me when I was doubtful, for all your help to make this book possible, and for inspiring so many of these words through your kindness and love;

My editor, Lori Draft, for your helpful and concise edits. Your work greatly improved the book, and you made it possible for a working mom's dream to come true;

My beta readers. Joey Sloand and Ephraim Cullen, thank you for taking the time to read and make suggestions. Your time was appreciated, and your suggestions were helpful in the polishing of my manuscript. To Jessica McAdam, for sharing in the excitement of writing with me as well as providing great insight and feedback. To Kelly Webb, for generously volunteering your time to edit my book and for making me feel like my book could be worthwhile. And a special thanks to Angela Varnon for also providing great edits, but more importantly, giving me the confidence to publish. Your love for the story made me excited to share it with others.

Thank you to my brother, Spencer Cook, for helping me start my website. And thank you to those friends and family who assisted with organizing the Book Cover Competition and got excited for me in my journey as an author. I truly appreciated all of your efforts and cherished the time I was able to spend with each of you.

To my readers, thank you for taking the time to read my work. I hope that as you enjoyed the story behind *Hidden Contempt* that you found value in its words and relationships.

ABOUT THE AUTHOR

Celeste Shirecliffe was born and raised in the golden hills of Santa Rosa, CA. After graduating early from Santa Rosa High School, she attended college at Brigham Young University. There she spent her most memorable days directing cameras for BYU sporting events on the Jumbotron—making sure the instant replays were ready and finding bashful couples for the kiss cam. She enjoys brainstorming  business plans and creative marketing tactics in her spare time and even won a category in BYU's competitive business plan competition.

After graduating with a degree in human development and a minor in business, she and her husband trekked across the country to North Carolina where her husband was accepted into UNC Dental School. Celeste works as a freelance video engineer and was delighted to bring to light some of the behind-the-scenes of the audiovisual world in her book, *Hidden Contempt*.

Celeste's aptitude for writing came early, as she entered and won a short story competition as a child for *Reading Rainbow*, a PBS children's program, and now she hones that ability by writing fiction novels as an adult. Celeste has a young daughter who loves books, and she hopes to write more novels that will address important and difficult topics in a dignified manner without the use of profanity or vulgarity that her daughter can one day read and enjoy.